Iris

BOOK 1 OF THE RYGOM NARRATIVES

AMY ENGLE

This is a work of fiction. Names, characters, places, and incidents either are the product of the author's imagination or are used fictitiously. Any resemblance to actual persons, living or dead, events, or locales is entirely coincidental.

Printed in the United States of America

Cover by Zybrena Porter

Acknowledgements

This book almost wasn't finished. There were dozens of times in the past ten years when I wanted to quit. But several wonderful people inspired me to continue.

First and foremost, I'd like to thank my parents, Jeff and Wendy Engle. They have been so supportive and encouraging over the years. I'm truly blessed to have them as my father and mother.

The greatest editor I've had the pleasure of working with was Dee Cawood. I'm pretty decent at grammar and punctuation, but Dee was able to find all the mistakes that I had made. The praise she gave me on the first draft solidified my confidence as a writer during a time when I struggled with fears of inadequacy. I also greatly value all her suggestions that helped me give the story better direction.

I would also like to thank Lori Ann Natsyn for reading not one but two drafts of *Iris*. Her comments assured me that this story was something people would enjoy.

Last but not least, I'd like to mention the magnificent Glenna Bigelow. She has been a strong role model throughout my entire life and has been an essential part of my revision process. I couldn't have done it without her.

There are so many others that I'd like to thank, but that would probably double the size of this book. To those of you that have listened intently as I've blabbered on about writing, I appreciate your support in that; it might have seemed like a small thing, but it meant the world to me.

Without any further ado, I present *Iris*. Enjoy!

Chapter 1

Three shadowed figures stood outlined by a green light, shining starkly against the black and grey panels of the hall. With their night sticks in one hand and detection equipment in the other, they peered through abandoned rooms in search of the fugitive. The emerald glow from their visors illuminated their paths without disturbing the building's inhabitants.

Not far from them was their target: an eighteen year-old woman, battered and stained with dirt and sweat—recently escaped from prison. Iris Kayn crouched behind a large piece of debris, watching the lights dance across the walls until they became dim.

Peeking around the side of her sanctuary, Iris determined how much distance was between her and the pursuers. When they were approximately fifty feet away, she crept slowly down the hall, careful not to slip in the sludge that lined the metal floor. More than once, she was tempted to pull her twin long knives from their sheaves, but she didn't dare risk creating any noise. In order to remain calm, she took slow breaths of the stagnant, refuse-smelling air; if her heart beat rose above a certain level, her assailants would detect it with their sensors.

From what Iris could tell, all three Agents were men; they had bulky, triangular torsos and massive upper arms. Their boot-clad feet echoed heavily through the corridor, no matter how gently they tried to tread.

The game of chase lasted a couple more moments until the Agents stopped at an intersection. The tallest of the men pointed at the squat, husky one with arms as thick as his legs and motioned to the left. To the gangly, slim Agent, he nodded right. The towering figure—most likely the squad captain—headed down the forward tunnel after taking one last look in Iris's direction.

Part of Iris wanted to turn back the way she had come, but she was sure that there were even more Agents behind her. Making up her mind, she pulled out her long knives and turned the right corner towards the skinny one. She found him a few apartments in, scanning the darkness with his instruments. Without hesitation, she thrust her blades through his back. Iris grabbed the body as it fell and gently laid it on the ground.

She then turned back and went after the shorter, bulkier Agent. Minutes passed as she stepped through the filth towards her second prey, until she finally reached the green glow. It seemed like it would be another effortless kill as she tailed the unsuspecting Agent. Iris drew closer, lifting her long knives and preparing to strike.

Before her blades could make contact with the man's skull, he spun and parried her attack with his night stick. The detection instruments fell to the rusty metal floor, causing a clang to echo down the intersecting hallways.

He blocked her strikes again and again, generating noise that awoke the nearby Underlings.

Iris knew it was only a matter of time before the final Agent came running up the passage; she needed to finish him quickly. With the flick of the wrist, she pinned the Agent's night stick against the wall and sliced her free knife across the man's throat. Blood spurt from the wound as he fell to the floor with a thump.

Foot-steps sounded down the corridor at a fast rate. Iris ducked out of sight just as just as the last Agent came into sight. The squad leader was slightly out of breath as he surveyed the scene, holding his broadsword out in front of him. He turned to resume the search of his fugitive.

After a few steps, he paused.

Iris couldn't tell what caused him to stop. She held her breath and hoped that she hadn't left any clues as to where she hid.

A blade was suddenly at her throat.

"Nice try, Miss Kayn," the squad captain said. "Drop your weapons and stand up slowly."

She moved as though to throw her blades down, but tightened her grip at the last moment. Iris flung her knives up to deflect the sword, but only hit air. Confused, she turned to see the captain swinging at her back. Instinctively, she fell to the floor, her face smashing into the hard metal. As she moved to roll away, something heavy landed on her shoulders. With a groan, Iris dropped her knives.

When she was no longer armed, the man got off her and kicked the blades away. The man tossed her a pair of hand cuffs. "You can either put those on or I'll beat you until you can't move—then I'll put then on you."

For a moment, Iris simply sat there on the cool metal floor. She wouldn't obey until she figured out how the squad leader had found her. She glanced around and noticed bloody footprints that tracked from the dead Agent to where she had knelt. Reluctantly, she secured the restraints to her wrists.

Her vision went blurry and then everything grew dark. The smell of grime and bodily fluids disappeared, as did the cold floor. The cuffs no longer cut into her skin and she couldn't feel the ragged, thread-bare clothes that covered her body; there weren't sensations of any kind.

A rush of feelings swarmed her brain. She sat on something soft and plush in a warm room. Light filled her eyes, blinding her temporarily as she blinked them into focus. She was in her study with a Simulation visor over her face. A curse tore from her lips as she stood, swinging a pair of imaginary knives at the absent foes.

"Iris! My pancakes are burning!"

Rushing down the hall, she yelled, "I'm coming!" Iris took the stairs two at a time and rushed into the kitchen. Her father stood over the smoking skillet. She pushed him away from the stove and began cleaning up the black mess. "Sorry, I'll have new pancakes ready in a few minutes." When she finished washing the skillet, she poured fresh batter into it. Iris placed the morning's news-disc in front of him before returning to the range. "Here you go."

Dr. Kayn took a seat at the table, slid the coin-sized disc into his OMNI, and poured himself a cup of coffee from the pot on the kitchen table.

When the pancakes were done, Iris slid them onto an empty plate and placed the dish in front of her father. She slid into the seat across from him and picked up an apple from the basket beside her. Feeling fatigues from her

Sim, she poured herself a mug half filled with coffee and half with sugar and milk.

"What's so important about these Simulations, anyways?" her father asked, looking up from his OMNI. "There are other things you could be doing. How long has it been since you picked up a book or spent time with Claire?"

"It's part of my Agency Project," Iris explained, trying to eat and talk at the same time. "And I speak to Claire every night before I go to bed."

Dr. Kayn gave her an irritated glare as he cut his pancakes. "*Talking* to Claire is different than *seeing* her." He took a deep breath before inquiring, "I know I should have asked earlier this spring, but what exactly is your Project about?"

"I'm finding faults with the Agency Instruction Simulations," Iris explained, confused as to why he was so interested in her work all of a sudden. "Normally, they are for strategy training, programmed to act in accordance with Protocol. In the one I was just running, I play a convict trying to escape from prison. My goal is to find holes in their security."

"Is there another Simulation that you can try and fix? It seems a little obsessive to repeat the same situation over and over again."

Iris clenched her teeth as she replied, "I've already *been* through all the other ones. I found several flaws, but most Sims are absolutely perfect and can't be improved in any way." How could she explain it in a way he would understand? "This is the last Sim and then my Project will be complete. I want to finish it before I begin Placement Testing. I don't want to divide my time between assignments and completing my Project. Besides, Claire is probably finished with hers by now."

"Her plans to improve the Optimized Media Network Interface?" Dr. Kayn pinched the bridge of his nose. "And would Claire's parents be okay with it if she sat for hours each night with her brain synced to an OMNI?"

"The Birch have *too many* children to know or care what all of them are doing."

"Iris Kayn!"

"I know." Air quoting, she said, "*It's rude to talk about friends in that way.*" She had only said what she did because she was jealous. Sometimes she wished she had seven brothers and sisters like Claire. Iris knew that there would have been more Kayn children if circumstances were different.

After he gulped down the last sip of his coffee, Dr. Kayn asked, "Have you taken your medicine?"

She cleared her plate and placed it in the dishwasher. "I'm about to." From a drawer next to the sink, Iris pulled out a box of syringes. "You *do* realize that I'm eighteen, making me old enough to remember my injections, right?" She tightly secured a band of rubber around her upper arm.

"Of course. I only ask out of habit. Starting tonight, you won't have me to remind you."

"And starting this afternoon, you'll no longer have someone to cook for you." Iris removed the cap off a syringe and then placed the three-inch needle in the crease of her elbow. "Have you figured out how to cope without me?" She pushed in the plunger and the clear liquid poured into her veins.

Dr. Kayn picked up his dirty plate and walked up to her. He took the syringe from her and discarded it in the trash pipe. "I was going to have Audrey do whatever I need."

"Dr. Taledon is your lab assistant, *not* your servant," Iris protested while flexing her elbow. "She doesn't like being told to cook, clean, and do your laundry. Remember what happened the last time you asked her?"

Leaving him to contemplate that memory, Iris went back upstairs. She dressed in her light grey Candidate uniform. The tailored blazer and pants fit snuggly. Iris had spent the past month breaking in her thick leather boots, wearing them around the apartment as much as possible. There were gloves that came with the uniform, although it was optional to wear them; they were meant for sparring and were strapped nicely to a utility belt when not in use. She tightly pulled her sandy-blonde hair back into a neat ponytail.

She arrived downstairs to see that her father was surprisingly ready for the day. He had dressed in his finest casual clothes: a blue and white striped collared shirt, khaki slacks, and black loafers. His light brown hair had been carefully combed over to hide the bald inches of skin above his forehead.

Dr. Norman Kayn stared at a picture of Iris's mother. Dr. Teresa Kayn was posed as though she were dancing, her blonde, flower-decorated hair flowing to the side of her smiling face. He placed the frame into the packed hover cart that took up the entire living room. "Are you sure you have enough syringes?" Norman shuffled into the kitchen and pulled out the box of needles. "Remember what happened that time that you missed a dose?"

She shuttered, re-experiencing the memory. "Yes, I remember. I have a four-month supply. I'll make sure I come and visit you before I run out." She took the box from him and placed it on the coffee table.

"Miss Birch still doesn't know, right?"

"No, she doesn't," Iris assured him. "Claire knows that I take supplements, but not the exact reason why. The prescription labels you made should help disguise them." She grabbed her pack and flung it onto her back so that it rested snugly between her shoulders. "Since they're simply high doses of calcium, Vitamin C, and other nutrients, I could just say that I need them for my rigorous exercise regimen. Relax. No one will discover our secret."

Dr. Kayn looked his daughter over. "It seems as though you've thought of everything."

He moved behind the hover cart and activated the hover consol. A soft whirl sounded from the mechanisms in the base that produced the propulsion to lift the load. The cart rose two inches in the air. Iris opened the front door and Norman pushed the cart out into the hall.

They strolled down the enclosed passage toward the main stairs. The floor was moist from the Morning Shower.

Over-head sprinklers continued dribbling water, indicating that they were nearly done with their cycle. A little river flowed down the sides of the walkway, washing away the daily accumulation of dirt and human dander. The warmth of overhead Solar Lamps evaporated the accumulating puddles of moisture.

About every minute or so, Dr. Kayn diverted his eyes from the walkway and rested his gaze on Iris's face.

Uncomfortable by his stare, Iris turned her attention to the plant beds in the neighbors' windows. Most contained genetically altered plant hybrids, like lily-bonsais, rose-vines, and daisy-bushes.

"Look, dad, I know you don't want me to go to the Agency," Iris eventually said. She had a speech planned for this moment. However, she found that her prepared words were more condescending than she had realized. So she improvised. "There's nothing you can do to change my mind. Being a Candidate for the Agency Training Program is an honor. I need to do this."

Dr. Kayn sighed, "You let me think that you only wanted the acknowledgement of being good enough for the AT Program. That's the only reason I permitted you to apply. I wouldn't have signed the parental consent form if I thought you seriously wanted to attend. I just worry about your health; what if you aren't good enough? You should have enrolled at the Conservatory as well, just in case the Agency doesn't work out."

Iris knew that her father had always wanted her to join him in his pathological disease research. Dr. Norman Kayn had dreamed they would work side by side, curing the atrocious Plagues that ran rampant through the Lower Regions of the Megacity. In an effort to persuade her, Dr. Kayn had scattered applications to the Conservatory here and there throughout the house. In turn, Iris always made a dramatic show of throwing them down the trash pipes when she discovered them.

Norman shook his head in defeat when she refused to reply. He adjusted the settings on the control panel to allow the hover mechanisms to float above the stair steps. At the top, he switched it back and entered the Sector Plaza.

The Plaza was a perfect cube, measuring one mile in all directions. Nanite-enforced steel beams held up the Train portion of the Transit System. The bases of these structures housed little independent food and commercial shops. Tables were set up around these areas for people to eat or unwind at after a long day of shopping. Larger establishments were arranged into a grid of networks that filled the remainder of the Sector; they rose four stories above the ground to the ceiling of the Sector. Narrow walkways connected the buildings at every floor level. At the heart of the Plaza were the Elevators—half a dozen traveled Down while another half dozen went Up.

The Kayns passed a few pedestrians on their way to the Transit Station where the Trains and Elevators intersected. Some eyed Iris's simple grey blazer and slacks and turned their noses up at her; there were people in the city that felt the government held too much power and that the AT Programs should be abandoned. Conversely, others smiled encouragingly at her as they passed.

When they reached the Transit Station, they went separate ways for a little while. Iris left to find Claire Birch at their designated Elevator and Norman took the hover cart to the Postal Booth.

Her friend chatted excitedly into her OMNI. Claire said good-bye to whoever she was speaking with and ended the call. "What's wrong?"

"Oh, I'm just a little frustrated with myself. I thought that I'd have my Project completed before moving to the Agency." Iris realized how irritated she really felt. It bubbled up in her as she confessed her feelings to her best friend. “How can I call myself a strategist if I can’t think my way out of a prison Simulation?”

“You’re being too difficult on yourself, Iris,” Claire chided, slipping stray strands of her chestnut brown hair behind her ears. “If it were simple, someone would have figured it out already. Don’t put yourself down just because you don’t meet your own high expectations. I could never do what you have done.”

Iris scoffed and shook her head. “Of course you wouldn’t be able to do my Project—just like I could never do yours. You’re going to be an Engineer, and I want to be an Enforcer; they are two completely different areas of expertise. What if I don’t have what it takes? There’s no way to know how good my competition is; I have no frame of reference of where my abilities lie. What if I lose all my sparring matches? What if all the other Candidates are stronger, faster, and more experienced than I am?”

“*All you can do is your best*,” Claire said, paraphrasing Mrs. Birch’s favorite expression. “Try and be a little more excited. You don’t sound like someone that’s been accepted into the most elite vocational program in the Megacity.”

Dr. Kayn appeared a short while later with the rest of the Birch family. He gently pulled Iris away from Claire.

"Your Elevator will be here soon. Can we chat until it comes?" He led her away from the rambunctious Birch children. "I know I haven't been very supportive of your decision. But I'm proud of you and I faith that you have what it takes to become an Agent." He wrapped his arms around her and held her tight.

A few feet away, Mrs. Birch wept hysterically. She clutched her eldest child so tightly that Claire's face turned purple. "Oh, Claire-Bear!"

Mr. Birch tried unsuccessfully to pry his wife from his daughter. The rest of the family was obliged to hug Claire from behind and awkwardly pat her back in farewell.

The 8:43 a.m. Transition occurred and the young ladies took out their OMNIs. One at a time, they pressed their OMNIs to the scanner on their designated Elevator. Their ticket files were transferred to the mechanisms in the door and they were admitted into the compartment. Iris and Claire entered after first waving one last goodbye to their loved ones.

Chapter 2

As their Elevator ascended out of the Transit Station, Claire Birch screamed, “Oh, Iris! I’ve never been so happy in my entire life.” She giggled uncontrollably for several seconds. Her fit only ceased when she took a seat next to her best friend. “I no longer have to watch my brothers and sisters, help them with their school work, or deal with their pestering.”

“Yes,” Iris replied calmly. “There’s something liberating about moving away from one’s parent. Well, ‘parents’ in your case. We only have to deal with our own problems from now on.”

Claire gave her friend a slap on the shoulder. “Stop looking so forlorn. We’ve been *selected for the honor of going through the Agency Training Program. Millions have applied, but only a few thousand are accepted.*” She was quite proud that she could quote the text she had read only the night before.

Iris laughed, shaking her head. “I had no idea that you knew so much about it—let alone could quote the introductory information.”

Tying up her rumpled brown hair, Claire said, “It wasn’t until last night that I learned those facts. There’s still plenty that I don't know, which I believe you'll be happy to fill me in on during our journey." She gave Iris a sly smile.

With a groan, Iris rolled her eyes. "Alright. Where would you like to start?"

"Wherever is fine," Claire shrugged, waving her hand passively as if she were sweeping something away. "Just keep it relevant and entertaining."

Iris rummaged through her pack and removed her OMNI and a case of data-discs. After flipping through the container, she slipped one of the small circles into the hard drive. "*The Agency of the Rygom,*" she read, "*makes, enforces, and interprets laws for its citizens. Without the Agency's ability to regulate life, the Megacity wouldn't thrive. For the past one hundred years, the Agency Training Program has readied young people for positions in the top occupations of Rygom.*"

"Yeah, yeah. I already know *those* things. Skip to the interesting stuff!"

Iris put her OMNI in her lap. "This is *important* information. You weren't raised in Upper Society, so you didn't grow up knowing anything about the Agency."

"Oh, you're going to bring *that* up, huh?" Claire turned away with a scowl.

It wasn't her fault she had been born in the Middle Zone. The Birches had moved to Society when Mr. Birch received a promotion at work five years ago. In order to help her acclimate to Society, Oscar and Helen had devised a plan.

*****

Claire walked alongside her Aunt Audrey as they made their way to the Kayn's house. Bored, she pulled out her OMNI and began mindlessly blasting alien creatures with her trigger-happy fingers.

"I still don't see why I have to spend time with this *Iris Kayn*. She's probably just some rich, fancy girl who's got her head stuck so far up her—"

"That's enough, young lady!" Her aunt's face turned bright red, the way it always did when Claire or any of her other nieces and nephews were aggravating. "Iris is a very pleasant young lady. She's also—" Audrey yanked Claire's OMNI from her hands. Without finishing her former thought, she said, "She just needs a friend her own age."

Upset at having her source entertainment taken away, Claire said, "That's the saddest thing I've ever heard: a thirteen-year-old that's unable to make her own friends?

She needs her daddy to arrange to have some stranger come over to play?"

"Look, Claire, your family has a rare opportunity of moving up in life. Your parents think that the best thing for you is to make friends with Miss Kayn. Her father has a lot of connections in this Megacity, as well as all the others. If you get along with Iris, it'll put you in circles you never knew existed."

Claire still wasn't thrilled with the idea, but she was beginning to see why it was so important. Putting on her best fake smile, she replied, "Yes, Aunt Audrey."

She wasn't really her aunt; Audrey was her father's cousin, but it was just easier to call her "aunt." Saying, "Second-cousin Audrey" was more than most of the Birch children could handle.

Audrey glided down hall after hall, dragging the unenthusiastic girl. At the Kayn's residence, she pulled out her OMNI and held it up to the door lock. They passed by half a dozen empty rooms before they reached a staircase. As they descended, Claire heard a series of thuds, grunts, and shouts. Turning into an open doorway, she saw the source of the noise.

A small, blonde girl stood opposite a tall, lean man with dark hair. They circled each other, their fists raised.

The man threw some punches, which the girl easily dodged before throwing her elbow at him. They went back and forth, alternating between attacking and defending. The girl was fast—zigzagging in and out of the man's reach. She kicked at him with her legs or knees and then quickly spun away quickly when she missed. A few of the strikes landed on her opponent, but they didn't seem to do any damage.

"Focus, Iris. Aim a little higher for the kidneys."

The man gave all sorts of advice when the girl messed up, which she did quite a bit. She stumbled over her feet, kept her hands too low, or had a shallow stance. But every time the teacher corrected her, she seemed improve.

"Enough flailing, Iris. Punch me!"

She sent her fist it at the man's ribs; there was a crack and then a high-pitched scream.

"Let me see." The self-defense teacher grabbed her hand and examined it. "Nothing is broken; it's just a bruise. Make sure you soak it in Epsom salt water. I'll be back tomorrow." He grabbed a duffle bag from the far wall and waved as he left.

The girl approached and held out her uninjured hand. "Hello. I'm Iris Kayn."

"Claire Birch." She politely shook Miss Kayn's outstretched hand.

Iris wiped a lump of sweaty hair from her brow. "What would you like to do today?"

Looking up at Audrey, Claire was uncertain about what to say. Her aunt gave her an encouraging nod before leaving the two girls alone.

"Well, what do you usually do for fun?" Claire asked.

"*Fun*?" Iris replied with uncertainty, the naïve smile disappearing.

"You know, things you enjoy doing. Recreational activities? Watching movies, shopping, playing games. Do you do any of those things?"

Iris gave her a blank stare. "I just started learning self-defense. Does that count?"

Claire sighed, "No, self-defense doesn't count as *fun*."

"But I *enjoy* it. I thought you said 'fun' was something you *enjoy* doing."

Speaking slowly, the former Zonese girl said, "Anything that requires *work* is not *fun*."

"*Everything* requires work," Miss Kayn stated, matter-of-factly. "Your muscles are always working to keep your body upright, to inhale oxygen, to pump blood, to blink—"

"I have no idea what you're talking about," Claire interrupted, shaking her head with a scowl.

"It's basic physiology."

She stared at the strange girl, trying to figure her out; Claire had a bizarre theory. "Are you a robot, or something?"

Iris laughed as though Claire had told a joke. "Silly! Robots are only used by Agents!"

Already regretting this arrangement, Claire took a step forward and put her arm around the girl's shoulder. "Iris, you have a lot to learn about the world. Now, take me to your room and I'll introduce you to on-line gaming."

*****

Iris's frown disappeared. "Sorry I upset you. I know that you still struggle with—"

"No," Claire interrupted. "You were right. We're beginning our Training at the Agency; I should know what the Agency is all about." She gave Iris an encouraging smile. "Would you please continue our lesson?"

Claire tried her best to listen diligently as Iris gestured at a three-dimensional model of the Sectors above her OMNI. She wanted to point out that the layout of the Agency fell under the *boring* category, but she didn't want to risk upsetting Iris any further. They were going to spend the next three years rooming together; bickering the whole way to their new life wouldn't be a good start.

They exited their compartment when it stopped at a Transit Station on the bottom Agency Sector.

A woman in a black uniform greeted them. "Welcome to the Agency." She eyed the light grey hue of their clothes. "May I see your Identification?" They held out their OMNIs as the woman scanned their ID files. "Good. Please wait over there for your Mentors." The lady pointed to a group of other eighteen year olds in dressed in the same uniforms.

Iris moved toward an empty table in the Plaza, but Claire stopped her.

"Where are you going? People are *this* way. It's time to socialize." She meandered to the nearest huddle, pulling Iris along with her.

A woman with short, red hair greeted them. "Hi. I'm Evelyn Sanders; call me *Eve*."

"*The* Evelyn Sanders?" Claire exclaimed in the form of a question. "As in the daughter of the OMNI tycoon, Byron Sanders? And your uncle is Mayor Cromford, right?" She smiled and extended her hand to the newcomer. "My name is Claire Birch. The quiet, timid girl beside me is Iris Kayn."

"Ah, *Iris Kayn*!" Eve exclaimed without looking at the offered hand. "The daughter of *Dr. Norman Kayn*, the Plague Curer? Are you following in your father's footsteps?"

"No, I'm hoping to get into the Enforcement Program," Iris replied, smiling awkwardly.

Eve eyed Iris. "Well, that makes two of us. But now I see the knives at your sides. I'm assuming that your ideal career lies in Local Police or Military Combat? I'd like to have some sort of administrative position; I'll probably be Placed as a Coordinator."

Iris wrung her hands and looked down at her feet, obviously forgetting that eye contact was the most important rule for socializing. "Actually," she sputtered, "I want to go into the Special Operations Branch. But I don't know if my skills are up to par for Spec Ops, so Security Patrol is my second choice."

"We must all do our *best* this summer during the Placement Tests." Eve turned to Claire and asked, "What about you, Miss Birch?"

"Engineering. I've been learning from my father's cousin, Dr. Audrey Taledon." Claire waited for some sign that Miss Sanders recognized her aunt's name, but there wasn't any. She continued, hoping to establish credibility of her skills. "I've worked in her laboratory since I was four."

"I imagine that there aren't very many *handsome* young men in the sciences," Miss Sanders frowned, changing the subject. "I admit that I chose the Enforcement Program because of the physical stature of the males. My cousin, Viola Cromford, assures me that there are many good-looking men in the Enforcement Program." She paused briefly before adding, "There's one in particular that I'm looking forward to spending time with."

Claire had begun to think that she wouldn't find anything in common with the young woman. However, the last comment tore away all hesitation about becoming close friends with her. "And who is this hunk of a man?"

"Alastair Vega," Miss Sanders replied with a swoon.

Pretending to not have heard of him, Claire asked, "Oh? Who is he?" She risked a side-ways glance at Iris, who was beginning to look even more nervous than usual.

"He's only the most successful Third-Year Trainee in the AT Program!" Miss Sanders said rather loudly. "Alastair has received top marks in every Advanced Class. Not to mention, he is the most *gorgeous* man you will ever see. Surely you have heard about him, Miss Kayn. Didn't your father use to work for Vega Industries?"

"Yes," Iris replied, wiping her hands on her uniform. "I have met Alastair Vega."

"That's so *wonderful* for you. I'm sure you'll get to have *a lot* of time with him, since you know him *so well.*" She spoke with a lot of energy, but there was a tone of agitation in her voice.

"It's nothing like that," Iris assured her. "I mean, I met him about five years ago. It surprised me that you said his name. Mr. Vega and I had a bit of a tiff and—"

"Aw, that's too bad," Miss Sander said, smoothing strands her short red hair. She smiled widely, a hint of relief in her bright eyes. "I'm sure there are other men that might prove to be more suitable boyfriend material."

At this point, Claire was tired of being ignored. She pointed at the small, pink stud below Miss Sander's ear. "Is that an implant, Eve?"

"Yeah, it's a verbal-converter; it transcribes my speech into a text file," the girl explained. She scanned Claire's face and neck. "Why haven't you had one installed yet? They make life so much easier. For my nineteenth birthday, my mom is going to buy me another one. I haven't decided what to get. Maybe a radio or a dream-scanner! Hey, we should go *together*."

Claire was dumbfounded. She had worked hard for years to hide her parents' financial burdens from those who knew her. Feeling self-conscious, she wanted to say that she was going to wait until she had *earned* an Agency implant through Service Hours.

She was interrupted by a loud chime.

The Candidates directed their attentions to the entrance of the Transit Station. A number of people clad in dark grey uniforms approached.

A young man with dark brown hair advanced and addressed the cluster of new recruits. "Greetings, Candidates. I hope everyone is having a great morning. The Third-Years behind me will be your Mentors this term."

He motioned to the older-looking group. Many of the men and women had a set of two grey implant studs placed somewhere on their face, neck, or hands.

"As I call out roommate pairs," the man explained, "listen for your name. Then come forward and meet your Mentor."

As groups of two were announced, the crowd began to shrink as the duos took off behind their Mentors. Eve Sanders and Beatrice Cromford followed Viola Cromford to a stairwell and walked downward. There was a Vega mentioned—a giant of a man with an amused look on his face—but it wasn't the one Iris had told Claire about. After a few minutes, only the two friends remained alone with the apparent leader of the Mentors.

He pulled out his OMNI and pressed a number of buttons. Clearly, he was assigned as their Mentor. Claire took a moment to study him.

His brown curls were neatly gelled to his head and tucked beneath his ears. Two grey implant studs sat behind his right jaw, one a lighter shade than the other. Miss Sanders had been right when she said the AT Program had attractive young men.

The young man looked up from his OMNI and moved toward the girls. "Iris Kayn? Claire Birch? I'm Alastair Vega."

Claire gave Iris a nudge as she stepped forward. "It's nice to meet you, Mentor Vega."

"Likewise, Miss Birch." He turned to Iris. "And, Miss Kayn! It's a delight to see you again. How long has it been?"

"Just over five years," replied Iris, coldly.

He didn't seem deterred by her unfriendly response. "That long? Well, I hope we can get reacquainted during

Placement Testing." He spun on his heel and turned towards the Elevators. "If you two ladies will please follow me, I'll take you on a little tour before we go to your Living Quarters."

They situated themselves in the Elevator, sitting in silence during the brief trip Up. Alastair spent most of the ride staring at Iris, making her even more uncomfortable. She kept her gaze on the blinking lights of the Elevator's control panel.

"You've been very quiet, Miss Kayn," Alastair said as they exited the pod.

"My friend is often like that," Claire commented, steering the man's attention away from Iris. "She seems happiest when in silent contemplation. I've found it's best to just leave her to her own thoughts."

For the first time since they were reacquainted, Alastair Vega's face wasn't the model of pleasantry. He narrowed his eyes at Iris, but continued addressing Claire. "The Agency Training Program is a place to socialize, network, and meet new people; she won't get far if she shies away from conversation."

Without looking at Iris, Claire flippantly said, "She's quieter than usual today; Iris really can be a chatter-box—when she's in the right mood."

The trio walked through the Plaza while Mr. Vega pointed out the information desk, the closest cafeteria, popular meeting spots, the shopping locality, study areas, and other important places.

He motioned to a building at the end of the avenue. “I’ll be with some friends at The Grey Circumstance club tonight. Come by and I’ll introduce you to some of the other Mentors.”

“Should I drag along Miss Melancholy over there?” Claire inquired, pointing at Iris.

“Of course. Hopefully her spirits will improve by then.”

“I’ll be there,” Iris retorted.

“That concludes the Plaza tour. I’ll take you to your apartment now.” Alastair gestured toward the West side of the Plaza and began walking in that direction. After heading down a series of passages, Alastair stopped at a door. He pulled out his OMNI and pressed it to the controls. The door opened and he strode into the room.

“You can get into our Living Quarters?” Iris gasped.

“Only this one time,” Alastair explained, gesturing for the girls to enter. “Your OMNIs need to be configured to the lock." Once inside, he moved to a three-foot square screen on the wall. "Good morning, ARHA."

The dark screen suddenly turned on, adding to the illumination of the room. A female voice came out of the speakers beside the screen. "Good morning, Alastair Vega."

"This is Iris Kayn and Claire Birch." He motioned to each girl as he said their names.

"Welcome Iris Kayn and Claire Birch. I am ARHA—Automatic Regulating House Assistant."

"Hello!" Claire said, ecstatic about meeting the artificial intelligence.

Alastair asked the screen, "ARHA, could you please configure their locks?"

"Very well, Alastair Vega. Iris Kayn, place your OMNI to my sensor." Iris did as she was told. ARHA asked Claire to do the same.

"Thank you, ARHA," the Mentor said. "That will be all for now."

"Good bye, Alastair Vega. Iris Kayn and Claire Birch, you may ask for my assistance at anytime." The screen went black.

Alastair Vega smiled at the empty monitor. "If you have any questions, just ask ARHA. If she is unable to assist you, she will call me and I'll help you if I can. I'll see you ladies tonight. Have fun moving in." Mr. Vega gave a slight bow and left the apartment.

Claire chuckled. "I had no idea that a scum bag could be so handsome!"

"I don't want to talk about him," Iris snapped, walking around their Living Quarters.

"ARHA?" Claire called out.

The wall screen changed from black to white. "How can I help you, Claire Birch?"

"Where's all our stuff?"

"According to the tracking signal," began the artificial intelligence, "your hover-carts will be delivered in a short while. In the meantime, perhaps I can answer any questions you may have."

Iris approached the screen. "When do we get our implants? I heard that the Agency gives out free ones to the Trainees."

"That's true, Iris Kayn. If you pass Placement Testing and become a First-Year Trainee, your Instructors will have Service Hour options that you may volunteer for. Once you have completed enough Hours, you will be eligible for an implant. You may only earn one free implant each year that you are a Trainee." ARHA's screen shifted from white to purple. “Please open your door; your hover carts are here. Enjoy the rest of your day, Iris Kayn and Claire Birch.” The screen faded to black.

The roommates retrieved their carts and pushed them into their Living Quarters. After pushing the carts down a wide staircase, they chose their rooms and then left each other to get settled.

Claire had started putting her clothes away when she had a thought on how to arrange her video games. She was halfway done with that when her focus shifted to checking her social media sites. After that, all thoughts of unpacking left when she had an epiphany about her Project.

Chapter 3

A clanking sound started Klev awake. Slowly, he blinked his eyes open to see a pair of Agents unlocking his cell. "Lom! Something has changed." He banged on the top of his bunk bed. "Look alive!"

Lom's snoring ceased, replaced with a gasp as he rolled off the lofted cot. "What's happening?" Sprawled on the floor, he scratched at his thinning, grey hair.

"We've got company." Klev stood abruptly. "What are you doing lying around still?"

The approaching Agents were stark contrasts to each other, and yet both had the same eyes, nose, and jaw line. The lady had dark curls that reached the middle of her back; she held herself as though she were the most important person in the Megacity. However, the male Agent had short, dark blonde hair and seemed bored with his situation.

"Your time is up, boys," the woman Agent said as she swung the barred door open. "You get to rejoin civilization." She stuck an index finger in the air and bent it toward her. With a smirk, she turned and walked away.

The man Agent gestured after the female, holding the cell door for them. "After you."

Klev and Lom shared confused stares, but followed the intimidating woman.

They passed dozens of prison cells; the other inmates whooped at them, cheering them on as they headed for the next phase of their lives.

"I can't believe it is over," Lom admitted, dusting off his prison uniform. "The past five years are all blurred together. Most days, I can't even remember why we were put here in the first place."

"Oh, I remember! We, um—I think that—" Klev racked his brain, but the memory escaped him. "We must have gotten sloppy! How could you have let that happen?"

Ignoring Klev's outburst, Lom said, "I hope our notebooks will help fill in the blanks."

Once at the Administrative Center, the Agent woman handed them each a wide box. "Here's your stuff. I still think we should have confiscated your weapons, but I guess the Agency Board wants you to have a shot at surviving."

"Stella, you don't have to tell them everything," the Agent man sighed.

"Oh, save it, Drew. They have the right to know that their lives might be in danger." The woman took off again. As she walked, she often glanced at Klev and Lom and gave them menacing grins.

Eventually, they made it out of the prison. Klev and Lom studied everything, trying to find something that looked familiar, but it all seemed new. They knew enough about Rygom to know that it wasn't Upper Society and nor was it the Lower Region. By process of elimination, they reasoned that they were in the Middle Zone.

Lom rummaged through his box; he picked up various notebooks and then threw them back when they weren't the one he was searching for. After looking at a couple dozen, he discovered the one written just before their prison sentence. "Here it is, Klev!" He showed his colleague the notebook.

As they walked through the Middle Zone, they skimmed through the details in the notebook. It was all foreign at first, but then the memories began to resurface.

*****

It was a refreshing change of scenery to be doing business outside the enclosed walls of the Rygom Megacity. Klev and Lom had enjoyed their previous task. They were sorry that they were so efficient that their expedition took two days less than anticipated. Klev scanned the valley surrounding the Megacity and scribbled a quick picture into one of their notebooks. On the horizon, the sun began to set behind the mountain. The dusk light bounced off the exterior of the Megacity.

"Do you think we'd get away with spending an extra night out here?" Lom asked, writing up a quick summary of their morning.

Klev turned away from his sketch with a sigh. "I'd like to stay out here longer, too, but I'm sure the Agency would find out. It's best to finish the job and move onto the next assignment."

There was a thump from their cargo crate as they moved to pick it up. Muffled, indistinct shouts came from inside.

"How are they awake already?" Klev growled. "They should have woken tonight."

"Perhaps we lost a day?" Lom replied, readying his stun baton. "Our memory isn't as good as it use to be." As quickly as the thought appeared in his head, it vanished from his consciousness.

The pair of mercenaries carefully opened the crate and zapped their captives. The first strike made the Dakonite girl child fall unconscious, but the woman remained awake.

Shaking her head with a groan, the woman huffed, "We've been taken before and we always get away!" Her thick accent was difficult to understand, but Klev and Lom had previous experience dealing with Torleans.

"Taken?" Klev shook his head. "You've haven't been *taken.* You're being *returned.*"

The woman from the Torlea Megacity let out a deep breath. "I'll give you one chance to set us free, or you'll regret accepting the job to bring us in." When she finished her threat, the mercenaries smacked their stun batons at her once more. The woman's face fell to her chin, her black, matted hair covering her dark-skinned face. The rest of her body hung limply in the restraints.

Lom stared guiltily at the small child beside the Torlean. The nameless girl—not more than six years old—was from the Dakon Megacity; she looked so helpless and innocent. It was hard to believe that the bronze-skinned girl was a dangerous fugitive. "I wonder why our employers want these two foreigners?" Lom thought out loud, holstering his stun baton.

"How should I know what they want with a Torlean and a Dakonite?" Klev responded, shutting the door. "We'll move the crate inside once I finish my picture. Who knows the next time we'll be outside?"

The mercenaries enjoyed the sunrise before turning back to their assignment. They lifted the crate and moved towards Rygom's entrance. For a thin woman and a tiny child, they were oddly difficult to lift.

As they approached, a group of black-clad Agents approached them.

Lom waved to them. "It's awfully nice of you to help with our load, gentlemen. It's quite heavy."

But the Agents made no move to help with the cargo. They unsheathed their weapons.

One of the men stepped forward; he had a couple dozen pins on his black blazer, clearly the captain of the squad. A long scar ran down his left forehead, skipped the eye, and continued across the check to his jaw line. "Put your hands up."

Klev removed a knife from his belt. "You got the moves to back up your words, *worm*?"

"I think there has been some miscommunication," Lom said in a calm voice. "You see, we've been employed by—"

"Step away from the cargo," the scar-faced Agent interrupted. His hands went to the belt at his hip and removed a gas grenade. When Klev and Lom didn't move, he hurled the can at them.

Smoke filled Klev's eyes as he clenched his mouth and nose shut. Lom had closed his eyes in time, but he had forgotten to hold his breath before fleeing. They rammed into each other, falling to the ground in a coughing fit. Their lungs burned and their eyes stun. But the pain didn't last long, for they soon lost consciousness.

*****

Lom searched for information about their last assignment, but the pages were missing. Prison must have done something to his brain since he couldn't remember his former employers. He had memories of working with Klev on countless missions, but the names of the other operators were gone from his mind. Rubbing his temple, he asked, "What are we gonna do, Klev?"

"I'll figure out something, Lom." Klev nudged his colleague. "I always do."

Klev was the brighter of the pair; both of them had agreed on it many years previous. His superior intellect helped him and his partner to get out of many tight spots. In addition, his fierce demeanor made him a more effective leader than follower. Lom was a typical side-kick. Although his skills were also legendary, his mind was nothing compared to Klev's. To make up for his *inferiority*, he followed his friend more loyally than any other person alive.

"There will be plenty of work in the Zone for us to do," Klev continued, motioning at the simple but comfortable-looking buildings all around him. "We'll have so many people wanting our services that we'll soon have to send people away!"

The female Agent named Stella laughed uncontrollably. "Oh, we're not leaving you in the Middle Zone! The only place for dangerous convicts is the Lower Region."

"The *Region*?" All Lom had were faint wisps of memories of that place. But there were enough little pieces to make him realize that it was not the sort of place anyone wanted to reside in.

"We'll be fine!" Klev sighed as he realized that jail had made his friend go soft.

It was perhaps best that they were headed to the deadliest area of the Rygom Megacity; it would refresh Lom's long-lost ferocity.

Drew, the male Agent, stepped past the convicts when they arrived at a private Elevator. He covered the screen as he entered a code into the panel. The Agent said, "Have a seat," as the pod opened.

Klev and Lom did as they were told. In the corner, they whispered as quietly as they could manage while the Agents pushed buttons on the Elevator's control screen.

"You think we can take them?" Klev asked, reaching for a knife hilt in his box.

"I—" Lom was interrupted as a strip of leather wound around his wrist, tying him up with Klev.

Stella pulled her whip tighter as she said, "No funny business."

Drew in turn removed throwing knives from his jacket and held them nonchalantly in front of him. "We might not be as famous as The Klev and Lom Duo, but I guarantee you that the Harding Siblings can take on two old geezers that have spent the past five years rotting in a prison cell."

Klev groaned as he held up his empty hands; Lom complied as well. Stella released her whip and chatted quietly with Drew. The former prisoners were silent as the Elevator descended through the Middle Zone, past the Market levels, and into the Lower Region.

It was worse than Lom had thought. Even without much light to see everything, he could still make out shapes of discarded metal and plastic that cluttered the floor. Glass-less windows showed the empty interiors of dust-filled buildings. The smell of body odors and refuse filled the stale air.

"Where are all the people?" Lom asked as he scanned the deserted Plaza.

"There's a small community of Underlings two Sectors West of here." Drew nodded in the direction. "I'd start there."

Stella gave them a wink. "Good luck, fellas!"

Klev put his box down and searched for his weapons. "I wonder what kind of valuables the Underlings have." He began strapping his various blades to different parts of his body. "I'm sure they'll have plenty of supplies."

Something about his friend's enthusiasm perked Lom up. "I think it'll be nice to meet decent folk again, Klev. Perhaps it'll be just the thing to help us get back on our feet."

"Yes, Lom. We'll just do what we have to in order to get out of Rygom." Klev let out a sigh as a pleasant memory surfaced. "I miss the Wexar outskirts—the warm beaches, clear blue oceans, and incredible sunsets! I'd like to retire there."

Lom nodded and picked up his box. "Yes, it was beautiful. But didn't we get into trouble with La Policía?"

Klev began walking west—in the direction the male Agent had indicated. "We've gotten into trouble with the governments of every Megacity, Lom. That shouldn't deter us from our dream."

"What about Moryth? I liked it there."

"No! That is the absolute one place we should *not* go. That and Torlea and Dakon."

Lom thought a moment before saying, "So that only leaves Rygom or Wexar."

"And we decided that we didn't want to stay here in Rygom, so than it must be Wexar." Klev looked expectantly at Lom. "What do you think, Lom?"

"Perfect, Klev! You always know best."

They chatted about the fragments of their scattered memories as they made their way to the Underling community. Occasionally, they disagreed about what happened on a particular mission. They would stop briefly to look through their notebooks to discover that they were discussing two or more different events that had become jumbled in their brains.

"No, no, *no*!" Klev shouted in frustration. "We never met Alterations that could control elements. Maybe we heard rumors when we were in Moryth, but I don't think they actually existed."

Lom shook his head. He flipped through the notebook in his hand. “It’s in here somewhere. The fire guy burned my forearm.” He awkwardly shifted his box so that he could pull his shirt sleeve away. “See that?”

Klev barely glanced at it before saying, “That’s not a burn; it’s a cut. You nearly lost that hand in a duel with that Rygom Agent.”

“Wasn’t that you, Klev?” Lom selected another notebook and began pursuing the wrinkled paper pages. “The thing with the element Alterations was after we impersonated scientists in Torlea.”

“I thought that was in Dakon.” Klev snatched to notebook from him.

“I’m pretty sure that we hadn’t had an assignment in Dakon yet.” Lom didn’t like fighting with Klev. His head ached from trying to fit the memory puzzle pieces together. The notebooks helped, but he was sure that many pages were missing.

They were too busy bickering to notice that they had arrived at their destination. Klev realized where they were as he collided with an orange, plastic tent.

“What is that?” Lom asked, peeking inside. “Oh, Klev! Something’s not right.”

"What are you talking about?" Klev slipped under the tent.

Figures in over-sized white bio-hazard suits rushed about, moving between decrepit buildings. Dirty people wearing tattered clothing lay on the ground, letting the suited people prick them with needles. A poor person passed by them, a sterile mask was over her mouth; she joined a group of others wearing the same face-coverings.

Lom followed him inside. They stuck to the shadows as they observed the Regioners.

The people in the suits continued organizing the tattered people into two groups—those who were given masks and those who were denied them. The mask people were ushered away in groups, leaving the mask-less crying in their filthy homes.

"What are they doing?" Lom asked.

Removing a pair of binoculars from his box, Klev moved to get a better look. "The white suit guys are testing blood, probably for some kind of disease. The people with the masks are healthy and are being taken away. The sick ones have to stay."

"Should we get out of here?"

Klev didn't answer right away. He waited patiently for Lom's short-term memory to vanish. When his partner's expectant expression changed to one of confusion, Klev said, "I think we should leave, Lom. We don't want to be taken, too."

"You have the best ideas, Klev!" Lom smiled as he followed him back to the tent flap.

When they reached the barrier, a light blinded them. Klev removed the knife from his hip and assumed a fighting stance. Lom stood casually behind him, holding his own blade.

"We don't want to harm you," a female voice said. "Please put your weapons down."

"Let us leave and we won't kill anyone," Klev threatened, slicing the air.

A figure in a biohazard suit approached them. "I just want to see if you're sick." The woman held up a syringe. "You'll barely feel a thing. I promise."

Klev glared at the needle. "The promise of a woman means nothing to me."

Lom put a hand on Klev's arm. "Perhaps we should hear her out."

"We can always leave if we don't like what she has to say," Klev said as he sheathed his knife. He looked at Lom's blade with a frown. "Put that thing away, Lom! You wanna scare our host?"

The woman stuck each of them in the arm with a different needle. She put their blood samples into a small machine. When a light turned green, she grinned. "You're both clean."

"Does that mean that we get white masks?" Lom asked.

The woman gestured at a canvass, orange tent. "Please follow me." Once inside, she removed her biohazard suit. Smoothing her burnt-orange dress, the blonde female introduced herself. "I am Nasiram Rush. I run this relocation clinic." She extended her hand and Klev shook it.

Without introducing himself, Klev said, "What's this on your wrist?" He pulled her hand closer to his face. A line of orange dots and dashes was inked into her skin. "It's your first name in Morse Code."

"Yes," she replied slowly as she ran a hand through her short blonde hair. "It's my *Signature*." Nasiram paused, tilting her head. "You don't know what that is?"

"Well, we know how to read the code," Lom replied, joining the conversation. He inspected what Nasiram called her *Signature*. "We just don't know why you felt the need to permanently tattoo your name on yourself."

"All Clan members must have one. It acts as an electronic identification marker. Signatures are required to enjoy certain facilities in the Lower Region and Market Levels."

Klev frowned. "That still doesn't make any sense. Start saying things we'll understand."

Nasiram's pleasing demeanor faltered for a moment. Before she answered, she took a breath and gave them a sympathetic smile. "I know this is all very confusing, but your questions can be answered later. Right now, I'd like to discuss with you some possibilities for your future."

Lom's ears perked at the mention of the future. "Oh? What did you have in mind?"

"Well, you two could come join the Amber Clan," she explained. "My husband is the Clan Lord, Dagnos Rush. We'll put you to work—help you get your life back on track. In the Amber Head Quarters, you'll live out your life safely away from the deadly Plague."

"Safe?" Klev sniffed. "We like to live on the edge!"

"What's this you say about work?" Lom asked, intrigued by a way to support themselves.

The woman removed a brochure from a briefcase and handed it to Lom. "The Amber Clan has many exciting entry-level jobs available for new recruits. If you work hard, you should receive a promotion within a few months."

Klev snatched the papers from Lom and looked them over. "All the pictures are of men and women stomping through the pipe-works. Do you expect us to be plumbers or something?"

"Plumbers? Goodness, no!" Nasiram laughed. She took the brochure back, turned a few pages in, and handed it to Lom once again. "It takes at least five years to work your way to that position. You'd start off in sanitation and move up from that."

Lom was intrigued by the idea. "We've never worked with sewage before. It'd be a great addition to our resume."

Turning a bright shade of red, Klev growled, "After all our years of experience in the most prestigious occupations, you're willing to throw all of it away to clean toilets! Lom, I am ashamed that you are considering this."

Nasiram put her hands up and softly said, "You haven't heard all the amenities we offer to our Clan members. If you let me finish explaining, I'm sure that you'll—"

"We're leaving," Klev interrupted. He hefted his box and walked away.

Lom nodded his head in respect to Nasiram as he departed. As he caught up to Klev, he whispered, "Are you sure it's wise to turn down work? It didn't have to be forever. I'm sure we could have left as soon as we had saved enough to retire."

"No, Lom. That sneaky woman wanted to mark us; those tattoos are a way of claiming people as property. Even if we had gotten away and had the ink removed, there would still be scars etched into our skin. I wouldn't want to live the rest of my life with a permanent reminder that I was owned by someone."

"I didn't realize all that," Lom apologized. "It's a good thing you made that decision for us. I suppose we should seek employment elsewhere." They walked in silence for several minutes. Lom eventually stopped and asked. "Where are we going?"

"I decided that we need to look for work. But we need to find people in order to find jobs."

"Fantastic idea, Klev! You always know what to do."

"Of course I do, Lom. So we'll just roam until we find some—" He paused before suddenly saying, "Hide!" Klev pushed Lom into a dark, empty building.

A group of people passed by. Lom thought it strange that everyone in the group wore different shades of purple, accented by gold jewelry. Their wrists were inked with purple dots and dashes.

"Who do you suppose they are?" Lom asked.

"Perhaps more of those Clan people," Klev answered. "They look rather fancy. Maybe they'll have better job opportunities. Let's see where they're headed."

Chapter 4

Her first evening at the Agency was proving to be less exciting than Iris had hoped. She had changed out of her stiff grey Candidate uniform and into comfortable clothes in order to ease the stressful task of unpacking. It had taken her over two weeks to get all her belongings into boxes and suitcases; she hoped it wouldn't take her *that long* to get it all put away.

Needing a change of scenery, she left her room and walked across the hall. She knocked on Claire's door. It whooshed open a moment later, revealing a disheveled version of her friend. "What happened in here?" Iris asked with a chuckle.

"What do you mean?" Claire turned away from her and sat at her desk. She began tinkering with lumps of plastic and wires.

"We've only been here a few hours and already your room looks like you've lived here for several years." Iris gestured at the piles of clothes all over the bed, the scrap metal that lay in a heap in the corner, the dirty dishes from lunch by the door, and the cases of discs stacked untidily on the bookshelves. "Did you bring *every* article of clothing you own?"

“Yes,” Claire said indignantly as she tossed a lump of wires to the far corner. “What’s wrong with that? I like clothes.”

“Just don’t embarrass me by showing up for Testing in your green halter dress.”

Claire sighed, but didn’t respond. She continued tinkering with the lump in her hands.

“Are you still fidgeting with your Project?” Iris asked, moving clothes so that she could sit on the bed. “The OMNI hover features are great the way they are.”

Speaking in a fast, excited voice, Claire rambled, “No, this afternoon I heard that most of the other Engineering Candidates are focusing on OMNI upgrades. I don’t want my Project to be just another model! I realized that I have to do something different. And that’s when it hit me: *Simulation implants*!”

“Simulation implants? I thought they were deemed dangerous by the Agency Board.”

“The creators didn’t use the right method,” Claire explained, leaning over her work. “They attempted to sync the human brain with the Sim technology by connecting the wires directly to the cerebrum, which then resulted in them hooking up the different processing centers in ways that led to hearing with the eyes, smelling with fingers, and all sorts of messed up sensory experiences."

"And you think you can fix that?" Iris asked, skeptically.

"One: don't connect with wires—use nanites. Two: attach directly to the sensory nerves at the base of the neck instead of cutting the brain open." Without any further explanation, Claire began frantically typing notes into her OMNI.

"I'm going to get some dinner. Want to come with?"

"Nah." Claire waved her away. "I just sent the Kitchens my dinner order. They'll be sending it to the pantry soon."

Iris narrowed her eyes. "What?"

"ARHA told me about the delivery service. But you have to order within a certain time. You just missed the cut-off. If you send in an order now, the food won't arrive until tomorrow morning."

"Alright, you have fun with your Project. I guess I'll just go to the Cafeteria by myself."

The Residential Halls were scattered with socializing Candidates. Iris ignored all she passed, looking intently at the map on her OMNI. Eventually, she found the nearest Cafeteria. The room was full of strangers. Iris recognized a few faces from earlier that morning, but she didn't really *know* any of them. At the well-stocked buffet line, Iris carefully measured out her food. When her tray contained everything she needed for a well-balanced meal, she made her way to the far side of the seating area, away from the other people. She consumed her meal while reading a data-disc on her OMNI.

Unfortunately, several young men decided to disrupt her peace. She tuned out most of what they said. It appeared that they had vid-discs they wanted to give Claire. They had each met Miss Birch sometime during their high school days and desired to "hang out" again.

Iris was use to being a shield between her friend and the creepy boys she dated for several years. She guaranteed them that she'd give the discs to Claire, knowing that the messages were just going to be erased and the discs reused. When they were gone, she got up and dumped the remainder of her dinner in the garbage pipe.

Minutes later, she entered her Living Quarters and found Claire setting up a gaming system in their common room. Iris smiled at her friend. "I met some of your old *friends* at the cafeteria," she added, moving to the couch. "They asked me to give you these." Removing the coin-sized vid-discs from her pocket, she tossed them onto the coffee table. Iris was about to head downstairs when she realized that she didn't want to return to the chore of unpacking "ARHA?"

The wall screen went from black to white. "How may I help you, Iris Kayn?"

She moved to the screen between the kitchenette and common room. "Can you tell me where the nearest Simulator is located?"

"They are mostly in the Classroom Levels. But they are not operational this summer."

Iris frowned. "Why not?"

"The Agency Board Members feel that the Candidates should focus on the talents they have, and not try and develop others. Since the Simulator's main goal is to help enhance any lacking skills, the Board feel that it is an unnecessary distraction from the focus of the Placement Tests. I am sorry, Iris Kayn, for any inconvenience."

"That's alright, ARHA. Thank you for your help." Iris descended the stairs as the wall screen faded to black.

Back in her room, she fiddled with the automated control panel. The sound system was even better than the one in her father's house. She inserted a sound-disc and tapped the *play* icon. Her mother's recorded voice gave a lecture on the use of nanites to cure diseases. The sounds were so clear that Iris thought that the woman was actually speaking to her. Of course, it was a stupid thing to think of—her mother being alive again—but Teresa Kayn's words soothed her agitation.

Iris went to her bathroom and located a syringe. She barely flinched as she stuck the three-inch needle into her elbow. The thick, clear substance caused an itchy sensation under her skin. Iris tossed the empty injector at a waste basket and massaged the medicine into her bloodstream.

The daily activity was a result of the same thing that had killed her mother. Teresa had been acquiring Plague samples from the Lower Region when she caught one of the deadly viruses; she had been several months along in her pregnancy at the time. Plague Three not only attacked her mother, but had infected Iris as an unborn baby. Her father had been unable to find the cure for that particular strand of Plague, but he had devised the medication to keep the virus from killing Iris.

Iris had wondered why she hadn't died along with her mother. It hadn't made any sense to her. When she asked her father, Norman gave her some complicated science answer, full of medical mumbo-jumbo that she didn't understand. He told her that she should be grateful to be alive.

That task was difficult to do the first thirteen years of her life. She was often ill and too sick to do normal childhood things. Every several months, her father would perform surgeries to remove diseased sections of muscles or bones, making her more and more frail. The countless hours of recovery had been spent alone in her room with piles of books and data-discs.

Shaking off the horrid childhood memories, Iris returned to the task of unpacking. She opened a bag that contained her picture frames. Many were of her parents on various trips or events they went to in their years together.

She stroked an image of her parents on their honeymoon. Teresa was dressed in a short cotton dress, enjoying a light rain at a wildlife preserve. Iris stared into the blue-grey eyes that her mother had passed onto her. Although her hair was also light like Teresa, Iris had gotten the darker shade of blonde from her father.

As Iris began placing her hard-backed books on a shelf, there was a loud knocking on her door.

"Let me in!" Claire shouted.

Iris pressed the button to open her bedroom door. "What is it?"

"Grab you bag and come with me."

With a sigh, Iris complied. "Where we are going?"

"If I told you, you wouldn't come." Claire grabbed her arm and dragged her up the stairs.

Iris could have gotten out of the grip if she wanted to, but she had promised years ago to never use her self-defense skills on Claire. "Is this anything like the time you convinced me to go swimming in the Mason's fountain?"

Claire chuckled. "Like I'd risk our reputation as Candidates on a thrill-seeking whim! No, we're not going to break any codes of decorum tonight." She opened the door of their Living Quarters and escorted Iris out into the Hall. "We're going shopping!"

"I thought we already established that you have more than enough clothes for the next three years," Iris complained. "What else could you possibly need?"

"Haven't I taught you anything? It doesn't matter how many clothes I have if I don't have something for a specific occasion. So shut up and help me find something I can wear to the club tonight."

Iris really didn't want to go with, but she decided that she could procrastinate on the rest of her unpacking.

At the nearest Sector Plaza, they found a department store and ventured to the clothing section.

Claire was unusually picky as they glanced through the racks. She only let Iris out of her sight when she slipped into the dressing room.

"You're not coming dressed like that, are you?" a man's voice asked from behind her.

Iris thought she had been addressed by a giant; he was at least a foot taller than her. A red tank top sat snuggly over his colossal chest.

"Excuse me?" she whispered, backing away.

Alastair Vega appeared a moment later, a wide smile on his lips. He wore a green silk shirt under a sleek black vest. "Good evening, Iris. I don't know if you remember my brother, Max."

Iris was taken aback at being called by her first name; she barely knew her Mentor. "Oh, of course." She gave him an awkward wave. If they were going to speak informally with one another, she figured that she should too. "It's a pleasure to see you again, Max."

"Likewise," the giant replied with lop-sided grin.

A question formed on her lips, but she wasn't sure if it was appropriate to ask or not. However, she decided to take a chance. "Now how do you have such a simple name like 'Max' while your brother has such a *pretentious* one?"

"Actually, my name is 'Maximus,' but I'd rather be called *Max*."

Claire returned, wearing an ensemble of a pink tube-top dress, a brown velvet belt, and white strappy heels. "Hey, it's the Vega boys! Good to see you again, Max."

Iris frowned. "When did you meet Max?"

"Oh, that's not important." Claire replied passively with a shrug. "Thanks for escorting us to the club. We are *so* excited to meet everyone. Aren't we, Iris?"

"Yes, of course." Iris put on her fake smile while wondering when the Vegas had offered to *escort* them. "But I'm not dressed for a club." She gestured at her dark blue sweatpants and purple T-shirt. "I'll just head home real fast and meet you guys over there later."

She began to walk away, but Claire stopped her.

"Just find something here. Oh, those are cute!" Claire darted to the nearest rack, pulled a bronze blouse and a pair of denim pants off their hangers, and flung them at Iris. She nodded at the changing room. "Let's go."

After dressing in their new clothes, they made their purchase at the register and arranged for the store to deliver their old ones to their Living Quarters.

The Vega brothers led them to The Grey Circumstance club. Music grew louder as they approached.

Colorful lights flashed on and off, contrasting against the different hues of grey in the marble walls.

In the center of the room was a foot-high stage, complete with color-changing light panels on the floor. Several Candidates and Trainees took turns free-styling in the middle. The dancers moved in time with the beat as the crowds cheered them on. Iris was grateful that Claire didn't urge her to take a turn.

Max motioned towards a raised dais at the far end of the room. A pair of red-headed females sat talking to two dark-haired Candidates. The women's frowns turned to smiles as they saw the Vegas.

"Save me from your boring Mentees, Max," the taller woman whispered as she hugged the giant Third-Year. Upon closer inspection, Iris recognized her as Viola Cromford.

"As my damsel commands." Max made a fancy bow before swooping Viola into his massive arms. After saying farewell to his companions, he carried the Mayor's daughter up a flight of stairs.

Eve Sanders remained alone on the dais with Max's Mentees, looking irritated. She cut off one of the boys midsentence by putting a finger in his face. "Hold that thought." Approaching Alastair, she said, "It's about time!"

She fluffed her short red hair and gave him a flirty wink. "Wanna dance, Al?"

Alastair smiled in reply. "I'd love to." He turned to Claire and Iris. "Make yourselves comfortable. I'll be back in a little bit." Taking Eve's hand, he led her to the color-changing dance floor.

Claire nudged Iris in the rib with her elbow and said in a low voice, "Don't be mad, Iris, but I'm going to *disappear* for awhile with the cute one." She nodded at a lean, dark-haired boy with creamy tan skin and thick lips. "Can you do me a favor and please keep the other guy busy."

Reluctantly, Iris nodded. For some reason, she had expected Claire to dial down her promiscuity once they had moved to the Agency. But she now realized that was too much to expect. "Have fun sucking his face off."

By the time Iris reached the dais, Claire had already introduced herself to the dark, handsome Candidate and was pulling him away from the platform. "My name is Garret Sanchez, by the way," the boy barely managed to say before he and Claire disappeared into one of the side rooms.

The remaining boy had short, medium brown hair and mud-colored eyes. "I guess we're stuck together. Still, I can't complain that I get the pretty blonde for my date." He patted the seat beside him. "The name's Simon Pyke."

"Hello. I'm Iris Kayn." She smiled awkwardly as she joined him. "How do you like the Agency?"

Simon Pyke chuckled. "You really want to talk about the Agency?"

Iris hesitated before saying, "I guess not. I just don't really know what I want to talk about."

"If that's the case, we don't have to talk at all." Pyke reached out and grabbed her hand.

The suddenness of the motion startled Iris. The pressure of his fingers around hers triggered a reflex. She tightly gripped his hand in response while her free palm made contact with his nose. Iris stood, pivoting so that she could ram Pyke into the table behind them. Still clutching his hand, she extended his elbow and pulled him into an arm-bar.

"Ah! Let go, you crazy woman!" he cried out. "What did I ever do to you?"

Iris realized that the club had stilled in the moments it took to subdue Pyke. The guests stared at her with wide eyes and confused expressions. People began to whisper and she heard her name spoken in hushed tones. All the attention made her face hot and sticky with perspiration.

"What happened?" Alastair asked as he ran to them.

Releasing Pyke, she took a couple raspy breaths. By the time she calmed herself, all of her acquaintances had reappeared. "We were talking and then he touched me and I couldn't help myself and I put him in the arm-bar and I—" She stopped as she realized that her rambling was getting her all riled up again.

Alastair's gaze turned hostile. "He *touched* you?"

"No!" Pyke held his arms up. "Not like *that*. I was just trying to hold her hand."

"Oh, Iris!" Claire growled, pulling her away from the group. "You can't attack a guy for coming onto you. Haven't I taught you anything?"

Iris stammered, "I—I didn't know that. I'm just not use to—I mean, that only ever happens when I'm training—" There were too many eyes on her; she couldn't think straight. An overwhelming urge to be alone consumed her. Without another word, she took off towards the club entrance, running as fast as she could from the judgmental gazes of her peers.

Chapter 5

It was a typical, quiet morning at the Headquarters of the Azure Rye Clan.

The Region tradesmen and merchants, with the exception of *one*, had already collected their wares and headed to the Market in the Middle Zone to sell.

Lord Tays Rye rummaged frantically through the various bins in his garage. "Where *are* you?" he called out to certain misplaced items, hoping that his pleas would be heard and that they would magically appear in response to his inquiry.

Most of his tools lay scattered about, covered in grease or rust. The completed orders were stacked in towering piles in every free space. Tays tried to create a walk-way as he sifted through boxes. He missed the days when he knew where everything was. After eight years of working in his garage, he would have thought that he'd know better than letting it get this disorganized.

*****

Thirteen-year-old Tays sat completely still as he watched Jux skillfully weave wires into an iron casing. He was afraid to breathe, worried that he might distract his tutor from his task. Tays made a point of internalizing every facet of the mechanical production as he watched with his keen eyes.

"Would you like to weld it close?" Jux asked him. "Come on. You're hand is even steadier than mine. Go ahead." He handed over the acetylene torch.

Slipping the tinted goggles over his eyes, Tays carefully brought the flame over to the object on the work table. It was a small, electronic key; he had helped build dozens of general apartment keys for Clan members, but this one was different. It was a special design that Jux had created for high-security vaults.

One by one, Tays put the tiny panel covers on the object and welded everything together. When he was done, he stepped back, pulled the goggles up onto his forehead, and examined his work. Satisfied, he passed it to Jux.

His tutor took the item and inspected it. With a chuckle, he said, "Great job, novice." Jux handed the key back to him. "Take this to your parents."

Tays clutched the warm metal tightly and went off sprinting down the Azure halls towards Rye Estate. Curiosity gripped him as he ran. Who was the key for? Were the Rye Leaders redoing the security systems again? Was there something exceedingly valuable that needed to be transferred from one Clan HQ to another? Thoughts about what the special item might be flooded his mind.

Outside the family library, Ebyx leaned against the wall, watching the entrance. The blonde triplet nodded in greeting as he approached. "I'm just waiting for Lady Vamila and Sirad. You can talk to them first, Master Tays."

"Thanks, Ebyx." Before he entered the library, he asked, "Why is my mother a *Lady*, but my father doesn't get a title?" Living with the Azures as a Regioner was still so strange to him, even after having been with them for several months. "Should he be a *Lord* since they are married?"

"Your mum is Lord Asdem's biological sister, which makes her Rye royalty. However, according to Region Law, your pa has no right to her title. But since you, Miss Rikani, and Master Mezik are Lady Vamila's children, you'll receive your titles when you turn sixteen."

Tays thought that he was beginning to understand. "So if cousins Tyvax and Koje were to marry either you or one of your sisters, you wouldn't get a title?"

The comment made Ebyx laugh. The triplet playfully ruffled his deep black hair. "That's right. And there's more to Lower Region politics, but I'm not the one to teach you. Now go on in and see your parents.

Inside the library, Vamila and Sirad sat cuddled on a couch, reading a massive Dickens novel together. When one finished the page, they would kiss the other on the cheek. The receiver of the kiss would then turn the page when they were ready to move on. Not wanting to interrupt his parents' custom, Tays stood in the doorway.

"Hey, son," his dad said, placing a bookmark in the middle of the thick book. "Did you have fun with Jux this afternoon?"

"Yeah, we finished making this." Tays approached them and gave the key to his mother.

"Oh, perfect timing!" Vamila turned to Sirad. "Let's go show him."

His parents led him down a series of corridors to the South side of the Clan HQ, near the loading docks. Vamila and Sirad stopped by a door that led to a storage facility. On the door was a lock of Jux's design.

"What's going on?" Tays asked. "Why did you put a high-tech lock on a storage unit?

"Because it's no longer a storage unit." Sirad moved forward and put the key in the lock without turning it. "Would you do the honors?"

Hesitantly, Tays placed his fingers around the key handle. The latch came undone with a beep and he pushed the heavy door open. Inside, tables and benches stood in straight rows. Along the walls, every kind of tool imaginable hung from hooks and sat on shelves in a neat order. Everything shone in the bright work light.

Finally catching on, Tays whispered, "This is all for me?"

"Yes," Lady Vamila said. "Jux says you have such a passion for fixing things and suggested that we give you your own workspace."

"Koen has agreed to start bringing us broken down appliances for you to repair," added his father. "Perhaps you could fix them up and sell them at Market. The triplets have agreed to escort you there when you have enough wares."

Tays was speechless. Once the shock wore off, he quickly hugged both of his parents and then ran into the room.

Grabbing a rusted vid player, some scrap wires, and a handful of tools, he set everything on a table and began refurbishing the unwanted junk into beautiful treasures.

*****

"Sir?" A man in a simple, faded navy suit emerged through the doorway with a confused look upon his face.

"What're you still doing here? Lady Rikani will be very unhappy to know that you didn't go to the shop today."

"Then we shan't *tell* my sister, Ulrian." Tays spun to face him, knocking over a bin in the process. Ignoring the spilled contents, the Azure Lord moved to another container. "I'm not playing hooky; I'm looking for the Agency's sample order. A Liaison is coming to pick it up after lunch."

"Might I offer a suggestion, Lord Tays?" the steward asked, joining the search for the special items. "Why don't you go ahead to The Sapphire Pawn? I'll stay behind and look for the order. When I find it, I'll bring it to you."

"That just might work." The Azure Lord stopped to think, analyzing if there was anything wrong with the plan. Finding a flaw, he asked, "What if Lady Rikani has a task for you?"

"I'll tell her that you've given me a job of the utmost importance," Ulrian replied, sifting through a tub of spare parts. "I'll make sure to tell her that it isn't any of her business so that she won't pry further. Is that alright, sir?"

"Yes, that'd be great." Tays gathered a pack and box from the nearest table and left his garage.

As he walked briskly down the corridors, he heard his twin sister screeching after him.

"What are you doing?" Rikani called without regarding the watchful eyes of the other Clan members. She came along side him and matched his brisk pace. "You were supposed to be at the shop *over an hour ago*!"

"How would you know if I was at The Sapphire Pawn or not?" he asked, not slowing down. "Are you checking up on me?"

"Janez told me you didn't leave with the others," she said, her displeasure becoming more evident with every second. "Stop! I need to talk to you, Tays." She finally got ahead of him and cut off his retreat.

"Kani, I've been on official shop business," Tays sighed. "And as you have nothing to do with my pawn shop, you can't keep me from my affairs."

"Where is Mezik?"

Tays all but dropped the box in his hands. "What?"

"Daleen called; he's not in class." Rikani's gaze bore into Tays. "Please tell me that you aren't smuggling him out to Market."

He carefully put his box on the ground and peered at his enraged twin. "I would never put our little brother in harm's way!"

She shook her head. "I'll just ask Ulrian to look for him."

Rikani turned to leave, but Tays grabbed her wrist and said, "Let the man have a break for once. You give him *too many* responsibilities."

Rikani glared at his hand, her face turning red. She exhaled sharply and nodded.

Tays picked up his box, and sprinted down the hall. He passed by several Clan members along the way. Myhus, the head chef, was attempting to convince the ragged hunter, Sokun, to bring back something other than rabbits for the stew; one of the security guards, Bilez, tried quite unsuccessfully to mediate their dispute. All the while, Tarek, a pompous merchant tycoon, gave unwanted advice to whomever he came into contact with; the jester, Mutof, walked behind the aging tradesman, mocking him as he made his way down the courtyard. The Azure Lord was pleased that all of those people were his sister's problems and not *his*.

Reaching the main Head Quarters entrance, he nodded to Hurez, who immediately snapped up from his slouching position. Tays leaned over to type in the pass-code on door's keyboard. The sound of soft footsteps made him stop. He turned around to see his little brother a few feet away.

"Did you finish fixing my radio?" Mezik asked, sounding oddly casual.

"You ditched school so that you could ask me that?" Tays put on his best authoritative stare, but he felt like an imposter. "You only gave it to me yesterday, Mez."

"But it's really *important*. When will it be ready?"

"I'll get to it as soon as I can, but it's not a high priority." Something twitched in the back of his mind. Tays looked the thirteen-year-old up and down, sensing there was more to the situation. "It's not just about the radio, is it?"

Mezik looked at his feet and asked, "Can I come with you today? To the shop and to see Market? I promise to stay close to you and not wander off."

"You know how Rikani and I feel about that. You can go in three years when you're sixteen." Tays mustered up as much authority he could in his voice. "But for now, you march yourself back to class." Tays turned to a security guard and asked, "Hurez, could you please escort him?"

"Fine." With a huff, Mezik followed his guide.

Tays entered the exit code; the door opened and then closed the moment he stepped through it. It was a short journey from his home to the Lower Region limits. Agent Sentries stood watch at the Elevators that led into the Middle Zone. Their black uniforms blended into the dark barriers that blocked off the Transit Station from the rest of the Plaza.

The nearest Agent Sentry held out his hands to Tays and took the box and pack from him. He searched through the contents to determine if there was anything dangerous. Another Sentry stuck a needle into Tays's elbow and drew a blood sample. He put a few drops into a machine. A light on the screen blinked green, indicating that Tays didn't have a Plague.

He was then allowed to proceed to the Elevator after paying a small toll and allowing a small machine scan the blue Signature tattooed around his left wrist. He took a seat in the compartment. The Elevator went Up several Sectors before Tays exited the dingy pod.

Market bustled with both Regioner and Zonese shoppers, all looking for the best deals. Vendors, dressed in their respected Clan colors, shouted promises of sales of the lowest prices.

Tays recognized his tenants, clad in silver and blue, trying to sell their goods to the Zonese. He smiled at them as he passed through the streets to where his shop stood.

Jotea unloaded her new paintings into her gallery with the help of her nephew, Zett. The Triplets were busy helping customers at their produce stands. Kagome was visible through the window of her chocolaterie, stocking the displays with freshly baked sweets.

Along the way, he walked by a popular Icterine café with a little patio that stuck out into the street.

An eleven-year-old boy wearing rust-orange suit with white fringe and buttons called out to him. "Tays! Come and sit with me, cousin. It's been such a long time since I've seen you." He waved over a server dressed in a brown and yellow uniform.

"Hi, Kumate," said Tays with an uncertain smile. "Is this your first time at Market?"

"Yeah, it is." The boy took a sip of his steaming drink. "I'm having so much fun. Mom wasn't very happy with the idea, but Dad managed to convince her." He gestured at the loitering waiter/ "So, how 'bout some coffee?"

"No, thank you. I have to go to work." He dismissed the loitering waiter. "Maybe another time."

"Dad, can we go to Tays' shop?" Kumate pleaded with the man next to him.

Like his son, Lord Dagnos Rush wore a gaudy suit of rust-orange and white. "Oh, I think that's a splendid idea; your mother wouldn't object to it. There isn't a safer place in all of Market than The Sapphire Pawn."

Tays tried to object. "Uncle Dagnos, I really have too many things to do today. Why don't you come next week?"

"Perhaps Kumate could help you?" suggested the Amber Leader.

"Oh, yes!" the boy replied, clearly full of too much caffeine. "Can I help you, *please*?"

"Alright, Kum, don't forget your treats." Lord Dagnos turned to a handsome young man sitting at the table next to him. He waved a hand in the other man's face. "Are you coming with us, Nuto?"

"Oh, why not. I can mope anywhere, can't I?" Lord Nuto Berge whined, wiping pastry crumbs off his straw-colored shirt.

"She isn't worth it, lad. You'll find another girl."

Nuto dropped a fist of coins on the table. "I don't want another girl."

At The Sapphire Pawn, a man with shoulder-length golden hair pulled a jade and bronze necklace out of a glass display case to show to an elderly woman in a frilly green gown. He smiled at Tays and raised his hand in greeting. "Excuse me, Lady Darrow." The man stepped away from the counter, leaving the elderly Leader alone to admire the jewelry. He pulled Tays aside. "I know it's my day off, but I thought I'd come in and give you a hand since the Agency Liaison coming this afternoon."

Tays should have known better than to think that his sales associate would stay home on an important day; Roteg was too dedicated to the success of The Sapphire Pawn. "Thanks. I'm pleased to see you have everything in order. Let me know if you need any help with Unmare's purchase."

Kumate busied himself by picking things up off the shelves, showing them to his father, and placing them in the exact same place he had taken them from. Nuto simply stood at the window, gazing out as though he was looking for someone.

Tays was curious about the woman that Lord Berge was breaking his heart over, but he couldn't bring himself to ask him. The newly established Icterine Clan Leader had just finished mourning the death of his adopted parents and was finally out his HQ after a year-long period of solitude. He didn't want to risk further distancing their friendship by prying into his personal matters.

Dagnos gave Nuto a pitying glance and whispered to Tays, "He met Soha last week; he's been pining for her ever since. He visits the Jade Head Quarters every day, but she refuses to see him."

"The Heir to the Jade Darrow Clan?"

Lord Rush nodded at Lady Unmare. "When the old lady over there croaks, Soha will become the Leader."

Clan politics held very little interest for Tays, so he rarely understood what was happening between the different families. But his uncle's remark sparked a bit of curiosity. "What does that have to do with anything?"

"If Soha were to marry Nuto, she'd have to go live with the Icterine Clan." Dagnos clarified. Lord Rush pulled him further away from the customers and added, "Since there aren't any other Berges, the Council won't let Nuto give up Leadership. However, rumor has it that Lady Unmare has a grandson. So Soha isn't the only Darrow Heir. She's *expendable*, so to speak. Because Soha doesn't know the financial state the Jades, she's decided that she'd rather be in control of her own Clan instead being married off to Nuto."

Tays tried to rack his brain around the intricate situation. "Does Unmare know about Lord Berge's feelings? Maybe she could persuade Soha. The Icterines are one of the richest Clans and everyone knows that the Jade Darrows are on the verge of bankruptcy."

Dagnos shook his head. "She's too intelligent to *not* suspect anything."

A whirling noise sounded across the room. Roteg motioned for Lady Unmare Darrow to place her right hand inside the noisy box. "I just need your Signature before you go." There was a series of beeps as the scanner spun around the green ink on her wrist.

Nuto turned away from the window with a sigh. The sight of the Jade Clan Leader snapped him back to reality. Color flushed into his cheeks. He dashed over to the counter and caught her attention. "Excuse me, Lady Unmare, but do you need some help carrying your bags home?"

"Why, yes, Lord Nuto," Unmare said, enthusiastically. "Thank you very much. If you have some free time, you can stay for lunch. I'm sure Soha would be happy to see you."

Lord Berge perked up at the invitation, losing all signs of heartache. "I'd love to. Goodbye, Tays. Dagnos. Don't eat all your treats in one day, Kumate." He grabbed the bags from the counter and left the store, bearing a large grin on his face.

"That *poor* man," Dagnos laughed.

"You never felt that way with Aunt Nasiram?" Tays asked, feeling concerned his relatives' marital status.

Lord Rush's face wrinkled in contemplation. "I guess I might've a long time ago. But we've been married over a dozen years. *Wishing* for a wife and *having* one are two completely different feelings; passion eventually burns out. You'll understand someday."

Tays didn't like the idea of falling out of love. It seemed like a difficult enough business to just find someone to share your life with, let alone worrying about the time when the adoration would stop. His experience in love was that not even the deepest treachery could break the strings of attachment. Even after a relationship ends, feelings for the other person continue, despite the circumstances that caused the rift.

His contemplations were interrupted as the shop doors flung open. "Lord Tays! I've found them," the Azure steward said, running forward. "They were under Lady Lurahi's electronic book readers. I don't know how they ended up there."

"Thank you, Ulrian." Tays took the box from him and carried it to the counter. "Did you tell my sister what you were up to?"

"Lady Rikani came into the garage once," Ulrian said, catching his breath, "She seemed to be looking for the Master Mezik. I was able to hide behind your motor bike." The steward gave a slight bow. "Good luck with the Agency, Lord Tays." He bowed again and left the shop.

"What's that?" Kumate asked, peeking into the box.

"It's an important order, Kum," Tays explained to his cousin. "An Agent is coming by to pick it up in a little while."

"Wow! Can I stay and meet them?"

Dagnos intervened. "I think we'd better head home now, son. Your mother will be frantic with worry. It was good to see you, Tays. I'll ask Nasiram when we can have you, Rikani, and Mezik over for dinner." Before he left, he added, "Of course, we'll take care of all the necessary safety precautions."

"I appreciate it. I'll have Rikani give Aunt Nas a call tonight." He turned to Kumate. "And you, little man, better take good care of yourself. Be careful when you come to Market. We wouldn't want you dragged off now, would we?" He hesitated before adding, "And could you do me a favor, Kum? Don't tell Mezik that you've been here today. He'd never speak to me again if he found out that his eleven year old cousin got to see Market before him."

Tays began his work after his relations left. There wasn't much to do with Roteg there as well. He tried to send his employee home, but it was futile.

"No offense, but I'm the better salesman," Roteg said. It wasn't a boast, merely a statement of fact. He sold circles around Tays. His charm and charisma were what brought in the money that held the business together. "By the way, I think you should *hire* someone to clean and stuff," Roteg added, restocking the jewelry cases. "Zett is looking for a little more work. Jotea is planning on opening the gallery later in the morning and closing earlier in the afternoon. He might be interested in helping a few hours every day. That way, you could sit in your garage all day and tinker to your heart's content."

"I wish I could piece things together like you can, Ro," Tays replied, ashamed of the thought that his employ was trying to take over his shop. "It sounds like you've got it all planned out. I'm assuming that we can *afford* to hire someone else?"

"As long as you leave the selling to me, then yes we can." Roteg looked him over, his brow furrowed in thought. "How ya doing, Tays?"

The Azure Lord tried to act like he didn't know what his employee was referring to. "Good, as always."

Roteg shook his head. "Don't give me that. The lovey-dovey brat that was in here earlier has got you thinking about *her*; don't deny it. I know how you get when you see Vian and me together. And you've been acting all depressed since you walked through the door."

"Yes, okay! I've been thinking about her. Not that I want to. I just can't help remembering—"

"Get a hold of yourself, Tays!" Roteg shouted as he punched Tays in the arm. "She *never* loved you. I don't even think she can love anyone. She used you. Remember that."

"That doesn't change the fact that *I* loved *her*. What would you have done if had been Vian that betrayed you? Would you be able to get over it so easily?" Tays rubbed his eyes to banish his mind's image of Exada.

Roteg shook his head. "You're right. I'd be a mess, like you were a few weeks ago."

"I don't want to discuss it anymore; talking about her just makes everything worse. Let's just go on with our day and stick to topics concerning the shop."

Roteg nodded and went on with his work, rearranging the display items.

Tays looked at the clock on the far wall and determined that there was still time to leave for awhile; the

Agency Liaison wouldn't be by for a couple hours. He called out to Roteg, told him that he was going to get lunch, and then left the shop to clear his head.

Chapter 6

Alastair Vega observed through the two-way glass as one of his Mentees ducked and dodged with ease through an Obstacle Course on the other side. A twinge of resentment flashed across his face as Iris Kayn gracefully jumped atop a toppled cargo box while deflecting a sedation dart with her twin knives. On the other hand, he admired the elegance of Miss Kayn's movements. Her blades swung fluidly through the air. Strands of her blonde hair fell out of her ponytail and wisped around her face. A spark of determination lit in her blue eyes; even filthy and covered in sweat, she was a thing of beauty.

Beside him, Max stood with his jaw dropped in amazement. After Miss Kayn completed an aerial somersault, his brother turned and said, "That girl is *good.* Have you ever seen anyone move like her? It's like watching a whirlwind." Max suddenly grew serious. "If only my Mentees had that kind of ability. I'd love to be able to train with someone like Miss Kayn."

Alastair ignored the voice in his head that told him to hide his feelings. "I'd trade *my* Mentees for Mr. Sanchez and Mr. Pyke in a heart-beat, but the Board won't let me switch." He stepped away from the window.

Thoughts of his first encounter with Iris Kayn ran through his mind.

*****

Strangers flitted about the ballroom of Vega Manor. Fifteen-year-old Alastair searched in vain for a familiar face.

Max seemed comfortable in his stuffy, expensive suit. Alastair approached him, laughing as his brother delivered the punch line of his famous joke about a salesman, the roof of a building, and an emergency call.

"That never gets old," Alastair sighed with a charming grin. He turned to the guests. "Please excuse us for a moment, ladies and gentlemen. Our father requires our attention."

Tobias Vega, stoic and stern-faced, stood with a light-haired man and lady. A little blonde girl, a couple years younger than Alastair and Max, timidly clung to the woman's hand. Her simple brown dress stood out against the elegant gowns and sleek suits. Still, she was quite pretty.

They were waved over by Tobias Vega to meet the guests. "These are my sons, Alastair and Maximus. Boys, meet the famous Dr. Norman Kayn and his research assistant, Dr. Audrey Taledon. And this is his lovely daughter, Iris."

Dr. Kayn reached over and shook the boys' hands. "Would you young men be kind enough to show my girl around? She doesn't know anyone here."

"We would be honored to escort her, Dr. Kayn." Al turned and addressed the small lady. "Would you be so kind as to come with us, Miss Kayn?" He offered his arm, flexing his bicep below his stuffy suit.

Iris accepted his arm, gasping lightly when Alastair moved her fingers to his upper arm. She followed them away from the crowded ballroom to the secluded library of Vega Manor.

The new scenery seemed to help Miss Kayn relax a bit. She bypassed the rows of fiction-discs and began perusing the antique books. Iris gingerly fingered their stiff bindings, a smile finally making it to her lips.

"What do you think?" Alastair whispered to Max. "I bet she'd let me."

Max looked Iris up and down as she inspected an encyclopedia. "She's certainly different than your usual girls. With how nervous she is, I doubt she's ever kissed a boy."

Iris stiffened. Her eyes peeked over the edge of the book in her hands.

"I think you're right." Alastair rubbed his jaw in thought. He looked the girl up and down, wondering what it would feel like to hold her in his arms. "It's been a while since I've made out with a chaste Societan girl. It'll be a great experience for *both* of us."

An OMNI beeped and Max pulled his device out. "Excuse me a moment, Miss Kayn. I have to go bring my father something." He bowed and left the room.

Alastair stared at the nervous girl for several moments, planning his move. Based on her stiff posture, she was obviously pretending not to have heard their conversation. He couldn't tell if that meant she was just waiting for him to come kiss her or if she was hoping he wouldn't do anything.

But of course she was waiting for him! What young lady didn't want a handsome young man to spontaneously kiss her? Every other time he had done it, he had received a positive reaction.

Slowly, he eased himself closer to her. She glanced up quickly before turning her back on him. Alastair read over her shoulder for a moment, skimming the text about the former United States. He grabbed the encyclopedia from her firm grasp and tossed it to the floor. Iris tensed, her back cringing as he put his arms around her. She gasped as he planted a firm kiss at the base of her neck.

"What are you doing?" Iris put a hand on top of his head and pushed lightly. "Stop."

"Just relax." His lips moved across her bare shoulder.

"Please," she begged. "Stop!" Iris smacked his arms, surprisingly hard for such a small girl. It startled him, causing his grip to loosen. She rushed away, but he grabbed her wrist.

Undeterred, Alastair said, "You'll enjoy it if you just calm down."

"*Let go!*" She yanked herself backwards. Miss Kayn fell to the floor, her head smacking against the corner of a book shelf. A smear of red shone against the wood.

Alastair ran out of the library and into the ballroom. "Help!" he shouted at the strangers. They all stared at him, not sure how to react. "Someone help me, please!" A moment later, Mr. Vega, Dr. Kayn, and Dr. Taledon appeared. He led them to the library. "It was an accident. Miss Kayn hit her head. She's bleeding!"

Iris sat up with her hand held to her bloody scalp. "It hurts!" she sobbed.

Dr. Kayn picked up his wounded daughter and disappeared, followed closely by Dr. Taledon. Tobias Vega remained behind, giving his son a disapproving glare.

*****

From down the hallway, someone asked, "Aw, is Mr. Perfect feeling envious?"

Alastair and Max turned to see Stella Harding strutting towards them in her tight, black leather outfit.

Drew Harding, wearing a looser but almost identical uniform, walked up behind her. He looked rather upset—as he usually did—at his big sister's teasing words. "Leave the poor guy alone, sis. You probably couldn't beat her either."

In an answer to the challenge, Stella pulled her whip from her side. The men instinctively ducked as she swung her weapon around the corridor, swatting at the near-by Solar Lamps. The spherical lights shattered in a spray of hot glass. "I'd be happy to prove my skills against hers. Her puny knives are no match for my whip."

"Geez, Stel," Drew sighed. "Do you have to destroy *everything* you come across?" He shook his head and mumbled something about self-control as he recorded the event of his sister's latest outburst in his OMNI. "Agent Vega isn't going to be happy when he hears about the damage from your tantrum."

"Stop over-reacting, Drew. They're just cheap bulbs." She wound up her weapon and placed it back on her hip. "Big *V* wanted me to remind you two Little *V's* about the meeting with the Azure scum in an hour." Stella frowned, clearly upset she was being used as a messenger.

"Oh, *no*," Alastair said with sarcasm. "I *completely* forgot about the Region meeting. Thank you *so much* for sweeping in and saving the day!"

"Shut it, Al," Stella scowled. "Apparently this account is very important and it can't be messed up. So get to it." She turned and left, swishing her dark hair as she strode down the hall.

"That woman needs an attitude adjustment," said Max with a grimace.

Drew nodded his head in agreement. Before leaving, he threw in one last reminder. "You're supposed to leave now if you want to make it there on time."

Max shook his head. "I can't believe father lets her get away with so much."

"She's attractive and she's good at what she does," Alastair replied, dismissively. "If either of those facts were different, I'm sure he'd keep her on a much tighter leash."

"We should throw her in a Sparring Ring with Miss Kayn; that should humble her."

Not wanting to talk about the women anymore, Alastair said, "We should get going."

The two young Vegas made their way out of the Agency, through the Upper Society floors, all the way to the lowest Sector Level of the Middle Zone where Market was held.

Alastair and Max removed their Branch pins from their pockets—the letters SO were in gold over a blue shield—and placed them on their lapels. As Mentors in the Agency Training Program, they didn't need to wear them while going about their normal duties. However, they were about to go on an official mission and therefore were required to identify themselves as Third-Year Special Operation Trainees of the Enforcement Branch.

On the journey Down, Al had studied a data-disc about the shop owner. Very little was known about the Azure Clan Leaders. Tays and Rikani Rye had begun co-ruling their Clan after a tragedy that killed half their family five years previous. There were hints that the twins use to be Societans when they were children, but there wasn't any solid evidence.

Alastair had been to several Market Plazas with his father and brother throughout his life. Although there was a bit of culture shock going to some of the more grungy places in the Megacity, their ventures had always been educational in one aspect of another.

Most of the shops sold inferior quality items, while other more reputable establishments managed to produce goods that had higher worth than ones in Upper Society.

The Sapphire Pawn was one such shop.

There was a further advantage of buying from such shops. The Agency's reputation was enhanced when word spread that it was helping the Region Renovation Act by supporting their merchants. On top of it all, products in Market were produced more cheaply and saved the tax-payers thousands of dollars every year. It was for quality, politics, and frugality that Tobias Vega had proposed that the Agency do business with the Regioners.

The Sapphire Pawn was only the beginning—the first wave in the ocean of their father's Mayoral Campaign to gain popularity with the voters. It would all start with the initial transaction between the pawn shop owner and Vega's sons. As they trekked through the streets on the Market, Alastair couldn't help but feel the pressure of the situation.

Consulting his OMNI map, Alastair realized that they were directed to the wrong location. He scanned the surroundings. The street lights were all but broken as they flickered from random pulses of electricity.

"What's going on? Is this a joke?" Max gave a half laugh. "It's not a very funny one, if you ask me. What's that Rye fellow up to?"

The lights went out completely. Alastair held up his OMNI and activated the flashlight; a moment later, that also went dark. A download bar appeared on the screen. From behind him, he could hear Max unsheathing his sword. Alastair resisted the urge to pull his out as well.

A woman's voice echoed through the halls. "Well, well, well. I wouldn't have thought that the Vega brothers would be afraid of the dark."

"*Afraid*?" Max scoffed. "Come out and we'll see who is afraid!"

"Calm down," Al whispered, stepping away from his brother's voice. He didn't want to be near his brother if he decided to start swinging blindly at the air. "You know, it's illegal to hack another person's OMNI. You could get into some serious trouble."

"Only if I get caught," the woman replied, still not visible.

"So that's why you lured us here?" Alastair scoffed. "To steal our personal information?"

"I just wanted to introduce myself." The lights blinked back to life. A woman dressed in red leather stood between Alastair and Max. Random black lines and shapes embellished her sleeveless top and knee-length shorts. Waves of platinum blonde hair draped across the front of her shoulders. "I am Exada of the Royal Steel Family." She gave them a bright red smile.

Alastair searched his mind for everything he knew about the Steels. None of the data-discs he had read ever mentioned a woman with that name. "Pleased to meet you, Miss Exada. How are you related to Queen Romisa?"

"Oh, that really doesn't matter at the moment." She paused for a moment before adding, "Perhaps we could get to know each other better—if you do a little something for me." Exada held up a pair of data discs. "In return, I'll also give you back the info I took off your OMNIs. Deal?"

"As much as I like doing things for pretty ladies," Max commented, sheathing his sword, "I'm not inclined to help someone who hacked our OMNIs." He crossed his arms across his wide chest, the way he did when he was tried to control his urge to hit something.

Exada laughed for several moments. With an amused sigh, she said, "I like you. I truly do, Maximus. With that said, I really hope it's not you."

"*Not me*? What are you talking about?"

"Oh? Did I go and say something out loud? Silly me!" She turned her attention to Alastair. Stepping towards him, she eyed Al from top to bottom. "But you, on the other hand, could be quite intriguing. I suppose I won't know for some time yet."

Growing irritated with Exada's cryptic words, Alastair held his hand up to stop her. "You said you wanted us to do something."

"It's simple really. Let me escort you gentlemen to the Sapphire Pawn. What's the harm in that?" Exada shrugged her shoulders as though she were trying to appear innocent, but it made her seem like she was hiding something.

Reluctantly, Alastair nodded. Exada's smile widened as she began walking down the deserted halls. She took them through a series of passages to a Market Plaza that bustled with crowds of hurried shoppers and energetic salespeople. All the while, Alastair and Max had their hands on their sword hilts.

Exada stopped by a building with white paneled walls. A marble walk-way led up to the front entrance where two silver-etched glass doors stood with sapphire-tinted handles shaped like chess pawns. The shop's name was painted blue over a metal plank that hung beneath the walk-way of the second story. From the looks of things, the three levels above the ground floor remained vacant, but they didn't seem as run down as the surrounding buildings.

The woman manually opened the door and gestured for the Vegas to step inside. The shop was empty of people except for a man who stood behind a counter.

"Mr. Rye?" Max inquired.

"Nope. I'm Roteg, a humble salesman." The man eyed their dark grey uniforms. "You must be from the Agency. Please wait a minute and—" He stopped as Exada joined them. "What are you doing here?"

"I've got something for Tays." Exada pulled out a disc from her pocket.

The salesman slowly reached for the disc as though it might be dangerous to touch. After a moment of hesitation, he yanked it from her hands and put it inside his jacket.

Exada turned to leave, but stopped. "I do hope you're treating my sister well, Roteg. If not—well, let's just say that I know how to return the favor." She removed two more discs from her pocket. "Speaking of returning, here you go." Exada tossed the discs to Alastair and Max before leaving the shop.

Roteg shook his head with a sigh. After a moment, he took on a more pleasant demeanor. “I’ll let Lord Tays know that you’re here.” He disappeared into a room behind the counter.

A few moments later, a figure appeared from the room where the salesman had gone. The newcomer stood had dark hair and green eyes with pasty white skin. He squared his shoulders and moved past the store counter.

Alastair cleared his throat before saying, “My name is Alastair; this is my brother, Max.”

“It’s a pleasure to meet you both,” the Azure Clan Leader said. “Though I’d been led to assume that I was going to be doing business with *Agen*t Vega.”

“Our father is a busy man,” Max replied.

“So he sends his sons? He must have great faith in your bargaining abilities.”

Alastair wasn’t sure how to respond. There was something uncomfortably familiar about the Clan Leader that made him feel uneasy. He simply nodded, hoping that it would be enough of a response.

“If you two are ready, then let’s begin. Please, have a seat.” The Azure Lord motioned to a table set with four chairs around it. He signaled for his associate to lock the shop doors. The motion exposed the man's left wrist; it had a series of blue dots and dashes inked in two rows.

A domineering female voice sounded at the front of the shop. "But I have business here. Let me inside this *instant*."

"I'm sorry, Queen Romisa," Roteg growled, bracing his weight against the shop door. "Lord Rye is in a very important meeting that can't be interrupted. You'll have to come back later this afternoon when he is free."

"Let her in, Roteg," the shop owner said. He shot his salesman an irritated look before putting a charming smile on his face. "And what can I do for you today, Your Majesty?"

The woman had hair of a deep brown shade and wore a bright red gown. A metal halo of the same color was woven into her ringlets. She looked around the shop's interior with a discerning eye. Her gaze eventually fell on the Vegas. "I don't wish to disturb you, Rye, but I was hoping that you would allow me to search your shop for a particular item I need."

Alastair examined the Region Monarch, trying to determine if the woman called Exada was telling the truth about being related to her. The colors of their features were considerably different, but there was a hint of similarity in their mannerisms. Perhaps Queen Romisa was Exada's aunt?

"If you tell me what you seek," the owner replied," I can tell you if I have it or not,"

"That seems like a good idea," admitted the Monarch. "But I'd rather you not know what I'm looking for—in case you don't have it."

"Whatever you like, Queen Romisa. Feel free to browse as long as you like, provided that my guests don't object to your presence." Lord Rye turned to Alastair, obviously waiting for an answer.

"That's perfectly fine with us," Alastair replied, recognizing the perfect advertising opportunity. "We have no wish to hide the fact that the Agency has decided to do business with the merchants of Market. Anyone may solicit our patronage, as long as their products are of excellent quality."

"Maybe it's time for my Clan to come on friendly terms with the Agency," said the monarch in red. "I'd be happy to welcome you two capable young gentlemen to the Crimson Steel Head Quarters."

"That'd be wonderful, Your Majesty." Alastair fished a data-disc from his jacket pocket and handed it over. "Please call at anytime to schedule an appointment."

“I’m much obliged.” The woman began her down the rows of shelves.

Tays Rye sent his salesman to the back room to fetch a metal briefcase. The man returned, handing over the case carefully. The shop owner entered a code then flipped open the locks. Inside sat a number of identical mechanical devices surrounded by plastic foam, their wires carefully tied together. He pushed the case across the table to where Alastair sat. “I hope Agent Vega finds these satisfactory. I fixed them based on the specifications he sent. If there are any problems, you know where to find me.”

Alastair moved to inspect the items. In the corner of his eye, he saw the Queen looking up curiously from the device she was holding. Her gaze shifted back to the item in her hands as soon as she noticed her watching him.

Pretending to know what he was looking at, Alastair picked up one of the gizmos. He fingered the paneling and gingerly turned the device over in his hands. “Everything looks in good order,” he lied. Alastair was only the Liaison; he had no idea what his father wished to purchase from the Regioners. He handed the man a credit-disc.

Rye gave it to his associate, who then inserted it into an outdated OMNI.

“All good,” Roteg said after a few moments.

"It appears that our business is complete. It's been a pleasure. Mr. Vega." Tays Rye gave a slight bow to Alastair, then did the same to Max. "You as well, Mr. Vega. Enjoy your day."

The two brothers said their goodbyes to Tays, Roteg, and the Region Queen and left. When they reached the next street, a figure moved to block their path. Al and Max tried to step around the man, but another appeared. They turned to go back the other way; a second pair of men emerged.

"Hello, Trainees," the first man said, eying their dark grey uniforms. "Do you mind if we ask you a few questions?"

The Vegas reached for their swords, but a series of clicks stopped them.

Alastair tightened his grasp on the case of recently-purchased goods. He glanced past the guns in the men's hands, attempting to see the Clan color of the Signatures on their wrists. But they wore black bands above their hands.

"I'm Lazr and this is Essin." He pointed at the others as he said, "That's Relyq and Jux."

"We are the LERJ Gang," Essin explained in a quiet but menacing voice. "Perhaps you might have heard of us?"

Good-natured as always, Max Vega addressed them. "It's always nice to meet Gangsters. Now if you don't mind, we'd like to be on our way. We've met more than enough Regioners for the day."

The Gang members laughed heartily as they lowered their weapons.

In a hushed tone, Alastair said, "Max, they're the rogue Agents that father told us about. They do whatever they can to keep the Agency out of the Lower Region."

"So you *have* heard of us?" Relyq smirked. "Good. That evens the field, *Vega*."

"Alright, we know who you are and you know who we are." Jux clapped his hands together. "Shall we get down to business?"

"Do you always begin your *business* meetings with a threat of violence?" Max scoffed.

Lazr smiled. He removed a vid-disc from his jacket and handed it to Alastair. "Please give this to your father for me. I believe he'll be *delighted* to receive this information."

Without another word, the Gangsters vanished into the shadows.

Curious about the disc, Alastair inserted it into his OMNI. He moved the screen so that Max could watch as well and then tapped the play icon.

The LERJ Gang appeared in the vid, looking disappointed.

"Uh-oh," said Jux with a frown, looking both amused and disappointed. The ginger-haired man shook his head and clicked his tongue. "You boys have tried to open something you're not *meant* to see."

"If you try to view this information again," Relyq added, "your OMNI's software will cease to exist."

Essin spoke next. "The material on this disc is meant for Tobias Vega's eyes only."

"Failure to deliver this to Agent Vega within two hours will result in the explosion of the disc," Lazr threatened.

The screen went black and the vid-disc automatically ejected.

Max cleared his throat. "So this has been a fascinating day. We had our OMNIs hacked, met royalty, made some money, and were threatened. I think that's more than enough excitement. Now let's get this explosive disc to father before we add being blown up to our list of activities."

Chapter 7

As Iris strolled purposefully towards the nearest gym, she pulled out her OMNI and inserted her ear amps. She inserted an audio-disc and pressed a few icons; loud, upbeat music sounded through the tiny speakers. The pounding notes helped raise her adrenaline levels, preparing her body for her upcoming workout.

The gym was empty, as was expected on a Saturday afternoon. After a week of Placement Testing, the Candidates were all recuperating; most would be dressing up and preparing to hit the popular hangout spots in the Plazas. If Claire had it her way, Iris would be doing something similar. However, Iris had vowed never to return to the Grey Circumstance. Instead, she was looking forward to having the gym to herself.

Iris glanced at the rows of treadmills. She thought about running on one of the machines, but she decided to run on the actual floor. Starting off slow, she began to jog. The resistance of the padded floor beneath her feet was greater than the moving path of the treadmill, giving her a more efficient workout.

Her breath became ragged as time passed. She lost track of the number of laps she ran. It was never her intent to run a certain amount; Iris usually pushed her legs just past their limit.

The muscles in her thighs and claves burned from exhaustion, but they continued to move. Her lungs stung as they struggled to intake enough oxygen to provide for her body's cells. Her heart thumped hard against her ribs. Part of Iris told her to stop and rest while another urged her forward with vast determination. Whenever she felt like stopping, she simply focused on the pounding beat and the repetition of the chorus lyrics.

Nobody seemed to understand why Iris pushed herself so hard; they couldn't comprehend her desire to overcome the physical ailments that racked her body. Up until her thirteenth year, she had spent most of her life cooped up in her study, feeding her brain while ignoring her flesh.

She supposed that she had Alastair to thank for awakening her drive to be strong. Shortly after their initial encounter, she told her father that she wanted to learn to defend herself. When it became evident that she had a knack for athleticism, she retained the services of a team of fitness experts.

Fatigue set in; her legs cramped and her chest ached. Pain overwhelmed the endorphins, influencing the brain to cease the taxing activity. Iris walked a cool-down lap, sat, and then stretched her sore muscles.

On the way back to her Living Quarters, she stopped by the nearest Cafeteria. Iris didn't feel like interacting with people, so she got her veggie wrap to go and ate it as she walked home.

"Have a nice work out?" Claire asked as Iris entered their common area. Her fingers flew across the game controller in her hands.

Iris sat on the couch next to her and watched as Claire's Amazon warrior fought off multiple KGB Officers. "Not as a good a work out as you're giving your character." She couldn't help but laugh when a group of cowboys arrived as reinforcements. "What are you playing?"

Claire huffed, "I know it's stupid; one of the guys I met today recommended it. The graphics are incredible, but the story line is awful. All the best fighters throughout history and fiction are pitted against each other in the all-out war between good and evil." Her scantily clad Amazon decapitated an alien robot before teleporting back to her homestead. "Honestly, I'm ready to go rogue and become a mercenary."

"Sounds interesting. I'll have to give it a try sometime."

"Well not tonight. You're coming to the Club with me."

Iris tried to make some excuse about being busy, but her friend wouldn't listen.

"Oh, Iris! Stop being so stubborn," Claire ordered as she shut her game off. "Everyone is bummed that you didn't come last night. You were the life of the party when you took on Pyke! Max thinks it would be funny if you went on stage and challenged people to sparring matches. We can set a new trend. Instead of dance-offs and singing contests, we'll have duels!"

"You really need to quit watching those competition shows," Iris said as her OMNI beeped.

She reached to answer it, but Claire grabbed her arm. "Do *not* answer that! I mean it, Iris. Your father needs to stop calling you every five minutes like his life is about to end." She scooped the OMNI from Iris' hand. "It's not healthy!"

"He's just lonely," Iris retorted, reaching for her OMNI. "You know, OMNI theft is a serious crime, punishable by banishment to the Lower Region."

A sly look came onto Claire's face. "Let's make a deal." She handed back Iris her OMNI. "If you can go the next hour without answering your father's calls, I'll do whatever you want for a *whole week.* You can make me go to the gym with you every night or force me to miss my shows or tell me to quit kissing strange boys—anything you want."

Intrigued, Iris asked, "And what will *I* have to do if I answer the call?"

The OMNI continued ringing.

"You'll come with me tonight, tomorrow night, and all next weekend to The Grey Circumstance without complaint. What do you say, Iris? Do we have a deal?" Claire stuck her empty hand out expectantly.

Iris thought carefully for a moment. It was a tempting proposal. She would enjoy keeping Claire from getting messed up with every cute Trainee boy she met. "You're *on.*"

After the two girls shook hands, Iris pressed the ignore icon on her OMNI and went to her room to wash up. She descended the stairs and took a refreshing shower. When she finished, her OMNI was beeping again. Iris picked it up and read the screen. She had dozens of missed calls, e-mails, and text and voice messages.

Claire called from above. "When I said 'answering your father's calls,' I also meant replying to his messages and/or e-mails."

"You didn't *specify*!" Iris shouted. "Something must be wrong. He has tried to contact me over thirty times in the past fifteen minutes. I'm answering and I don't care if that makes me loose the bet." She pressed the accept button on her OMNI.

"Iris! I was so worried when you didn't respond to my calls. Are you alright? Are you safe?"

"Yes, Dad, I'm fine," she assured him. "What's the emergency?"

"Claire called me and told me that she thought something was wrong."

Suddenly suspicious, Iris asked, "When did she call you?"

"Awhile ago. Maybe twenty minutes."

"Claire!" Iris flew out of her room. "You set me up!"

Her roommate looked down at her from the top of the staircase, an amused expression on her face. She gave Iris a wink and stepped away from the railing.

Dr. Kayn very loudly asked, *"Iris? Is everything alright?*

"Yeah, everything is *excellent*," she lied, taking a deep breath.

"You shouldn't yell at Claire; she was just being a good friend."

"Yes, Dad. Whatever you say. Good night." Iris ended the call without waiting for her father to say anything else.

"Time to glam up," Claire said with a devious smile as she descended the stairs. "I'm leaving in one hour, whether you're ready or not. Unless you want to be dragged to The Grey Circumstance wearing your fluffy robe, I suggest you go get changed." She entered her room and the door closed behind her.

Iris reluctantly went back to her bedroom and began getting ready for the evening. She didn't have many clothes that Claire felt were "appropriate for the club," but she didn't care. After selecting her favorite midnight blue flare jeans from her wardrobe, she put on a plain black T-shirt over her white camisole. To complete her grungy look, she slipped her well-worn brown, knee-high suede boots over her jeans. She left her slightly-damp hair loose to let it air-dry.

After one last glance in the mirror, she went across the hall to see if Claire had any last minute fashion advice. Iris pressed the chime button on her best friend's door control panel.

From inside the room, Claire said, “Open.”

“I didn’t know we could do that,” Iris said as she entered.

“You’d know a lot more if you went to The Grey Circumstance more often.” Claire sat on her bed, strapping on her golden sandals. Her brown hair fell in waves to her collar bone. A maroon, ¾ sleeve dress fit tightly across her torso, exposing the slightest amount of cleavage. Forest green tights with white pinstripes covered her legs. “The Candidates trade the tidbits of information they come across, and Mentors pass along their knowledge of the Agency. I think I’ve learned more about the Agency at The Grey Circumstance these two weeks than I learned from you in the past several months.”

Iris made no attempt to hide her chagrin as Claire tried to entice her curiosity.

“If you’re going with a more casual look, at least let me put a little makeup on you.” Claire pulled Iris into her bathroom. “Mascara and eye liner will really make your eyes pop.” She pulled out a couple of tubes from a bag on the bathroom counter and began putting black goop around Iris’s eyes. “*There*. Now you’re gorgeous.” She stepped aside and let Iris look at herself.

"You're right; my eyes *do* look better," Iris consented. "Thanks. Now can we go and get this night over with?"

At the Grey Circumstance, Iris scanned the crowds for familiar faces. She recognized most of the Candidates and Trainees that she saw, but none were people she wanted to know better. Claire led her past the entrance into the main room.

People pushed chairs and tables together while others brought trays of drinks for their group. Couples broke off from their friends to find couches in the dark, secluded corners. Some simply sat and stared at the dancing figures on the color-changing dance floor, sipping their beverages.

There was performer that stood out amongst the rest. In comparison, the others looked as though they were fresh out of Dance 101. The girl spun, leapt, and krumped, all while throwing in the occasional gymnastic move. But it was more than ability that set her apart; her attitude was confident as her body moved like the dance steps were the most natural thing in the world. There was something familiar about the girl; closer examination made Iris realize that it was Beatrice Cromford.

A pair of drunk Third-Years nearly knocked her over as they passed; their half-empty glasses fell from their hands and spilled on Iris's shoes. "Are you sure you want to spend your night being pushed around by complete strangers?"

"No, I don't. That's why we're going to the Vega Balcony." Claire pointed towards the ceiling.

"They have their own balcony?"

"Only *certain* people are allowed on the second floor. It's a good thing our Mentor has good connections. Alastair and Max share a balcony with Viola and a few other Mentors, but everyone calls it the Vega Balcony."

"Why didn't we go to the balcony that *first* night?"

"It's wasn't as crowded; most of the Candidates were too tired from moving in." Claire walked towards the stairs that led to the second landing. "There are going to be a lot of important people up there so try not to embarrass me."

At the top of the stairs was a barrier. Claire showed an attendant the Identification file on her OMNI and motioned for Iris to do the same. The man pressed a series of buttons on the barrier and then ushered the ladies through. Iris followed as Claire expertly maneuvered between clusters of partiers, down a hallway full of doors.

"If you were so worried about me embarrassing you, you shouldn't have *tricked* me into coming," Iris pouted, tucking her OMNI in a boot.

Claire turned to face her. "Okay, I believe one of the conditions was that you not complain." She resumed strolling to a door at the end of the hall and knocked. "I've got a lot of flirting to do this evening and I don't need you turning the mood all serious. You can stay with Alastair. He seems *fond* of you."

Viola Cromford answered the door. "Ah, Claire! We were wondering if you were going to show up. And Iris! Come on in."

"Thanks, Vi," Claire replied with a satisfied smile. "By the way, I *love* your outfit."

The Mayor's eldest daughter wore a violet long-sleeve blouse and black slacks. Her height was extended by silver heels. Viola thanked Claire before mingling with other clubbers.

"Iris!" Alastair Vega called from a couch across the noisy room. "You made it! Have a seat." He patted the cushion beside him. His white dress pants and sleek, yellow collared shirt showed off his muscular form. A metallic blue tie completed his look.

Iris did as she was told and even put a smile on her face. If he could pretend to be friendly with her, then she could play along.

Eve Sanders sat on the other side of Alastair. The grin on her face instantly turned to a frown, but changed back as quickly as it had distorted. Her short red curls had an extra measure of bounce in them. She fidgeted with her baby blue halter top and smoothed down her black and beige plaid skirt. Her rose pink flats *accidentally* kicked Alastair in the shins. “I’m so sorry, Al. Did I hurt you?” Miss Sanders leaned forward and gently caressed Alastair’s shin.

“That’s okay, Eve.” Alastair pushed her hand away and turned to Iris. “So, what have you been up to?”

Uncomfortable with his close proximity, Iris scooted to the far end of the sofa. She kept her gaze on everything but her Mentor. “I’ve been busy training and studying. The Placement Tests are more difficult than I had thought.”

“Yes,” Eve said, loudly. “I’ve found my Tests to be challenging as well, but I think I’ve been proficient in enough skills to make it into the Coordinator Branch.”

“That’s wonderful, Eve,” Alastair said without looking at her.

"You know, I'm thinking of going by '*Evelyn.*' It just sounds more mature. 'Eve' is a bit childish. Don't you think? Alastair!"

"Hmm? What was that?" He turned away from Iris and gave Eve a confused look.

"I said that I want to be called '*Evelyn*' now."

"Oh, that's great." Alastair returned his attention to Iris. "I'm glad that you came tonight." Suddenly remembering something, Alastair stood and called over to where Claire was conversing with a group of men. "I owe you a beverage. What shall it be?" He approached a high counter covered in a series of crystal glasses and liquid fruit mixes.

"A watermelon slushy, please," Claire replied, strolling over to him. "Thanks, Al!"

"Why does Alastair owe Claire a beverage?" Iris asked.

"He bet her that she couldn't get you to come again," Eve replied with a sigh. "We all thought that Al would win, of course. You left in such a hurry last week. In my opinion, Simon Pyke had what was coming to him."

"I doubt he'll make it past Placement Testing," Alastair said, returning to his place between Iris and Eve. He put a clear bowl full of dried fruit on the short table in front of the couch. "Pyke has little skill. We don't need the likes him in the Agency Training Program."

Picking up pieces of dehydrated pineapple and cranberries, Iris cautiously asked, "So no one thinks I'm a freak or anything? People have been giving me strange looks ever since that night." She tried very hard not to show how disappointed she was that her best friend betrayed her for a fruity drink.

"Maybe people give you looks because you're just so darn stunning." Max joined the group, sitting on the couch across from Iris. "Your loveliness could be what makes them stare. But then again, it could be the circulating rumors that you're an Alteration."

"Really?" Claire took the seat on the other side of Max, a pink slushy in her hands. "I suppose that *could* be possible. But I'm afraid the gossip about my friend is completely unfounded. Having spent the past week living with her, I think I'd know if my roommate was a genetically-altered super-human."

"So tell us, Iris. Are you a superhero?" Max inquired, teasingly. "Will you save us all from the hostile, power-hungry Regioners with your laser-vision, invulnerability, mind control, and teleportation?"

Feeling rather witty all of a sudden, Iris replied, "If I were a super hero, do you think I'd have time to sit here and chat with you powerless beings? I'd be out in the bowels of the Megacity, slaying the evil Gangsters and Clan Leaders in order to bring justice upon the Lower Region."

"I guess that answers the question. Now we can spread rumors that Iris is *not* an Alteration. Then we will see which reputation will prevail."

Viola took a seat next to the giant Vega. Smoothing her violet blouse, she deviously pulled it down to expose another inch of cleavage. "Oh, Max, you come up with the craziest schemes." She flirtatiously slapped him on the shoulder.

"And where is your charming sister, Vi?" Max craned his head to look past the crowds of people. "Where is the exquisite Beatrice?"

"She's probably down stairs, showing off her dance moves," Viola scoffed, leaning against Max. "Bea promised to join us as soon as she finished 'wiping the floor with the amateurs.' Whatever."

"And here I am, as *promised*." Beatrice arrived, wearing a pair of black leggings that were laced together down the sides with yellow ribbons and a lime green shrug over a dark grey shirt. She kicked off her orange sandals and crossed her legs. Her hair had black, brown, and red streaks mixed with the blonde. A single bead of perspiration dripped down her forehead.

Max frowned at her. “What did you do to your beautiful flaxen hair?”

“I dyed it for a performance that I’m training for,” Beatrice replied, shaking her multi-colored mane. “Don’t worry; it’ll wash out in a week or two. In the meantime, I have to carry a note from my costume designer around with me to show any Agents that asks about my breach in dress code.” She pulled a laminated card from between her bra. “Besides, I think my new look helped draw a larger crowd for tonight’s dance-off.”

“How was the competition this evening, little sis?” Viola asked with a hint of mockery. “Did you make anyone give up on having a dancing career?”

Beatrice eased herself onto the floor and did a set of cool-down stretches. “Oh, don’t ask me about that, Vi! If you really want to know, you can watch it on The Grey Circumstance’s website.” She seemed to notice Iris for the first time. “So, the Alteration has finally decided to grace us with her presence.”

"Actually," Alastair commented, "we were just saying how Iris couldn't *possibly* be an Alteration. We'll have to start respecting the fact that her skills purely come from hard work and dedication."

"Oh. Pity." Beatrice twisted towards Iris and said, "I rather enjoyed the tales the other Candidates have been spreading, especially the one that depicts you as a spy from the Dakon Megacity. There are numerous variations, but the most popular version is that you were spawned in a Petri dish and spent your early years locked up in a dungeon to develop a ruthless personality. People are also saying that you have come to infiltrate the Agency and take it down one Branch at a time until it's vulnerable. Then the Dakon military will sweep in and destroy Rygom." She smashed her fist into the couch arm for emphasis.

"That's only your favorite version because you started it, Bea," Eve laughed.

"Shush, coz!" Beatrice exclaimed, standing abruptly. "Not everyone knows that." Miss Cromford cast a glance at Iris. "I meant no harm with this little fabrication. I had hoped it would help enhance your reputation."

Iris swallowed her disdain before saying, "I would appreciate it if you would stop trying to help. It hasn't had the impact that you imagined. People give me hostile glares." She had tried to voice her concerns carefully, but they sounded accusatory. After a moment of uncomfortable silence, she added, "If you wish to help me, Beatrice, maybe you could begin a counter-rumor?"

"If that is what you want, then fine," Bea replied with a smile. "We're all friends here; I don't wish to put a stain on your name."

Beside her, Alastair looked at his OMNI and said, "It's almost time for closing. We should head out of here before everyone else does. It was a pleasure seeing you tonight, Iris. Night, everyone." He stood and walked out of the balcony room.

"Why do we need to leave before the club closes?" Iris asked as her best friend dragged her out of the Vega Balcony.

"A bunch of Agents come and kick everyone out at 11:30 pm," Claire explained. "It's crazy! There are always people running everywhere. It's difficult to get back to the Living Quarters before the Midnight Curfew."

They reached the front doors as a number of black-clad Agents entered The Grey Circumstance. The Harding siblings were up front, wielding their weapons. Having seen the brother and sister duo around the Agency, Iris knew that she needed to stay as far away from them as she could. She moved forward cautiously, ducking as low as she could manage without being trampled by the horde of party-goers.

Stella flicked her wrist at a panicked Second-Year; her whip caught the poor Trainee by the ankle. "I love it when they try to run!" Miss Harding shouted to no one in particular.

"All non-Agents not in their Living Quarters within the next thirty minutes will spend the night in a jail cell," Drew announced to the chaotic mob. A group of Candidates were too busy talking to hear the message, so Mr. Harding punished the cluster by pinning them to their chairs with a handful of throwing knives.

As Stella moved through the crowd, her gaze suddenly fell on Iris. The woman moved toward her, flinging her whip at anyone who moved too close. "Let's see if I can catch Little Miss Perfect."

Iris felt a rush of air as the psychotic woman's whip cracked past her head. "What's her problem?"

"I think it's part of Testing," Claire explained, taking off her heels. "If you get caught, your score goes down." She pulled Iris outside to the Plaza outside the Grey Circumstance, easily maneuvering around the picnic table obstacles. "We should have left sooner."

Chapter 8

Everything was green with bronze trimmings. The Jades made a huge fuss to prove to other Clans that they were still financially stable, even though everyone knew that they weren't.

"What beautiful decorations, Unmare." Flattery never came easy for Lady Rikani Rye, but she attempted it as best as she could. She smoothed down the lacy ruffles of her powder blue dress, stroking silver beaded embroidery. "Darrow Villa is quite splendid today."

It had become traditional for the female Clan Leaders to put on shows for each other during their monthly private parties. The Ladies often said things they didn't mean to those they didn't trust or like. At these gatherings—more often than not—a friendly comment from someone was a mask for one's true feelings.

"Why thank you, Rikani." Lady Unmare Darrow took a sip of her tea from a forest green china cup and turned to a young lady in a violet gown. "I hope you like the furnishings as well, Belana, although they aren't as grand as those found at your Palace; the Tyrian Clan is so elegant."

"I appreciate your praise, madam," replied Lady Belana Lynch. The eighteen-year-old Tyrian Leader adjusted the gold tiara on her head. "I trust your grandson will like my home as well—when he comes to visit tomorrow. Please make sure he keeps his commitment *this* time."

"Once again, I apologize for his rude actions," Unmare said. "I'm sorry to say that he is a little restless at the moment. But I'll demand that he does his obligation to his esteemed fiancé." The Jade Leader turned to her granddaughter. "Soha, ensure that your brother keeps the appointment."

"Yes, Gran-mama." Soha replied with her usual haughty tone. "And I'll make sure he looks his absolute *best* when he goes to see Lady Belana."

Queen Romisa Steel, dressed in red and black, seemed absolutely delighted with the conversation. "How fortunate you are to soon have this wonderful, charming young woman as a granddaughter." Queen Romisa Steel gestured at the Tyrian Leader. "I hope my Matevak is lucky in finding a wife just like her."

"Oh, Romisa, if your son is as talented and charming as I've heard," Unmare sighed, "I'm quite sure he'll find a delightful little wife. If only my dear Soha could find a husband. I've told her to encourage the attentions of that delightful Nuto Berge; he simply dotes on her."

"Gran-mama, I *can't* marry him," Soha said in a strained voice. "I *can't* give up my claim to the Jade Clan. My brother can't lead. It's his place to marry Belana and become a Tyrian."

Rikani almost felt bad for Soha. The Darrow Heir was nearing thirty and had no other prospective husbands. But then she remembered that Soha wasn't stupid; she must have some sort of plan for the love-sick Nuto.

Unmare gave her granddaughter a stern look. "Yes. Thank you, Soha, for that pretty speech, but I think we should move on to another subject." She addressed a radiant, middle-aged woman with red hair, wearing a grey silk shirt and pink skirt. "You're very quiet today, Lurahi. How are things with the Magenta Clan?"

"It's very boring at present," answered Lady Lurahi Bray. "Everything is running so smoothly. I sit in my parlor and read for hours most days. I've just finished rereading my favorite Shakespeare play—"

"Oh, Lurahi! Don't talk about literature!" Queen Romisa set down her tea cup on its saucer. "Save it for your book club; it isn't a thing to converse with in this particular company."

"My apologies, Your Majesty. I have nothing else to say, then. Perhaps I should leave you alone to your gossip." She rose from her seat, lifting the edges of her gown as she glided away from the table. "Good day, Ladies."

"Lurahi!" said Rikani, standing up quickly. "My Aunt Nasiram had hoped you'd have time to talk with her this evening; I'm sure that she would love to discuss novels and plays with you." She hoped that the tone of her words portrayed genuine sincerity instead of false pleasantries. They gave slight bows to each other and Lurahi left the room.

"Where *is* Nasiram today?" the Region Queen asked. "I'm missing her company this morning. Is she out consoling your brother, Lady Rye?"

"I don't know what you're talking about," Rikani said as she returned to her seat.

"You know *exactly* what I'm referring to, dear," Romisa said with a sly, red smile. "Everyone knows about Lord Rye's little fling with my darling niece."

Rikani suppressed the urge to fling her cup of hot tea in the Region Monarch's face. Instead, she took a deep sip before continuing, “It’s just idle gossip. Besides, Tays’s love life isn’t anyone’s business.”

There was an awkward silence. The Ladies sipped their tea and ate their little scones, waiting for someone else to bring up another subject.

The quiet was disturbed by the appearance of a servant dressed in green and bronze. He passed a paper card to Soha and said, “Lord Nuto is waiting in the entrance hall. He wishes to speak with you, Miss Darrow.”

Putting on a wide smile, Soha said, “Tell him that I’m busy entertaining guests and I can’t leave.”

“Of course you can!” Unmare shouted. “Go at once, my girl, and talk with him. I don’t need you here.”

With a grimace, Soha stormed out of the room.

“Their relationship is so very romantic,” Belana commented, fanning herself. “Soha is going to lose Nuto if she doesn’t get off her high-horse and see him as often as she can.”

Rikani couldn’t take any more of their love talk. She took out her OMNI and pretended to get an urgent message from her steward. As she tried to excuse herself, Romisa had one last remark for her.

“Say hello to Vian for me,” the Crimson Leader smirked. “Tell her that we all miss her so dearly. Make sure she understands that she could come and visit us anytime she wishes."

The only thing Rikani could do was nod before turning her back on the Ladies. She wanted to say something malicious, but she had promised Tays that she would hold her tongue when she was with the female Clan leaders. Rikani couldn't believe there had been a time when she longed to attend the Ladies' tea parties.

*****

Fifteen-year old Rikani sat at a window overlooking the Azure's exterior courtyard. A battered old book with a ripped cover lay in her lap unopened. She was bored beyond belief, anxiously awaiting the return of her mother and aunts instead of working on her studies.

Three figures emerged in the distance; Vamila, Jomiq, and Nasiram appeared below, all dressed up in their finest gowns and jewelry. Oily colors smudged their pale faces. The two eldest wore blue and the other orange. Rikani wished for the day when she would be able to attend tea parties with the Clan Ladies and eat pastries over idle gossip.

Rikani rushed down the halls and stairways to greet the women. She wrapped her arms around her mother. "How was your party? Tell me *all* about it."

"Oh, the usual," Aunt Nasiram sighed. "Desa kept telling me how to bring up my son, as though she knew *everything* about raising children! I was close to smacking my mother-in-law upside the head, right over Princess Romisa's brunch spread."

"Calm down, Nas," Aunt Jomiq ordered her sister-in-law. "Desa was only trying to help; she'll be dead in a couple years and only wants to be involved in the raising of her grandson. Personally, I wish *I* had had more help with my two boys."

"I just want that old hag to mind her own business," Nasiram pouted. "Vamila, you agree with me, right?"

"Please don't drag me into it." Rikani's mother stepped away from her sister and sister-in-law, taking her daughter's hand. "Come with me, my dear, and help me change."

Aunt Nas stopped them. "Kani, where's Kumate?"

"He's with everyone at the park," Rikani replied over her shoulder. "Oh, except Koje; apparently he challenged Tyvax to some kind of physical challenge and ended up in the hospital wing with Dr. Darreth."

Jomiq's face went white as she processed the news; she rushed off to where her eldest son lay injured. Nasiram also left Rikani and Vamila to go find her own child.

"Are you going to tell me how Romisa's tea party went?" Rikani asked.

"Yes, but not yet." Vamila looked anxiously around her at nearby Azures. "As you know the gossip found at the Clan get-togethers is for Leaders' and Heirs' ears only."

They continued walking until they reached Lady Vamila's lavatory.

As Rikani began unbuttoning her mother's gown, she said, "No more delaying. What's the latest piece of news?"

"Oh, not much," Vamila answered, casually. "Only a new Clan Lady."

Rikani gasped at the information. "Is it the Princess? Has Matolin finally given up his throne? Is she going to be Queen now? Or, is Miss Lizra taking over for Unmare?"

"Neither," her mother replied, slipping into a simpler dress. "Kasta Bray has sold the Magenta Clan to a young woman named Lurahi. She is a Societan who use to be an acquaintance of our family."

"Mom, why can't you ever just tell me what you want to say? Just say it! Who *is* this woman?"

"You know her as Madeline."

"Madeline Cromford?"

It was fairly common for a disgraced Societan to purchase Leadership of a Clan when they were exiled to the Lower Region, but Rikani would have never guessed that the Mayor's wife would be among the outcasts.

"What could the Mayor's wife have possibly done to deserve shame?" she asked as she hung the frilly dress up in her parents' closet.

The door opened and Sirad entered. "Is it true, Mila? Does it have anything to do with—"

Vamila interrupted her husband. "Not now, my love."

Rikani popped her head out of the closet. "Why won't you say something in front of me?" She felt hurt at the realization that her parents didn't tell her everything.

Sirad moved to his daughter and gave her a firm hug. He kissed her on the forehead before explaining, "Sometimes we don't say things in order to protect you, Kani. It will all make sense when you're older."

*****

On the way out of the Darrow Villa, Rikani passed by Soha in the hall, sitting uncomfortably on a bench beside Nuto. Lord Berge did all the talking; he described his plans to commission a pool to be built in the Icterine HQ. Soha listened, but she clearly wasn't interested in a word he said. Her hazel eyes glanced about the room and only occasionally met with his.

Rikani couldn't help but feel sorry for the poor man. It was obvious that Nuto liked Soha very much. Nevertheless, Miss Darrow would no doubt rip his still-beating-heart out of his chest and hold it for ransom.

Lady Rye gave them a nod of farewell. After a short walk to the Jade HQ entrance, she stepped outside and headed home.

The path that led to the nearest Plaza was lined with planters of trees, bushes, and flower beds. As she strode down the lane, a foot sticking out of a hedge made her stop. Rikani peered around the shrub to see a young man lying at the base of the grassy planter, a novel in his hand.

"Can I help you?" he asked, looking up from his book. His green eyes seemed more amused than upset at his solitary being interrupted.

"Sorry, I was just leaving when I saw your boot lying here; I was curious if there was a leg attached or if someone had merely lost their shoe." She gave the man a smile, hoping to diffuse her embarrassment.

"And what would you have done if it had just been the boot?" the man replied. "Donated it to the local charity or would you have simply thrown it away?"

Rikani thought a moment as she casually moved closer to the stranger. "I'm not sure. I probably would have tried to find the owner—even if that meant I had to go back to the Darrow Villa."

The man closed the novel and sat up. "You don't like the Darrows?"

"Unmare is alright, but I'm not fond of Soha." She glanced at his left wrist to see if he was a Jade; the ink of his Signature was indeed green. "And what do you think of your ruling family?"

"Well, *Lady Rye*," he said after noting her Signature—two rows of blue lines and dots, "I'm about as acquainted with the Darrows as I care to be. The old Lady prefers to preserve the façade of being wealthy without concern about how her spending will affect Miss Soha's rule. I'm afraid the poor girl is quite unaware of how broke her *Gran-mama* is."

She didn't want to talk about a serious thing such as that with someone she hardly knew, so she changed the subject. Kneeling down, she said, "You seem to have the advantage over me. You know my name without telling me yours."

He extended his hand to her. "I'm Brak. Pleased to meet you."

"Rikani." She shook the offered hand. "Now that the pleasantries are out of the way, might I ask you what book you were pouring over when I interrupted you?"

Brak slid the book behind his back. "I'd rather you didn't."

"What title could make you ashamed to tell a stranger that you're reading it?"

With a groan, he showed her the cover and said, "It's *The Dwarf and the Dryad.*"

Rikani suddenly burst out laughing. "That silly romance fantasy?"

"See? That's why I didn't want to say anything." Brak set the book down beside him as he admitted, "A friend is making me read it; apparently, I'm going to be *quizzed.*"

"Are you sure you want to be friends with someone who likes that junk?"

"How cynical you are!" Brak laughed. "I can't just break off a relationship with someone because they have poor tastes in literature."

"I'm sorry, but that is frivolous nonsense. I don't see how so many people could read that rubbish." At that moment, her OMNI buzzed. "Excuse me one second." She stood and took a few steps away from him. She read the message on the screen and then said, "Not that I haven't enjoyed chatting with you, but I have to go."

"Well, milady, may I walk you home? I'd like to talk to you some more."

They strolled together down the long pathways, through Sector after Sector. Topics of all subjects were touched on: hobbies, the standard of living in their respective Clans, feelings on the Agency's Rehabilitating Act, etc… The more they conversed, the more Rikani liked him. Brak was pleasant, well-informed, sympathetic, and extremely good-looking. After only knowing him half an hour, she could see herself falling madly in love with the Jade man.

In a short while, they were at the Azure Rye HQ. Rikani didn't want to say good-bye. The two of them stood awkwardly by the front entrance for several seconds, until the door swung open.

"Lady Rye!" Ulrian shouted through the opening. "You're needed in the administrative center, immediately!" He turned and ran back down the corridor.

Rikani gave a slight bow to Brak. "Duty calls. I'll see you around." She clamored in after her steward and made her way towards the sound of Ulrian's frantic running. He had disappeared up ahead rather quickly, but

Rikani knew the halls of the HQ better than most of her Clan Members.

Before she took a step into her office, she heard the sound of shouting and bickering. Aril, Ebyx, and Otum were situated next to the reception desk, waiting for the two raised voices to come to a conclusion. Ulrian unnecessarily pointed at Rikani's office and then left her to take care of the mess.

"You three can go back to your greenhouse," she told the triplets. "I'll come find you once I've solved this." Rikani took a deep breath and entered her workplace.

Tays stood in the corner of the room; he was trapped by a woman in a light blue business suit, who pointed a sharp writing implement in his face. The instant her twin brother saw her, he shouted, "Kani! Call off your vicious secretary! She's about to take my head off!"

"Vian, put the pen away," Rikani ordered her assistant. She asked Tays, "What did you do this time?"

"I didn't *do* anything," Tays snapped. He pointed at her disordered desk. "I was sitting here like you told me and then your little lap dog comes in and tells me I've got to resolve a dispute. Like I've ever settled a row before!"

"You were filling in for her this morning," Vian shouted, her face becoming an even deeper shade of pink. "That means you have her responsibilities."

"*No*," Tays replied, dragging out the vowel sound. "I've been told that all I have to do is sit here and play figure head while Rikani goes to her girly party. I wasn't told that I needed to do anything else other than pretend to be authoritative." He pushed past her to safety behind Rikani.

"You're impossible." Vian made a threatening jab at Tays as he slipped by her. "Lady Rikani, he tried to pass the responsibility onto *me*. He told me to go take care of it and then he continued to sit and fiddle with his little doohickeys. As if I have any authority over the Clan!" The administrative assistant threw up her hands in exasperation. She seemed to have finished her rant, but then remembered another of Tays's offenses. "Oh, and he called me a *bloody Crimson*!"

Rikani sighed, "I'll take care of this, Vian. Please get back to work." Turning slowly to Tays, she said, "You called her a *bloody Crimson*?" She tried to ask it calmly, but it came out as a growl.

"Yeah, that probably crossed a line," Tays admitted with a shameful shrug. He began tossing his gears and tools into a rough sack. "That's when Vian came at me. Thankfully you intervened when you did. Otherwise, I'd be squirting blood right now and on my way to Dr. Darreth."

"I just can't believe you, Tays." Rikani rubbed her temples. "I leave you in charge for one morning and you ignore your duties. On top of it all, you insult my employee."

"It shouldn't be *that* insulting. She *is* a Crimson."

"That's not the point, Tays! She doesn't *want* to be a Crimson. If her Aunt Romisa had given her consent to removing the red Signature, Vian would be an Azure now and be happily married to Roteg." Rikani smacked her brother in the arm, hoping that it would help the concept sink in. "I have to take care of the Trips' problem. Go apologize to Vian for the way you treated her—*after* clean the grease off my desk. *Then* you may go back to your garage and play with your thingamabobs."

Rikani didn't wait to listen to the apology; Vian would tell her later if he didn't say that he was sorry. She strode down the series of hallways to the triplet's greenhouse.

Taking in the grimace on her face, several Clan Members stood aside and let her pass unhindered. A few of her tenants turned down a different corridor suddenly when they saw her coming toward them. Rikani resented the fact that they steered clear of her when they met in the passages, but she didn't have time to dwell on it at the moment.

"What did the cooks do *this time*?" Rikani asked as she entered the Trip's greenhouse.

"We *do* have a minor complaint with Haben," Aril said, whipping her red braids over her shoulders. "But it's nothing new. Myhus said he'd deal with it."

"Yeah, Haben still wants more tomatoes than we have available to give him," Ebyx added, bending over a patch of cabbages. Through the cascade of her blonde hair, she said, "He misses cooking in his old restaurant in Market, so he wants to only make greasy, carb-filled Italian dishes."

"That's not the main problem." Otum rummaged through some papers on the desk along the far wall of the greenhouse. "We're trying to decide where to put our second greenhouse." She placed the forms in Rikani's hands.

The Rye Clan Leader rarely handled building projects; she didn't have the proper instruction in that field to make informed decisions. She flipped through the pages, but hadn't the slightest idea of what to make of it. "Do you three really need me for this? You should speak with the contractors."

"Colbert won't authorize anything without your consent." Aril looked as though she was about to explode. "He wants you to go with him to a seminar about the new Renovation Act. After the fiasco with the bathroom refurbishing, Colbert doesn't want to risk anymore delays."

Rikani nodded her head, doing her best to remain positive. "Okay, I'll make an appointment with him to go to the meeting. Thank you for bringing this issue to my attention."

Otum took the papers back, placed them into a satchel, and handed it over to Rikani. "Oh, wait!" The brunette Trip looked over Lady Rikani's exhausted expression. "Please take some apples."

Ebyx, who was closest to the orchard, picked a few pieces of the fruit and placed them in the satchel. "Thank you for the help, and I hope the rest of your day goes better."

Rikani took her leave and made her way to back to her office. She placed one of the apples on Vian's desk and said, "For your trouble." She thought of mentioning Romisa's greeting from earlier, but decided that it wouldn't be very prudent of her to bring it up.

"Thank you, milady." Vian was about to turn back to her work, but she gasped as she remembered something. "A letter came for you. It was handed to Kagome on her way back from Market by a Jade man." The administrative assistant handed it over. "I can take care of everything else for today if you're tired; you can go home for the day."

"Do I look that *awful*?" Rikani asked."Fine. I'll take some time off, but only if you take vacation day tomorrow and spend some time with Roteg."

"If that's your bargain to taking a break, then I accept. Now go and read your love letter."

Rikani moved to break the envelope's seal, but she stopped. "Why do you think this is a *love letter*?"

"It was the look on your face when I told you about it," Vian smiled. "I know it isn't any of my business, but would you care to tell me who it's from?"

Her cheeks felt hot. Rikani cleared her throat and tucked the letter into the satchel the triplets had given her. "I don't care to tell *anyone* about it. At the moment, it's only a little infatuation. Don't speak of it to me anymore."

Rikani to her bedroom in Rye Estate. She tore open the envelope and pulled the letter out.

Lady Rye,

We've only been parted for a mere hour, and yet I find that I can't stop thinking about you. If it isn't too much trouble, I'd like to see you again. There is an abandoned school between the Jade and Azure Head Quarters that I often like to visit to clear my head. Will you do me the honor of meeting me there tomorrow night at 8?

Yours truly,

Brak

PS: See other side for the map to our rendezvous.

Rikani read and reread the letter several times. How was she going to bear the time until she could see him again? The minutes passed too slowly. She played with the idea of writing him a note back, except that she realized it would make her appear desperate.

After a little thought, she made up her mind to not dive right into the relationship. They would be friends first, meeting privately away from gossiping on-lookers.

Chapter 9

Covered by a thick plaid sheet, Evelyn Sanders lay face-down on a padded table. Her left arm was exposed at her side. A Massage Agent rubbed lotion onto the forearm and began manipulating the soft tissues. In Eve's right hand was her OMNI—with which she was messaging Beatrice, who was lounging on the table beside her.

Positioned on her back, Bea was sprawled across a compression table. Tiny rollers pushed into her vertebral column, causing her body to rock up and down. All the while, another Massage Agent gently rubbed ice cubes around her swollen knee joint. Bea cocked her head to the right, peering through her once-again blonde hair to look at Eve as her hands flew over the screen's keypad.

The cousins would have had their conversation aloud if it weren't for the Therapists and two of their fellow Trainees.

Goody-two-shoes Iris Kayn winced as a Chiropractor Agent twisted and cranked her ankle bones back into place. In the far corner of the room, the *so-called* engineering prodigy, Claire Birch, was reluctantly letting an Acupuncture Agent stick her with tiny needles.

Miss Sanders and the youngest Miss Cromford refused to let their discussion be hindered by the presence of the ones they were gossiping about.

Eve: *Are you sure he feels that way?*

Bea: *Yes. Viola heard him say it yesterday. Alastair regrets signing up as a Mentor. That means he has no real feelings for Iris. It's time for you to swoop in and make him realize that you are the woman he is looking for.*

The Massage Agent pushed too hard into the top of Eve's elbow.

"Hurt me again, and you can kiss your tip good-bye," Miss Sanders snapped. Turning back to her OMNI, she replied to Bea's last message.

Eve: *Do you really think Alastair would like me over Iris or Claire? Every Test they complete only brings those two more notoriety. I see nothing special in them, but they have the admiration of all the men!*

Bea: *Nonsense. You just need to try harder.*

Eve: *I HAVE been trying. I sit by Al at every meal and at the club. I call and message him all the time, but he barely replies.*

Bea: *You know, I don't think Iris is interested in Al; it's almost like she's avoiding him.*

That did little to comfort her. Eve took her frustration out on the Therapist. "Seriously, didn't anyone teach you proper pressure? You're rubbing too lightly. Work that knot out or I'll *personally* make sure that the Agency takes your license away."

Eve: *What if Iris is playing hard-to-get?*

Bea: *Be patient. Placement Testing isn't over yet. After classes begin and his Mentees get a hang of their schedule, they won't need him as much. Then you can make your move. In the meantime, enjoy your massage.*

Putting down her OMNI, Eve closed her eyes. She breathed deeply and tried to get herself to relax. Part of her mind told her she was crazy for feeling the way she did about Alastair since he didn't seem to reciprocate her affection. But the fact that she had such a strong attraction to him silenced the thought.

What else could it be if not love?

*****

Eve Sanders' sixteenth birthday party was turning out to be as epic as her parents had promised her. She just wished that Byron and Claudia hadn't also invited adults to the celebration.

"Sorry about that," Eve replied to the huddle of her closest peers. "I tried to talk my parents out of having their friends over. But they like any excuse to have guests."

Several drunken couples—including Mr. and Mrs. Sanders—were making fools of themselves on the dance floor, insisting on performing out-dated dance moves. The teens reluctantly made room for them; they didn't look happy at being out-shone by a bunch of old-timers.

Fed up with her parents stealing attention from her, Eve made a plan to rotate people through a more exclusive festivity in her bedroom.

"We'll go in shifts to sneak away," Eve explained to her friends. "Check your OMNIS regularly to see the updated schedules. Pass the word onto the others and add every teen you see to our private chat."

They agreed to the plan, hoping to get some much-needed relief from their chaperones.

Eve was about to head to her room when she bumped into someone. She looked up to see a young man who was a good foot taller than her. Dark brown waves fell in a mess over his ears. Eve let out a low gasp as she recognized Alastair Vega. Her cheeks felt hot as she stared at her secret crush, very aware of how close he was to her.

Eve let out a squeaky, "Hi."

"I know you, right?" He looked over her face and extended a hand. "You go to Jefferson Academy, don't you? I'm Alastair Vega."

"I know," Eve replied, losing her poise once again. "I've seen you around." Regaining her composure, she accepted his outstretched hand. "Evelyn Sanders."

"Oh, you're the birthday girl." Alastair let out a nervous chuckle. "Sorry. I guess it's weird to attend a birthday party where you don't know the person of honor. My dad sent me to represent the family. So here I am."

Eve ran a hand through her red curls. She began walking backwards through the halls, heading in the direction her bedroom. "Well, it's nice to finally make your acquaintance."

Alastair relaxed a little as he caught up to her. "I wonder why we've never met before."

Once he joined her, she faced forward and strolled normally. "I'm only going to be a sophomore this year and you'll be a senior, so we just never had any classes together. And I know your name because, well, *everyone* at school knows who you are." Eve stopped blabbering, mentally telling herself to shut up.

There was a crowd forming outside her bedroom door. Eve pushed past them and used her OMNI to disable the lock. Alastair entered after her, but quickly shut the door before anyone else could come in.

"What are you—"

"I just want some alone time with the birthday girl," Alastair interrupted. He plopped onto the bed and patted the comforter next to him.

Eve hesitantly joined him. "Did you have anything specific in mind—I mean, that you wanted to do? There isn't much to do here except try on clothes or browse social media. Would you—"

There was a knocking at the door. "Evie?" her mom called in a loud voice. "Are you in there? You're missing your party!"

"Hide!" Eve jumped off the bed and motioned for him to go into her closest. She opened the door to see her red-faced parents leaning in the doorway. "I'll be right out. I'm changing dresses. I saw another girl with one that looked like mine."

Byron frowned at his daughter. "But we paid a lot of money for that one from a professional designer. Claudia, get a new designer for our Pumpkin."

"First thing in the morning!" Claudia pushed past her daughter. She moved too quickly for her inebriated state, so she was a little unsteady on her feet. "Now, let's see if we can't find something just as extravagant in your closest, Evie."

"No!"

They stared at her, confused by her outburst.

"I've already found one. It's in the steamer now, so it'll be just a couple more minutes. So go back to the party and enjoy yourselves." Eve ushered her parents through the door.

Alastair poked his head out of the closest. "We should probably rejoin everyone. We can always hang out at school or do something afterwards." He leaned over and kissed her on the cheek. "Happy birthday, Miss Sanders."

They parted awkwardly, saying good-bye half a dozen times before Alastair finally exited the room.

*****

Eve's OMNI beeped, signaling an incoming call.

Viola's name spread across the screen. Reluctantly, Eve answered. "What is it, Vi?"

"Where are you? I've been looking for you for fifteen minutes! Is Beatrice with you? She won't answer her OMNI."

"We're in the Body Work Clinic. What's wrong?"

"Nothing's wrong, *but I have something I want to show you. I'll be right over."* There was a click as the call ended.

"Why did you have to answer the call from my sister?" Beatrice groaned, easing herself off the compression table. She wrapped herself in a robe and tipped her Therapist. "Viola is going to make us go look at the stupid latest invention from the experiment group she manages."

"Sorry; I didn't know any better." Eve sat up and dismissed her incompetent Therapist. "There's no escaping it now."

The doors to the Body Work Clinic opened to reveal Viola Cromford. She motioned across the room for Iris Kayn and Claire Birch to come over as well. Eve wanted to give the other Candidates a nasty look to show them that they weren't welcome, but that would hardly be appropriate. She had to accept the fact that her cousin enjoyed the company of the intrusive relationship-destroyers. Reaching under the massage table, she grabbed her robe and wrapped it around herself, covering her undershirt and shorts.

Beatrice scowled at Viola as she tied the strings of her robe. "Let me guess: you won't tell us what we're going to see until *after* we're there?"

"I think you'll really like this one," Viola replied, placing her arm around her little sister.

The group walked past the rows of massage and adjustment tables, most of which were occupied by injured or stressed Trainees. They trailed behind Viola, who eventually led them to a warehouse full of boxes, metal contraptions, and men in lab coats.

"Welcome to the Improvement Center!" Miss Cromford exclaimed with pride, gesturing towards the room.

"Do you actually *work* on the experiments yourself, Vi?" Claire asked, glancing through shelves of old technologies side-by-side with new models. She scowled as the lab-coated men shooed her away.

Viola shook her head awkwardly as she tied the long red strands into a messy tail. "No, I only *oversee* the projects. Since I'm in the Management Branch, one of my Requirements is to direct a Center or a Guild to gain experience. The Improvement Center seemed like the most fun."

"Which experiment are we going to be testing?" Iris asked in a quiet voice.

Eve groaned, "Testing? Isn't human testing *illegal*?"

Viola ignored her. "We'll be trying the new Bubble Sauna. It's through here, in Testing Room 2." She nodded toward a door and ushered them in.

The Bubble Sauna looked like an oversized, eight-sided hot tub. There were a series of jets in each porcelain seat. A metal grate covered the center of the floor. The eldest Miss Cromford walked over and pushed a button. That caused one side of the tub to slide down, exposing a set of steps. The ladies uncovered themselves down to their undershorts and shirts. They climbed in and each took a seat.

"This doesn't look like a sauna," Eve remarked, noticing the lack of covering. "It just looks like a hot tub."

"It's more than a sauna." Viola pushed a button and the walls rose towards the ceiling.

The roof—which the other women assumed was simply a part of the ceiling—came down and enclosed the entire tub. It was dark for a second, but then a dozen dim lights blinked to life. The air suddenly became very warm as a red glow came up from the grate on the ground. Water dripped from the covering onto the hot grate, causing sizzling steam to waft into the enclosure.

Viola stood carefully and pulled two tiny bottles from a compartment in the roof. She poured a few drops of each liquid onto the grate. Soon, the air was full of sweet, aromatic smells. "Chamomile and lavender oils for relaxation."

Eve wasn't a very patient person; she itched to ask about the jets that sat at her back, except that she feared that might show the others how irritated she really was.

Timid Iris was the first to begin a conversation. "How was your dance last night, Bea?"

"The performance was wonderful!" Beatrice replied without the slightest hint that she had bad-mouthed Miss Kayn only minutes ago. "The crowd called for an encore and I was obliged to obey."

"Several Performing Arts Coordinators just happened to be there as well," Eve added, leaning back in her seat. "I wonder how much influence Uncle Jay had in their attendance."

Moving away from Eve's comment, Beatrice said, "You all should've been there. It was the most spectacular Theatre I have ever danced in! They want me to come back for another show." Beatrice's mood suddenly became more subdued. "But my choreographer has pneumonia. If I decide to accept the Theatre's invitation, I'll have to arrange everything by myself."

"I'm sure it'll work out," Claire assured her. She gave Bea a pat on the back, smiling her deceptively charming grin. "I've seen the videos of your dance-offs. If I'm not mistaken, you design *those* routines yourself."

Beatrice nodded. "I guess you're right. I'll just have to work hard to channel my creativity and think of something completely original."

"Let us know if we can help you," Iris added.

In an effort to capture everyone's attention, Eve said, "I heard a new Alteration rumor."

"Really?" Claire inquired, unenthusiastically. "Please don't tell me there's more nonsense about Iris being a secret spy?"

"No, but one of the Candidates *must* be an Alteration," Eve urged. "The Agency Board plans to tighten Security during the Placement Assembly next month. People are saying that each Candidate will have to undergo a thorough Medical Exam before being admitted to the Stadium."

"What kind of procedures will they do during this Medical Exam?" Iris asked, sounding slightly more upset than usual.

"Whatever they do, it'll be to make sure every Trainee is completely normal—anatomically and physiologically." Eve removed a pair of pins from a pocket in her undershorts and fixed them in her short red curls. "Based on the stories about Alterations, they are said to have different types of cells and such—things that would give them special powers."

"Oh, Evelyn," Viola scoffed, shaking her head. "The stories about Alterations are circulated to keep criminals at bay. If there's the threat of a super being that could be unleashed to track people down, law-breakers would be much less likely to commit crimes."

The water ceased to trickle down, ending the steam. Miss Cromford stood and tapped several buttons on the sauna's control panel. With a click, the grate disappeared as the floor closed up. And then gallons of warm water gushed out of the jets positioned in the seats and in the ceiling.

Viola pulled out a different bottle from the above compartment. The smell of peppermint filled the moist air. "Mint scents act as energy stimulants and pain-relievers."

Eve hadn't given up her case about Alterations. "All stories have some basis of truth. Surely with all our technological advancements, we would have figured out how to make humans stronger. Maybe they *have* discovered how to make people more physically efficient." With a shrug, she added, "It's too bad that Alteration Research is illegal."

The water level no longer rose, but the jets continued to shoot streams of water at the ladies' backs in a therapeutic fashion.

"My father says that too many people died during experimentation," Iris whispered as she leaned into the jets. "Our bodies aren't compatible with the extreme changes. We can adapt to gradual modifications, but not with the proposed ideas and theories of modern scientists."

"How does your dad know so much about it?" Viola inquired. "I thought he was involved in with Plague Research."

"He is," Miss Kayn admitted with a nod. "Father also consulted with a number of Alteration Surgeons. Many had hoped Alteration advancements would bring about the end of the Plagues."

There was a lull in the discussion, during which Viola fiddled with the control panel. The water drained through slits at the bases of the seats. When the tub had drained, the jets began spouting white suds. Soon, the whole sauna was full of bubbles. The ladies giggled like little children as they ran their fingers through the soapy mass around them.

Beatrice suddenly exclaimed, "Vi, this is *truly* an inspiration." She stood and moved across the sea of suds, her hands spread in front of her. "Imagine this: The whole stage is filled with bubbles. More and more keep appearing and piling up in hills. The lights dim. Different colors of light then shine on the stage—blues and greens and pinks. I sneak onto the stage, hiding below a mound of bubbles at stage-left." Bea knelt down and pulled suds over to conceal her. From below the bubbles, she resumed her description of the scene. "The music starts, but I'm not visible yet. When the audience least expects it, I pop out and—" Leaping up, Beatrice twirled on the spot. She lost her balance on the slippery surface of the tub's floor and crashed to the floor.

Eve rushed over, stepping very carefully so as to not fall as well. "Bea, are you alright?"

The other girls began moving the bubbles to the far end of the sauna in order to get a better look at Beatrice. They shook her, but she remained motionless.

Viola activated a warm shower in the sauna. The water poured from the ceiling and washed the bubbles away. Bea's wrist was crumpled under her body, her hand beginning to swell. Eve carefully stepped out of the Bubble Sauna and called the Agency Emergency Line on her OMNI.

Later that afternoon, Mayor Jay Cromford and his new wife, Sophia, arrived at the Hospital shortly after receiving the horrid news. They alternately fussed over Beatrice and demanded to know every detailed that led to the incident.

Throughout the next several hours, there were a number of visitors. Many of Bea's acquaintances called her OMNI and offered her words of encouragement in her troubling time. Alastair and Max Vega came to wish Beatrice a speedy recovery. Iris and Claire remained for several hours, but they were sent home by a nurse who insisted that only immediate family could remain overnight.

Just before midnight, Eve was down the hall, preparing for the next week's Placement Tests when she heard the mayor and his second wife bickering with Viola. As usual, Vi0 was reprimanded for being frivolous with her littler sister's health.

In an attempt to defend herself, Viola said, "I couldn't have known that Bea would be stupid enough to fall."

"Beatrice dances *everywhere* she goes. You should know that!" the mayor growled. "I would have thought by now that you'd keep her from activities that aren't compatible with dancing."

"How can she hope to get into a Program now?" the new Mrs. Cromford added.

"She still has singing and acting," Viola protested, clenching her fists as though trying to control her temper.

"That's not enough for Beatrice!" Mayor Cromford exploded, his intense blue eyes boring down on his eldest daughter. "What? Are you so jealous of her talent that you have to sabotage her at every turn?"

His tone of voice didn't have any effect on Viola. She stood there, glaring back at him.

When Vi didn't reply, Sophia took over the conversation. "Beatrice is lucky that we brought the Coordinators to her performance last week. They might be willing to overlook the injury. I just hope that media doesn't learn of this. They'd just *love* to run a story about the mayor's envious daughter who seriously injured her younger sister in a fit of rage."

Jay shook his head. “We have to be more careful; we can’t give the press any reason to support Tobias in the election. I’m sure that his boys know better than to make spectacles of themselves.”

He took his wife’s hand returned to Bea’s room before Viola could retaliate.

Chapter 10

Two feet from Iris's head, an electronic device beeped. The sound wasn't loud, but it was enough to bring her back to consciousness. Slowly, she stretched her arms out from her coiled body and searched the darkness for the source of the noise. When her fingers discovered the OMNI, she picked it up and turned it around in her palm.

With a wipe across the screen, the gadget ceased beeping. Iris didn't bother stepping out of bed. Instead, she rotated her hips so that she could roll off the mattress and onto the wool rug. Her honey-blonde hair fell over her shoulders and face. She centered herself in the middle of the mat and then proceeded to twist her limbs into different poses. Her joints cracked and popped as they were pulled and pushed within their range of motion. When every body part was stretched in every possible way, she stood and began to get ready for the long day ahead.

In her bathroom, Iris removed a syringe from the box, took the cap off, and stuck the needle into her elbow. The clear liquid poured into her veins as she pushed the plunger down. She rubbed ointment over the injection site and then put on a bit of liquid bandage; the little red dot would disappear in an hour's time, leaving not even the slightest hint of a scar.

While flexing her hand and elbow to help her veins push the medicine to her heart, she brushed her hair with the opposite hand. After eliminating the snares and neatly pulling back her long hair, she washed her face and returned to her room. Iris quickly changed out of her sleeping attire and dressed in the simple, light grey uniform. She strapped her belt around her waist and attached two long blades to it.

Breakfast was waiting upstairs in the pantry; Iris and Claire had ordered the meal the night before—as was the custom. Setting her pack on the floor, Iris grabbed her plate with granola bar, a plain bagel, and blackberry cream cheese. A fruit and veggie smoothie sat in the refrigerated section of the pantry. Iris took her seat at the kitchen table and chairs as Claire came trudging up the stairs.

"What do you think would happen if I just stayed in bed one of these days?" Claire asked with a yawn.

"You'd probably fail Placement Testing and be kicked out of the Agency." They had the same conversation every morning and Iris was getting sick of reminding her friend that she could still fail, despite her talent and intellect.

Claire rubbed her eyes as she pulled out her own breakfast and joined Iris at the table. “I was up until 3 am working on Project 4.”

Iris let her friend drone on about her latest Project while she checked her OMNI for updated scores. She had done well on the fitness and agility Tests so far, but the Coordinators had just begun measuring a Trainee’s mental capacity and understanding. ARHA reported that she was passing, but wouldn’t say anything about her score in relation to the other Candidates. The lack of knowledge led to an atmosphere of fierce competition.

In a month, there would be a ceremony to announce which Candidates were selected for each Program, based on their aptitude and scores. During the Placement Assembly, she would officially be indoctrinated as a First-Year-Trainee of the Agency—but only if she passed.

Iris finished her breakfast and placed the empty dishes in the proper chute. She pulled out a pack of mints and offered one to Claire, who quickly scarfed down her vanilla yogurt.

Claire took the mint and asked, “Do you need to go back to the Body Work Clinic?”

Iris following her friend’s gaze to her arm. “Huh?”

"You keep flexing your hand; you flex it *every* morning and evening. Did you hurt it or something?" Claire walked toward her. "Take off your jacket." When Iris didn't comply, she huffed and began rolling up the sleeve.

Pulling back, Iris said, "It's fine!" She grabbed Claire's fingers, but had to stop herself before she snapped her friend's digits.

"You always say *fine* when you're really *not*." Claire slapped away Iris's hand and continued pushing the blazer fabric away from the forearm. "If the muscle is cramping, you should put pressure on it; that's what all the Massage Agents tell me."

Growing desperate, Iris blurted out, "You're going to wrinkle my uniform!"

"It's wrinkle-free fabric, silly. Hold still and let me help." Claire rubbed her palm up and down the forearm. "I don't feel anything. Where's the spasm?" She yanked the sleeve up to the bicep and gasped. "What happened?"

Iris yanked the fabric down to cover the prick mark. "It's from an injection."

"Steroids? Are you crazy!" Claire smacked Iris on the arm. "You're jeopardizing your career to bulk up?"

"No, not steroids. S*upplements*. I need extra vitamins and minerals to give me energy."

Claire reluctantly let go of her. She tossed her trash into the chute. "That *better* be all. I don't want to risk my future career by lying for you."

The two women stepped out of their Living Quarters and went their separate ways to their respective Testing Areas. Iris looked over her shoulder. As soon as Claire passed someone in the hall, she was back to her old self, chatting with whomever she met.

Iris made her way to her assigned classroom for the day. Other Enforcement Candidates stood about, waiting for details on their Test for the day. They chatted easily amongst themselves. Iris wanted to join in, but she hardly knew any of them. She had studied their public records the first week of Placement Testing and knew what each individual was good and bad at. If she was a betting person, she'd confidently gamble money on who would pass and who would fail any given task. But the statistical knowledge did little to help her engage in successful conversations with her peers.

Thankfully, she didn't have to wait long before the ARHA screens in the room flashed on. The Candidates noticed the shining display almost instantly and ceased talking. Nothing happened at first. And then the monitor flashed back and forth between white and black as though the artificial intelligence was flipping on and off.

When the screen remained white, ARHA spoke in quicker, more urgent voice than normal. “We have an emergency in the Lower Region. All available Enforcement Agents report for duty at their Stations and await further instructions. Candidates, remain where you are until a Mentor or Coordinator gives you orders.” The computer panel went black after twice repeating the same message.

There was a mix of panic and excitement in the group as the Candidates speculated what was happening. Some believed that another Megacity was attacking Rygom while others simply assumed that an accident had occurred in a lab somewhere. Iris refused to listen to any of the theories; they would know soon enough what had happened.

One of the Placement Coordinators entered the room. Agent Chase Mitchell had been present at all of her Tests. He was a pleasant fellow who was always helpful in explaining the dynamics of the Agency. But today his face was grave as he approached the Candidates. “I must ask you to calm yourselves. All available Squads are being sent to contain a *situation* in the Lower Region. Placement Testing for Enforcement Candidates has been canceled for the day since most of the Coordinators have left Upper Society."

"What about us?" a Candidate asked from the back of the room.

"If you wish to take the day off, you may do so. However, we are asking for volunteers to join a Squad of Third-Year Trainees to provide back up for the Enforcers. It'll be dangerous and we can't force you to come. Your decision *will not* affect your Testing scores."

There was a murmur in the crowd as the Candidates discussed the matter with their friends. None seemed to be willing to go unless someone else would go with them. In the end, Iris came forward and volunteered to join the Squad. The room fell silent for a moment and then a dozen others consented to go as well. Only a handful decided that they were too *busy* to come.

Agent Mitchell handed out data-discs with medical waivers along with instructions on their assignment. OMNIs were pulled out and the group quickly signed the contracts and read about the mission. Shortly, they loaded into Elevators that led straight to the Lower Region.

As they descended, Iris approached the Coordinator. "I'm still figuring out all the terminology. What's the difference between Underlings, Regioners, Gangs, and Clans?"

"All Agents should be able to distinguish between them," Agent Mitchell replied. "*Regioner* is a general term used for anyone who lives in the Lower Region levels below Market. *Clans* are organized groups of people that live in the Region, each ruled by their own Leader. *Gangs* are much smaller than Clans, usually ruled by three to six outlaws who trying to gain as much power as the Clan Leaders. *Underlings* are anyone who don't belong to either a Clan or Gang; these are the people that are generally stricken with a Plague."

The Candidates quickly took notes in their OMNIs about the distinctions. They spent the rest of their descent reading and re-reading the briefing on coin-sized data-discs.

Earlier that morning, several dozen groups of bandits, led by various Gangs, declared war on the Clans. The Clan Leaders had pleaded with the Agency for aid, saying that the violence in the Lower Region levels would create so much damage that it would affect every Sector of the Rygom; the structures holding the Megacity up might break and cause the higher levels to sink and collapse should the Agency refuse to help.

They emerged from the Elevators to find a group of Third-Year Trainees scattered in a run-down Plaza, huddled in defensive positions.

Iris scanned the faces and realized that they were all Mentors. This knowledge loosened some of the anxiety she felt about volunteering for a dangerous mission; surely the Agency wouldn't give their Enforcement Candidates and Mentees difficult tasks.

Agent Mitchell explained that he needed to rendezvous with the rest of the Coordinators and that the Candidates would remain behind with the Mentors.

As she walked through figures clad in dark grey, she noticed Alastair Vega giving orders to some of peers. He looked up as she approached. "I see that an invasion force doesn't scare Iris Kayn. Come to help, huh?"

"What do you need me to do?"

He waited a moment as the other Candidates formed a circle around him. "I'm Vega 1 and I'm in charge of this unit. We are to hold this Elevator at all costs. Scouts will alert us if any bandits make it past the Enforcers."

Alastair motioned over their heads and a Mentor brought over a hover-table covered in tiny, metallic figurines. Alastair began arranging the figures within a holo-map of the area to show where he wanted everyone to stand if they received word of an upcoming attack.

"We'll begin the battle in four lines," Vega 1 instructed. "Shield Agents with spears will be in front; Melees, crouch behind them. Make windows between the shields so the Archers can shoot through the empty spaces. When the Scouts return, they'll be in the center, using their equipment to watch for an ambush. After the skirmish begins and the bandits are mixed in amongst our ranks, the Shields will part, allowing the Melees to move into the gaps and join the battle. Then the Shields on the sides will curve and begin to surround—"

"Time to rock and roll, Al!" Max interrupted, coming out of a nearby tunnel. He wore a badge on his shoulder that said, *Vega 2*. "They're coming from the North. The *party* will start in less than ten minutes."

There was a scuttle as the Agents arranged themselves in the fashion that Vega 1 had showed. The sound of steel scraping against steel echoed through the Plaza as the men and women pulled out their weapons. The remaining scouts returned to the Squad and moved to the back of the lines.

Max planted himself by Iris' side. "Is it okay if I stay by you?" He nodded at her twin long knives and gave her one of his goofy smiles. "I've seen you wield those things; I'm pretty sure I have a better chance at surviving if I'm under your protection."

"Are you sure you *need* protection? You look like you can take on a dozen adversaries at once if you had to."

"Perhaps," he smirked, nudging her on the shoulder. "But I still like my odds of sticking with you." Max gave her a wink before turning to scan far Plaza walls. Despite his cheery, easy-going persona, he seemed to be legitimately concerned about the upcoming battle as he unsheathed his broadsword.

Soon, the Underling bandits became visible in the distance. The mob was more than twice the size of their small Agency Squad. The brown-splotched men and women came sprinting out doorways along the North of the Plaza. They gripped crude, rusty blades in their grimy hands. Some had plates of metal strapped to their torsos to protect their vital organs, but most wore no armor at all.

Four figures in black signaled orders at the horde—supposedly the Gang members that instigated the invasion.

"Not good," Max moaned.

"What?" Iris knew that the situation wasn't ideal, but there must have been something serious if it made Max become downright pessimistic.

"That's the LERJ Gang. Al and I met them recently. They almost blew us up." He exhaled sharply and then he was back to his normal self. "This is going to be more interesting than I thought!"

The bandits rushed through the Plaza, filling the enclosed area with the sound of battle cries. As they reached the Squad of Trainees and Candidates, they crashed against the wall of shields, swinging their weapons at the barriers. However, that made it easy for the Archers to attack; they easily took out a dozen bandits in the first volley.

Iris and the other Melee fighters picked off any stragglers that managed to break the line of shield-wielders. As promised, she made sure to keep an eye on Max as he fought off three assailants at once. The Gangsters had singled him out as the most dangerous due to his size, so they focused their attacks on him. Iris sliced a knife down the back of one and stabbed the other blade into the gut with the other. Max nodded in thanks after smashing his massive fist into the face of the remaining bandit.

After mere minutes, the battle was over. Cheers echoed through the Plaza as the Squad congratulated themselves on their victory. Iris didn't feel like celebrating; something was wrong. Why would the Gangsters think they had a shot at defeating them? It was a fool move and she was sure that the Gangs were smarter than that.

And then it hit her. "There's no black clothing in the pile," she whispered, still processing her revelation. "Where are the Bosses? Does anyone see them?

The sound of an explosion reverberated through the Plaza. That is, it sounded like an explosion to her. Her Squad was already taking cover when Iris discovered the cause the noise. Led by the Gangsters, fifty bandits stood scattered in the exposed windows above her head. Each held machines that Iris had only seen in pictures on the web—firearms.

"Firearms are *illegal*!" she unnecessarily stated. Iris knew she needed to move, but she was too shocked to take cover. "How do they have so many?"

"*Iris*!" Max shouted as he flung himself at her. He put his hands on her shoulders and pushed her towards the nearest abandoned building. "I guess it's *my* turn to save you. Don't—" He stopped short, his gaze going blank before he fell forward. His face smashed into the cold, metal floor. Dark liquid dripped out of a hole in his back.

As she watched, another hole appeared, and then another. Iris tore her gaze away and took cover in a condemned building. She looked around and noticed that some of the Candidates lay on the ground with bandages wrapped around various bloody limbs.

Alastair looked up at her, seemingly unaware of what just happened. He returned her gaze, his eyes slowly comprehending that there was a tragedy. "Report."

"I'm so sorry, Alastair" she whispered, trying to keep her composure together. "I couldn't—." Iris took a deep breath. How could she tell him that his brother died because she froze? "Vega 2 didn't make it."

The cool, confident look in Alastair's eyes was replaced with the look of blank shock. He stood and peered into the body-ridden Plaza. "Max is—*dead*?"

"What are your orders?" Iris asked, trying to distract him from his grief.

He didn't answer; he just kept staring out at Max's body.

"Alastair! We need you to tell us what to do!" She grabbed the front of his blazer and pulled him back to the shelter. "You're in command. Command us! How do we defeat ranged firearms with only our melee weapons?" When he still didn't respond, she punched him in the face.

"What?" Alastair blinked at her, holding his cheek. "Iris, I can't do this. It doesn't mean anything. Why doesn't it matter anymore? It should, but I—"

With a sigh, Iris said, "I have a plan. Can I take over?" One of the Mentors began to protest, but Iris pulled out her knives, flicked her wrists, and disarmed him. "I've read all your files and none of you have the tactical skills to ensure our victory. So I'm putting myself in charge of this Squad. Does anyone else have a problem with that?"

The rest of the group fell silent and held up their hands up in indifference.

Iris walked away from the group and tried to think of a way to make the guns irrelevant. Shortly, she returned to the group.

"Do we have any explosives?" Iris asked the Squad.

There was a series of head shakes, but one woman nodded her head.

She knelt by a woman whose leg was being wrapped by a Field Medic Trainee. "What do we have, Basset?"

"We don't *technically* have any explosives, Kayn," she explained, wincing as blood seeped through the white bandages. "But I know I can build some with parts and materials from our equipment."

"How long will that take?"

"Probably ten minutes."

"Good. Go ahead and get started," Iris ordered. "Anyone with explosives experience, help Basset. All others will attend to the wounded. Vega, come with me."

"Where are we going?" Alastair asked, following her down a corridor.

Iris needed to get him away from Max's corpse; he was useless just standing there, staring at his deceased brother. "We need to find a way to get to the bandits' building."

They spent the next few minutes searching for intact passageways between the different Plaza buildings. The architecture was similar to that in Upper Society; everything connected in one way or another. Most of the rooms were corroded or had their steel walls ripped from their frame. Eventually, they found a series of covered walkways that led to the bandits' structures.

They followed their own footprints in the grease and grime back to where the Squad remained hidden.

"Is everything ready, Basset?" Iris inquired, trying to sound confident.

The woman looked up from a mass of wires she had been inspecting. "We have eight explosives prepared."

"Hoffman, go with Vega," Iris ordered. "He'll show you where to put them. Finch and Moretti, stay here and look after the wounded. I want the rest of you to follow me."

Iris led the remaining uninjured squad members upstairs to the second level. She could see the bandits across the way, one floor up. Purposefully, she stepped too close to the open wall of the walkway to let them see where they stood.

A few shots were fired, but none managed to hit her. She scooted back and signaled for the others to retreat. They ascended another stairway so that they were on an equal level with the Underlings. A gap in the walk way hindered them from running across to slash the throats of the outlaws.

"We have to keep their attention on us," Iris explained. "Find a plank that we can push over the hole in the walk. It has to be long enough that we can still push it while hiding behind these walls."

She didn't intend to have her squad run through gunfire; she just needed the bandits to *think* that that was her plan. A plank was soon found from amongst the debris of the abandoned buildings. Just like Iris had thought, bullets shot through the air as her Squad positioned the length of wood across the walkway.

Her plan was working. She peeked through a small hole to see all twenty of the remaining bandits out in the windowsills, vigorously shooting in her direction. The black-clad Gangster Bosses continued to bark orders over the noise of their guns.

Fire burst out of every opening of the building. Metal bent from the blast of the bombs.

Cries of horror sounded barely audible over the noise of the explosion. Scorched bodies fell three stories to the ground floor of the Plaza.

As Iris moved to regroup with her Squad, an all-too familiar void-sensation occurred. She felt the scene of the Lower Region melt away as she was pulled back into the real world. All around her, the Enforcement Candidates awoke from a Simulation that they didn't know they had been in.

"Wait! That was a Test?" Basset cried.

A Candidate that hadn't volunteered looked as though he was having a panic attack. "I would have gone if I had known what was going on! Does it affect my Testing score?"

"How did they put us in a Sim?" Hoffman asked Finch.

Agent Mitchell raised his hands and motioned for everyone to be silent. "Thank you for partaking in this Simulation Test. The Agency Board will review the results. All questions may be sent to my OMNI. At the moment, I'm not allowed to discuss anything further." Without another word, he left the classroom.

The Candidates dispersed soon after, looking rather ragged from the events of the morning.

Iris was the last to leave; she didn't want to deal with the unsettling stares of her peers.

As she walked behind the crowds, two hands slid between her arms and torso, raked across the front of her shoulders, and hooked around her head to the nape of her neck. Iris was about to maneuver out of the hold when she realized who was behind her.

"Guess who's back from the dead!" Max chuckled from behind her. "Why didn't you protect me? I thought we were friends," he playfully pouted as he let her out of his hold.

"I wish I could've stopped the bullets with my mind. Sadly, I'm not a metal-manipulating Alteration."

"No worries," Max said as he pulled her in for a quick hug. "Don't make a big deal about it to Alastair. We didn't know what was going on either, so he really thought that I had died. But good job at taking over! Just don't let the victory go to your head!" He walked away and joined a group of Third-Years.

Iris nodded in greeting as saw Alastair come around a corner up ahead. He paused for a moment when he noticed her. His eyes still had remnants of the anguish he had endured before spun on his heels to venture the opposite way.

Chapter 11

Renowned nanoengineer Dr. Audrey Taledon stood at her work station in Dr. Kayn's laboratory. She carefully placed a black cube into the machine before her and a foggy, dark mass squirted into the clear mechanism. Audrey added a grey cube; it reacted the same way, releasing its contents into the black goop that already lay in the machine.

The doctor waited a moment, hoping something would happen. After a few minutes, she gave up watching. She held up her OMNI and spoke into the receiver.

"Nanite concoction 34 is a failure; it doesn't react with Plague number 5. The two masses remain separate, even though they intermingle." She ended the recording and played it back. Her disappointments were piling up. Audrey was beginning to feel more and more apathetic every time one of her theories died. She put her OMNI down on her desk and left the lab.

Norman sat in his private study, pining over pictures of his wife and daughter. "How did the trial go?" he asked, sounding completely uninterested.

Dr. Taledon paused, surprised that Dr. Kayn had remembered about trial # 34. She decided that she needed to be fir, with Norman today. "Why don't you come over to the lab and see for yourself?"

He turned to face her. "Audrey, you're my assistant. Tell me what I want to know."

"Yes, I'm your *assistant*, not some *minion* you can send to do your bidding," she chided, taking the pictures away. "How can I *assist* you if you don't do any *work*?"

She knew she had him. Dr. Kayn hadn't done anything constructive in a month and a half. Ever since his daughter had moved to the Agency, Norman had been absent-minded—clueless as to what went on in the house. At first, he had meandered about the laboratory, picking up random items, walking about the room, and then placing them somewhere else without realizing the frustration this caused his assistant. After two weeks, Audrey sent him up to his private study to rest; he hadn't left since.

There he sat in a month's worth of filth. Air fresheners had been laid about the room to counteract the smells of body odor and other stenches that came from uneaten food that the maid was unable to clear. The poor Zonese girl had been accused of interrupting Dr. Kayn's "important work"—as he called it—and was forbidden to enter the room again. She brought him food and fresh clothes every day, but they remained untouched where they had been placed.

Norman stayed planted at his desk, except during secret nightly excursions to raid his secret stash of booze. The whole situation was too familiar to Dr. Taledon. It was a repeat of what had happened almost seventeen years previous.

*****

Anxiety gripped Audrey; she couldn't believe she had accepted the position as Dr. Norman Kayn's assistant. There was a small amount of pride that went with being asked to work with a legend, despite the fact that it was masked by the grief she still felt at the death of her idol.

Although she had only met the woman once, Audrey felt as though Teresa was as good as any advisor. Only months ago, she had completed her degree in nanoengineering through the virtual lessons that had been created by the brilliant Dr. Teresa Kayn. The husband was nice enough. She had met him a few times at various dinners the Academy had held, but she didn't know him on a personal level.

And there was the child—a little girl, now two years old—who had lost her mother. Audrey felt that she may never be able to look at Iris without the feeling of loss.

Dr. Kayn answered the door. He gave her a faint smile then motioned for her to come in. A putrid smell filled the air. Room after room was stuffy from the accumulation of dust. Dirty dishes sat piled in the kitchen sink, clothes flowed out of the laundry room into the hall, the bathroom smelled of refuse, and wilted flowers and potted plants accented every room. Empty liquor bottles lay in scattered piles, some broken as though they had been thrown to the ground.

Reluctantly, she followed the man to the lab, hoping that it was cleaner than the rest of the rooms. She was wrong. There was a sticky residue on everything. White flakes of some unidentifiable mixture were caked to the floor. A burning, rancid smell drifted through the vents.

Dr. Taledon exploded. "What kind of researcher are you? How can you work in this environment? Have you no decency? I *refuse* to be here unless everything is pristine and hygienic!" She began to storm out, but stopped. Dr. Norman had slunk to the floor and began to sob. "Oh, stop it. You're a grown man, for heaven's sake!"

Audrey looked for a tissue to offer him, but the box had green slime on it. She walked over to the distraught researcher and patted his back comfortingly as the tears continued to flow.

"It's alright," Audrey cooed, feeling compelled to calm the hysterical man. "Calm down. I'll stay, but you *have* to hire a house cleaner. And I mean *right now*." She removed her OMNI from her lab coat and made the call to the Organization of Domestics that handled those sorts of things.

"Thank you for coming, Dr. Taledon," Norman whispered, wiping his eyes and nose with his fingers. "I haven't been very capable since—"

"Please pull yourself together," she ordered. "Now, where is your daughter?"

"Iris is over there." He pointed at the far corner of the lab.

The girl lay in an old tub that was stuffed with blankets. An empty sip cup sat beside her. Her clothes looked as though they hadn't been changed in days. Audrey was surprised that the girl wasn't screaming.

"She won't disturb us," Dr. Kayn said as pulled himself to his feet. "I gave her a mild sedative to keep her asleep."

"You gave a toddler a *sedative*?" Audrey screeched in disbelief as she charged towards the make-shift crib. She leaned over the lip of the tub and stroked the child's warm forehead. In a softer voice, she added, "I have another rule: No more putting drugs in Iris."

"Well, I sort of need to give her some medicine." He looked as though he wanted to share something with her, but he didn't say anything more.

"Okay. But you can't give her anymore sedatives to make her sleep. If you're unable to take care of your daughter properly, you'll need to hire a nanny." With Norman's approval, Audrey made the call for a child-care provider, as well as a gardener. After that, she said, "I can't do anything today except clean. We can start our research tomorrow."

"Whatever you think is right. I'll be in my study." Dr. Kayn began to leave, bur Audrey grabbed his arm.

"*Wrong!* You'll be here with me, dealing with this mess." She gestured at the wrecked lab with her free hand. "The Organization of Domestics is sending someone over right now to take care of Iris. They said they'll send a fleet of maids to sanitize and tidy the rest of the apartment, but I don't trust them to care for our workspace."

Audrey went in search of cleaning supplies. She discovered some rags in the laundry room, along with some disinfectant sprays. Returning to the lab, she tossed Norman a handful and told him to get started.

It was a shaky beginning to their professional association, but overtime, their working relationship excelled. But what really kept Dr. Taledon from running away screaming was something Dr. Kayn said at the end of that first day: "If there were a way to save Teresa, would you do it? No matter what?"

*****

"When are you going to tell her?" Audrey asked, pulling Norman out of his chair.

"Never, if I can help it." He steadied himself in his chair. "Iris doesn't need to know."

"Of course she *needs* to know! It's her life; Iris has a *right* to know."

She wanted to carry on with her rant, but the *urging* in the back of her mind started pressing on her inhibitions. Audrey took a deep breath to help her fight for control. But as Norman walked to the lab, her arm reached out of its own volition and took a picture frame from the desk.

Audrey didn't need the picture; she already had half a dozen photos of Teresa. The darkness in her gained control, forbidding her to put it back. Without meaning to, her fingers slipped the frame into her coat pocket.

"*Which* secret are you talking about?" he asked when she didn't continue.

Audrey shook her head, willing herself to recover from her episode. "I suppose I'm talking about *both* of them. I had no hand in the first one, but you pulled me into the second. I'm tempted to call her right now and tell her the whole thing." She pulled her OMNI out and searched for Iris's number.

"You can't do that!" Norman lunged at her and took her OMNI. "There's no reason to. As long as she continues to take her injections, everything will be fine. My previous doubts on the matter were unfounded. The Agency will *never* discover the truth."

She easily got her OMNI back. "What if they do? Iris should know so she can be prepared. The Agency is tightening security. If they look closely enough, they'll find—"

"They won't find *anything*," he snapped. "Stop all this nonsense and let me work."

"Norman, you haven't worked for a month and a half!" Audrey sighed. "*I* do all the work. *I* do all the preparation. *I* do all the testing. You just sit here, driving yourself crazy with thinking of Teresa and Iris. Guilt is eating at you. You feel responsible for what happened to your wife and culpable about what you did to your daughter."

"That's enough!" There was more strength in his voice than Audrey had heard in a long time. He turned his gaze away and then walked across the hall to his bedroom. There was a click as the door locked.

Audrey wasn't going to get anywhere with Norman that day. "We'll discuss this more tomorrow!" To release some of her anger, she kicked at the door.

With a huff, she went back to the lab, turned off the equipment, and gathered her belongings. It was a little early to be leaving for the day, but she knew that she wouldn't be able to get anything else done with Norman acting like an infant. Anyways, she had work to do at her office in Vega Industries.

She had her *own* studies that she ran—other than the Plague trials she did with Dr. Kayn. Her latest feat involved a new type of nanite to treat cancer. There were plenty of different versions of a cancer-curing nanites, but most had awful side effects. Audrey had been asked to use her experience with Plague nanites to find more suitable treatments for cancer. Compared to curing the highly-resistant viruses, finding a simpler cure to a nearly-cured disease was the easiest thing she had ever done. After a year of work, only a few more types of cancer remained.

When Audrey reached Vega Industries, she signed in and went to her laboratory. Her work area was clean and well organized—just how she liked it. As soon as she began setting up for an experiment, there was a beep at the door. She walked over and pressed the lock release button.

The door opened and in strode Tobias Vega. "Good afternoon, Dr. Taledon."

"Good afternoon, Agent Vega. What can I do for you?"

He took a seat in *her* desk chair and motioned for her sit across from him. "I've been told very startling news by several of the interns. They've noticed that some of your files go missing, occasionally for a whole week before turning up again. Since everything eventually comes back, I haven't been too concerned. However, the frequency of these occurrences and the length of the disappearances have greatly *increased* in the past couple weeks. It has made me curious about what is *really* happening. Would you care to enlighten me?"

Audrey cleared her throat. "I assure you that it is nothing *illegal*."

Tobias leaned back in his chair and stared at her, searching her face. "I never said that I suspect anything *criminal*, doctor. I'm simply interested in understanding the circumstances. Vega Industries has no policies against our researchers taking their work home, but the situation has too many discrepancies for me to continue ignoring it."

She had planned many explanations in her head and yet she already knew that Vega would never believe her, no matter what she said; the man was renowned for his ability to detect truth in people's eyes. Still, she had nothing to lose. The cost of the truth was her financial security. If her lie wasn't believed, the same thing would happen, except she'd be able keep the world from learning her iniquity.

Audrey didn't want to meet the man's gaze, but she knew that looking elsewhere would automatically giver her away. "I brought the files home to read. Browsing them before bed allowed my subconscious to ruminate on the day's findings. It normally resulted in an epiphany the following day."

He pulled out his OMNI and pressed a few icons. That's an unusual story, Dr. Taledon. There's just one flaw—the timestamps on the files. My records don't show the files being opened after work hours."

"Well, I—"

"You're clearly not willing to provide me with the truth," Vega interrupted. He stood and looked down at her. "Since you lack integrity in this matter, I'm afraid I have to terminate your position at this company. You have half an hour to pack your things and leave the premises." Without another word, he walked to the door and left the lab.

Audrey wanted to scream profanities at the empty room, but it wouldn't help her case. She began packing up her things while spouting out curses in her head.

Losing her job shouldn't have bothered her. Many other research companies had tried to pry her away from Kayn and Vega over the years; she was the best nanoengineer in Rygom and everyone knew it.

However, being dismissed from such a large corporation would stain her reputation. Tobias would likely slander her name to all her potential future employers.

Banishing the negative thoughts of her former employer, she set about packing her things. Her laboratory was emptied within the time-frame. She picked up the data-discs on her last trial. Debating about what she should do, she weighed all the consequences for each scenario she might possibly play out. The files held nothing but failed experiments, and yet she couldn't bring herself to give it over to Vega. She gained nothing from withholding the information and yet she couldn't help the overwhelming urge to stash the files in her bag. But taking them would be legally disastrous for her.

There was only one solution. Audrey pulled out a number of discs full of false information that she had been fabricating since the first day she started working for Vega; Norman had warned her about working with Tobias, telling her to come up with a contingency plan in case things went wrong.

Audrey had spent the past year creating a quantity of data-discs that contained faked trials which she knew wouldn't end up working, entering bogus results to make the trials appear successful. When she completed a false trial, she hid the discs behind various panels in her lab walls. It would take the next researcher a few months to perform the secondary trials and discover the errors.

She placed the *real* files underneath the pile of *false* data and left her laboratory. Audrey slipped into the incinerator room and dumped the true data-discs in a fire tube. Putting a scowl on her face, she tossed the false trials at the Verification Department administrator.

On her way home, she couldn't shake the feeling that someone was watching her. Not wanting to be like the idiots in the cinema that dismiss the sensation, she glanced behind her. Societans with their OMNIs in front of their faces strolled across the crowded Plaza. She memorized the faces and then resumed her commute.

The next Plaza over, she scanned the crowds to determine if any of them had been in the previous one. Sure enough, she saw a familiar-looking woman in a white dress suit, standing at the other end of the food court. When the mysterious woman became aware that she had been spotted, she lowered her OMNI and walked forward. As she approached, Audrey recognized her as Mayor Cromford's new wife.

"Good afternoon, Sophia. To what do I owe the pleasure?"

"Dr. Taledon, you're in awfully good spirits for someone who just lost her job." She grinned at Audrey's shocked expression. "Yes, I know that Tobias has let you go. Don't worry; the reason is irrelevant to my husband."

"And what does Jay want from me? Perhaps information on my former-employer?"

"It's *so* refreshing to do business with someone who isn't a brainless nit-wit," Mrs. Cromford said with a wink. "Yes, of course Jay-Jay is interested in Agent Vega. Would you be so good as to accompany me to the Mayoral Mansion?" Sofia moved toward the Transit Station. When Audrey didn't come, she asked, "Do you really think it's wise to upset the Mayor of Rygom?"

Audrey huffed as she caught up to her. She didn't think that she knew anything of importance; she was just a researcher. It wasn't like Vega had even invited her to a secret meeting or shared vital information with his contracted doctors.

Once at the Mayoral Mansion, Sophia Cromford led her down a series of halls, occasionally using her OMNI to open locked doors.

Eventually, Audrey entered the lavish, yet simple, workplace of the mayor.

From across the office, Jay looked up from his computer and welcomed her. "Dr. Taledon! I was so *very* sorry to hear the sad business at Vega Industries today."

Sophia linked an arm around Audrey's and guided her to the opposite end of the room. "You can skip the pleasantries, Jay-Jay; she was perceptive enough to already discover what you want." She left her at the end of the desk and moved toward her husband.

"I still think an explanation is in order, Soph." Mayor Cromford took his seat and leaned back. "You see, I've noticed that the number of Vega's employees has increasingly declined that past few months. Tobias is a careful man, but I got to thinking that maybe a few of his former workers might be willing to reveal something *useful.* So I've had Sophia watch the company for disgruntled employees."

"Is this because he's running against you in the election?" Audrey asked, skeptically. "What makes you think that he'd get rid of anyone that might know anything against him?"

Jay clicked his tongue. "No, no, Dr. Taledon. I'm not looking for *illegal* activity—just *unusual.* I have a survey that I'd like you to complete. If your answers help me piece together my Vega puzzle, I'd be rather grateful."

Fishing through the desk, Sophie produced a data-disc and handed it over. "In case you didn't figure it out, *being grateful* means that we'll give you *financial compensation.*"

"Yeah, I got that, too," Audrey replied, insulted that the haughty woman thought it necessary to spell everything out for her. She put on a false smile and took the disc. "I'm still not convinced that I'll be helpful."

"Just answer the questions as best you can," Jay replied. "Any information you give us might possibly help us save your niece."

Audrey froze as she began to stand, processing what was said. She had four nieces From the context of the situation, Mayor Cromford most likely meant Claire. What kind of trouble had she gotten into at the Agency?

"That got her attention," Sophia remarked, sitting on Jay's lap. "She's asking herself what on earth we could possibly mean."

Jay kissed his wife on the cheek as he wrapped his arms around her. He snuggled his face into her short, platinum blonde hair and whispered, "I thought you were going to be more kind to our guests, Soph."

"Sorry, Jay-Jay; I'll try harder."

Reclaiming her tongue, Audrey said, "Alright, tell me. How will answering your questionnaire help Claire?"

"Agent Vega has taken a vested interest in Miss Birch," the Mayor replied, his bright eyes losing a hint of their sparkle. "He personally assigned his eldest son as her Mentor. We're not *quite* sure what plans he has for her."

"Other than the fact that she's an inventive genius?" Audrey asked, walking around the room to hide her agitation. She felt the *urge* rise up again as she felt Norman's picture frame within her lab coat pocket. "Maybe Tobias sees that having Claire and Alastair form a strong bond would be beneficial to his son's future?"

Mayor Cromford sighed. "That's what we thought at first, but things can never be taken at face-value with

Tobias. Years of dealing with him have taught me that he always has a deeper agenda. He has a plan for Claire and I'd like to know what it is."

"Why aren't you concerned about Iris Kayn? She is *also* Alastair's Mentee."

"Yes, Miss Kayn is a very talented young lady, but I've determined that she is only around to keep Alastair on his toes."

Audrey felt the urge rise up again. She turned her back to the Cromfords and began examining a collection of political advertisements. The historical slogans ranged from holo-screens to ancient metal buttons. Before she could calm herself down, her hand slipped a badge into her shirt sleeve.

"By helping us keep Vega out of office, we'll prevent him from the nefarious scheme he has involving Miss Birch. I do hope you'll reconsider. My offer stands until the week of the election."

The Mayor rang a bell and a large man appeared, waving his hand for Audrey to follow.

Minutes later, Audrey was back in the Plaza; no one noticed that one of Cromford's political antiques was tucked inside her shirt sleeve.

Secluded in a Train pod, she put the badge in her bag and inserted the tiny data-disc into her OMNI. Still hesitant, she glanced through the survey and scoffed at the absurdity of the questions. Audrey briefly thought about typing out answers to the questions. She certainly would have been justified at providing Jay with information on Tobias.

In the end, she smashed the disc and discarded it as she exited the Train.

Chapter 12

The last thing Tobias Vega wanted to do that afternoon was to sit and watch Candidates trying to impress him with their *skill*. The word was used too loosely. "Skill" implied that there was some semblance of talent; these boys and girls had no such thing. Tobias was tempted to just take a nap and then fail everyone. But the other Agency Board Members would want to see his notes and figure out why so many didn't pass.

No, he was forced to watch these mediocre fighters clumsily block attacks from the Dueling Dummies in the Sparring Ring. Robotic arms swung heavy weapons at the frightened Candidates who were two heartbeats away from passing out. Some of the youths simply swatted their swords or axes or spears every which way in a dizzying fashion, hoping to hit something. All they ended up doing was knocking themselves off balance so that they fell over backwards at the lightest tap from their opponents.

The Dueling Dummies consisted of a human-like skeleton made of a pliable metal that could be sliced through by steel like bone. Flesh-colored plastic prosthetics covered the robotic limbs, providing the representation of a mock-human. The figures even wore dingy clothes similar to what the barbaric Underlings wore in order to make the situation seem more real to the Candidates. The Dummies were programmed with the most basic sparring strikes with their respective weapons. The aim of the Test was for the Candidates to disable a set of them single-handedly. None so far had managed to destroy a single robot.

Laughing to himself, Tobias typed an overly insulting note into his OMNI. A rather clumsy boy had managed to hit himself in the kidneys as he swung his num-chucks at a spear-wielding Dueling Dummy. Agent Vega dismissed the disastrous Pyke from the Testing Area and summoned the next incompetent fool. Time passed and each shaking, grey-clad idiot blurred into the next. He tried to keep accurate notes to appease the other Board Members.

The only Candidate that he looked forward to watching was Miss Iris Kayn. Alastair and Max had told him that she was a vision of speed and dexterity as she moved from opponent to opponent. Of course, she couldn't possibly be as talented as Alastair or Maximus; he had raised his two boys in the Sparring Ring since they were four years old.

At one point, Stella Harding came by. She sat directly next to him on the couch; her thigh pressed firmly against his. “I would *love* to get in there and teach those kids a thing or two,” she hissed, staring maliciously at the one-way mirror, her whip in hand. In a milder tone, she asked, “Will you let me, Big V? Will you let me in there with them?” Stella batted her long lashes at him.

“No. This is still only the Placement Testing; you must wait another week before you begin tormenting First-Year Trainees.” Tobias gave her a sly smile. “Was there something you needed, Stel?”

“I’m your *body-guard*,” she replied, proudly. Stella gripped her weapon. “As such, I’m very diligent in my duties. What if one of those brutes has been recruited as assassin? They might come crashing through this glass panel and stab you through the heart if I weren’t here to stop them.”

He patted the hilt at to his side. “I can handle myself.”

Stella poured herself a cup of tea. “I also thought you might want some company. You spend too much time by yourself, Big V.”

“You’re right. I’d be happy for a little company. Perhaps this *evening*?”

"Yes, sir." She put down her cup of tea and stood. As she strutted out of the Observation Room, she presented him with a flirtatious smile.

A little known secret about the Placement Testing was that every Test began with the most incompetent Candidates first, leaving the most skilled for last. It was a tactic to get the Coordinators to stay the whole time. A Candidate's skill level was originally determined during the Application Process and then became a more accurate tool to measure potential as the Test Results were factored in. This system was the reason that Iris was the last one to be Tested that day.

Tobias anxiously waited for the young lady's turn as the skill level of the others increased.

*****

"New Candidates are new *threats*," Tobias shouted at his sons as they clashed swords. "Unknown potential will be coming to our doorstep and you must be ready for anything." He signaled for the Hardings to throw in their own attacks as well. His four protégés engaged in a free-for-all battle in the Sparring Ring. Tobias paced nearby, giving feedback. "Drop your weight. Block higher. Breathe!" He pulled his own sword out and lunged at his eldest son.

Alastair barely stumbled out of the way, only to step into the path of Drew's throwing knives. The small blades nicked the side of his arm. He checked his skin to see the depth of the cut, but it was shallow. "If only we each had a set of nanite armor."

"Always be aware of your surroundings," Tobias scolded. "Then you won't need armor."

The Vega boys were nearing the end of their second year in the Agency Training Program. Tobias frowned at how complacent Alastair and Maximus had become.

They claimed that their finals got in the way of their practice time, but it was clearly all the frivolous time at The Grey Circumstance that was to blame. When Tobias had tried to ban Alastair and Maximus from the club, they pointed out that their outings were crucial networking opportunities, an imperative step towards their future careers. He had no choice but to let them continue attending wasting their weekend night gossiping about the Agency with pretty girls.

Across the Sparring Ring, Maximus grappled with Stella, trying to take away her whip. She deftly stepped out of the way, teasingly swatting at the back of his knees. An opportunity presented itself; she pulled out a leather strap, wrapped it around one of his wrists, and then another.

"Strength isn't the mark of the best fighter," Tobias said, directing his comment at his younger son. "Dexterity, speed, and precision need to be implemented as well." From the corner of his eye, he saw his sons exchange an exasperated look.

Alastair cut through Maximus's bonds and regrouped. They moved into better positions and worked together to swat Stella's whip away with their swords. Before they could subdue her, a spray of jagged metal shards flew towards Alastair, electrifying the air. Drew prepared to flick another set of shuriken, but Maximus hit him from behind with his massive fists.

Drew crumpled to the ground. "Yeah, that's just what I needed, Max—broken ribs."

"It's your own fault." Maximus motioned at his large frame. "How did you not see me?"

Tobias pulled up Drew's shirt and examined the injury. "It's only a bruise."

"I suppose that's the end of our fun," Stella pouted, retrieving her whip.

"Yes. I think it's time to pass out the assignments." Tobias walked across the Sparring Ring to where his case sat by the entrance.

Alastair joined them, sheathing his sword. He whispered something to Maximus—most likely a witty retort, congratulating him for finding a way to end their practice early.

Removing a pair of data-discs, Tobias said, "I know you'll both be disappointed with your Mentees, but the decisions were made by the *whole* Agency Board. There is a reason for their selection and it's not your place to question their motives." He handed the discs to his sons.

Without another word, he gave the boxes to the Hardings. After several years of service to Agent Vega, they knew he wanted them to hand out the rest of the assignments to the other soon-to-be Third-Years that had signed up to be Mentors. Stella and Drew put away their weapons and went about their task.

The boys' faces reflected shock as they read the files, but they didn't groan like Tobias expected them to. They both took a deep breath and simultaneously asked each other, "Do you want to switch?"

"Switching isn't allowed! Weren't you listening to me?" Tobias asked with an exasperated sigh. "The Board wants *you* to guide those Candidates during Placement Testing."

"But Simon Pyke and Garret Sanchez are the most incompetent buffoons the Agency has ever seen," Maximus groaned, wiping sweat from his forehead. "I'll be the laughing stock of the Mentors!"

"I wouldn't mind Pyke and Sanchez," Alastair said with a shrug. "Perhaps a few months with one of the top Trainees might straighten them out."

"Who do you have?" Maximus asked his brother.

"Iris Kayn and Claire Birch."

"Their preliminary scores were off the chart; they'd be great Mentees!"

Tobias cleared his throat, reminding his boys that he was still there. "Don't make me repeat myself again. Now go do the background checks; they're due in a week."

There was something about messing with his sons' head that gave Tobias sense of pleasure. Maximus and Alastair were sure to spend the rest of the day arguing about who would have an easier summer. As long as they were focusing on the unfairness of the situation, they would remain blind to his intentions.

*****

Miss Kayn's turn with the Dummies came up. She strode in and moved confidently to the middle of the Sparring Ring. A pair of long knives sat snuggly in her hands. Iris was a fairly pretty young lady, her blonde hair tied back neatly in a tail. There was also something fierce in her appearance. A fire burned in her blue eyes—a sort of vicious determination. She looked straight forward into the glass that separated them, though she wouldn't be able to see him.

Tobias pushed a button in front of him and a set of four Dummies were released into the ring. Iris had a distinct advantage with her twin blades. She blocked with one while striking with the other. The entire skirmish lasted less than a minute. After she had destroyed all four, she resumed her original position in the center of the Ring.

Iris looked disappointed when Tobias dismissed her through the intercom. Returning her knives to their sheaves, she strode away.

Collecting his things, Tobias left the Observation Room. Drew Harding waited outside, clearly standing guard at his sister's orders. As Tobias began to walk towards Vega Manor, Drew followed a few paces behind him.

Out of nowhere, Iris Kayn intercepted him. "I'm sorry for approaching you this way, but I have to know—what did I do wrong?" All the appearance of the gruff warrior had dissipated. The woman before him was a nervous wreck, rather juvenile in appearance the way her eyes pleaded for a response.

"*Wrong*, Miss Kayn?" Tobias asked. "What makes you think you did anything *wrong*?"

"You dismissed me after only *one* set. Was it because I did irreversible damage to the Dueling Dummies?"

"Should I remove her, Agent Vega?" Drew asked, stepping in between them.

"No, Mr. Harding. I can handle this." Tobias turned to Iris. "You know that I can't discuss the Testing Method with Candidates, Miss Kayn. Now, go on back to your Living Quarters. I'm late for a dinner meeting."

"Is that why you wouldn't let me continue? Did I take too long?"

"Miss Kayn!"

"I apologize, sir. Good-bye." She quickly disappeared around the corner.

"That girl has self-esteem issues," Drew sighed. "That's such a pity."

"I don't need your services tonight," Tobias snapped. "You may go home as well."

"Are you sure I can't escort you to Vega Manor, sir?" the young man asked. "Ever since you announced that you're running for Mayor, the hate messages have tripled."

"Fine. Patrol the outside of my home, but do *not*—under any circumstances—enter."

Tobias only kept the Hardings around to show the world that he was untouchable. Deep down, he despised having people follow him around everywhere he went.

Luckily, Alastair and Maximus were old enough to run several of his operations for him. They'd soon be taking regular trips to the Region for him, but that was only the beginning of his plans. With the help of a little manipulation and conspiracy, Rygom would soon be under his control.

His sons were waiting for him in the massive, gaudy dining room. Dishes had been set out on the neatly prepared table.

"Father, Byron Sanders came by this afternoon." Maximus heaped scoops of various side dishes onto his plate. "He seemed very upset, mumbling something about contacting you this evening."

"Thank you, Maximus." He turned to his eldest son. "I Tested that beautiful little Mentee of yours—Miss Kayn." Tobias had little appetite, but he always insisted in sitting down with his sons for at least one meal every day. "Your compliments regarding her skills were inadequate. Perhaps you need to spend more time with her to get a better understanding of her capabilities."

Alastair grunted in reply.

"I want you to organize a field trip down to Market—under the guise of an academic outing. After Placement Testing, of course. Bring Maximus and Viola along, too, as well as their Mentees."

"I have a feeling that my Mentees won't pass Placement Testing," Maximus remarked with a scowl. "May I still come along, too?"

Tobias couldn't help the amused expression that came to his face. "Yes, you may. The Agency Board never planned on those two imbeciles to make it into a Program. The only reason Sanchez and Pyke were accepted into the Testing stage was because of some threats from their parents. I had to agree to let one of my sons be their Mentor as part of the deal. The Board won't blame you for their failures."

The rest of the meal was eaten in silence. Agent Vega shortly retired to his private study, only to find Stella stretched out on a wide couch in the corner. A bowl of vegetable stew sat nearly empty on an end table beside her. She let out a loud yawn as she stretched her arms.

"Stel, I thought we agreed to meet later on tonight."

"We did," she consented, sitting up. "However, I had nothing else better to do this evening but stand guard as you do your business."

"I'm expecting a call from Byron Sanders; you shouldn't be here for that." Tobias sat in his over-stuffed armchair at his desk, trying to ignore the scent of her perfume that wafted through the room.

"You mean that you don't *want* me tonight?" She walked over to him and began to massage his shoulders.

"That's not what I said," he replied, leaning back in his chair. Tobias put a hand on hers to stop the massage. "Take that dirty bowl to the kitchen and then wait for me in the library. I'll call when I'm ready for you."

Without another word, Stella picked up her dish and went to leave. Before she did so, she strode over to him and gave him a firm kiss on the mouth.

Tobias stared after her until the door closed. A part of him wanted to call her back and ignore the fact that the richest man in Rygom wished to speak with him. However, duty won out. Since Byron Sanders owned one of the largest OMNI manufacturing companies, he was one of the most influential people in the entire Megacity; Tobias owed it to his reputation to listen to what Byron had to say.

He spent the next several minutes going over his notes for the day. Finally, his OMNI beeped, showing Byron's number on the incoming call screen. After connecting his OMNI to the wall monitor, he accepted the vid-call.

A handsome man in his late 40s sat behind a large ebony desk. His pale blonde hair shone in the light of the over-sized office. "Good evening, Tobias. I hope I'm not interrupting."

"Not at all, Byron," Tobias assured him. "To what do I owe the pleasure of your call?"

"I wanted to pay my respects, seeing as you are going to be running in the next election."

After inspecting the man's expression, he said, "We both know that isn't what you wanted to say. Don't play politics with me. Go ahead and say what's on your mind."

Mr. Sanders' cheery mood suddenly dissipated. "I've heard the most alarming rumor—that there's an Alteration amongst the Candidates. Do you know anything about it? Is there any truth in what they say?"

Vega hid his worry behind a vague response. "Depends on what people are saying."

"Tobias, be frank with me. Do you have any reason to suspect a Candidate of being an Alteration?"

"None, whatsoever," Tobias shrugged. "Alterations are an impossibility. As you know, my company used to lead the world in Alteration research. A few advancements were made; however, there weren't enough successes to make the public happy. More importantly, there were too many health problems with the subjects—too many deaths. We scrapped the technology over twenty years ago, as ordered by the Agency at the time."

"Were any of the other Megacities able to produce positive effects?" Byron asked, sounding too suspicious for his own good.

"No. Rygom led Alteration technology. We had our spies in the top clinics of Dakon, Moryth, Wexar, and Torlea. But there were no successful results. Every subject eventually died as a result of the procedures and surgeries."

There was a long silence as the two men glared at each other through the screen.

"Was there anything else you wanted, Byron?" Agent Vega asked, noticing something odd about Sanders' mannerism.

"Yes. I'm thinking about supporting you in your campaign."

Tobias chucked, very amused at his old friend's joke.

"I'm perfectly serious, Vega. It's about time that Cromford left Office."

"But he's your brother-in-law," Tobias said, unnecessarily. "You've supported him in all his past elections. How is this one any different?"

"That's just it; he's no longer family," Sanders replied, shaking his head with a frown. "He divorced Madeline shortly after he was reelected six years ago, breaking ties with my family."

In the background, there was a loud bang as a door closed. "Is that Tobias?" a woman's voice asked.

"Claudia!" Mr. Sanders' image disappeared from the wall screen. He whispered at his wife, but his words were still distinguishable. "I told you that I was in an important meeting. Get out."

"I just want to ask him about how our little girl is doing."

"He can't disclose information like that." Mr. Sanders reappeared in the monitor. He paused a second before adding, "I have an idea: you should go visit her this second!"

"I would love to, but she refuses to see me or tell me *anything*!"

Byron's voice dropped to an even lower register. "Stop being so dramatic. Go and wait for me in the bedroom. I'll be there soon."

A figure with red hair appeared on the screen. "Hi, Toby!" Bright make-up covered the woman's face, making it impossible to tell Claudia's natural skin color. "If you think you can get away with it, just message me Eve's Test results. Thanks!"

"Goodnight, Claudia," Tobias shouted as she pranced out of sight.

An annoyed expression spread across Byron's face as he returned to his desk chair. "Tobias, the Alteration issue is *very* important. As long as you're sure that none exist, I can guarantee my support. However, I'd like to do some more investigating first. Can I come by tomorrow to discuss the details in a more private setting?"

"Of course. I'll have my assistant call your office in the morning to set something up." Tobias ended the call and spoke at the door. "You can come in now."

"How did you know I was listening?" Stella asked, striding into the room.

"You *always* listen in on my calls, Stel," Tobias replied as she plopped into his lap. He placed his hands on her hips and squeezed. "Besides, I could smell your delicious perfume."

"I love it when you lie to make a business deal." Stella leaned over and gave Tobias a long kiss.

After returning the embrace, he asked, "What do you think about taking money from Byron Sanders? How will the voters interpret me accepting support from my opponent's ex-wife's sister's husband? Would it be the right move on my part?"

"I think you are making it more complicated than it is," Stella scolded, sliding her hands down his arms. "It shows that the richest man in the Megacity no longer trusts the current Mayor. That gives you a major advantage. Besides, do you have any idea what we could do with money that came from Sanders?"

"You're right," he consented, stroking her low back. "I have no reason to be worried. There's no proof that Alterations are possible. We'll just have to be careful."

"Now, can we get out of this stuffy office and go someplace more *comfortable*?"

Tobias let Stella lead him to his bedchamber. Thoughts of being Mayor flitted through his head along the walk, but vanished the second he reached his room.

Chapter 13

The upcoming Placement Assembly had the Candidates in a mixed state of anticipation and sheer horror.

Iris Kayn absently swung her long knives when no one was near in an effort to sooth her nerves. She empathized with her peers as she strolled down the halls of the Living Quarters.; the past two months had pushed them past their limits with the almost-cruel Tests, determining who had what it took to become one of the best of brightest of Rygom's Agency.

Within a few hours, their fate would be revealed. Iris wanted to be confident, but she really only felt like throwing up.

She was on her way to her Living Quarters when she received a frenzied call from Claire. "*Help! I'm stuck in the Gym with some messed up Dueling Dummies. I don't how much longer I can—.*"

Taking off in a sprint, Iris headed for the Gym. She nearly crashed into half a dozen dazed Candidates along the way.

Mere minutes later, she burst through the door to the Gym. Iris barely saw the blade that nearly took her head off before she ducked out of the way. She pulled her knives up in time to block the next attack from a robot.

Claire cried out as she awkwardly fended off a Dummy with a dumbbell.

Iris rushed in the direction of the sound, slicing at whatever got in her way. She destroyed those Dummies and positioned herself between the remaining half-dozen."Claire, get out of here!" Iris was able to block the next set of attacks, but she couldn't find any opportunities to go on the offensive.

"We have another problem!" Claire shouted from behind her. "The door is locked."

"Then pull the control panel apart and disconnect the lock!"

Claire cursed, causing Iris to divert her attention to her. Iris winced as an axe nicked her arm. A small stream of blood oozed through her grey uniform. She parried the next attack before sinking her knives into the Dummy's artificial flesh.

Turning her attention back to Claire, she realized that the remaining Dummies had decided to go after the weakest of the pair. Iris dashed forward and fended them off.

"The mechanisms were replaced with a bolt," Claire explained. "I haven't seen a lock like this in years. Aunt Audrey taught me about these outdated locks, but it's a bit different than the ones I use to fiddle with."

"Figure it out. More Dummies are being activated." Fatigue began to set in, but Iris pushed past it.

Groaning, Claire said, "My hands are shaking. I can't—"

"I'll protect you, but you have to get us out of here."

"I thought the Agency was supposed to be safe," Claire mumbled as she returned to her task. "Stupid Dummies. I'd like to gut the insides of these things and see what made them go wrong." She continued rambling on for several moments before letting out a cry of success. "I owe Audrey a huge thank you."

Iris pushed her through the door and slammed it behind them. Gasping for air, she slumped to the floor.

"What was that all about?" Claire asked, gasping. "I could have *died!*"

"I think this was one last Test before the Placement Assembly. Perhaps it's to make sure that we don't become complacent."

Iris and Claire walked carefully to the nearest Emergency Room, half-expecting the floor to melt or spikes to shoot from the walls. They passed other nervous, sweat-covered Candidates along their way, who seemed to share their paranoid thoughts.

One figure in the crowd stood out; he stood tall with his shoulders back as he strode through the crowds of shuffling Candidates.

"I'll be right back," Iris told Claire before chasing after the figure. "Alastair!"

The man turned, a blank expression on his face. "Miss Kayn, as your Mentor, you must refer to me as *Mr. Vega*."

Confused, she asked, "Are you upset with me?"

He didn't answer; he walked into an empty classroom and motioned for her to follow. Alastair stared at her, his eyes growing hostile.

"Please, tell me what I did. I didn't mean to cause you any offense." Iris knew that she wasn't the easiest person to get along with, but she had been attempting to make a better effort in befriending her peers. "I apologize for whatever is bothering you."

He turned his back on her and inhaled deeply. "Do you have any idea how hard I worked to set those records?"

"*Records*? What you are talking about?"

Alastair turned to face her. "Two days ago, you took a series of timed Tests. Above the arena, a time blinked on the screen beside another one. You completed all the tasks within the shown minutes, beating the record time—my time!" His hands came up suddenly, as if he wanted to strangle her.

Iris took a few steps back. "I thought that I had to beat that time in order to pass the Test. I'm so sorry. If I had known that it was your ultimate record, I would have never tried to—"

"See? That's the thing; you *were* able to beat it. It doesn't matter if you *meant* to disgrace me or not, but you are *able* to." Alastair sighed and leaned against the wall. "I've spent my entire life training to join the Agency; I *live* in the Training Center. And you come along and beat me without even realizing it. You, who has only been learning self-defense for a measly *five* years!"

Iris didn't know what to say. She apologized one last time and left.

At the Emergency Room, Claire clenched as a Nurse Agent injected her with a mild sedative. "Is everything okay? What did Alastair say to you? Your eyes are all red."

Ignoring her, Iris shrugged off her jacket and waited for someone to sew up her cut.

A Nurse pulled back a divider sheet. Eve lay with her hands wrapped in bandages. "Did Alastair finally tell you off?" Her smile disappeared as the Nurse roughly pulled at the strips of cloth.

"It's none of your business, Sanders," Claire retorted.

"Oh, but it sort of is," Eve replied, shaking a free hand. "You see, after Miss Kayn broke Alastair's records, he stumbled upon me—literally—as he strode out of the Observation Room. I took him out to dinner and did what I could to console him. But the poor man had been through a lot. He seemed resolved to cut you out of his personal life entirely."

Iris tried to ignore the vicious woman. As a Nurse tended to her arm, she reflected on her relationship with Alastair Vega—how she loathed him at the beginning of Placement Testing and then grew to care for him as an acquaintance the past couple weeks.

"I think," Eve remarked as she jumped off the table, "it would perhaps be best for both sides if you two just stayed away from each other from now on." She washed her hands in a sink and addressed the Nurse. "My hands still hurt. I thought the Menthol Wrap was supposed to get rid of the throbbing."

The stern-faced healer tossed the bandages in the trash. "You typed nearly two thousand words in an hour. Your muscles will need a little more time to heal."

"I didn't do this to myself. ARHA said that someone hacked my OMNI and that it would explode if I didn't stop typing—and they had to be real words, too! What kind of Test is that, anyway? It didn't do anything productive! What was the point?"

The Nurse didn't look up from her next patient. "I'm sorry, Miss Sanders, but I know nothing of your Testing. I just heal people and send them on their way. Now get out of my Emergency Room."

Eve gave the Nurse a dark look, but did as the woman instructed.

After Iris and Claire were treated, they made their way to the closest cafeteria and grabbed some lunch. Through the crowd of grey clothing, they saw the Vegas, Cromfords, Miss Sanders, and two other Candidates sitting at their usual bench. They were about to locate a different table on the other side of the room when Max and Viola waved them over. The mood during the mealwas mixed with hostility, unease, and contentment. Iris and Claire sat beside the two smiling Third-Years without glancing at the others.

"I see you made it through your morning," Alastair muttered, taking a bite of his casserole.

"We were worried that you wouldn't make it in time," Max said in a much nicer tone. "Claire, I can't believe you knew how to pick that archaic lock! I told Alastair to find something a little easier for a Final Assessment, but it seems my worries were unfounded."

Claire choked on a dumpling. She coughed before managing to ask, "Wait, *Mentors* plan those awful tasks?"

"Well," Viola replied, "we make *suggestions* to the Coordinators. But they are the ones that get the last say in what happens. It takes a lot of work to pull it off without anyone knowing. The Mentors are under a lot of pressure to keep information about the Final from the Mentees. I heard about a guy that leaked information and was forced to run away to the Lower Region."

Iris and Claire quickly gulped down their soup and salad as the others chatted. The mood seemed to lighten a bit when the others changed the subject.

Eve monopolized Alastair's attention. Viola laughed as she shared inside jokes with Max. Beatrice massaged her newly-healed wrist. Max's Mentees, Simon

Pyke and Garrett Sanchez, sat at the opposite end of the table, looking smug and cocky.

At a quarter to 1:00, a bell rang. All the Mentees and Candidates stood and made their way to the Stadium. Once at the entrance, Iris and Claire presented their OMNI identification files. They were shepherded into a body scanner. After that, Agents from the Medical Branch took a blood sample.

Iris inhaled sharply as a woman in a white coat pricked her finger. She hoped that the machinery was looking at DNA instead of whether or not the eighteen year olds had diseases in their blood. A small light on the mechanism blinked green, allowing her to go to the next area. The Nurse impatiently handed them their respective metal tickets and gave an annoyed gesture for them to move on.

She let out a sigh of relief. The past week had been tense as she wondered if the Agency would discover her health secret. Releived, Iris looked at the seat number on her ticket and said, "Section 4, Row B, Seat 1."

"That's weird. I'm two over. I wonder who is sitting between us."

Claire's question was answered when they reached their seats. Sitting in Section 4, Row B, Seat 2 was Alastair

Vega. Iris braced herself for more harsh words from him. To her astonishment, Alastair smiled at her when she took her seat next to him.

She grinned awkwardly back at him. “Does this mean that you aren’t mad at me anymore?”

“Not in the least,” he whispered through clenched teeth. “It has been pointed out to me that *both* our public images are stained when other people see us not getting along. So I decided that I am going to *act* civil towards you when we’re around other people.” For a second, his eyes flashed angrily at her, but they instantly went back to being cheerful.

Eve, Viola, and Beatrice sat in Seats 4, 5, and 6, respectively. Max was sandwiched between his Mentees in Seats 7-9. They all had a great view of the platform that had been erected in the center of the Stadium

The first few dozen rows by the stage were filled with all the Candidates and their Mentors. Men and women dressed in straight black—Agent Instructors and Coordinators—sat behind them. The Stadium grew calm and silent as a bell chimed to signal the beginning of the Assembly.

On the platform, six of the seven wooden chairs were filled with the Agency Board Members, all dressed in black suits. From left to right sat Marshal Brawn, Amos Romaine, Henry Weldon, Josiah Morrow, Byron Sanders, and Tobias Vega.

The empty seat should have held Mayor Jay Cromford, but he was nowhere to be seen.

There was applause as a confident-looking man in a white suit with well-groomed blonde and grey hair meandered through the crowd. He grabbed the occasional hand, baring an eager smile. Mayor Cromford called out greetings, wishing luck to all he passed as he descended.

Beside her, Alastair grunted. A scowl covered his lips as Jay Cromford came closer. The Mayor approached their seats, reaching out his hand towards Alastair. There was a moment of hesitation when Alastair looked as though he was going to refuse the offer. The Third-Year Trainee reluctantly accepted the offered gesture.

Mayor Cromford made his way down to the platform, granted one last wave to the audience, and eased into the last empty chair.

A sturdy-built man appearing to be in his mid-60s moved to center stage and spoke into the Audio-Transducer. "Welcome honored Candidates to our prestigious Placement Assembly. As you are all aware, I am Director Marshal Brawn. I would like to begin by congratulating each and every one of you for making it this far in our selection process. As I call your name, come up front in an orderly fashion to the front of the stage and face your peers."

Director Brawn began listing off names. Candidates stood and filed down the steps to the floor of the Stadium.

Iris wasn't sure if she should hope to be called or not. There was a startling lack of pomp as the names were hastily read off; there wasn't mention about Programs or Branches or anything else. She tried to catch the eye of Alastair for reassurance, but he continued to stare ahead of him.

When their names were called, Max's Mentees stood and went with the others. As the last name was said, Iris noticed that about half the Trainees were up front. A flood of figures in black uniforms came onto the field and surrounded the standing Candidates.

"I would like everyone," Director Brawn continued, "that is still sitting to applaud these young men and women for their effort as they are escorted from the premises forever."

Scattered clapping echoed around the Stadium. There was a mass confusion as reality hit those that had failed Placement Testing. Many broke down in anguish, sobbing uncontrollably. Several were so distraught that pairs of Agents had to physically remove them from the Stadium.

“Now that the unpleasantness is done,” Director Brawn continued with a grin, “I would like to proceed with the ceremony. As the rest of you are smart enough to figure out, you have all made it into the Agency Training Program. Congratulations! You are now officially First-Year Trainees!”

A sigh of relief shot out of Iris. She carefully smoothed her uniform and took deep breaths to calm herself. It barely registered that the Board Director began calling off names again. Her attention snapped back to the Stadium when she heard Claire’s name announced.

“Miss Claire Birch: Engineering Program—Experimental Branch.”

Standing with poise, Claire carefully hid her excitement. Alastair whispered, “Congratulations!” as she passed him. Iris gave her a big hug.

Claire proudly strode down the steps towards the platform. When she reached the stage, she was passed along the line of Board Members. When she returned to her seat, she pulled out a small pin from the box she had been given. She carefully attached it to her uniform lapel. Iris could barely make out the image—it appeared to be a group of pewter tools forming to make the letter "*E*" over a green square plane.

The rest of the names blurred into each other. Iris politely clapped for all the Candidates that successfully Tested into the Agency Training Program.

Beatrice Cromford miraculously made it into the Dancing Branch of the Performance Program despite the injury she was still recovering from. On the stage, her father gave her a hug and a kiss instead of the traditional handshake. When she came back to her seat, a purple pin in the shape of a leaping figure holding a silver letter "*D*" was attached to her lapel.

When her name was called, she was thrilled to hear what Program and Branch she was Placed in. "Miss Iris Kayn: Enforcement Program—Special Operations Branch." She stood and walked to the platform.

The Agency Board Members gave her well-wishes and assured her that they knew she would fit wonderfully into Spec Ops.

When she reached Tobias Vega, he gave her a smile similar to the ones given by the other Board Members. However, his grin seemed to have a different subtext. He looked as though he knew something—some terrible secret.

No, Iris decided that she was just imagining things. She tried to hide the apprehension she felt, but she failed miserably. Iris felt her up-turned lips fall to a worried frown. Blood rushed to her cheeks. She quickly dipped her head in respect and moved down the line. At the end of the row, Mayor Cromford handed her the box containing her own pin. She thanked him and went back to her seat.

Fumbling open the box, she removed its contents. It was a blue shield the size of her thumbnail, identifying her as a Trainee in the Enforcement Program. Over the shield were the letters "*SO*" in gold for Special Operations. Iris carefully pinned it to the corner of the right lapel of her uniform. The pin looked oddly familiar, as if she had seen it before.

Her eyes wandered and they landed on Alastair's left lapel. There were a number of badges across his chest, but the little blue shield stood out. On it were the same letters as on hers.

Alastair was also a Trainee in the Special Operations Branch of the Enforcement Program. As a Third-Year, he would likely be an Aide for many of her classes. With his new-found loathing, Iris worried that his feelings about her might cause some problems of her

Training. She had begun to hope their interaction would be minimal now that she had made it into the Program, but it seemed as though they were going to remain in close proximity.

He turned and looked her square in the face. A glint in his gaze showed that he noticed her sudden realization. Alastair appeared to be forming plans behind his mysterious green eyes.

Chapter 14

A half-empty bottle of rum in his hand, Norman stared blankly at the screen in front of him. He took a large gulp without removing his gaze off the facts that flashed across the monitor. The data slowly scrolled down. He had spent the past four days in his laboratory, watching the stream of information, hoping to see something he might have missed.

But it was all in vain.

"*He knows*," Norman slurred. "He knows what I've done. Oh, Resa!" Shaky sobs burst out of him, accompanied by a fountain of tears. "I ruined our daughter's life in the hopes of saving you."

Norman turned to the comatose figure lying along the far wall. Dr. Teresa Kayn lay frozen on a table, hooked up to a variety of machines. Except for a few wrinkle lines on her cheeks and forehead, she looked just as she did the day she gave birth to Iris. Norman sat by her side, leaned over, and tenderly brushed her face with his fingers. The heat from his hands vanished, sucked into Teresa's cold body.

"How did we come to this, Resa? How did you catch a Plague? You were always so careful. When I first saw you this way, my grief consumed me and I did stupid things. I experimented on Iris and now Vega knows. It's only a matter of time before he takes our girl away and confiscates all our research. He probably already knows that you aren't *dead*."

*****

"Norman!"

Facts and statistics from the latest studies on nanite research flashed across the screen, being fed to the monitor from Dr. Kayn's OMNI. Data-discs sat scattered on the desk in jumbled piles. Half-eaten take-out food lay just out of reach from the weary scientist.

"Did you hear me, Doc? It's time!"

For the first moment in hours, Norman Kayn was wide awake. "Where are you, darling?" He stood and walked out of his study.

"I'm downstairs, ready to go. You know, where you should be!"

In an instant, he was down the steps and in the living room. Bags and a suitcase stood lumped in a pile next to the front door—more luggage than was needed for a one-night stay.

Dr. Teresa Kayn stood leaning against the archway to the kitchen, her dirty-blonde hair tied up messily in a bun. Her belly was swollen with the presence of their unborn child. A twinge of pain flashed across her eyes.

"Okay, here we go. Off to the hospital!" Panicking, he opened the door for her and grabbed their luggage. "Are you sure we have everything? Your clothes? The baby's things?"

"Yes!" Teresa shouted. "We have enough to last us a week. Now, let's *go*."

The journey from their apartment to the Hospital took them less than ten minutes. A team of nurses, headed by an OB-GYN, surrounded them upon arrival. Dr. Teresa Kayn was carried off to the Delivery Wing without her loving husband.

Norman walked hurriedly down corridor after corridor, directed by the various staff members and signs that he came across. He finally reached his destination, out of breath and red-faced. An elderly woman behind a large desk gave him the room number where he could place their belongings and then advised him to wait there for his wife and baby.

The longer he sat there in that empty room, the greater Norman's anxiety grew. His eyes were fixed on the door, watching for any sign of movement.

Occasionally, a perky nurse would pop in and ask if he needed anything. Norman ordered pot after pot of black coffee, hoping it would settle his nerves. But no amount of caffeine in the Megacity could relieve his fears.

A physician walked in slowly, a screen chart in his hand. The look on his face was solemn. Norman hoped he was only imagining the hint of sorrow in the man's eyes.

"How is she? How is my wife? And my baby? Boy or girl? Where are they?"

"I need you to come with me, Dr. Kayn."

They walked down a long hallway; every step was agony. Norman was concerned about where he was being taken. Eventually, the physician led him a room with a large silver plaque that said, "Quarantine."

Norman gazed through a wide window into the room. Teresa lay unconscious on a bed, tubes sticking out of her arms and face, attached to a range of medical equipment. Nurses in protective gloves and masks hurried about the room, stabbing her with needles and hooking her up to even more electronics in the room.

"What's going on?" Norman asked, peering through the viewing window. "She *is* alive, right? I see her chest rising and falling."

The doctor averted his gaze. “Not quite. The machines are allowing her organs to work.”

“How did this happen? How did her labor cause this?”

“It wasn’t labor that did this to Mrs. Kayn.”

“*Dr.* Kayn,” Norman corrected. “Her name is *Dr.* Kayn.”

“I apologize. It appears—” He paused for a moment before continuing. “It appears that Dr. Kayn has a *Plague*.”

Norman couldn’t believe what the physician was telling him. Dearest Teresa couldn’t possibly have caught the virus that rampaged through the bowels of the Megacity. No. It had to be something else.

But there his beauty lay, hanging onto the last inch of her life. Their child was somewhere else in the massive series of rooms and halls in the hospital—never to know the passionate words her mother spoke, the way Resa walked with elegant grace, nor the never-ending wisdom that flowed from her sharp mind.

Tears poured relentlessly down his cheeks as he watched and waited for his true love to wake.

*****

Caught in an alcohol-induced stupor, Norman barely noticed that his OMNI beeped. He stumbled back to his desk and answered without looking at the screen. "Iris?"

"*No*," answered a deep voice. "*Dr. Kayn, this is Byron Sanders*."

"I can't talk right now," Norman slurred. "I'm waiting for my daughter to call me to tell me about her Placement Assembly."

"*May I please come in*?" Mr. Sanders asked with a tone of impatience.

"Alright, I'll be down in a second." Norman ended the call. He pushed a few buttons at his desk and his wife disappeared into the wall.

Warily making his way down the steep stairs to the main floor, Norman tried to make himself look sober. He smoothed his hair down, fixed the collar of his shirt, and rubbed the wetness from his cheeks.

Dr. Kayn was apprehensive about meeting Mr. Sanders. Like all Societans, se had heard about the family and their prosperous OMNI production company. But he had never met any of the people themselves. Iris had talked once or twice about the snobbish daughter and that was the extent of his connection to the Sanders. He wondered what sort of urgent business would bring the patriarch to his doorstep.

As the door opened, Mr. Sanders held up a bottle. "I hope you're a scotch man."

Norman, in turn, moved to the kitchen to fetch some glasses. "To what do I owe the pleasure of your company?"

"I've been researching the progression of Alteration technology," Byron replied, entering the kitchen. He placed the bottle on the counter and took a seat at the bar stool. "Everyone seems to think that they are impossible, but I wanted to get an expert's opinion."

Blood rushed out of Norman's face. "And what makes you think I'm an *expert*?" He set down a pair of crystal glasses.

"I didn't mean to imply that you were an expert in that field," Sanders corrected, pouring both of them a large drink. "There don't seem to be any experts of Alterations; they've all run away to die in the Lower Region. I simply meant that you have such a *grand* reputation in this Megacity for your success with curing several strings of the Plague. I was hoping for your professional belief on the subject."

"As I'm sure you've been told, humans don't have the capabilities to handle radical changes in their physiology," Norman explained as he began pacing around the room. He took a few sips to calm his nerves. "The body rejects foreign substances by sending immune cells to destroy the supposed *invaders*. The immune cells end up destroying good tissue in the battle. Most of the Alterations died, but some were saved by removing the changes before their important organ systems shut down. I've heard that the experience was very painful and emotionally traumatizing."

Byron leaned forward on his stool, scrutinizing the researcher. "Do you know where I could find some of the survivors? I would love to get their perspective."

"As far as I know, they all moved to other Megacities to start new lives. I wish I could give you more information, Mr. Sanders, but I'm afraid that's all I can tell you." After a pause he added, "Might I ask why a man such as yourself would be interested in such a concept?"

"It's a political matter. I know that kind of thing doesn't interest you, so I shan't bore you with the details."

Norman held up his glass as though to toast the man. "I wish you luck in your investigation, but I'm still not sure why you are conducting this search yourself. Aren't there people you could hire to ask questions?"

Byron set down the glass, his barely-touched scotch nearly spilling out. “I inherited my OMNI production company from my father; it was never what I wanted to do. I’ve let my company run *itself*. I collect the profits, which sponsors my moon-lighting investigations. Uncovering secrets is the passion of my life.”

“It’s important for a man to follow his passion.” Not wanting to continue the conversation, Norman closed the scotch and moved the bottle to one of his stashes above the fridge. “Now, you must excuse me. I have a lot of work to do this evening.”

“Well, thank you, Dr. Kayn. You have been very helpful.” Sanders pulled out two discs and handed them to Norman. “Here’s my contact information and some credits for your time.”

Norman showed the man out after slipping the credit-disc back into the man’s hand. He said good-bye and closed the door behind him. Letting out a sigh, he finished Byron’s scotch and he went back to his laboratory.

He pushed in the command to reveal Teresa’s hiding place and went to sit by her side.

“I let paranoia get the better of me earlier.” Norman rubbed his forehead. “Do you remember when I talked about that Byron Sanders? He was just here, asking questions. I told him what I told the authorities twenty years ago. It's all political; it's always—*always* political," Norman scoffed, sitting beside his beloved. "For two decades, I have kept your family's secret, but I don't know how much longer it will stay that way. What about Iris? Can I protect your family's good name at the cost of our daughter's life?"

Full of despair, he left her side and went to grab a bottle of rum from a floor safe. When he turned, he stopped. Standing in front of him was Dr. Taledon.

Audrey stood with her hands on her hips, looking disgusted at what she just heard. Her pale face grew pink and she clenched her jaw. Growling, she said, "It's not right to save *dead* people's reputation for the sake of a *living* person."

Norman shook his head. "I didn't say—I mean—I was only speculating."

"I can't believe you would even think that!" Dr. Taledon spat. "Iris is your *daughter*. She didn't turn herself into what she is; you did that. You need to make things right."

"Yes, I know your stance on the subject," he sighed, wiping his sweaty hands on his pants. "You think that I should just spill out all my sins to my daughter and hope she'll forgive me. No, this must be done carefully."

"You can't let *Tobias* be the one to reveal everything to her."

"The trail ends cold. Resa's family covered their tracks carefully."

"Don't say that as though you actually believe it. Vega *must* know that you're doing something off record. It's only a matter of time before he figures it out. He's going to get into this laboratory and get his grubby hands on a hundred years of research." Biting her lip in agitation, Audrey entered the commands that put Teresa back behind the wall.

Norman reached out his hands as he said, "Leave her out! I want her to hear what we say; it helps her understand what's going on."

"*She is not here*," Dr. Taledon replied, slowly. "That's just her body kept alive by machines. It's too dangerous to keep her out." She looked over the information on the lab monitor. "Now, have you decided to do any trials today?"

Dr. Kayn shook his head. "I was going to, but I remembered that Iris has her Placement Assembly today. Teresa and I have been waiting for her to call."

"I suggest we try and get some work done while we wait. You can hear your OMNI ring when she calls." She handed him some data-discs. "I managed to smuggle out the results for my past few studies. There is some promising data."

With a groan of frustration, Norman let Audrey lead him over to his work station. He inserted the discs into the computer and pulled up the files and documents. Squinting to read the data, he couldn't understand Dr. Taledon's intentions. Confused, Norman asked, "Why am I re-running this trial?"

"It would look suspicious if I randomly showed up with these results at the Department of Disease Prevention," Audrey explained, sounding more annoyed than usual. "I need to have a fresh study with a new date marker on the results."

"And why does this affect me? This isn't my field of research. Why would the DDP believe I created a nanite that destroyed cancer?"

"They wouldn't." Audrey inserted a data-disc in the computer. "Oh, come on, Norman! Trust me on this. I need you to agree to this before I show you the results. You owe me one for mixing me up with this whole Iris mess." She began to click through other research files on the wall screen. "When I create a new nanite, I always mix it with other diseases besides just cancer. I hope I'll accidentally find a cure for something else in the process. There was a trial that I ran that came up with an interesting result when put with Plague 7."

Norman's interest was suddenly piqued. "*Plague 7*, did you say? What happened?" He came over to where Audrey stood and stared at the screen in disbelief. "Your hypothesized cancer-killing-nanite did *that*?"

"Yes. I'll let you claim this discovery if you tell Iris what we did to her."

"I really hate your ultimatums, Audrey," Norman sighed, slumping into a firm laboratory chair. "I need to think about it."

"Then we'll skip this trial until you make up your mind. In the meantime, let's run my other studies." Audrey fished samples of four different nanite tubes from her briefcase. "Could you please prepare the Plague Petri dishes?"

He did as he was told. As Norman carefully arranged the dishes for each Plague, he wondered when the roles of head researcher and assistant were reversed. He took the tray of viruses over to Audrey's work area. She injected a mass of nanites into the small glass containers while Norman put labels on each.

When they finished, he grew anxious since Iris still hadn't called him. He cleaned his hands and went to pick up his OMNI. Selecting the appropriate number, he hit the call button. A moment later, Iris's voice came on the transceiver.

"Hi, Dad."

"How's my wonderful little girl?"

"All grown up."

"How did the Placement Assembly go? Are you coming home or are you officially leaving your old man?"

Iris then spent the next several minutes describing all the events of her day, beginning with a startling tale involving a surprise Dummy attack, and ending with the results of the Assembly.

After processing the information, the first thing Norman said was, "I'm glad that Alastair chump has finally decided to leave you alone. Those Vegas are nothing but bad news."

"I agree with your father," Audrey affirmed.

"Hello, Dr. Taledon!" Iris responded. *"Sorry that I didn't call earlier; it's been a busy afternoon. There has been a lot of last-minute preparation before classes start*

next week. We're getting ready for the beginning-of-the-year banquet, so we can't talk for very long—"

There was the sound of a short scuffle. Claire's voice came through the OMNI next. *"Hi, Aunt Audrey. Dr. Kayn. Would you please pass on to my family that I was Placed into the* Experimental Branch *of the* Engineering Program*? Now, Iris and I must go. There's only an hour until the banquet and I still need to do her hair and make-up. We'll talk to everyone tomorrow afternoon. Good—"*

"Sorry about that," Iris said when she regained possession of her OMNI.

"Well, I hope you have fun, Iris," he muttered, wiping a Petri-dish clean. "Just remember that there is room here if you feel like coming back home."

"I know, Dad. Oh, I need to go now. I love you!"

"I love you, too. Contact me tomorrow and tell me all about your first day of Training," Norman instructed before the call was ended. He fought back fresh tears when the call cut off. As Audrey gave him a sympathetic hug, he broke down as she soothingly patted his back.

Chapter 15

Trying to look busy, Rikani strolled down the halls of her Clan's Head Quarters. Even when she was off the clock, the Rye Leader was always sought after to solve her people's problems. Most days, she was okay with going from person to person at all hours of the day.

But Sunday evening was her time off.

As she walked, she messaged her assistant, reviewing with Vian the tasks that needed to be completed.

Vian texted, "*It might take awhile to adjust Jotea's contract; I'm still finalizing everything with Lady Lurahi for the Market Library. The landlord isn't being very cooperative about the location; he won't show us any appropriate buildings.*"

The fact that one more thing was going wrong nearly knocked Rikani over the deep end. She knew that the delay wasn't Vian's fault, so she replied as calmly as she could manage.

Rikani sent a short reply. "*I'll talk to Lurahi. Send Mr. Guile a message, saying that I'll be by his office after lunch tomorrow.*" Hoping that was the end of the matter, she returned her OMNI to her pocket. But a moment later, it beeped again.

Vian: *Your schedule has you reprimanding Zobin after lunch.*

Rikani: *Right. The New Blue View tabloid is getting a little out of hand again. Have you searched the eviction bylaws?*

Vian: *Yeah, you can't kick someone out of the Azures for bad-mouthing the Clan.*

Rikani: *Whose stupid idea was it to include a free-speech clause! So I have no authority to get rid of him?*

Vian: *Sorry, no. But I'll keep looking.*

Rikani: *I'll handle Zobin later. Push that meeting back so I have time to negotiate with Mr. Guile.*

She switched her OMNI to vibrate, hoping that it would minimize the number of interruptions. As much as Rikani enjoyed ruling one of the most productive Clan in the Lower Region, she wished she had a helpmate.

Ulrian and Vian did a lot of work for her, but it wasn't the same as having someone else to help make decisions. Tays was supposed to help facilitate the running of the Azures, but he loathed responsibility. Even if she had more assistance, Rikani had been groomed to run the Clan ever since she moved out of Upper Society; she couldn't see herself trusting anyone else to share the power with.

*****

Eleven year old Remy Parson had a hard time adapting to her new life in the Lower Region. Transitioning from Upper Society to the Azure Clan was a difficult change. The hardest thing was getting used to her new name. It felt odd to have strangers reverently call her Miss Rikani Rye.

She had a fit when her mother had told her to change her name. "Why can't I still be *Remy*? That's my name."

In the end, her father gave her the name 'Rikani' and put an end to it.

Troy didn't mind switching lives; he liked the idea that they were starting over. He went out of his way to introduce himself as *Tays*. Their parents changed their names to *Vamila* and *Sirad*. To Remy, they were still *Mom* and *Dad*. Little Derek had no qualms of being called *Mezik*; being three, he simply thought it was a nickname.

Vamila had explained to her children that someone did bad business with Daddy and hurt the company. They ran out of money and now had to go live with their uncle, aunt, and cousins, and become Heirs to the Azure Rye Clan.

Grandma Rye had loved a Societan man. They met in Market for years, spending every moment they could together. As they had children, they alternated taking a child to raise. The eldest, Asdem, remained in the Lower Region to become the next Rye Heir. When Vamila was born, she went to Upper Society with her father, Grandpa Parson. Lastly, Nasiram stayed with the Azures and lived there until she married Dagnos. There was probably a lot more to the story, but that was all that Remy and Troy were told when their parents moved them into Rye Manor.

And now all three siblings had been reunited. Vamila's kids got along with their cousins, although they only met up about once or twice a week. Koje and Tyvax were off doing who knew what in Market with their respective "friends." Little Kumate, being a one-year-old, stayed within Nasiram's eyesight almost every moment of the day.

Her siblings weren't exact the best companions either. One of the Azures, Jux, took Tays away all day to show him how to make and fix things. And Mezik was constantly running off to all the corners of the HQ.

To keep her busy, Uncle Asdem had started giving Rikani private lessons every day. She sat at a desk and watched strange videos for hours on end—vids about business, finance, philosophy, and a number of other subjects. All the while, the Rye Clan Leader sat across from her, trying to find more and more videos for her to view.

"Why am I doing this?" she asked him one day.

"Because my own sons will run our Clan into the ground," Asdem replied, looking up from his screen. "I'll need my wonderfully intelligent niece to keep an eye on her rowdy cousins when I'm dead."

Rikani frowned at her uncle. "That's both flattering and morbid." She closed out a video of an actor reciting quotes of John Locke and selected another from her electronic mail. "But I'm not in line to rule. Koje and Tyvax will be upset if I subvert their authority. I don't want them to hate me, uncle."

"Don't worry about that. By the time I'm done with you, you'll know how to manipulate those two idiots into doing whatever you want. And they'll think it was all their idea."

"I don't know if I—"

"Oh, you'll do it," Asdem interrupted with a nod. "You're still young, Rikani. But I guarantee that in a couple years, you're going to love telling other people what to do."

*****

Despite having dozens of people at her disposal, she had yet to find someone she could share her burden of running an entire Clan. But that was beginning to change. Rikani had finally met a man with sound judgment and a strong work ethic.

She spent a lot of her time thinking about Brak, even when she rushed about the HQ and dealt with everyone's problems.

Brak had agreed to keep their relationship a secret for the time being. She felt the need to fully process her feelings for the man before she considered telling her family about him. Rikani used to be open about her feelings for men, but experience had taught her to keep her mouth shut until the relationship grew more serious.

"Is everything alright, Lady Rikani?"

The sound of Ulrian's voice snapped her out of her memory. "Yes, thank you. Why? Do I look like I'm *not* alright?"

"You looked pretty upset as you strode past me," the steward replied, concern evident on his face. He gestured at the surrounding architecture. "I've been following you for two corridors. Don't you know you're in the men's residential area?"

"Oh!" Rikani searched the corridor to see if any of her male Clan members noticed that she was in the *Men Only* quadrant. She turned back to Ulrian. "What's the shortest way out of here?" Rikani followed her trusty steward back to the common passages of the Azure Head Quarters.

She peered at her time piece. *8:15 .pm*. Quickly, Rikani ran down the hall after hall until she made it to the HQ entrance.

All three of the Azure security guards stood in a straight line, blocking the exit door of the HQ. They looked rather concerned as a scrawny figure with dark brown hair tried to push past them.

"I have to get out!" Mezik shouted at them as he faked to the left. The adults went to block him, but he was already at the control panel.

"Geez, that boy's fast." Hurez barely grabbed Mezik as the door swooshed open.

"Master Mezik, how do you know the pass code?" asked the head guard, Bilez. He helped lift and position the boy over Hurez's shoulder.

Mezik's feet kicked wildly in the air."Like I would tell you!"

"Now, Master Mezik," Janez said in her calm, caring voice, "your brother and sister have left us very clear instructions not to let you out of the Azure HQ."

"We certainly have." Rikani folded her arms and scowled.

Her youngest brother flinched at the sound of Kani's voice.

Rikani took the skinny child in her arms and lowered his to the ground. "I'm getting tired of your breakout attempts, Mez. Do you want me to lock you in your room until you're sixteen? So help me, I'll do whatever it takes to keep your *safe*."

"I can be safe out in the Market, Kani. Just send Bilez or Hurez with me. I promise I'll stay right by their side every moment!" Growling with frustration, Mezik turned and kicked at the floor. "It's unfair! Kumate gets to go to Market, and he's two years younger than me. *Two years*! Why does he get to go when I'm stuck here?"

Her face sank as she heard those words. She adopted her stern, authoritative voice as she said, "Mez, I know you are upset. But you have to believe me when I say that Market can be dangerous, especially to young Heirs like you." Softening, Rikani stroked his shaggy hair and added, "Even if you aren't harmed, you could be kidnapped and held for ransom. Although Tays and I would pay anything to save you, a price might be too big to pay *and* keep control of the Azure Clan."

"Yeah, yeah, I know. The Crimson scum have been trying to take over the Azures for years," he said with a huff. "But you've always been able to outsmart Queen Romisa and the sinister Pavoc."

Rikani pulled him in for a gentle hug. "That doesn't mean that they won't find a way to take the Clan away from us. Please, Mez. Promise me you won't try and get out anymore."

"I promise." Mezik's eyes glanced at everything but her, indicating that he was lying.

"Now, I have to go. Can you manage to stay out of trouble at least until I get home?" Rikani gave him a quick peck on the cheek. Before she left the HQ, she texted Vian to change the pass code for the main door's control panel. She thanked the security guards for keeping an eye on Mez and then finally left the Azure Clan.

Running as fast as she was able, Rikani made it to the old run-down school half an hour past the designated time.

"Brak?" she called out to the shadows.

"I was beginning to wonder if you were going to show up," he said, stepping away from a crumpling wall.

"Sorry I'm late. There was so much Clan business—"

He stopped her mouth with a tender kiss. "No apology necessary. I'm just glad you're here now." Brak folded her in his arms, his lips moving to her forehead.

Rikani buried her face in his chest, inhaling his scent. When Brak began to pull away from her, she clutched at him. "What's that smell?" She sniffed his shirt. "It's sweet. Are you wearing perfume?"

"No. Of course not." He held his shirt to his nose. "It's probably Soha Darrow; I ran into her a few times today." Changing the topic too quickly, he asked. "How was your week?"

Suspicions ran through Rikani's head, but she pushed them out of her mind. She only had a few hours a week with Brak and she didn't want to spend them interrogating him. "Well, Vian and I have been working on this contract with—"

He put his fingers on her mouth. "I don't want to hear about work tonight." Brak took Rikani's hand. "I want to know what you do for *fun*; how do you spend your *free time*?"

Rikani hesitated; she didn't get all that much time to herself.

With a sigh, Brak asked, "Will you do something for me, Ri?"

Uncertain about his request, she took her hand from his. "D*epends*. What do you want me to do?"

"I want you to do something that you *never* dreamed you would ever do," Brak instructed, as though it was the easiest thing in the world. "Then come back here and tell me about it."

"What do I get in return?"

"I'll let you ask me one question—anything you like—and I'll answer it with one-hundred percent *honesty*." He paused briefly before adding, "I'll even let you ask your question right now."

Rikani thought for a moment. Brak was often very secretive when she asked him certain personal questions. It was a tempting offer. But how would she know if he were really telling the truth? There was something off about the way he said, "I'll answer it with one-hundred percent *honesty*." The fear of infidelity raced through her mind. In the end, her fondness for him made her banish the dreadful feeling; she decided to comply with his wishes.

"Okay, you win," she said, spinning back around. "I'll do something completely out of the ordinary—for me at least. As for the other part of our bargain, I want to know if I'm your *first* love."

Brak suddenly burst out laughing. "You could have asked me anything and that's your question! Well, Ri, you wasted your wild card. My answer is: yes, you *are* my first love."

She stared at him, looking closely for any sign that he might be lying. His eyes gazed back, full of affection and sincerity. In that moment, she knew he was being completely truthful. Leaning forward and up, she gave him a kiss. "I just thought of something fun that I want to do."

"Really?" he asked, seductively.

"No, not like *that*. I'd like to spend a day at Market with you."

He pulled back again and averted his gaze. "I don't know, Ri."

"What's the problem?"

Hesitantly, Brak said, "I'm a little nervous about being in public with you." With some firmness, he added, "We only get so much time together every week and I don't want to waste it. I mean, we can't do the same things in *public* as we can do in *private*."

Rikani wasn't sure how to take that comment. Brak had always insisted that they see each other away from their respective HQ's. It was strange—like he wanted to avoid seeing someone. But she couldn't determine if it was someone she wasn't *supposed* to meet or if it was someone he didn't *want* to meet. She decided it was about time to figure out which it was.

"I think we've spent plenty of time getting to know each other. Now I want us to do some sort of activity for our meeting next week—as a true couple. You said I should do something new and fun and I plan on doing just that with you."

"Your happiness is all I want." He hugged her gently. "But I can't next Sunday; I have an appointment that I can't cancel. How about the following week? Does that work?"

Reluctantly, she nodded. Rikani almost began to wonder what sort of appointment would cause him to cancel their weekly get-together. But she reminded herself to stop being a suspicious girlfriend. She grew determined to enjoy the rest of her night with him, silencing the thought that something might be very wrong with their relationship.

Chapter 16

Scanning the History room, Iris looked for two empty seats near the front of the class. She started to descend the stairs of the lecture hall, but Claire walked to the back rows of desks. Torn between sitting by herself near the Instructor and being at the far end of the room, Iris eventually chose to join her friend.

Eve Sanders and Beatrice Cromford were already sitting in the area. "I just know that I'm going to be so bored in this class," Eve complained, twirling a short braid with her fingers. "Why do I need to know history?"

"It's important to understand what has happened in the past," Iris explained, "so that we understand where we come from."

Claire nodded as she applied a fresh coat of chap stick. "Yes. Mistakes are often averted by looking at how things have occurred in history. In order to avoid repeating those events, we need to study the patterns and—"

"I'm going to stop you there," Miss Sanders interrupted, holding up a carefully-manicured hand. "Life today is *much* different than it was even a generation ago."

Beatrice leaned forward and said, "It's true, Eve! Studying history and what came before us helps us improve

Society." She popped her wrist gently as she added, "For example, with my dance and music, if I know what has been done in the past, I can take it and make it into something new. We can't go forward without first looking back."

"That's very philosophical, Bea," Claire replied, sounding astonished. "Are you sure you chose the right career path?"

Eve looked as though she was about to say something snide, but she was interrupted when a woman dressed in all black entered into the room. Her face was covered in freckles, making her look younger than she seemed to be. Her brown hair was pulled back into a neat braided bun. She set a large portfolio on her desk when she reached the front of the class and began speaking.

"Welcome, First-Years, to *Megacity History*. I am your History Instructor this term, Agent Haley Snow." She opened her portfolio and removed a disc. "I hope you all brought your text-discs to class. For today *only*, I'll let you read off a peer's screen if you didn't bring one. In the future, unprepared Trainees will receive extra assignments to make up for forgetting materials. See the syllabus file in ARHA's database for a list of all other classroom requirements, as well as any disciplinary tasks that may be given to you for failure to meet my expectations. Now, please insert the disc entitled, '*From the Ground Up: Volume 1 of the History of Megacities,*' and turn to entry one."

The History Instructor paused, allowing the unprepared Trainees search through their profiles in ARHA's database. There was a series of shuffling sounds as the First-Years rummaged through their packs to pull out their text-discs.

Not surprisingly, Claire nudged Iris and asked if she could share her screen. She scooted her chair over; her OMNI was in her hand, ready to take notes.

Iris pulled out her own OMNI and opened the textbook.

Agent Snow began the lecture. "The idea for a Megacity came from the renowned architect, Dr. Doyle Rygom. He proposed it as a solution for housing shortages and land management. Instead of spreading the city limits across the plane of Earth's surface, he suggested building upward into the atmosphere. His self-contained structures would provide livable circumstances for humans, animals, and plants—"

Loud beeps interrupted Agent Snow. She looked down at her desk and tapped an icon. "Miss Sanders?" The

Instructor looked in Eve's direction. "Please refrain from messaging during my class. The fact that you, 'Wonder what Alastair is doing at this moment,' is irrelevant to your education. It is also a distraction to Miss Cromford." Agent Snow then addressed the rest of the class. "I receive all messages sent in my classroom. If you wish for your conversations to remain private, save your personal life for your free time."

The room went silent. A moment later, there was a series of shuffles as the Trainees tucked their OMNIs away.

Resuming her lecture, Agent Snow said, "Many people said Doyle Rygom's Megacities wouldn't be able to stand with so much weight over the supports. What they didn't know was that Rygom's friend and colleague, Sabian Torlea, had developed a nanite that reinforced steel at the molecular level. These nanites rearranged the molecules to form a more sturdy structure of steel. To keep the support pillars and beams in good condition, stations of nanites were placed at the centers of the supports."

Agent Snow's desk let out another beep. With an agitated frown, the History Instructor went and looked to see who had dared to send a message in her class.

After scanning the message, she let out a chuckle. "That's a good question. Miss Birch asks, 'Is it true that the decay in the Lower Region has left certain nanite stations inoperable?' Yes, that is correct. In the process of expansion, the Agency has ignored the Lower Region. Since the Middle Zone and Upper Society are situated above the Region's supports, this is a problem that our engineers have been trying to fix for many years. It's ultimately what prompted the creation of the Renovation Act. But we'll study that later on this term."

The remainder of class time was spent reading about the other influential people that worked with Doyle Rygom to make Megacities a reality. Louis Dakon owned the construction company that built the first Megacity, Clint Wexar developed the utility systems, and Ellie Moryth was a politician and philanthropist who convinced people to move to the Megacities. Without them, Dr. Rygom would never have succeeded. Later on, the major Megacities of the world were named after them: Rygom, Torlea, Dakon, Wexar, and Moryth.

These were things Iris already knew, but she enjoyed hearing it from a fresh perspective, especially coming from one who was so passionate about history. Iris's tutors used to always give dry, monotone speeches without any feeling. Agent Snow clearly enjoyed her work, even if she was a strict Instructor.

At the end of class, Iris and Claire parted ways. There was still a bit of time before her next class, but Iris wanted to get there early. She wished Claire luck with the rest of her morning and promised to find her for lunch.

Rounding the corner to the Sparring Ring, Iris could hear the other Enforcement Trainees talking excitedly. As soon as she entered the Ring, the conversation dropped to a series of whispers. Eyes fixed on her from every direction. At the center of the largest group stood Eve Sanders, sharing gossip with other First-Years from the Coordinating Branch.

Iris tried to ignore Eve, but her name was mentioned frequently in a volume above a whisper. She took a seat in the bleachers as far away from her peers as possible.

At precisely 10:15 a.m., two male Agents dressed in all black strode into the Sparring Ring. They were followed by another figure, covered from head to toe in a black combat suit. Layers of armor plates connected flawlessly together while still allowing for full muscle range of motion.

Iris had always wanted to try on a combat suit, wishing to know how it felt to be completely protected in a state-of-the-art armor. She had only ever worn low-grade plates that were available for regular citizens, but they were weak and had vulnerable areas exposed.

The man in the armor remained close to the entrance while the other two Agents walked to the middle of the Ring.

Iris recognized both of them.

The eldest of the two, a middle-aged man with a scar on face, was Agent Brant Thomas—the Agency's top Sparring Instructor.

The other was Agent Chase Mitchell, one of the Coordinators during her Placement Tests. Iris thought he was a kind, compassionate man. Agent Mitchell jokingly said it was because he was still new to the Agency and had not yet been *corrupted* by his profession.

Agent Thomas called the class to order, the scar running along his forehead, eye, and cheek twitching as he spoke. He needlessly introduced himself and his assistant. Some of the females giggled as Agent Mitchell waved a greeting to the class. Chase gave Iris a wink and turned his attention back to the Instructor.

"We're starting the term off with a little match," Agent Thomas continued. "Agent Mitchell is sending a number to everyone's OMNI. Once a number is selected, the chosen First-Year gets the opportunity to experience the latest design of the revolutionary combat suits."

A wave of awe spread through the class. They turned their attentions to the third Agent clad in the armor. Hushed whispers filled the room.

Iris's OMNI beeped and she opened the file that had been sent to her. The screen read *12*. She repeated the number over and over in her head, hoping to hear it said aloud. The Trainees around her had their fingers crossed, their eyes shut tight in anticipation.

After a moment of suspense, Agent Thomas read out, "Twelve," and waited to see who the lucky winner was.

Taking a deep breath to calm down, Iris stood and walked to the center of the Sparring Ring. She presented her OMNI to the Instructor to prove that she had received the correct number. Agent Mitchell then motioned for her to follow him out of the Ring.

Sitting in the locker room—heavily guarded by four Agents—was a suit of light grey combat armor.

Iris gingerly fingered the smooth surface. On the outside, the nanite material was firm and impenetrable. But when pushed from the inside, the metal plates shifted where touched. The interior sections of the armor always stayed a millimeter from an object or flesh. When the wearer moved, it stirred with the person while still maintaining the hard, exterior shell.

"Let me help you with that," Agent Mitchell offered.

She gave him a startled look and backed away from him.

"Oh, no, I mean—" He stumbled over his words. Taking a deep breath, he explained, "You can put the suit on *over* your uniform." The Coordinator held up the armor and motioned for her to step through the opening. "If you're not careful, the armor will be lopsided and uneven."

After removing her knives from her hips, Iris carefully placed one booted foot into the leg of material. The plates shifted, shrinking or expanding as they allowed for the mass. When she put her other foot in, Agent Mitchell slowly pulled the armor up to her torso. Next, Iris' hands slid through the sleeves; there was a soft and cold sensation over her hands as the armor hovered above her skin. Her head disappeared as the helmet covered her face and scalp. Despite the tinted screen in front of her eyes, Iris's peripheral vision was unhindered.

"Any chance you could help even further and tell me who my opponent is?" Iris asked, her voice barely muffled by the stream-line helmet.

"I could, but I won't," Agent Mitchell commented, shaking his head. "Besides, it wouldn't make any difference knowing who they are." He gestured for her to follow him. "Good luck, Miss Kayn."

When they returned to the Sparring Ring, scattered applause echoed through the room. Her opponent stood poised at the far end of the Ring, holding a broadsword.

"Welcome, First-Years, to today's match." Agent Thomas's voice came through speakers located in the walls and ceiling. "Miss Kayn will go up against our sword-bearing Sparring Champion with her twin long knives. Please watch carefully as the battle progresses; a three-page paper is due tomorrow about your observations."

Iris took a deep breath and faced her opponent. She stepped into defensive stance, holding up her blades.

The swordsman likewise prepared for the match, keeping his gaze on Iris as he raised his weapon. He gave her a slight bow and—without a moment of hesitation—moved in to attack. At first, his strikes were slow and weak, testing her reaction time and power. Iris only put forth enough effort to fend off his blows.

The first minute was very boring, but then Iris turned things up a notch. Although the mystery Champion had the advantage of greater reach, Iris had *two* weapons instead of one. She began swinging both her blades at his chest and head. With small, strong flicks of his wrist, he deflected them all and then lunged forward with his own set of attacks.

His blows met her knives in a series of clangs.

In the background, the audience grew more animated. People stood and cheered; the noise was so deafening that Iris couldn't tell who they were rooting for. She tried to drown out their chants, focusing on the sounds coming from her opponent.

A few grunts escaped the Sparring Champion's mouth as they skirmished, but Iris couldn't match a voice to the sounds. Images of the men she knew from the Agency flashed in Iris's head. She shifted through the images as she attempted to match it with the figure striking at her. It felt like an impossible task; she couldn't get an accurate visual of the Champion's frame due the armor. For all she knew, they could have been *a woman*

Iris smothered her curiosity and focused on what she was doing. She continued exchanging blows with the

Champion. Their resolve never weakened—even after they both began to show signs of fatigue.

The strikes became more frenzied and frantic as time went on. But the Champion still retained control of their sword. One of the swings hit Iris's knives with such force that it caused her to stumble backward. They took the opportunity to bring the blade across her armored ribs. There was a loud crack as the two metals clashed.

Although Iris barely felt the impact, she looked down to inspect the armor. To her relief, there was only a tiny scratch where the Champion had sliced her. She thrust her fist into his helmet to try and create some space between them.

On contact, the armor over her knuckles shattered—as did the front of the Champion's helmet.

Trickles of blood ran through the ragged armor—over the hands that had been instinctively raised to the site of pain. Iris tried to get a look at her opponent's face, but she was soon pulled backward by Agent Mitchell.

Agent Thomas came up to look at the awful wound. He put a towel over the man's face and escorted him out of the room.

In the absence of the Instructor, Agent Mitchell spoke the class. "Take your seats. Agent Thomas will be back shortly. Begin writing your three-page essay now." He then took Iris to the back room to help her out of her armor.

"Am I in trouble?" Iris asked, slightly out of breath.

"No," Agent Mitchell assured her as he carefully pried off the nanite armor. "You didn't know that only the armor can smash through another combat suits,"

Iris held out her hands and the material fell of her shoulders. "I was just trying to get some space."

Chase Mitchell seemed oddly amused by something. "Well, you've had quite an interesting first day: defeating the Agency's Sparring Champion, destroying a pair of billion dollar combat suits—"

"I ruined something worth a billion dollars?"

"No, not at all!" he laughed, running his hands through his shaggy brown hair. "It cost about one billion dollars to *create* the suit, but it costs next to nothing to *repair* it."

Iris was beginning to feel a little better about her first day of classes, but a question still itched at her. She wiped lumps of sweaty hair from her forehead and asked, "Agent Mitchell, do I get to know who that was now?"

"No, I'm sorry, darling. I'm afraid that's confidential information."

"Why does everything have to be so secretive?" Groaning, she returned her knives to their sheaves.

Agent Mitchell didn't respond. He pulled off the last section of the combat suit and then motioned for her to follow him back to the Sparring Ring.

Iris then took her seat in the most secluded part of the risers.

A moment later, Eve came casually walking up and took a seat on the bench beside er. "So, did you get a good look at that Sparring Champion?" she asked, acting as though she was Iris' closest friend.

"No," Iris responded, pulling out her OMNI. She began typing up her homework as she said, "They put their hands up before I could see who they were."

"That's too bad," Eve sighed, moving closer. "I guess you're pretty lucky to get chosen to fight. And then you won the match on a fluke. I bet you feel pretty happy." She stood and gave her a smirk. "Well, this has been fun. We should talk more often. See you later."

Iris checked her schedule to confirm that she had Equipment Basics next. If she remembered correctly, she didn't know anyone in that class. She was looking forward to not having to socialize for an hour. Not caring that she was covered in sweat, Iris made her way through the halls of classrooms, hoping that the rest of her day would be relatively uneventful.

Chapter 17

A series of jagged red lines covered Alastair's left cheek. The cuts had clotted and stopped bleeding, leaving an ugly mess of grated skin. The burning sensation disappeared, replaced by a chilling numb after he was given a pain-relieving injection.

When the swelling died down, a Medical Agent cleaned the wound. She touched his shoulder and pulled him to face another way. "This will help stimulate new skin growth," the elderly woman explained as she gently rubbed an oily salve into the cuts. "In a couple weeks, there won't be any trace of scars."

"*A couple weeks*? Do you have anything more instant?"

"No, Mr. Vega. I'm sorry." She began taping gauze to his cheek. "This is as quick as it works. The cuts are deep and will take time to heal without a scar." The woman finished with the bandage and handed him a tube of the clear medicine. "Apply this ointment to the damaged area twice a day—morning and night. If you apply it more often than that, the new skin will generate too quickly and you will end up with lumpy growths on your handsome face."

Agent Thomas dismissed the Medical Agent and began carefully removing what was left of the nanite armor. The pieces stretched and expanded beneath the pressure of his fingers. "I don't think that Miss Kayn meant to smash in your helmet. It was her first time in the combat suit."

Alastair picked up the helmet and examined the shattered area. "Whatever her intentions were, they have no bearing on the fact that her fist managed to get past my defenses. Her jab was quicker than my eye."

Agent Thomas checked a message on his OMNI. "It's time to go."

"I can't leave looking like this!" he shouted, indignant that the Sparring Instructor would suggest such a thing. "Everyone will know it was me in the battle armor." Alastair thought carefully. Pulling out him own OMNI, he speed-dialed his brother.

"Hey, bro," Max answered.

"I need your help." Alastair conveyed a list of items for Max to bring him, insisting that everything be kept a complete secret.

Several minutes later, Max joined Alastair and Agent Thomas in a private room of the Hospital Wing. He pulled the pack from his shoulders and handed over the contents. Alastair removed his old civilian clothes from the bag, which barely fit him: a red flannel T-shirt, ratty jeans, and a musty brown hat. He quickly changed and placed his uniform in Max's pack.

"Agent Thomas, please take a different route to Vega Manor," Alastair instructed, wrapping a scarf around his face. "Max, grab hold of my arm and pull me along as though I'm just a stupid Trainee caught out of uniform during class hours."

The two men did as Alastair said, respecting his need to protect his reputation. A few people glanced his way as he was half-dragged home. Occasionally, he would pretend to resist. This only made Max smile, clearly seeming to enjoy his brother's misfortune.

Once at Vega Manor, Alastair put on his dark-grey blazer and slacks and made his way to his father's library.

Mayor Jay Cromford and Director Marshal Brawn formed a circle around the room with Agents Thomas and Mitchell. The rest of the Agency Board Members were shown on screens above Tobias's desk. The Hardings stood on either side of the door, doing their duty as bodyguards.

As Alastair entered the room, Stella gave him a look that seemed to say *I'll tease you about this later.*

"Come in." Tobias Vega motioned to the pair of chairs. When Al and Max had taken their seats, he added,

"Alastair, it looks like you will need to be confined to your Living Quarters until your cuts heal. Maximus can spread the rumor that you are busy making plans for your upcoming *field trip* to Market." Tobias didn't wait for them to respond. "We can't have all the Agents and Trainees believing that you can be bested by an ambitious First-Year."

Confused, Alastair asked, "Then why did you arrange for me to spar with her today?" He could feel his self-control melt away as his temper rose within him. "What did you hope to gain by it? What is so special about Miss Kayn? You seem more interested in her abilities than all the other Trainees. What about Miss Birch, the engineering prodigy? Why didn't you ask me to keep a closer eye on her? She was my Mentee, too. She seems to be a greater asset to the Agency than Miss Kayn."

"Too many questions, young Vega," the Board Director cautioned him with a stern expression. "All you need to know is that we are doing what is in the best interest of the Agency and the Rygom Megacity."

"I'm just a pawn in your political games?" The idea of being manipulated made Alastair's blood boil. He longed to claw at the itchy gauze taped to his cheek, but resisted due to the fact that it would make him look childish; he needed to maintain some semblance of maturity. "This is ridiculous! I agreed to keep an eye on her, so I want to know what's in it for me. How is this going to further my career?"

"We will ensure you a position as Captain when you complete your Training, plus regular promotions should you continue to be useful. I foresee you becoming a General by your thirtieth birthday."

This calmed Alastair a bit. He took a deep breath and said, "In that case, I apologize for my failure today. I'll try harder in the future to not disappoint you."

"Son, nobody said that you *failed* today," Tobias replied with a chuckle. "You couldn't have done better. Even though you lost your match with Miss Kayn, we learned much about her fighting ability. We wanted to see how she fares against a living, intellectual being instead of those mindless Dueling Dummies." After a pause, he asked, "What is *your* assessment of her abilities?"

"She has strong instincts; I don't think she's aware how powerful they really are." Alastair tried to hide his resentment, but he felt some of the hostility seep into his words. "Her technique is well above average, although it's still limited. But twin knives are the best weapon for her because they work efficiently with her natural speed."

"And what about her *strength*?" Director Brawn asked.

"The only person that has ever hit me harder was Max," Alastair admitted, feeling the bitterness once again rise in him.

"Thank you, Alastair," the Board Director said. "Maximus, what do you think?"

"I agree with my brother," Max replied, solemnly.

"You've spent a lot of time with her socially. How does she behave outside of Training?"

"She is fairly charming, despite some social awkwardness. The key to getting her out of her shell is to first show interest in her career goals. It's something she feels comfortable talking about and so she opens up. After that, she isn't as nervous and is more willing to discuss other topics."

"Do you agree, Alastair?" Tobias asked.

Al shrugged, hesitant about the best way to answer. "I'm not sure. She has always seemed extremely timid around me."

"Then work on fixing that," Tobias ordered. "Maybe your intimidating demeanor towards her makes her unable to confide in you. I heard you've been upset about her breaking your Obstacle Course Records. It's essential to our plan for you two to get along. Get rid of your wounded ego and put on a friendly face."

"Sir." Alastair chose his next words carefully. "I mean no disrespect, but I don't think you have chosen the right person for this task. Max would be a better fit for getting close to Miss Kayn. They already have a steady friendship. I don't think I can *convincingly* be her friend."

"No, Alastair, it has to be *you*," Director Brawn insisted. "Focus on the plans for your field trip. Your father will provide you with the details you need to know." Brawn stood up, as did Agents Thomas and Mitchell. "If you'll excuse us, we have other matters to deal with. Good day."

They left the room, escorted by Stella and Drew Harding. The Board members on the screen disappeared a moment later. Mayor Cromford made no indication that he was ready to leave. Tobias turned to his sons and dismissed them with a wave of the hand.

The Vega boys gave slight bows as they exited. They walked down the long corridors to their wing of Vega Manor and turned into their private library.

Max plopped onto his desk chair and took out his OMNI. "I still can't believe father hasn't found the bug in his study." He thick fingers gingerly connected his personal device to a larger computer.

Alastair rolled his chair up to his brother's desk. Through the speakers, they heard the conversation between their father and the mayor.

Cromford: *Is everything in place? I'm concerned that her* feelings *toward you might motivate her to hinder the arrangement. What makes you sure she will cooperate?*

Vega: *Trust me; I have sufficient leverage against her.*

The word "leverage" enticed Alastair; it implied that his father was doing something sneaky, under-handed, and possibly illegal. Al reached forward, checked that the conversation was being recorded, and turned up the volume.

Cromford: *Come on, Tobias. Tell me. We're all in this together. I need to know what power you have over that woman.*

Vega: *She wants to see her son; she won't risk upsetting me with failure.*

Cromford: *So she* is *the mother of one of your boys? Which one, if I might ask?*

Max nudged Alastair. Al nodded and scooted closer to the speaker, hoping that their father would divulge something useful.

Vega: *You're asking an awful lot of questions today, Jay. Too much information can be* bad *for you.*

Cromford: *Alright, fine; I can be satisfied with that for now. Did she tell you how she's going to carry out* her side *of the bargain? Tobias, I'm in a very delicate place right now; we both are. If things go poorly, it could mean the end for* both *of our careers.*

Vega: *Yes, I've heard the rumors: a third Mayoral contestant! Someone free of this dreadful industry. Do you have any idea who it is?*

Cromford: *Perhaps a businessman who is new to politics. The public likes new blood.*

Vega: *We'll deal with it when it becomes more than just gossip. For now, we have other problems to deal with.*

Cromford: *One problem at a time? Sounds good to me. Keep me informed.*

The conversation ended, leaving the Vega boys troubled by what they had just learned.

"Whose mother do you think is plotting with father?" Max asked, disconnecting his OMNI from the computer.

Over the years, there had been much speculation between the boys as to who their mothers were. Tidbits of information were revealed through their carefully planted listening devices, but there was never enough information to confirm their theories.

*****

It was hard enough being seven, but not having a mother made the age especially difficult on Alastair. He watched the other children his age interact with the adults in their lives; they all had someone to go to when they were upset by something.

"Do you ever wish we had mothers?" Al asked his half-brother one day during their video game time.

"Sometimes," Max replied as his avatar slashed at zombified animals. "I think it'd be nice to have someone on our side when father tries to get us to do crazy things."

Nodding his head, Al said, "Yeah, like yesterday when he caught us watching old movies instead of studying." He paused the virtual battle and rubbed his knees as he remembered the five miles they had to run as punishment.

Determined to learn who his mother was, Alastair hatched a plan. From then on at their father's fancy dinner parties, Al and Max discretely took saliva samples from all the women in Society. Max *borrowed* an analysis machine from Vega Industries and they tested their DNA against the women's. Twelve months later, they still had no leads as to who their mothers were.

"Now what?" Al asked as the last of their theories died. He burned the last of the DNA swabs. "Should we start sampling Zonese women?"

Max shook his head. "Nah. Father would *never* consort with lowly women."

"Perhaps we missed something. We should run everything again." With a sigh, Al suggested, "What about Regioners? Some of the Clan Leaders have a lot of power. And many Regioners use to live in Society."

"I don't like the idea that we have Region blood," Max replied, his face scrunched up in disgust. "I'd rather believe that we missed something. It could be that our mothers are dead."

Alastair shivered. "I'd rather not go corpse-hunting."

The door to their library slid open and the Vega boys quickly turned back to their computers, pretending to write their seven-page reports on aerial battle strategy.

"Why aren't you finished?" their father asked, looking at their screens with distaste. "You've had ten hours."

Max cleared his throat, the tell-tale sign that he was about to lie.

Not wanting to earn a punishment for distorting the truth, Alastair said, "We were thinking about what it would be like to have mothers."

Tobias's eyes narrowed. "And what's wrong with *just a father*?"

"We didn't mean any disrespect," Max said, suddenly.

Alastair motioned for him to be quiet. "We just noticed that most families have more than one parent."

"What about Gina and Ross?" Agent Vega asked. "They spend just as much time with you as I do."

"The Hardings are *wonderful* guardians," Alastair lied with a grin. In fact, Gina and Ross should never have been allowed to breed, especially since they spawned the horrid Stella. "However, we're curious who our mothers were. I mean, we know how babies are born—"

"Yes!" Max interrupted. "Gina told us all the *disgusting* details about it." He let out a loud sigh. "I couldn't look a girl for weeks afterwards."

Tobias frowned. "*Gina* told you? I specifically told Ross to explain it."

Alastair scratched his arm, diverting his eyes to the floor. "Well, um, Ross was going to. Then Gina seemed really rather excited about telling us, so he just let her."

"It was *very* unpleasant," Max added as he shook his head and groaned.

"Yes, you've already stated your view, Maximus." Tobias paused and took a deep breath. "Alastair, you're right. There needs to be a man and a woman to make a baby."

"Gina said that some kids have *two* dads or *two* moms," Max commented, wringing his hands as he thought. He shook his head as though processing the information was too much to handle. "But Ross stopped her from explaining how that happens."

"Yes. That can occur, too."

Confused, Al rubbed at his brain as he tried to understand. "So does that mean that we actually have more *fathers*?"

With a laugh, Tobias said, "I made each of you with two different women. However, I felt like I was enough of a parent to be adequate for you. So I've kept your mothers out of our lives so that they don't taint you; they're in no position to raise you *properly*."

"So do they *want* to see us?" Max asked, agitated. "And what do you mean by *taint*?"

As he always did, Tobias dodged the question. "I think that's sufficient bonding time for today, boys. Now I want your reports in half an hour."

*****

Alastair broke out of the memory emotionally exhausted. In response to his brother's questions, he said, "At this point, I don't care who our mothers are. I'm more concerned about whatever Father is plotting. The plan he has with Mayor Cromford seems suspicious; Father doesn't give important tasks like that to just anyone. This woman—whoever she is—must be either really influential or well connected."

"She might be both," Max offered. "Father likes that combination, especially when dealing with women who produced his offspring. From what I've heard on the listening bug, both our mothers were cunning and powerful."

"You're probably right." Alastair absent-mindedly scratched at his bandage. "I wonder if those same qualities are what made our mothers disappear. What if our mothers felt that they reached a place of power higher than Father when they conceived us? They would be able to turn their sons against Tobias. What if he foresaw that and got rid of the women so he would have sole parental rights?"

"If that's the case, I hope he gets Stella pregnant," Max spat. "Then we'll be rid of her."

Alastair shook his head. "As much as I like the idea of Stella going away, I don't want to see another sibling within Father's clutches."

"Good point," Max admitted. "And speaking of Stella, when should we use that information to our advantage?"

"We should confront him *soon*. But not yet. When we do, he'll know we have listening devices in his study. He'll find and remove them; then we won't be able to eavesdrop on his private conversations. We should wait until we really need something from him before we attempt blackmail."

"That's why you are the *smart* brother; you think things through."

"Yeah. I'm the brains. You're the muscle," Al laughed. "We're the unstoppable Vega brothers!"

"Well, for the next few days, I'll be the *lone* brother. It isn't going to be the same without you at Training," Max sulked, his chair creaking as he leaned back in it.

"Keep me posted on everything that happens. No detail is too small." Alastair instructed. He stopped himself from scratching at the bandage on his cheek. Instead, he put all his focus into his next plan. "And you'll have to convince everyone why I am too busy to leave Vega Manor. Make this Field Trip sound enticing, without giving out too many details. And any rumors about today's true dealings must be hushed up. Can I count on you, Max?"

"Of course, Al. What are brothers for? By the end of the week, it'll be every Trainee's greatest wish to come with us to Market."

Chapter 18

Klev and Lom were *professionals*. Their resumes included the most extraordinary skills people could possess. Wanted throughout the world, their quick-thinking always managed to get the job done.

Of course, there were many non-believers. People called them "delusional kooks" or "over-confident frauds." Klev thought those people were jealous lunatics, while Lom simply pitied them for their lack of vision. These two men had very little training in the way of careers or vocations, but they were adaptable.

No one understood the reason for the duo's success. Many guessed they were Alterations. But Klev and Lom refused to limit themselves by only one title. If anyone asked what they did, they would simply reply, "We are *Professionals of Everything*."

Despite their years of success, they were running out of job opportunities. A few recent mishaps resulted in a diminished reputation. Their stint in prison had just ended and they were determined to turn their life back around. Klev and Lom were in search for the perfect career to help them get back on their feet.

After they had snuck back to the Middle Zone, a kind pawn shop owner had recommended that they search the job-boards in the Market Sectors. They had already checked half a dozen, but none had any decent occupations that were worthy of their extensive resumes.

Klev and Lom hefted their packs onto their backs. They had traded a couple small items for them when they became tired of hefting boxes around for miles.

As they approached the next job board, a group of men came up to them.

The figures were clad in all black, making Klev and Lom fear that the Agency was after them again.

The duo backed away, trying to remember all the times they had fought in the military. The memories that flooded through their brains were scattered, but it was enough to give them the confidence to step into defensive positions.

"Whoa! There's no need for that," commented one of the strangers, raising his empty hands. "Do you mind if we have a little chat." He motioned towards an empty building.

Klev and Lom exchanged anxious looks. They reluctantly let the men lead them inside.

Once completely surrounded, the former-mercenaries made observations about the four well-armed men. They each had a different hair color: brown, blonde, black, or red. Dressed in matching black leather uniforms, they even wore the same white patch with the word *LERJ* embroidered into their right lapels. Klev and Lom racked their brains, but they were at a loss as to what Branch of the Agency *LERJ* was.

"What do you want?" Lom inquired, his fingers discreetly feeling for the knife at his side.

"We couldn't believe it when we heard that the great Klev and Lom had finally been released," said the black-haired men.

"Have you been following us?" Klev asked.

"Not at all," a man with red hair assured them. "We've been *monitoring* you."

"We wanted to keep an eye on Rygom's most dangerous duo," replied the blonde.

The first man to speak—who had brown hair—gave his associates a cautious glare. "We were simply curious about you two. There have been rumors about what caused your downfall. Some say it was just a misunderstanding between you and the Agency Enforcers. Others say you turned rogue and decided to conduct your own covert missions without the proper authorization."

"And you're here to confirm or disprove the hearsay?" Lom asked.

"Only if you're willing to cooperate," the wild-eyed ginger said in a threatening manner. For emphasis, he menacingly rubbed his hands together.

Klev and Lom contemplated the implications of telling what happened. They had no idea who the mystery men were; telling the wrong people might ruin their attempts to rehabilitate.

*****

Klev and Lom strolled casually through the piles of fresh corpses. As they passed wooden buildings that remained fire-free, they lobbed lit explosives through the broken windows and continued on their way.

In the distance, a Megacity sat snuggled within the forested mountains. Almost a perfect cube, Wexar cast a long shadow amongst the nearby shoreline. The survivors ran screaming towards the covered, well-armed metropolis—away from the pair of mercenaries that had torched their farming town to the ground.

The smoke parted above Klev and Lom as a helicopter descended. They entered the chopper and handed over their weapons. A small file-box remained in Klev's care, despite the protestations of the Squad Captain.

"This is for Agent Thomas, and for him *only*," Klev explained, giving the woman a menacing glare. "I'll hand it to no one but him."

On the flight back to Rygom, Lom wrote detailed descriptions of their exploits in one of his notebooks. He enjoyed reading his journals to help him relive their adventures and learn how to better himself to make future missions more successful.

Klev sat in stoic silence, with the exception of occasionally reminding his colleague to include certain details that he thought Lom might have overlooked.

Back at the Agency, they were greeted by Agent Thomas. Wearing his usual scar-marked frown, he took the box from Klev. "I'm sorely disappointed in you men. Agent Vega expressly told you to be more careful about who you kill on your missions. He is worried about your recklessness. Since you haven't heeded our warnings, we have no choice but to suspend you for a month."

"A *month*!" Klev took a step toward his manager. Blades scratched against their sheaths as a dozen Enforcement Agents wielded their weapons. Taking a breath, Klev calmly said, “Alright. If the wise Agent Vega feels that is necessary, Lom and I will bow to his wishes.”

Agent Thomas gave him one of his rare smiles. “Good. It will give you two plenty of time to recuperate after your surgery.”

Lom cocked his head in confusion. “What kind of surgery? Are we going to get some new implants? If so, I’d love the one that gives an instant adrenaline boost. Is that one finally available?”

“No, not an implant surgery.” Agent Thomas nodded at the squad and half a dozen men came forward with restraints. Once the mercenaries were secured, he continued. “We have decided to do a little memory modification on you. Don’t worry; you’ll still retain all your skills. We are simply going to adjust your personalities in order to tame your violent tendencies.”

“I don’t see how cutting up our brains will make us better at our jobs,” Klev growled, pulling at the restraints. “What if the surgeon slips and we become brain-dead? Then you’d lose your two greatest assets.”

Agent Thomas’s face became emotionless. “It’s better than the alternative. We can’t risk you losing control and destroying half the world.” He waved his hand in front of him and the squad escorted Klev and Lom away.

"It's been nice knowing you, old friend," Lom sighed, unable to expel the feeling that things would never be the same again.

*****

Deciding to mix the truth with lies, Klev said, "Our memories about that incident are gone; we think they wiped our minds to keep us from figuring out what really happened."

The blonde rubbed his stubbly chin. "I bet that's made you quite angry with the Agency."

"Is there a burning fire of injustice raging through your entire being?" asked the short, dark-haired one.

Lom raised his hands and tried to diffuse the situation. "We just want to move on."

Klev's approach was a little more aggressive. "Nothing you say will make us go back to the Agency!"

Something amused the four men and they chuckled lightly.

"Thanks for clearing that up," commented the brunette man. He turned to leave without saying another word and signaled for the others to follow. Each of the three remaining men gave Klev and Lom one last threatening look before walking away.

"What was that all about?" Lom asked, releasing the hold on his knife.

Klev was at a loss for words. Why would the Agency send people after them like that? They had completed their required years in prison and didn't owe the government anything anymore. With a shrug, he went about returning to their original task.

Once they reached the next Market Plaza, Klev stopped in front of a job-board and turned to his partner. "I'll keep watch as you look through the ads. I don't want anyone coming in and stealing our last chance." He faced the bustling Plaza and put his most intimidating expression on his face to scare people away. "What's it say, Lom?"

Lom started at the top of the list and began scanning the want-ads. "Lady Unmare Darrow is looking for an Administrative Coordinator."

"No!" Klev scoffed. "Administrative duties are beneath our skill set. What else?"

"Lord Nuto Berge wants a Medical Surgeon. Oh, it'd be just like our time in Torlea."

"Am I the only one that remembers what really happened to us in Torlea?" Klev asked, shaking his head at the distant memory.

Lom began flipping through one of their notebooks. "What did we do?"

"Check it later. First, we gotta find a new career."

"Do you wanna be in the legal profession again?"

"Nah. My law knowledge is pretty rusty," Klev admitted. "Plus, the rules down here is different than in Upper Society."

Shaking his head, Lom added, "Yeah, and I think it has too much drama: you say that someone is guilty and they say that they aren't, then you change your verdict and someone else insists that the person really is guilty."

"Is there anything in the Performing Arts, Lom? I really miss that."

"No, sorry. But the Agency is—"

"What did I say about working for the *Agency*?" Klev shouted, spinning to face his colleague. "We can't do government work anymore!"

Lom returned his attention to the board. "Oh, this looks promising." He read the information clearly, trying to remember every detail. "The Crimson Clan is looking for *hired muscle*. Do you wanna check it out?"

"Hired muscle, huh?" Klev spun around and stared at the advertisement. "Write down the info and we'll contact these *Crimsons*."

Pulling out a wrinkled notepad, Lom carefully wrote down every word from the advertisement. When he was done, he turned to Klev. "It doesn't say where the Crimsons are located."

Klev thought for a moment before saying, "We'll have to ask around and see if anyone can tell us."

The duo began making inquiries into the location of the Crimsons. They weren't entirely sure who those people were, so they were a bit confused when no one would answer their questions.

"Maybe we need to give them a little more *persuasion*," Klev thought out loud as he pulled out a knife. "Come on. Let's corner one of them."

Lom followed, removing his blade from his belt.

They wandered down a small side-street, searching for a loner. It was several minutes before they spotted one: a young man in his late teens. Klev and Lom approached him and showed their knives.

"Hello," greeted Lom. "We have a few questions for you and we'd appreciate it if you'd give us some answers."

The frightened boy nodded and held up his hands. A glowing blue tattoo wrapped around his left wrist. The dots and dashes appeared to be a similar style to the Morse code that all the Regioners had; males seemed to have it on their left wrists, while women had it on their right. Looking carefully at the series, Lom concluded that the tattoo said, "Zett."

"How can I help you?" The young man's gaze shifted nervously between them.

Klev pushed the man with the "Zett" tattoo against the wall and placed the edge of his blade at the man's neck. "We're looking for the Crimsons. Tell us who they are."

"They're a Clan in the Lower Region—the Crimson Steels."

"How do we get there?" Lom held out his notepad, ready to write down the information.

"Go Down three Sectors, head North for four, and then West for two," the youth quickly explained in a quick but shuttering voice.

Klev removed the blade from the man's throat, but kept the knife in front of him. "You seem to know a lot about these people. Why wouldn't anyone tell us anything without a little persuasion?"

The young man took a step back. "Nobody likes the Crimsons; they're vicious and cruel. I think you'll fit in nicely."

"If we wanted to speak to their boss, who should we ask for?" Lom asked kindly.

"Queen Romisa Steel is the Leader. But her steward, Pavoc, runs most of the day-to-day business."

"What do you think, Lom?" Klev asked, looking the boy up and down. He ran a finger along the side of his knife to ensure that the blade was indeed still sharp. "Should we kill him now that we have information?"

Lom shook his head. "No, Klev. He has been most helpful; we probably should let him go now. Killing him would be unnecessary. And it might put the Agency on our trail."

"We *shouldn't* kill him, Lom. What a stupid idea! We don't want the Agency to start looking for us again. Think before you speak, partner." Klev turned to Zett. "Get outta here before I change my mind."

"Sorry, Klev," Lom apologized. "I just got all caught up in the moment. Let's go find those Crimsons." He stashed the notebook in his jacket and picked up his pack.

Two hours later, they were stumbling deep through the debris-ridden passages of the Lower Region. Due to Lom's carefully scribbled notes, they only managed to get lost a handful of times.

Eventually, they spotted some red splashed across the grey scene. Scarlett banners hung from holey walls. A giant cardinal rug ran down the center of the hall. Maroon lamps lit the way. A sentry stood outside the entrance. Their uniform was armor tinted a hue of red over black leather clothing.

The guards stopped them and asked to see their Signatures.

Klev took the notebook from Lom and wrote his name on the paper. He tucked his pen behind his ear before showing page to the guards.

The armored men burst into laughter. "Show me your left hands," commanded the captain. Klev and Lom obeyed. When the captain looked over their wrists, he said, "You don't belong to a Clan. What's your business here?"

"We've come to see Pavoc about a job advertisement we saw in Market," Lom replied with a smile.

"Do you have an appointment?"

Looking over the notebook, Klev said, "There wasn't anything in the advertisement about making an appointment. It just said that the Crimsons were looking for *hired muscle*."

"You're here about becoming a Snatcher?" the captain asked, skeptically.

"Um, sure, if that's what the ad was about."

The captain motioned to a pair of guards. "Show these clowns to Pavoc. Whether or not he likes them, I still get two points on my recruitment file."

Klev and Lom were led a short distance to a large office.

One of their escorts said, "The Captain discovered these two Underlings outside the HQ. They said they are here about a job advertisement."

"What's an Underling?" Lom whispered to Klev, who shrugged his shoulders in equal confusion. They both knew they had heard the term before, but could place where they had come across it.

A tall chair swiveled around and a man appeared. Pavoc stood and came closer. He inspected the men and sent the guards away. "What makes you think you are *capable* of the Snatcher position?"

"We have a résumé," Lom said, searching through his pack. After a few seconds, he removed a crumpled folder and handed over a packet of papers.

Master Pavoc scanned the faded, wrinkled pages. "There's only *one* for the *both* of you?"

Klev stepped forward. "Although we are *two* people, we have almost identical skill sets. But when one of us lacks in one thing, the other makes up for it. Everything listed in there is our combined talents."

Master Pavoc put up a hand and pointed back towards Lom.

Getting the hint, Klev stepped to where his partner stood and waited patiently.

After several minutes, Pavoc said, "You've had quite a few different careers these past fifteen years. I'll contact your references to make sure your résumé is accurate. Please go back the way you came and tell the guards that you need to receive your Signatures." He turned back to his desk as he said, "I'll be in touch."

They bowed again and exited the room.

"I think that went pretty good, Klev. Don't you think?"

"Yes, Lom. I believe we've found our new home. Let's just hope it works out better than our previous one."

Chapter 19

Iris was excited to finally do some studying. There had been almost no time during the summer to pour over books. Her time had been consumed with preparing her body for the physical trials of Placement Testing. As much as she loved pushing the limits of her strength, her mind missed reading.

In the Agency library, she visited a database computer in the lobby and searched for the location of the book downloads required for her classes. Many of the First-Years complained when the Instructors kept adding more texts for them to get for classes. It didn't really bother Iris; she loved the idea of soaking up more knowledge.

Once she found all her texts in the database, she synched her OMNI with the library's computer and saved the directions to her screen.

She entered the main aisle and stopped. Iris was amazed by the sheer size of the library. Shelves ran on forever in every direction. Awakening her OMNI, she began searching for the first text file. It was easier to find than she thought; the directions were so explicit that it was impossible not to find it.

Removing a blank text-disc from her pocket, she inserted it into her OMNI and connected her OMNI to the port below the text file. She pressed the "download" icon and the file was instantly copied. After taking out the disc, she went to find the next file. She repeated the process five more times, finding and then downloading the texts to date-discs to be read at a later time.

The remaining book file proved to be more difficult to locate than the others. Its position seemed to be in the middle of a labyrinth of shelves. She turned left, left, right, left, right, right in circles until she became so lost that she forgot which turn she was on.

She was about to call for help when she heard the sound of footsteps. Quickly, she moved towards the other people in the maze. Soon, the steps stopped and were replaced by a thud. Up ahead, she saw a shelf tremble as another thud sounded. She made her way towards it and looked on the other side.

A man pressed a woman against a wall of information, their arms wrapped tightly around each other. They shared a passionate kiss. Iris knew that she shouldn't be standing there. But her brain stopped working for a second, her body frozen in the middle of the row of shelves.

Before she could walk away, the woman whispered, "We've been spotted."

The man turned, dropping his lover. "Iris?"

"Oh, hi, Max! I was just looking for a text," she replied, averting her gaze. "I'll just let you get back to your love-making."

"Do something," Viola ordered in a whisper, smoothing her long red hair.

Max walked up to Iris. Hesitantly, he said, "Um, I know you're not exactly a wicked gossip, but I need you to keep this a secret; Vi and I are sort of forbidden from being romantically involved."

"Why does it need to be a secret?" Iris asked, feeling very confused.

Mr. Vega moved back to Miss Cromford. "Honey, perhaps you should go. I'll take care of this."

Viola nodded, gave him a quick kiss, and then left.

Turning to Iris, Max said, "Since our fathers are opponents in the Mayoral Election, we can't have a romantic relationship."

"But you're good friends in *public*. Doesn't that bother your fathers?"

"They aren't happy about it, but they think they can use our friendship to their advantages. After all, Jay and

Tobias have been pals most of their lives. However, *dating* is completely out of the question."

Iris knew it was none of her business, so she decided not to ask any more questions. "I can keep a secret."

"Good," Max sighed with his goofy smile. "I know that our *Romeo and Juliet* relationship isn't the best idea, but I can't help myself. I love her. Maybe we can come out of this better than the star-crossed lovers; we know not to *kill* ourselves if the other dies. We can avoid that mess, at least."

Unable to help herself, Iris began giggling. "You're comparing yourselves to Shakespeare's most famous lovers?"

He joined in her laughter. "See? I knew you had a lighter side."

"What's that suppose to mean?"

"Well, you're always so uptight and serious all the time. Every once in awhile, you need to joke around. It'll keep you sane."

Iris returned to her task of finding her last text file. She tapped uselessly at icons on her OMNI screen, trying to discover some sort of blueprints in the library's webpage. Stopping at a dead-end, she went back to her original route.

Max looked confused as trailed behind her. At yet, he managed to portray his natural amusement through his baffle expression. "Iris, I think you're one of the few people that actually go to the library for *books*. Most people save themselves the trouble by just purchasing what they need instead of braving the knowledge labyrinth."

"Is that why you bring Viola here?" Iris teased. "Making out in the library is such a cliché, Max."

"It's the one of the few places where we can meet in secret," Max admitted with a shrug. "Like I said, nobody comes here. Al and I practically grew up here, so I know where just about everything is."

"Really? Then can you help me find this book on Julius Caesar's military strategy?" Iris held up her OMNI to show him the book annotation.

Max quickly scanned the screen. "Easy. It's back this way." He expertly led her down a series of aisles. Of course, it probably also helped that he only needed to stand on his toes to see over the massive shelves. "It's a good read. I had to memorize it when I was ten. Alastair and I received a rather extensive education growing up. We've been bred to be the top Enforcers in the Agency. Our father's reputation depends on it."

"But is it what *you* want?"

His good-humor suddenly disappeared as he admitted, "I have no idea what I want—other than wanting Vi. But I know what I *don't* want: my father to be disappointed."

Iris was silent a moment. She wasn't sure if she should share what was about to come out of her mouth; she said it anyways. "My father wanted me to be scientist like him. Except I knew that it would *kill* me to be in a lab all day. So I chose another career."

"It's never been an option for Al and me." Max's face brightened up as quickly as it had darkened. "But it's refreshing to see that you have enough courage to choose your own path." He reached up and pointed at a text file on the top of the shelf. "You want that one."

Nodding, she pulled over a ladder and went to work downloading the book into her OMNI. When she came back down, Max began leading her out of the maze. Iris was amazed by how easily he maneuvered down the passages. They walked in silence for several moments. Iris was about to bring up another topic when they reached the library lobby.

"Thank you for everything. And sorry, again, about earlier." Iris began to walk away, but she stopped and turned back to him. "If I might offer a little advice: I think you should come out with your secret. Romeo and Juliet died because they hid their love from the world. Maybe your fathers will understand." With a wink, she walked off towards her Living Quarters, feeling rather nerdy as she eagerly looked forward to a late-night of studying.

Once she reached her Living Quarters, Iris instantly regretted not staying in the library to read. Claire sat on the couch, sucking the face off some Second-Year Trainee.

With a sigh, Iris entered their common room. She wished that she had walked in on Claire working on yet another crazy Project instead of once again watching a pair of horny Trainees in the middle of amorous activities.

"Oh, Iris!" Claire said, pulling away from the man. "Sorry. We probably should—"

"That's ok," Iris replied without looking directly at the couple. "I'm going downstairs. Feel free to continue."

Her friend spoke to her before she could descend the stairs. "No, the mood's over. Besides, I should get back to studying. And Project 7 is being temperamental." She turned to the man seated next to her. "Thanks for a great afternoon. See ya." Claire waved at him and moved towards Iris. She gave her the *please get rid of him* face as she passed her on the stairs.

Iris gave the poor man a sympathetic smile. "Sorry to throw you out like this."

The Second-Year frowned and stood slowly. "Is there any chance she'd want to see me again?" he asked, creepily rubbing his lips with a finger.

Shaking her head, Iris moved to the door and motioned for him to leave. With him gone, she made her way down the steps. She was about her room when she decided that she wanted to confront Claire about her promiscuous behavior.

She knocked on her friend's door and it opened a moment later. After two months of living there, Claire's room looked a million times worse than the day they moved in. Iris felt that perhaps Residential Mentors might be upset if they saw Miss Birch's room. She almost said something about it, but realized that bringing up too many issues at once might weaken her arguments. The messiness could wait.

"How'd it go upstairs?" Claire asked, not taking her attention from her work.

"Like most of the *other* men you've brought home," Iris replied, clearing a space to sit on Claire's bed. "He was thoroughly distressed that you didn't really like him."

"I *liked* him alright. But since classes started two weeks ago, I have a lot more choices with the Second-Years all moved in; I don't want to settle with *one* before I've tried *a few others*. Anyways, there are plenty guys willing to come back for more." Claire paused before adding, "If you want, I'll point out the best kissers the next time we're at The Grey Circumstance."

"Thank you, but no. I'd rather not introduce any more boy drama into my life."

Turning her back to her newest Project, Claire sighed, "Maybe if you lived a little more *flamboyantly*, I wouldn't have to let you live vicariously through my romantic exploits."

Giving up, Iris left the room. She disliked how Claire always made her hate her life. All the boy talk made her seriously think about going out and kissing the first guy she saw. She hadn't had any social-inspiration from her friend in weeks, so she made up her mind to follow the impulse.

Iris ascended the stair with a skip. She banished the melancholy from her attitude and left her Living Quarters.

The halls were empty save for a couple female Trainees. She briefly considered participating in the time-honored tradition of experimenting with same-sex, but she wasn't feeling *that* adventurous.

At the Plaza, her eyes skimmed the crowds. There were a few scattered males, but most of them were either middle-aged or already paired with someone. Iris wasn't particularly in the mood to begin a romantic escapade with an older man nor start a fight by kissing someone's boyfriend. Giving up, she abruptly turned to go back to her apartment.

But as she spun, she ran into someone. "Oh, I'm sorry—" her apology stopped short as she saw who she bumped into. "Mentor Vega."

Alastair had a hint of a smile on his lips. "Good afternoon. How are you?"

"I'm good—jut walking around *aimlessly*," she replied with nervous grin. Of course the first available man she came across was Alastair Vega! She had gotten herself all riled up to try something different and he had to go and ruin it.

He cleared his throat. "So I haven't seen you since the Placement Assembly."

Iris nodded. “Yes, when you said you were going to do your best to tolerate me, even though you actually hate me.” She put on the biggest smile she could manage.

“Look, I’m sorry about all that,” he groaned, his charming demeanor faltering. Alastair looked like he was going to say something, but he quickly clamped his mouth shut. After several awkward moments of silence, he continued. “I’ve been busy planning a field trip to Market. I hope you and Claire will be able to come with me and Max. Viola is coming, as well, with her Mentees. I’ll send you the details when they’re firmed up.”

“Great,” she replied, flatly. “Well, I’m done wandering, so I’m gonna head back to my place.” She quickly retreated back to the safety of her Living Quarters.

Chapter 20

Ignoring the piles of work on her desk, Rikani spent her afternoon trying to apply her make-up appropriately. Since she rarely had occasions to freshen her appearance, she was a fairly out of practice; she had to keep wiping everything off to try again.

"Got plans tonight?" Vian asked as she poked her head in.

Rikani looked away from her mirror—mascara only on one eye. "Why do you ask?"

"Just the pretty dress, clown paint on your face, and freshly-lacquered toes peeping out of your new sandals. Is it the secret-note-guy?"

Turning back to her mirror, Rikani resumed applying eye liner. "His name is Brak. "

Vian intervened, taking the cosmetics away. She expertly removed the oily smudges as she said, "Hmm. Why does that name sound familiar?" Searching through a bag of make-up, she selected a lipstick. "Maybe I met him when I was still a Crimson."

After her hair was pinned up, Rikani checked her image. "I *do* look stunning, don't I?" she asked, looking at the mirror with scrutiny. "Remember: no telling Tays."

"No telling me *what*?" Tays strolled in, covered in his usual grease stains.

Vian moved menacingly towards him, her hand discretely reaching for a pair of scissors on Rikani's desk. "That is absolutely none of your business."

Tays held up his hands in surrender. However, he seemed to take Vian's ferocity more calmly than last time. "Kani, call off your guard dog. You can keep your secret if it means I won't have my eyes gouged out."

Rikani motioned for her administrator to leave. "What do you want, Tays?"

"I need help in my garage tonight. The Agency just put in a large order, so I need more hands." He rubbed his oily fingers together and then smeared them on the front of his shirt.

Rikani shook her head. "Okay, then hire Zett to assist you. Problem solved. And I have to go now." Her twin brother tried to hug her, but she held her hands out to stop him. "You're dirty; don't touch me."

On the way to the HQ entrance, Rikani waved off everyone that approached her. She normally didn't ignore her Clan members like that, but she figured that she had sacrificed enough the past five years. Even though there was a time when everything rested on her, she now had plenty of reliable employees that could handle any disaster that happened that evening.

*****

Sixteen-year-old Rikani refused to cry in front of the Clan members. She strode confidently through the crowds of agitated Azures, who were simply trying to have their problems solved.

"Excuse me," she said as pushed past the people waiting outside Rye Estate. "I'll go talk to him," she assured the worried masses.

Slipping inside, Rikani turned the bolt and headed down the hall of residential rooms.

Knocking at the last door, she waited for a response. When she heard none, she entered anyway. "Lord Asdem?"

"Jomiq? Is that you?" her uncle called from the dim room. "Jo?"

"No, it's *Kani.*" She moved towards his hunched frame on a small sofa. Rikani almost reminded him that Aunt Jomiq was dead, but she didn't want to risk getting him even more upset. "When are you coming out? Everyone is worried."

He didn't say anything. His eyes lay on her—a blank stare.

"Please, Uncle Asdem. Please! We need you. Ulrian's doing everything he can, but he doesn't have the authority that you do."

"They're gone, aren't they?" he mumbled, laying his head on the arm of the sofa.

The door opened and Aril entered. "Is he coming back?"

"I don't think so," Rikani replied, pulling her cousin-in-law across the room. "Without him, that only leaves me and Tays to take care of everything." Rikani broke out into tears. "We don't know what we're doing, Aril."

"You'll figure everything out, Kani," the red-headed triplet assured her. "I'll help you, and so will Ebyx and Otum. We won't let the Azure Clan crumble."

Rikani dried her eyes. "How are *you* holding up?"

"It's weird waking up in the morning without Tyvax. Sometimes I tell myself that he's just gone on business. But know that's a lie." Aril gave her a hug and held her tight.

After taking one last look at her grieving uncle, Rikani left. Without a word, she moved passed the Azures outside Rye Estate. Feeling utterly alone, she made her way down the stairs and corridors that led to the HQ entrance. She stepped outside and slammed the door behind her.

Not entirely sure where she was going, she trudged down a trail surrounded by piles of junk metal and plastic. Tears streamed over her cheeks unchecked. Her parents were dead; she'd never realized how awful it was to be an orphan. Many times in her childhood she had wished she had no parents, but now she regretted that feeling.

Consumed by her grief, she didn't realize where she was. To her left was a group of Snatchers from the Crimson Clan. They didn't seem to see her, so she had time to hide inside a hollowed-out building. When the cluster got closer, Rikani could hear what they said.

"Pavoc isn't going to be happy," the oldest-looking one said to his companions. "We should've collected more Underlings this month."

"Do you think he'll fire us, Janez?" the younger man asked as he stopped in his tracks.

"Either that or kick us out of the Clan," replied the woman. "What'll we do if that happens?"

"We could start a Gang," suggested man 1, shaking his grey head. "What do you think, Hurez?"

The second man shook his head. "Maybe, Bilez. That might bring us a bit of respect."

"We aren't ruthless enough to be Snatcher's," the woman sobbed. "How are we going run a Gang?"

Rikani felt sorry for the trio, even though their occupation was to force people into slavery. Still, she had an idea of how to fix their problem. She slowly moved out of her hiding place, making a little noise so they would notice her.

"Um, hi. My name's Rikani Rye." She waved her hand at them. "I heard your whole conversation and I've been moved by your situation. If you're kicked out of the Crimson Clan, I'd like you to come join the Azures." She shook a step closer. "If you ever find yourself in need of a home, please don't hesitate to contact me."

*****

At the entrance, Bilez, Hurez, and Janez stood around the door, speaking quietly amongst themselves.

"He *must* be mistaken," Hurez insisted.

"I almost wished he *was* telling the truth," added Janez in her motherly tone. "She deserves a break."

Bilez waved his hands in disgust at the giant door. "Lady Rikani is better off without him. She doesn't need any young rascals lying to her about being in love. I thought she learned that lesson from Lord Tays's mistake."

"What did you do?" Rikani growled as she reached her security guards.

"We sent away that rogue before he could break your heart," Janez replied sweetly, as if she had just done her a favor.

Hurez stepped forward. "He won't be coming around again, milady."

"I gave him a stern talking-to," Bilez added.

Without another word, Rikani flung herself through the doors, determined to catch Brak before he got too far. But a pair of arms grabbed her and pulled her to the side. She looked up to see her boyfriend's grinning face.

"Brak! I was worried that my guards had scared you off."

"It'll take more than three grumpy soldiers to keep me from you." He leaned in and kissed her while gently stroking her cheeks.

On the surface, Brak looked his usual self. As they walked journeyed up to Market, he spoke lively, smiled at everything she said, and caressed her hand affectionately. But there was something off about him.

Briefly, Rikani considered what Bilez had said. Was it possible that he was only using her? Was he making her fall in love so that he could someday take all her money?

She saw it all the time. The Clan Leaders had to be cautious about who they let get close. The Lower Region was full of fortune hunters—people raised in the wealthy Upper Society that had experienced infamous humiliation and were seeking to reclaim a position of power and prosperity.

Rikani decided to let the feeling slide for the moment. It was her first official date with Brak and she didn't want to ruin it by being too guarded.

Upon reaching the level below Market, Rikani and Brak presented their fingers for a blood test and their wrists for a Signature scan. When the Agent Sentries determined that neither of them was infected with the Plague nor dangerous criminals, they let them pass to the Elevators.

The ride down was relatively uneventful—except for a bit of hand-holding and kissing. The pod doors opened as they reached the Market Transit Station.

Leaving the Elevators, Brak led her down a series of corridors and halls, past establishments of all sizes and sorts. They reached a vein of moving sidewalks. After passing through a handful of Plazas, they eventually stepped off. A short walk further, they entered a quaint bookstore.

Upon further examination, Rikani gasped. "Why did you bring me here?"

"I want to buy you a book," he replied, looking confused. "Go ahead and choose whatever you like."

"Brak, this is a *Gang-owned* shop." She turned to leave, but a tall man blocked her path.

"Lady Rikani! What an unexpected pleasure."

"Hello, Essin," she said as gently as she could manage. "We were just leaving."

"I couldn't let you do that," the Gang Boss said in his gentle voice. "Lazr would be quite upset if he learned that you were here without having a little chat."

Another man came down a staircase. He was a bit shorter than Essin, but he still looked formidable. "Lazr has already been alerted to your presence, Lady Rikani." He came a bit closer. "Perhaps you would like to wait for him in his office."

"Thank you, Relyq, but I'd prefer to be on my way." Rikani turned to face Brak. "What were you thinking?"

"I didn't know these guys were Gangsters," Brak assured her. He wrapped an arm around her waist, as though trying to comfort her. "I swear, Ri! I've been coming here for *years*. They're pleasant enough fellows."

"They're *violent criminals*!"

A third member appeared from the basement—this one more familiar to her than the others. "Well, if it isn't my favorite Clan Leader."

"Jux! Surely *you* wouldn't keep me here against my will."

"*Against your will*? Goodness, no!" The former Azure member laughed heartily, running his hands through his red hair. "We simply have a proposition for you. Please, come and sit."

Rikani raised an eyebrow. "There is nothing that you could say that I'd be interested in hearing."

"That's rather unfortunate," said a voice from behind her.

It had always freaked Rikani out the way the former Agents could move around with eerie silence. She turned to see Lazr standing in the doorway, a firearm strapped to his hip.

"I have information that will greatly benefit you," the LERJ boss added, moving through the rows of book shelves. His hand motioned upward, causing Rikani to break her stare on his gun. "Let's go to my office. Essin and Relyq can keep your boyfriend company while Jux gets us some refreshments."

Years of dealing with Lazr had taught Rikani that what he said was always done. Without another protest, she followed him to a spacious room in the back of the bookstore. When told to sit, she lowered herself onto a comfy chair.

"Now, Lady Rikani," Lazr began, "I'm quite familiar with your brother's attempt to create a treaty with the Agency. Don't bother looking surprised." He sat on the edge of his desk and gave her a wink. "There is very little that happens in Market that I don't know about; something this big couldn't have stayed secret."

Jux then entered with a plate of food. Rikani waved it away. Lazr picked a handful of grapes.

"And you want a portion of the profits? Is that what this is? Extortion?"

"No, not at all. I want you to find a way to make the deal *fail*," Lazr explained with a tone of casualty. He gave Jux a look and the lackey left with a slight nod of his head.

"I won't do anything that jeopardizes the prosperity of my Clan."

Rikani stood to leave, but Lazr raised a hand. "I'm offering a similar contract to the Rye Clan, in exchange for refusing to work with the Agency."

"How could I benefit from a deal with you? You're not as influential as the government."

"I don't pretend to be," Lazr admitted. "However, my associates and I still have many powerful connections in Upper Society. In addition, we have quite a following in the Middle Zone and Lower Region. But I will freely admit that the Agency's influence is still greater than my own." He was quiet a moment as popped a few grapes into his mouth. "By accepting the Agency's terms, you'd be forever shackled to them. They'd eventually resume their hold over the Lower Region; I don't want them to reclaim power here."

"Well, you've given me a lot to think about," she said, standing to leave. "I'd appreciate the chance to think about this for a few days."

"Of course, milady," Lazr smiled yet again. He stood and moved to the back of the office. His hand moved as though it were going to open the door, but it simply rested on the frame. "I'll keep in touch. Now, go enjoy the rest of your evening with that handsome Jade."

Once she nodded that she understood, Lazr made a show of pushing the door ajar and gesturing through it.

As Rikani headed for the store entrance, she gave Brak an angry glare.

He immediately fell in step behind her.

When they were half a Plaza away, Rikani spun around. "I understand that you didn't realize what kind of establishment you took me to. I'm trying not to be mad at you, but I'm not very happy right now. If you have any intention of taking me to a Crimson-owned business or something run by the Tyrians, then let's just end this date now."

"Ri, I can't say how sorry I am. I thought they were simple businessmen." Brak hesitantly reached for her mid back. "I wanted to keep it a secret. However, based on recent events, perhaps it's wise to get approval first."

"What are you talking about?"

"There's this little Icterine café that I enjoy frequenting. I know it's near a lot of Azure shops; I hope it's okay to be out where your Clan Members might see us."

She nodded and let him hold her hand as they walked to the nearest Transit Station.

They took a quick Train ride to their destination. The café was bustling with patrons of all walks of life. Much to Rikani's thanks, the faces belonged to strangers. They got a table in the back corner where smell of coffee wafted from the kitchen.

"Vanilla latte," Rikani ordered from the yellow-clad waitress.

Brak asked for a regular coffee with two sugars and banana nut scone to share. "I know getting coffee is the most lame, mundane date ever. But it's nice for a *first* date, right?"

A barista gave them their pastry and left.

"Definitely better than visiting a crime boss." Rikani smiled, amazed at how quickly she was recovering from the earlier ordeal.

A pair of hands suddenly seized her shoulders. Fear that the LERJ Gang followed them consumed her. She shrieked and turned to see who was holding her. To her relief, it was just the Icterine Clan Leader, Nuto Berge.

"Why can't you say hello like a normal person?"

Although he was clad in his usual yellow and brown suit, he somehow seemed less forlorn than usual. "Sorry, Rikani. I couldn't resist." He looked across the table and stared at Brak. "I'm glad to see you're out enjoying yourself this evening."

"Hello, Lord Nuto," Brak said, bowing his head.

"I just wanted to say thank you." The Icterine Clan Lord clapped a hand on Brak's shoulder.

Curious, Rikani asked, "What did you do for him?"

"Nothing," Brak replied a little too quickly.

Nuto shook his head as he sat down. "It's hardly *nothing*! Your help with Miss Soha has been absolutely wonderful!"

Rikani turned to Brak. "Care to expand on that?"

He shrugged. "His Lordship would write Miss Soha Darrow love letters, give them to me, and then I'd pass them along to her."

Lord Berge motioned for a waiter's attention. "Add their bill to my tab; they should always receive the greatest attention." He turned back to the couple. "You two have a pleasant evening. Order whatever else you want." He dashed off, waving to everyone he met as he left the café.

"For someone who claims to have honorable intentions, you sure seem to have some powerful contacts," Rikani teased. "Are you a part of Lady Bray's book club, as well? Or maybe you're also a liaison between Lady Belana and Miss Soha's brother?"

Brak cleared his throat. "What can I say? People flock to me." Suddenly, he said, "Sorry. I'll be back in a minute." He shot out of his chair and exited through the side door.

"Maybe he's getting me a present," Rikani said to quietly herself. She took a few bites from the scone, trying to imagine what sort of apology gift he was purchasing. "Such a sweet man."

A moment later, a series of shadows covered her table.

She twisted in her seat to see Soha Darrow and Belana Lynch.

"How good it is to see you, Ri-Ri!" Belana exclaimed as she plopped down at the table. "Soha and I were just talking about how we never see you anymore."

"Oh, you know, I have a Clan to run," Rikani answered.

"That shouldn't take *that* much of your time," Soha commented, pulling a chair over. "Don't you have people that can make all those decisions?"

Rikani nervously picked at the crumbs on her table. "I prefer handle matters myself."

"Well, we all do things differently, I suppose," the Jade Heir sighed with indifference. "Otherwise, what's the point of having the different Clans?"

Belana waved drastically at a barista. Before the woman could make it over, the Tyrian Leader shouted, "We'll have our usual!" She turned around and grinned at Rikani. "So, are you free for a girls' night, Ri-Ri?"

"I'm afraid I already have plans," Rikani replied.

"Sitting by yourself alone in a café isn't *real* plans," the Tyrian Clan Leader chided. "Come on! We'll go buy some clothes, paint each other's nails, and then watch a romance vid. It'll be fun. Exada says she hasn't seen you in a few months."

The mention of the Queen's niece made Rikani freeze. She wiped all emotion from her face before she resolved to make a carefully worded reply.

However, the Jade Heir spoke before she could open her mouth. "Belana, she obviously wants to be alone right now," Soha said, looking oddly cheerful. "We can do all that by ourselves, like we *always* do."

"We should be doing things *together*, Soha," Belana whined. "Ri-Ri has probably been feeling left out. Help me persuade her."

The barista returned, carrying the two drinks for Rikani and Brak.

"Oh, so you *do* have plans!" Belana cried, clapping her hands. "Who's the lucky fella?"

"No one," Rikani lied. "I'm taking this to Tays." She stood to leave, but the other women followed her.

"We'll walk with you," Soha said as a waitress brought them their order.

They strolled down the street, sipping their drinks. Belana began chattering about local gossip regarding different Clans. Rikani barely listened; she was too worried that Brak would leave once he discovered she was gone.

When they reached a secluded street, Soha shushed Belana. "Alright, Ladies. I have the biggest piece of news you'll ever hear."

"That's doubtful," Belana scoffed, "but you can tell me anyways."

"There's a Societan that's about to be busted for being an Alteration," Soha explained.

"Shut your face!" Lady Lynch smacked the Darrow Heir on the arm. "Are you sure?"

"Like I said, it's only rumors. But multiple sources assure me that there's definitely a super-being in Rygom." Soha looked at Rikani. "What do you think about that, Rye?"

Alteration talk had always made Rikani uneasy. She didn't like the idea of a person with super powers set loose in the Lower Region. Control was hard enough to have when dealing with *regular* people. When Alterations were thrown into the mix, it messed up the scale.

"There have been Alteration rumors for nearly fifty years," Rikani replied. She sipped her coffee before adding, "What makes this time any different from past scares?"

Soha gave her a sly grin. "Let's just say my sources are more *legitimate* than the usual gossipers."

Wanting to get away from the sinister Jade Heir and Tyrian Leader, Rikani said, "You know what? I forgot that Tays is at his shop. So I'll see you ladies some other time. Enjoy your girls' night." She strode quickly in the opposite direction.

Back at the café, Brak sat at their table. "Where did you go?"

"I don't want to talk about it." She handed him his coffee.

He must have sensed the displeasure in her voice. "Was it worse than the bookstore?"

"I'm not certain," Rikani admitted, stirring her drink. "I had to endure rumors about Alterations. The whole idea of it really bothers me."

"I'm sure there is nothing to *these* rumors."

Rikani narrowed her eyes. "You said there was probably nothing in *these* rumors. That implies that there is something to *other* rumors, right?"

He shook his head. "If it makes you uncomfortable, maybe we shouldn't talk about it."

"What are you hiding?"

Brak sighed. "I should have told you sooner. I was born a Societan. Before you freak out, I'm not a gold-digger. I was only five when my parents were disgraced, so I don't remember what Upper Society is like." He took a breath and looked away. "The reason my family was exiled was because they were connected to Alteration research. My parents kept secret the horrors of what happened to the test subjects."

"I've heard the stories—the frightful deaths."

"That's *mostly* true. See, when the scientists began altering human anatomy, they didn't realize the toll it took on a person's nervous system." Brak lowered his voice. "The Alterations could survive for a short period, provided that they didn't over-tax themselves."

"That isn't much different than what most people know. What did your family discover?"

"They learned that if someone were to reinforce the nervous system, then the Alterations would survive longer and live relatively normal lives."

"And?"

"Alteration research had already been deemed inhumane, but my family continued their research. When, the Agency found out, my family was ruined. I've lived in the Lower Region ever since."

Rikani leaned over and put her hands on his. "So you're saying that someone might have completed your family's research?"

"Maybe. For the sake of everyone's safety, let's hope the rumors are false."

Chapter 21

It was rather humiliating for Mezik Rye to be escorted home once again by Ulrian. He thought his most recent escape plan would be fool-proof. Who'd have thought that the fool would be the one to catch him? Mutof would pay for his betrayal!

Mezik felt like a fool himself. Why did he always need to play the hero? It was all the radio's fault; it drove him to go out and try to save all the poor wretches he heard on the other line. If he had any intelligence, Mezik knew he should go straight to his room and smash it to pieces.

But the thought of not having the radio unsettled him.

Ulrian ushered him past several Azures on the way to Rye Manor. The pedestrians stared and whispered behind their hands.

Vyruk strolled towards the HQ entrance with a bag of gadgets that supposedly were going to increase the security system. The Clan teacher, Daleen—recently returned from Market—had a cart full of school supplies. In the pasture, Rutab and Lavina tended to their herds. Bast wandered mindlessly, trying to find his way back home. The courtyard bustled as Kagome passed out free samples of her newest chocolate candies. Jotea and Zett rearranged a series of paintings near the residential halls.

All waved hello to him, but a twisted sense of judgment shone in their eyes.

Mezik's OMNI beeped; he checked it to see a message from Chera.

Chera: *So, what are you going to buy me? It's rude to not get a girl a present when you go on a trip :D*

Mezik: *I'm not getting you anything, Chera!*

He sighed audibly, catching Ulrian's attention. "Is the teacher's daughter giving you troubles?" the steward asked, a highly amused smile on his face.

"She's annoying," Mez replied as his OMNI signaled another in-coming message.

Chera: *Wait, you didn't make it to Market? :-(*

Mezik: *No, I got caught. AGAIN!*

Chera: S*orry, Mez. When you eventually get there, you'd better bring back a gift! :P*

Mezik: *Whatever. I have to go.*

Chera: *On your way to punishment, eh? I hope Lady Rikani isn't too angry with you. I'd hate it if she stopped letting you come to school ;)*

In a fit of frustration, he lashed out at his classmate.

Mezik: *Ok, stop with the emoticons. They're really annoying!*

Chera: *My bad. I'll try to tone it down. Just let me know when you're out of your punishment so we can hang out!*

Although Chera was fun to be with sometimes, she had begun acting strangely about a year ago. When he asked her about her behavior, her cheeks turned red and she changed the subject. He would have liked to find another kid to play with, but there were few options; there weren't many Azure children his own age.

Ulrian looked over the boy's appearance and asked, "What was your plan anyways?"

"Don't you recognize me?" Mezik asked, gesturing at his face. "I'm Uncle Asdem! I put on this fake beard and raided his closet. I tried finding stacked shoes, but there's not a pair to be found in HQ. That was the big flaw in my plan; I'm not tall enough to pass as him." He stepped onto the tips of his toes, trying to make himself bigger.

"You also look *nothing* like him," Ulrian chuckled, removing the hat Mezik had borrowed from the Azure Elder. "No wonder Mutof caught you. Besides, Asdem hasn't been out of Rye Estate in years."

Not caring about the looks of the Azures anymore, Mezik shouted, "I can't wait to be sixteen! Only three more years in this prison!"

Ulrian stopped suddenly and put his hand on Mezik's shoulder. "Lady Rikani and Lord Tays keep you at Head Quarters for a reason, young Master. Someday you will realize that this is a blessing."

"What could you possibly know about being *stifled*?" Mezik muttered.

"Honestly, very little. I grew up in Upper Society," Ulrian admitted. "My parents taught me that the world was mine to be had. So I ran wild. All the while, a part of me wished someone would care enough to set boundaries. I did anything and everything without a thought to the consequences."

"That sounds like the best life ever! How'd you lose it?"

Ulrian didn't answer right away. When the steward continued, there was a note of sorrow in his voice. "I realized that there was more to life than living for the next pleasure. After my parents died, I sold the company and moved down here. Lord Asdem took me in."

Mezik gagged at the realization of Ulrian's words. "You gave it up *on purpose*? What kind of an idiot are you?"

Ulrian sighed and continued walking. "It was the smartest thing I've ever done."

Part of why Mezik hated being smothered by his brother and sister was the fact that they didn't tell him anything about their past. They would say that it didn't matter anymore and then began talking about something else. Having only been three years old when his family moved from Society to the Region, Mezik knew little about the reasons for the relocation. He wanted *answers* and he wouldn't get them stuck in the HQ.

And his radio was someday going to help him with that.

*****

Life in Rye Manor was becoming unbearable. Tays had just broken up with his crazy girlfriend and Rikani constantly berated him for laying around and moping all day.

Mezik was at least grateful that their attention was elsewhere other than him.

Bored, he went exploring the old storage rooms in the basement. A pile of boxes in the corner seemed out of place; there wasn't any dust on them. Inside were mostly girls' clothes and weird, effeminate knick-knacks. Mezik was about to leave when he found an interesting machine—a black, metal box covered in buttons.

He played with it a minute before discovering the power knob. A screeching static fizzed out of a pair of speakers. Messing with a dial, he got lowered the volume. Mezik wondered why his family still had such an archaic mechanism.

Curiosity got the better of him. He took it up to his room and began fiddling with it.

Mezik didn't have the mechanical intelligence that Tays did, but he was determined to at least discover its function.

Another dial changed the static to a woman's voice. She seemed frantic as she spoke. "*No, no, no! I can't! I know things have gotten bad, but I can make them better. Just wait and you'll see that he's really a great guy*." There was a scuffle and a man began shouting.

Unable to hear anymore, Mezik turned the dial.

"*…like that? Yeah, baby*!" A man breathed loudly as a woman moaned.

While trying to a get a better signal, he went too far and the radio switched to another channel.

"*I don't know what to do with him.*"

It was Rikani's voice. Mezik turned the volume back up.

"*He just sits in his room all day, Aunt Nas. What should I do?*"

"*Buy him a girl from the Stroke Vice Gang?*" Nasiram offered.

"*I'm not going to hire a prostitute for my love-sick brother,*" Kani scoffed. "*Besides, I don't want to owe that Gang anything.*"

"*Maybe the Trips will take him to the country to their family's farm. The fresh air could do him some good.*" Nasiram said something unintelligible away from the transceiver—probably scolding Kumate about something. "*We could all go; I've been telling Dagnos that we need a vacation.*"

Mezik normally drowned out the nonsense when his relatives spoke. He didn't much care to listen to their phones conversations, either. Changing the channel once again, he heard a conversation of someone who appeared to be in trouble. Someone had been taken by Snatchers and was attempting to contact the Agency. But the Enforcers didn't seem all that interested.

Another channel had a young woman whose purse had been stolen.

Channel after channel was full people needing help. With nothing else to do, Mezik took it upon himself to try and help a few of them. But first he needed to get out of the Azure HQ.

*****

He was thoughtful for a moment. "How angry are Kani and Tays?" Mezik knew he'd find out soon enough, but sometimes hearing it from someone else helped him prepare.

Ulrian was quiet for a moment. The longer the silence lasted, the more nervous Mezik felt. Eventually, the trusty steward said, "Let's just say that your life is about to get even more restrictive. I think your next escape plan will be trying to get out of the Manor because you're about to be put under house-arrest."

Mezik groaned, "Don't they see that the more they contain me the more I want freedom!"

"Apparently not. When I was a Societan, the more freedom my parents gave me, the more I wanted them to set limits. I suppose it can be said of the opposite." Ulrian paused before he added, "I'll talk to your brother and sister." Before he left, he said, "*Don't* run off again."

At Rye Estate, Mezik waited in the front parlor as Ulrian went off in search of the Lord and Lady. While he waited, he continued to pick at the stubble glued to his face.

He managed to remove most of the chunks when Tays came strolling down the halls. Casually, he tilted his head at Mez, turned around, and headed back in the direction he came from.

Catching up to him, Mezik asked, "Why don't you look pissed?"

Tays' laid back demeanor was what made him Mezik's favorite sibling, but he should have been angrier than he appeared. "I'm letting Rikani be mad enough for the both of us," Tays explained rather calmly. "She's about ready to chain you to your bedpost, but I'm all for getting you a tracking bracelet so that we know where you are at all times."

"Both treatments are demeaning. What am I to you? Some disobedient puppy?"

"Well, if you don't want us to treat you like that, then don't *act* like it." Tays playfully ruffled Mezik's shaggy brown hair as though he were petting him. "We'll give you back your human rights when you learn to use them responsibly."

Mezik could hear Rikani shouting from down the hall. He stopped walking and asked, "Do I *really* have to go in there? Kani sounds like she's gonna murder me."

Tays held the door open and the volume of the shrieks magnified. "In you go."

Taking a deep breath, Mezik prepared to face the dragon.

Chapter 22

As she walked down the halls of a Middle Zone Sector, Iris couldn't help feeling uneasy. She had never been to camp before; her father said it was an unnecessary waste of time that was better spent learning. Even though she wasn't going to *be* a camper, she was still excited to see her first campground.

"Why aren't the Third-Years coming?" Iris asked.

"They aren't *coming*?" Eve Sanders squealed in disbelief. "Then why did I agree to do this stupid thing? I only said I'd come because I thought *he'd* be here."

Beatrice rolled her eyes. "Goodness, Eve! You're acting like you haven't seen him in months. It's only been a couple weeks." She turned to Iris. "Al, Max, and Viola finished their Service Hours by being Mentors this past summer; they don't need to escort us everywhere anymore."

"If you get enough Hours," Claire interrupted, "you get a free Agency implant."

"Oh, big whoop," Evelyn sighed. "I've already got an implant. I might as well turn around now and go back home."

Iris cleared her throat. "That wouldn't look good on your record; to sign up for Service Hours and not show up is a serious matter to the Board." She hated being the voice of reason in the group, but someone had to.

"No one asked you," Eve snapped, crossing her arms.

The group of First-Years walked the rest of the way in silence. As they drew closer to their destination, Iris noticed a change in the air. There was a strong scent of pollen and an increase of moisture as they emerged into a dense forest, complete with a ground of soil and crunchy pine-needles.

Eve was the first to interrupt the silence. "Great! I can never wear these shoes again."

"They still *look* clean," commented Claire.

"They've touched dirt now," the legatee complained. "We'll have to stop by a clothing store on the way home."

"You'll probably need a whole new outfit by the end of the day," Beatrice chuckled, tossing a handful of pine needles at her cousin. "Perhaps the camp counselors have a hose we can spray you down with."

Iris and Claire joined in with their own laughter.

The mockery only made Eve's mood drop even lower. From the look on her face, Iris inferred that the red-haired girl was close to pounding someone.

"I just want to get this day over with," Eve pouted. "Where do we need to check-in?"

"Agent Snow said that she'd meet us at the front office." Iris pulled out her OMNI, found a map of the camp, and located administrator lodge. She pointed north towards a large, sparkling lake. "That way."

Iris took in all the scenery around them. There was something beautiful about the greenery. Nothing was as fancy as the hybrid plants used to decorate Upper Society, but the simplicity of the forest vegetation was appealing to her senses.

"I still think we should have gone to that old folks' home to sing," Beatrice commented before vaulting over a giant boulder.

Eve rolled her eyes, clearly becoming more agitated the further into the forest they roamed. "Not everything in life can be chance to perform, Bea. Besides, the rest of us don't like making spectacles of ourselves in front of strangers."

"Yeah, we all know you prefer to do it in front of people you *know*," Bea teased.

Claire moved closer to Iris and whispered, "What's the matter with them?"

"I think Eve is just upset about not seeing Alastair for awhile," Iris replied with a shrug. "I have no idea what would make Bea so cranky. Perhaps living together has made them sick of each other?"

Up ahead, the two cousins stop bickering enough to realize that they were being talked about.

"What are you whispering?" Eve demanded.

"We were wondering what crawled up your butt and died," Iris said in reply.

Claire spun on her, brown eyes wide in shock. Through clenched teeth, she murmured, "We don't say things like that."

Iris sputtered, "Oh! I'm sorry. Did I use that phrase incorrectly?"

"No, that was used in perfect context. But you didn't need to tell them what we were saying."

"My bad." Iris turned back to Eve and Bea. "We're just concerned about—" She was at a loss of what to say to get out of her predicament. "Um—"

Beatrice nonchalantly waved her off. "Never mind. Let's just get to the office."

Minutes later, they stood in front of a rustic, wooden building that looked as though it was built centuries ago.

Agent Haley Snow, their Rygom History Instructor, sat cross-legged on a log out front with her eyes closed. As they approached, she opened her lids and said, "Ah, welcome to Camp Stone Lake! Are you ready to get your hands dirty?"

"We have to get our hands *dirty*!" Eve cringed, folding her arms across her body. "Nobody mentioned the unsanitary work conditions for Service Hours."

"Stop being such a priss," Bea snapped.

Iris moved in front of the bickering cousins and asked the Service Hour Organizer, "What are our assignments, Agent Snow?"

"Well, the craft counselor is sick with food poisoning. Who would like to take his place?"

"Children have germs," said Eve in a hushed voice.

Claire averted her eyes, obviously not desiring to be in charge of kids ever again. Iris thought of volunteering, but she didn't want to be separated from her friend. In the end, Beatrice was sent off to help a group of five-year-olds paint nature scenes.

After Agent Snow made the arrangements for Bea to be a counselor, she motioned for the remaining Trainees to follow her. "Isn't it wonderful? This forest was first planted by Rygom's Designers as a memorial to the outside world. With the Megacity closed off to nature, most of its inhabitants would go their entire lives without seeing the splendor of the natural world."

The History Instructor led them down a steep hill. When they arrived at their destination, the three First-Years immediately decided that Beatrice had the easier job.

Before them was a run-down park. There was a fine layer of dust covering most of the playground except where hand prints and shoe marks were visible. Bits of paint showed that the area was once colorful.

"Can I change my mind and switch places with Bea?" Eve asked Agent Snow.

"No, you cannot," the History Instructor replied curtly. She moved forward to show the First-Years what they needed to do. "This campsite hasn't been thoroughly cleaned in awhile. One of you will need to wipe down all this equipment. Another will go behind them and put a fresh coat of paint." She nodded to a pile of tools laid out on a tarp. "The third person will be shoveling out the old dirt so that some fresh sand can be laid in."

"Agent Snow, 'fresh sand' is an oxymoron," Eve sighed.

"You're right; it is. 'Sand that isn't full of trash,' is what I should have said." The Agent turned to leave, but she had one last comment. "You have six hours; better get started."

Once Agent Snow was gone, Eve called out, "I'll be the supervisor. Now get to work!"

"That wasn't one of the options," Claire said, picking up a rag and a pail of soapy water. "I'll clean, Iris will paint, and *you'll* shovel out the littered dirt."

The two responsible First-Years began their work immediately.

Eve just stood there, staring at a shovel on the ground.

After a few minutes of Miss Sanders not contributing, Claire said, "The purpose of Service Hours is about getting out of your comfort bubble and doing things that you never thought you'd do." She began wiping down a tire swing. "You can't go your entire life without getting a little dirty."

"Speak for yourself, Zonese," Eve muttered, glaring at Claire. "Yeah, I know your little secret. It's pretty obvious that you weren't born a Societan. I'm amazed that you thought you were hiding it at all."

Eve had crossed the boundary between being unpleasant and out-right verbally abusive. Iris wanted to step in, but she wasn't sure how to save her friend from embarrassment. If she needed help, Claire would have given her some sort of look. But none appeared. So Iris returned back to her work.

"I wonder why the Agency went against their normal policy of keeping Middle Zonese out of the Training Program," Eve mused, walking purposefully towards where Claire was hunched over. "Sure, they were probably fascinated in your skill in creating little doo-dads. But you can't be *too* great, can you? You never enrolled at the Prodigy Academy."

"That doesn't mean anything," Claire said in a low voice as she moved to a kiddy-slide. "I was pursued by the Prodigy Academy. However, I declined their offer."

"Why would you do that?"

Claire clenched her fists, clearly trying to calm herself down. "Why are you so interested in my personal life?"

Eve met Claire's glare. "I like knowing everything about everyone in my social circle."

Unable to keep silent anymore, Iris stood up. "What's your problem, Sanders? Stop berating her for something she had no control over. Are you so unhappy with your own life that you have to make everyone else feel like crap?"

"I don't know what you're talking about," Eve scoffed, flipping her short red curls. "I have a *wonderful* life."

"No life is *perfect*," Iris retorted, her hands clenching as rage gripped her.

"Only people with awful lives can say something so ridiculous." Eve narrowed her eyes. "I use to think you had it all, too, Iris Kayn. But I'm starting to think there's more to *your* life than we all know."

"My life sucks because my mom died when I was born. There! That's the unhappiness that surrounds my father and me."

"Yes, you lack maternal love. That doesn't mean your life stinks. Plenty of *alive* mothers ignore their children and their needs. If anything, you're lucky that she's dead; that way you didn't have to deal with the emotional scars of her neglect."

Iris couldn't control her temper anymore. Her hand went to the paint brush in her bucket. Flicking her wrist, red paint flew across the empty space between them.

There was a high shrill as the bright color splashed all over Eve's pristine grey uniform. "What'd you do that for?" Her hand felt behind her ear. "You better hope you didn't damage my implant!"

A group of children dressed in sports uniforms were passing by. Their attention fell on the three First-Year Trainees and they moved to get a better look at the red mess.

One girl pointed at the women and let out a blood-curdling shriek.

Beatrice moved to comfort the screaming child. "It's okay. It's just paint—not blood."

"No, that's not it," a boy cried. "There's an Alteration."

"What are you talking about?" The fill-in-counselor looked up at the eighteen-year-old women. Beatrice seemed rather amused at the sight of Eve dripping with paint. "Oh, no! They're just my friends from the Agency."

"The woman covered in red has an implant," another camper replied with disgust.

Eve narrowed her eyes at the children. "Just because I have an implant doesn't mean I'm an Alteration."

"That's not what my mom says!" shouted the girl that had screamed. "She says that implants are the beginning stages to creating Alterations."

"That doesn't mean that she *is* one," Bea Cromford assured the children, putting a hand on the girl's shoulder. She turned to the Iris and Claire. "Perhaps you should take Eve back to the front office. I'll meet you up there shortly."

Iris nodded and set down her paint supplies. She backed away slowly, motioning for Claire and Eve to follow.

The stares of the children unnerved her, looking as though they would chase after them.

As if reading her mind, a handful of children started running toward the decrepit playground. Iris, Eve, and Claire ran as best they could through the forest back to the front office.

Rocks whizzed past their heads as they dodged around trees.

Hysterical, Eve kept yelling, "They're going to kill us!" as she glanced behind her. "We're going to die!" She tripped over a root and landed face-down in the dirt. Scrambling to her feet, she ran through a low tree and got her hair caught in a branch. "Don't leave me!" she called after Iris and Claire.

After what had happed at the playground, Iris was more than happy to let the little devils stone the stuck-up woman. But she had a change of heart. Going back, she snapped the branch and grabbed Eve's shoulders.

When they caught up with Claire, Beatrice was already waiting in front of the office building.

Out of nowhere, Agent Snow appeared in a motor vehicle. She motioned for them to get in and then sped off. "I'm sorry. I forgot to check if any of you had implants. It seems to be a rather touchy subject for the Zonese."

"*Touchy*?" Eve shrieked, trying to get the twigs and leaves out of her tangles curls. "They tried to kill us with *rocks*!"

Agent Snow gave them tickets for the Transit Station as she dropped them off at the edge of the forest. "Sorry again, Miss Sanders. For my mistake, I will ensure that all of you get credit for the hours you signed up for. Hopefully next time goes a bit smoother and you can complete your tasks."

When the History Instructor was gone, Eve insisted that they stop at a motel to let her get cleaned up before returning home. She sent her three companions off to get her some toiletries from a near-by store and a fresh set of clothes.

Iris, Claire, and Bea didn't protest, deciding that their revenge would be best served in buying her a generic brand of clothes and the value version of soap. Much to their collective surprise, Eve freshened up with the cheap soap and wore the unfashionable clothes without any complaint.

Sensing that she had been properly punished for her harsh words, they laid off Eve for the entire journey home.

Chapter 23

Audrey peeked over her shoulder to make sure that no one was watching. She tightened the scarf about her head, further hiding her face. A pair of dark glasses covered her eyes and a portion of her cheeks.

Nervous, she hopped into a Down Elevator that led out of Upper Society.

Perhaps her plan wasn't a very smart idea; it had made complete sense after a few hours of drowning her sorrows in Norman's secret stash of vodka. But now that she was sober, she saw the idiocy of it.

Her financial problems were getting worse. No one would hire her now that her name was tainted.

Well, that wasn't entirely true. A company in the Middle Zone had offered her a job a couple days ago, but that was out of the question since Societans weren't permitted to work in the Zone. She would have had to relinquish her status and move away from Society.

But with her reduced circumstances, it was a tempting offer.

Unless she could help it, Audrey decided to stay where she was. It was tough to cut back to only necessities; money was tight with her savings account quickly draining.

She needed to economize better. That was when she decided to purchase things from Market.

Activists of the Restoration Act encouraged Societans to openly purchase things from the Regioners that sold their goods in the Market Sectors below the Zone. Unfortunately, most of the wealthy considered it *taboo* to buy anything not produced in the higher levels of the Megacity. She was already one scandal away from being a public outcast. So Audrey had covered herself up as well as she could and took off to the Region to buy cheap groceries.

Up until a couple years ago, Societans didn't care about where goods were purchased. Families often took trips to the Market Sectors. But then *incidents* began to occur, causing rumors of unsafe traveling conditions to spread through the higher levels of the Megacity. Ever since then, Societans kept their distance.

As she grew closer to her destination, Audrey wondered how she would get all her supplies back home. She didn't want to make this excursion regularly, but that might not be an option. There was no way she'd be able to bring home more than a week's groceries without arousing suspicion. The neighbors were terrible gossips who were completely aware of her situation. If they saw her coming home with a large load of bags, they'd put the pieces together to determine the truth. So she resolved that she would go every couple of days, buying just a couple sacks of items at a time.

Once at her destination, she began moving uncertainly towards a group of shops at the nearest Plaza. Thankfully, none of the faces she passed were familiar. Still, she kept her scarf around her head.

Mingling amongst the vendors and consumers, she browsed the prices. Audrey's jaw dropped when she read the tags; most items were one-tenth the price of those she was used to spending. It took a lot of self-restraint to not squander all her money in one place. She limited herself to one or two things from each shop.

Soon, her bags were fairly full while a majority of her wallet's contents remained. She was about to leave when a quaint little fruit stand caught her eye. Cautiously, she picked up a berry and examined it.

"Those are the *best* raspberries in all of Market," said a voice behind her.

Audrey turned to see a man in his late-thirties, dressed in a simple blue suit. "Are you the produce stand owner?"

"No, I'm just watching it while the proprietors run errands." He gestured at the small berries. "Go ahead and try one."

Audrey held the red fruit to her lips and took a bite. Flavor exploded on her tongue. "Mmmm. Ah, that's good. I'll take a quarter-pound." She eyed the other types of produce. "Can I sample more fruits, please?"

"Yes. There are veggies and herbs, too." He paused for a second before adding, "Is this your first time at Market?"

Cautiously, Audrey asked, "Why do you ask that?"

The vender looked her up and down as he said, "Most everyone in the Lower Region and Middle Zone has tried produce from this stand." From the corner of her eye, she saw him look intently at her face. "You're a Societan, I bet."

"Keep your voice down." Audrey pulled her scarf tighter. "I can't be seen here."

He pointed at silky material. "If that's the case, I'd lose the handkerchief. We see all sorts of Societans trying to sneak down here without letting their acquaintances know; they always try to hide their identities with things like trench coats and bulky hats. Personally, I don't understand what the big deal is."

Audrey hesitantly raised her hand to her head. With a pull on the knot, the scarf came off.

"Much better. You fit right in now," the man said with a wink.

"Well, I feel like an idiot. No wonder I've been getting strange looks all day." Before she could say anything else, her OMNI beeped. Audrey looked and the screen and groaned. "Sorry, I just need to message my boss really quick." She tapped the message icon.

Norman: *Can you get me something while you're at Market?*

Audrey: *How did you know where I was going?*

Norman: *Mr. Birch told me.*

Audrey*: How did he know? I didn't tell anyone.*

Norman: *Oscar used his accounting abilities to estimate how long you'd last on your savings. That plus the fact that you mysteriously didn't show up for work today made it obvious that you went to Market.*

She re-read the last message since it didn't make any sense.

Audrey: *It's the weekend; I don't work on Saturdays.*

Norman: *Saturday? Oh, that explains why I'm out of tequila. Speaking of, would you mind getting me some while you're out?*

After years of working for Dr. Kayn, she still had yet to find a way to keep the man from thinking that she was his *personal* assistant rather than his *lab* assistant. Being direct rarely helped, but it was a sufficient form of stress-release.

Audrey: *I'm not your booze lackey. Go to the liquor store yourself.*

She closed out of the message center and silenced her OMNI.

When she turned back to the fruit stand, the man had a smirk on his face. "You Societans are all the same—can't go *five* minutes without looking at your OMNI." Changing the subject back, he asked, "Did you want anything else?"

"I'm afraid I've bought all the food I can buy for now. But I'll be back some other time. Will you be running this venue again anytime soon?"

The man shook his head. "Probably not. Like I said before, I'm just doing a favor for the owners. They are—" He was interrupted by the appearance of three women. "Ah, welcome back, Trips."

"I trust everything went smoothly," said the red-head.

"Absolutely, Aril."

A brunette stepped forward, bearing a small envelop. "Here's for your troubles, Ulrian."

"No, thank you," he replied, raising his hands in protest. "I couldn't possibly take that, Otum. I'm always happy to help."

"We appreciate it," the blonde assured him. "Let us know if we do anything for you."

"I sure will, Ebyx. Good day." He stepped away with a slight bow.

"So, you're name is *Ulrian*?" Audrey raised an eyebrow at him, not at all concerned that he was tagging along with her. "That's interesting."

"Yeah, Regioners usually get to name themselves. They tend to choose made-up names over more traditional ones." After a second he added, "Oh, I guess we forgot to introduce ourselves."

"Well, I'm—"

"No, you don't need to tell me your name. I'd hate for someone else to overhear and report it to Society."

She chuckled, "I don't think I care anymore. I'm Audrey."

"It's a pleasure to *meet* you."

The tone of his voice was amused, as though he knew something she didn't. She suddenly felt like she had seen him before.

*****

Having been surrounded by nanoticians her entire life, Audrey Taledon had nothing to fear on her first day of classes at Kleinmann University. She probably knew more about the miniature, specialized robots than half her professors. Her parents were some of the leading nano-researchers in the entire Megacity of Rygom and had begun teaching her the secrets of the science early in life.

But soon she was to meet her idol—the foremost expert in the field. Well, she wasn't really going to *meet* her; the woman was too busy with her research to actually teach classes. Dr. Teresa Kayn had created a series of hologram courses for the University. To learn from her was something Audrey had dreamed of since she was a child. Even her parents—who were rarely impressed with anyone—conceded that their combined knowledge of nanites was inferior to Dr. Kayn's.

Audrey entered the science building twenty minutes before the beginning of class and took a seat at the front of the lecture hall. While she waited for the period to begin, she reviewed the class syllabus on her OMNI. The seats around her began to fill up and conversations started up. Instead of joining in, she continued staring at the small screen in her hands. She had no wish to divert her attention from academics by socializing at school.

Someone tapped the back of her shoulder and she reluctantly lowered her OMNI. Without turning to face the interrupter, she asked, "What is it?"

"I heard a rumor that the daughter of Doctors Chet and Ramona Taledon is in this class," a boy whispered, leaning over the chairs beside her. He knelt onto his knees and rested his arms along the backs of the chairs. "Do you have any idea who that might be?"

"Why do you care?"

"Great things are expected of her. I'd like to get to know her *now* before she's famous."

Audrey turned around in her seat and scoffed. "You're a fame hunter."

The boy had ruffled brown hair that fell into his dark green eyes. He gave her a lob-sided grin. "Guilty as charged, Miss Taledon."

"You already know who I am?"

"You just confirmed my suspicion," the boy laughed. He climbed over the rows of seats and sat at the desk next to her. "Usually when two people meet, they introduce themselves. I know who you are, but I haven't had the opportunity to introduce myself."

"I have no wish to know who you are," Audrey replied, returning her gaze to her OMNI.

He draped an arm around her shoulder, his fingers running through her long, blonde hair. "I'll tell you anyways. If you *still* don't care after that, I'll leave you alone."

She pushed him away. "Save yourself the trouble and let me go back to ignoring you."

Dismissing Audrey's negative behavior, he introduced himself. "Ulysses Mason."

She had been determined to not react no matter what he said, but she couldn't help looking back at him. "*Mason*? As in *Mason Commerce*?" The Taledons had been trying for years to get a contracting position at Mason Commerce. But the owners refused to buy into nanite technology. "Your parents think nanites are a dead end. Why are you in Nanites 101?"

"Unlike mom and dad, I believe they hold a lot of promise." Ulysses' hand trailed down to the small of Audrey's back. "I want to learn about nanites and then report back on the benefits."

Audrey was beginning to rethink the possibility of a friendship with this Ulysses fellow. She allowed the Mason boy to continue stroking her back while she carefully planned her next words. Trying to sound playful, she said, "Well, if there is anything I can do to help with that, let me know."

"I already told you how. We should *get to know* each other better." The boy moved his hand to her knee and slid it up her thigh.

"What are you doing!" She grabbed his hand and tossed it back at him.

"Giving you a *hint*."

"So if we are *intimate*," Audrey whispered, "you would talk *your* parents into giving *my* parents a contract?"

"You *are* a smart girl!"

Audrey picked up her things. "You're a pig!" She made her way down the row of desks and walked down the aisle to a desk at the back of the room just as the class began. She reordered her things in front of her just as the hologram of Dr. Teresa Kayn began to speak.

*****

"You're Ulysses Mason," Audrey stated as a wave of queasiness crashed through her.

"So you *do* remember me." Ulrian's pleasant demeanor faltered for a moment. His cheeks reddened as he averted his gaze. "I'm rather ashamed of our first meeting; I was a different person back then."

After a brief pause, she said, "Well, you seem to be a philanthropist *now*. Perhaps you could make it up to me and give me more Market tips."

"It'd be my pleasure. I know a great little café we could go to and talk."

Unsure of why she was willing to spend her afternoon with a Regioner who used to be a classmate, she walked alongside of him and listened to his information. She scolded herself for wanting to spend time with him, and yet another part of her brain memorized the image of his smile and the sound of his voice. Perhaps this young man was what she needed to distract herself from her troubles. He was a pleasant fellow and his manner made him easy to talk to.

Ulrian took her to a café that was full of yellow items: sunflower vines, star figurines, bumble bee caricatures, etc… The walls, furniture, and glassware were all different shades of that color, mixed with splashes of brown wood accents. When she was done gawking, they ordered and took a seat in a corner booth.

"So, Audrey, are you thinking about relocating to Market?" he asked, picking at a lemon poppy seed muffin.

"No, of course not. I love Upper Society."

"I didn't ask if you *loved* Society," Ulrian sighed, steeling a bite of her chocolate chip banana bread. "*Everyone* loves Society. I asked if you were thinking of moving here."

Suspicious of his intentions, Audrey inquired, "Why do you ask?"

"Well, it's a common pattern for Societans who visit Market. They enter into financial difficulties and begin economizing by buying from Market. Soon, things are too tight and they have no choice but to move. I've seen it dozens of times."

"I have no immediate plans to relocate. Things are *perfect*. Things are just—"

A barista interrupted their conversation as he dropped off their coffee.

Ulrian stared at her for an uncomfortable amount of time, casually sipping his drink before saying, "Did you know that you shrug your shoulders when you lie? You've shrugged them twice now since we've—" He stopped short and sighed. "Sorry, I didn't mean to profile you; it just sort of happens. You probably want nothing more than to just run off now."

Audrey was torn. She was worried that she was beginning to grow too comfortable with this man. But she didn't want to leave. Snuggling back into the booth's cushion, she resumed drinking her coffee. "So if you're not the produce vender, what kind of a job do you have?"

"Do you *really* wanna share specifics about our lives?" Ulrian asked skeptically. "I may never see you again. But it's kinda weird to swap personal information with a stranger."

"You're right," Audrey consented. She ripped off another corner of her muffin, but didn't feel like eating it. "We don't need to talk about that stuff. I'll just sit here and wait for you to make another inappropriate profiling comment."

Ulrian laughed so hard that his hand shook and his drink spilled. "I'm sure another one will come out if we wait long enough." He paused as his OMNI beeped. Ulrian pushed a button and the sound ceased. "I've had a pleasant time, Miss Audrey, but I'm afraid I have an important appointment."

"Well, thank you for the coffee and the tips." She offered him her hand.

Ulrian took her palm gingerly and covered it with both of his. “The owner has been insiting on repaying a favor. Our snacks have merely helped him feel better about not being indebted to me. But you are very welcome. I hope we can do this again should you make another visit to Market.”

When he was gone, Audrey gathered her bags and left the quaint, yellow café. She was about to make her way to the Transit station when a glimpse of red hair caught her attention.

Curious as to why the sight would affect her so strongly, she impulsively moved to get a better view of the face behind the distinguished mane. The woman wore a simple but stylish grey dress hemmed with pink lace. She held a thin book up to her nose, supposedly inspecting the cover.

A man in an orange suit stood beside her. He seemed agitated and yet the woman spoke calmly. “You’re seeing strings that aren’t there, Dagnos. Unmare’s inquiries won’t directly affect us. So what if she wants to find her other granddaughter?”

“Based on Lizra’s past, I’d say that we have *plenty* to worry about.” The man called Dagnos wiped sweat from his brow before continuing, “Why can’t you see it, Lurahi?

You know better than anyone what happens when schemes are set in motion. This could upset the division of power through the Clans."

"Lizra was not Unmare's eldest child. Therefore, Clan Leadership should not pass to either of her children. The older daughter's line will inherit the title."

"And what will happen the other two grandchildren?" Dagnos asked.

Lurahi sighed, "Oh, Lord Rush! They both have prospective spouses. They'll be fine."

"If you're not concerned, I'll stop pestering you. Good day, Lady Bray." The orange-clothed man scowled as he walked away. He didn't seem to care when he saw that Audrey was eavesdropping; he tilted his head in respect and continued on his way.

A woman in her late twenties stepped forward and took the aged tome from the pink and grey woman. She gently tucked the book into a wide bag along with three identical volumes. "Shall we pay Lazr a visit, milady? Essin tells me that they have a new shipment in from Moryth."

"Not today, Hawa." Picking up another book, Lurahi tucked it under her arm.

As the woman moved to leave, Audrey recognized her face. Without thinking, she moved forwards. She finally caught up to the pink woman a block down the street. "Madeline!"

Madeline Cromford froze. Without turning, she said, "It's been a long time since I've been called me by that name, Dr. Taledon."

"I'm sorry to bother you, Madel—"

"Call me *Lady Bray*," she interrupted. "Or *Lurahi*; it doesn't matter." She tilted her head, motioning for Audrey to follow. Addressing her assistant, she said, "Hawa, go ahead and prepare my conservatory. We'll be along in a bit."

Audrey trailed after the lady, apologizing for calling her by the wrong name. "I'm aware of the Regioners' custom of choosing their own names, but I had assumed that former Societans might keep them as a status symbol."

"I've never heard of a Societan who didn't change their name once disgraced. And I suppose you probably want to change your name now."

Confused, Audrey asked, "Why would I want to—" She suddenly realized what Lurahi meant. "Oh, I'm still a Societan." Audrey held up her right hand and pulled her sleeve down to show that she didn't have a Signature tattooed to her wrist. "I'm just *visiting* Market. Some say that it's nearly fashionable to buy and trade here."

Lurahi laughed. "You're a rather awful liar, Dr. Taledon; you should work on that." Blunt as ever, she commented, "I was almost convinced that your condition finally got you into trouble."

"No, I'm not in any trouble at the moment," Audrey assured her before realizing what Lurahi insinuated. "Wait! What *condition*?"

"Oh, sorry. I forgot that you think no one knows."

"I realize that *some* people know, but how do *you*?"

"You and your parents came to a little party Jay and I threw together to celebrate our fifteenth wedding anniversary," Lurahi explained. "You snuck into my library and took a book. I was rather annoyed when I saw you lift one of my more precious volumes. But he next day, I found it on a window sill by the gardens."

Audrey wanted to apologize, but Lady Lurahi wasn't done with her story.

"Intrigued, I began asking around if any of my friends had things disappear and reappear. They all thought the question was odd, but several admitted that they had little items vanish and then materialize in the strangest places. Some of my more superstitious companions believed they had attracted a Poltergeist."

Once again, Audrey asked for forgiveness. Embarrassed, she said, "I can't help it. I just have an *urge* to—"

"No need to explain. Just be careful or else you'll end up down here."

They continued walking for a short distance, talking about all the things that had happened since Madeline Cromford became Lady Lurahi Bray. When they reached the conservatory, Audrey was invited over for tea and scones.

Hawa brought in a tray of treats and left.

"I suppose everyone is wondering what happened between the Mayor and his ex-wife," Lurahi said before taking a sip of her Earl Grey. "Not that you'd ever bring up such question. No matter. I'd like to tell someone my story. Would you mind listening? I think you might benefit from the tale."

"That's not necessary, Lurahi," Audrey insisted. "I don't need to know the circumstances around your exile."

"Someone else should know the details, Dr. Taledon. In case something happens to me, I'd like someone with credibility to circulate it." She set her tea cup down and folded her hands in her lap. "To put it simply, my exile is due to blackmail. I over-heard too much about the wrong person and they proceeded to ruin my life."

"Was it Mayor Cromford?" Audrey asked.

"My husband was involved, but he wasn't the grand puppet master." Lurahi paused and took in a deep breath. "To this day, I hardly know what to make of the information. It must be extremely important if they were willing to frame *me*."

Intrigued, Audrey set her own cup down, no longer interested in the soothing taste of tea. "I thought you said you were being blackmailed?"

Lurahi put her cup down and stared absently at her massive book collection. "Yes. That, too. I was framed for someone's murder. In order to ensure that I wouldn't tell anyone what I heard, my loving husband warned me of the plot and helped me flee to the Lower Region. However, he said he'd tell the Agency where to find me if I ever made the information public."

Suddenly unsure about the situation, Audrey held up her hands as she said, "Then you can't possibly expect to tell me what happened. I don't want you to get into trouble."

"I suppose you're right. We can stop for today. Just know that I'm not the only person to be falsely accused of something; others have been wrongfully sentenced to a life in the Plague-infested Region." Lady Bray stood and walked Audrey to the door. "I *do* hope you'll come visit again, Dr. Taledon. There's so much of my narrative left to tell."

Chapter 24

"If you wipe down the counter anymore, the glossy finish will come off," Zett groaned.

"Why don't you try to relax for the next few hours, Tays?" Roteg offered in a gentle manner. "The Agent Liaisons won't be here for awhile.

Tays tossed his dust cloth over the counter and said, "Don't talk to me like I'm an infant. You think I'm going a little overboard with the whole situation? Fine. I agree with you. But considering the circumstances, I believe my concern is warranted."

"How long has it been since you were a Societan?" Zett asked as he gathered his cleaning supplies.

"Almost ten years," Tays replied, unsure of why the boy was asking.

"Why is impressing the Agents so important to you? They're stuffy, self-absorbed snobs. Is it because you think they might let you back into Upper Society?"

"No, I can never go back," the Azure Lord sighed. "Rikani, Mezik, and I are stuck in the Region for the rest of our lives."

"But that ain't so bad, Tays," Roteg commented, playfully punching his boss's arm. "You guys lead your own Clan; you're making a difference down here. I'd rather be an Azure than be in any other Clan."

"I think I'd rather die than be a Crimson," added Zett. He turned to his fellow employee. "Don't you agree, Ro?"

"Aw, kid, don't get me started on those conniving, dominating thieves."

"Don't call me *kid*. I'm 19."

"That's still young." Roteg ruffled the boy's hair.

Zett swatted his hand away as he said, "You're only a few years older than me!" Turning to his boss, he said, "Lord Tays, I think you and Lady Rikani would do a much better job ruling the Region than Romisa. Can't you hold some sort of Clan Court session and impeach the Crimson Leader or something like that?"

"Thanks for the vote of confidence," Tays sighed. "But it takes more than popularity to be the Region Monarch."

His new employee said something else, but Tays was no longer paying attention.

*****

"I still can't believe this is happening," Tays said to his sales associate, feeling overwhelmed on his first official day of being a shop owner.

"It took a lot of work to get it looking presentable," Roteg replied, sorting through the boxes of merchandise. "The effort shows. I think we are gonna keep quite busy with this little enterprise."

Tays ceremoniously flipped the sign to open. Part of him expected a crowd of people to flock inside, but he knew that wasn't reasonable. He tried to keep himself busy—tinkering at his worktable at the far end of the shop. Although there was plenty of stock available, he hoped that soon wouldn't be the case. Besides, he had been told that working on various odds and ends while browsers shopped was a good marketing scheme; he could explain what he was doing to shoppers, increasing his reputation as a mechanic.

Roteg came over to see what he was up to. Tays showed him a few simple techniques about wiring power cells to hardware—nothing too complicated. Since it was all they had to do with the shop being empty of customers, they soon became engrossed with their work.

When the doors suddenly swung open, they both started, dropping their gadgets. Two women stepped through the doors. By the looks of them, they were sisters—both with light blonde hair and alluring blue eyes. They were covered in grime, but the boys barely noticed;

they stood captivated by the frightened gazes of the women.

Finally, Roteg got up the nerve to introduce himself and Tays. The strangers bowed while conspicuously putting their right hands behind their backs. The eldest told them their names: Vian and Exada.

"We don't mean to intrude," Vian apologized, moving away from the wide windows. "But we needed a place to lie low for awhile."

"Of course," Roteg replied with an enthusiastic smile. "Stay as long as you wish. Would you like to wash up?" He rushed to the back room and returned with some damp hot cloths and dry towels.

Vian and Exada wrapped the towels around their shivering bodies. They then wiped their faces using only their left hands. They thanked Roteg and returned the cloths.

"Is there something wrong with your right hands," Tays asked.

"No, they're fine," Exada said in a low, shaky voice.

"Please, you have no need to be ashamed of your Clan; you don't have to hide your Signatures. It doesn't matter what Clan you are from. We won't kick you out or anything."

Exada shared a look with her sister before asking, "Do you promise?"

"Yes. I promise I won't force you out of my shop."

After a moment, Vian slowly showed her arm. Red ink marked her right wrist, identifying her as a Crimson. Exada revealed her Signature, too. The ink was the same color, but it was arranged in a different pattern of dots and dashes.

"We saw the blue sign out front. We almost went somewhere else. But we didn't have a choice. I know that Azures and Crimsons don't usually get along," Vian rambled, sniffing back tears. She clamped her eyes shut shivered under the towel. After taking a calming breath, she added, "I was worried you might get upset."

"We're not going to let that stupid feud keep us from being hospitable," Roteg assured her with a charming smile.

In fairness, Roteg and Tays held out their hands as well.

Exada looked at Tays's Signature carefully, noticing the second row of glowing blue ink. "Oh, you're a Rye?"

"Yeah, against my will," Tays chuckled as Exada fingered his Signature. "If it were up to me, I'd be some regular, working-class Regioner like my friend, Roteg, over there. This shop is my attempt to be someone other than *Lord Tays Rye*."

Roteg had taken Vian down the aisles of spare parts and miscellaneous electronics. They spoke in quiet but animated voices, taking turns giving embarrassed smiles as the other talked.

"Isn't Lady Rikani the Azure Leader?" Exada asked, casually perusing a counter of restored antiques. "I thought only Leaders and Heirs have the two rows of ink. You aren't an Heir, are you?"

"No. Lady Rikani is my sister," Tays said, fidgeting with a pile of broken OMNI's. He eased the back covers off the communication devices in preparation of wiping their memory banks. "The Azures have a different law about Leadership. Anyone with Rye blood is able to be involved with running the Clan—as long as they are over sixteen."

"Hey, Tays," Roteg interrupted. "Can I speak to you for a second?" He inclined his head to the far corner of the shop.

"Yeah. Give me a sec." Tays turned to Exada. "I'll be right back. Feel free to browse through the store." He walked over to Roteg, giving Vian a polite smile as he passed her. "What is it?"

"I've been talking with Vian about their position. It seems they're trying to get away from their abusive father."

"*Abusive*? What kind of abuse?"

Roteg rubbed his forehead—the way he did when he was agitated. "I don't know for sure. It could be physical, emotional, or both. It doesn't matter what *kind* of abuse. They need a place to stay for awhile."

"You want me to ask Rikani if we can bring them home?"

"Yeah. We can't let those beautiful damsels go back to their father." Roteg's eyes constantly moved towards Vian.

"We can't officially make them Azures; they still have the red Signatures," Tays sighed. "I doubt Romisa will authorize the Signature removal for girls that ran away from home. She almost never lets her Crimsons leave."

"But they can still live at HQ. Having different ink never stopped Rutab; he still has his violet Tyrian Signature."

"Alright," Tays consented, pulling his OMNI from his pocket. "I'll go call Kani—so long as the girls *would like* to come home with us; I'd rather not be accused of kidnapping a pair of pretty ladies."

Roteg strode over to where the girls stood. "How would you two like to come live with the Azures?"

"Oh, Roteg!" Vian gasped. She held her hand to her lips as tears began rolling down her blushing cheeks. "We couldn't ask you to take us in. If our father ever found out, the hostility between our Clans would never end."

"Well, then we'll have to make sure he never finds out where you are."

*****

"You have a visitor." Roteg nodded at a muscular, red-headed man that had entered the shop.

Tays didn't know whether to be delighted or angry at the sight of the man. "Jux?"

"Hey, sorry to burst in on you like this, but we need to talk." The normally good-natured man looked nervous.

"If this is about supporting your Gang—"

"No, I'm not here about that." Jux took a few steps closer to him. "It's about your little Agency friends that are coming by today. Lazr is very concerned."

"Oh, I bet he is," Tays growled, clenching his fists.

"Listen to me!" the Gangster urged. "You have no idea what you are getting into. Lazr isn't the kind of man to ignore people who support the Agency."

"I know very well what kind of man he is," Tays snapped, unable to control the rage he felt for the LERJ Boss. "You can crawl back to him and tell him that I'm not interested in what he has to say."

"You can tell it to his face."

Tays nearly fell over. "He's coming *here*? I thought I made it clear I didn't want any of you anywhere near my shop. I'm barely tolerating *your* presence."

Jux's expression turned smug. "Yeah. Cuz without me, this little place wouldn't be here."

"I'm aware of that," Tays replied as calmly as he could manage. "Just go tell your Boss I got your message."

"There's no need." Lazr leaned casually in the doorway of The Sapphire Pawn. His two other lackeys stood on either side of him. "I've already heard your answer. However, I'd appreciate it if you'd reconsider."

"Lazr, if any of your men mess up my shop, I swear I'll—"

"You'll *wha*t?" the Gang boss laughed. "You can't do anything to me."

Tays reached under his work bench and pulled out a handgun. Essin and Relyq moved in front of Lazr. They pulled out their own firearms, prepared to take Tays out the second his hand flinched towards the trigger.

"Careful, Tays. Those things are illegal," Lazr warned.

"Not in the Market."

"Once the Agency regains its hold down here, they'll be banned everywhere."

Tays cocked his gun. "If that's your excuse to keep me from partnering with the Agency, you need to work on your persuasion skills."

"My point is that this little thing called *freedom* will be permanently squashed," the LERJ boss explained. "You see, down here we have the liberty to do as we please. There aren't any Enforcers lurking around, suppressing the wills and urges of the masses. Once you start trying to get back in favor with the government, they'll swarm through every hole—every hallway—suffocating us, squeezing us dry until we become completely complacent to their will."

"That's a very cynical point of view." Tays lowered his weapon, but he kept it in front of him in case he needed to use it. "I don't care for your little conspiracy theory."

Lazr's calm demeanor waivered. "It's not a *theory*; it's a *fact*!"

"I don't know what they did to you to make you so upset. I've had nothing but *friendly* dealings with them. I need to do what's right for my Clan."

"You're making a mistake, Rye." Lazr called to his men as he left the store.

Jux gave Tays a pleading look just before he followed after the Boss.

After the men had left, Zett tentatively asked, "Who were those men?"

"They're the LERJ Gang," Roteg said with disgust.

As his employees conversed about their visitors, Tays returned his handgun to its hiding place under the table. He'd have to find a new place for the firearm now that Lazr and his lackeys knew where he kept it.

"I just met *Gangsters*? Cool!"

Roteg narrowed his eyes at Zett. "You shouldn't be so excited, kid."

"Why are they called LERJ?"

"It stands for the members' names: Lazr, Essin, Relyq, and Jux. They all used to be Agents until something happened to them." Roteg seemed to anticipate what Tays had been thinking since he reached under the table and retrieved the gun. "Tays, I'm gonna go put this in the *other* hiding spot." He disappeared into the back room.

"What made the LERJ guys go from working for the government to hating it?" Zett asked, mimicking how the Gangsters quickly upholstered their firearms.

"No one knows. Jux almost told me once, though," Tays replied with a shrug.

"How do you know him?"

"He was my tutor. If it weren't for Jux, I wouldn't have this shop."

"So he taught you all the mechanical stuff you use to repair and create things? I always thought it came to you *naturall*y."

"Some of it does," Tays shrugged. "But you can't do what I do without some of it being shown to you."

"Alright, squirt," Roteg said. "That's enough prodding for information. Go and get some refreshments for our guests. They should be arriving shortly. Kagome has some stuff set aside in her chocolaterie across the way; so do the Trips. Oh, and bring us some sandwiches from that tasty café run by that Icterine fellow. I'm starving."

Looking disappointed at the idea of being left out of a conversation, Zett grabbed some money from the cash register and left the shop.

Roteg cleared a space on the counter for Zett to place the treats when he returned. “So you still haven’t filled me in on what’s happening this afternoon. What does the Agency hope to gain by this little arrangement?”

“Tobias Vega is running against Jay Cromford for Mayor,” Tays explained, flipping the “OPEN” sign to “CLOSED.” The Azure Lord moved to lock the door to keep shoppers from entering. “Agent Vega hopes to show the voters that he’s interested in rehabilitating the Lower Region. He will do that by sending his sons and their friends down here to promote economical relations.”

“And we’re gonna show them that we’re a safe bet for their money?”

“It’s a little more complicated than that, but yes.”

Chapter 25

Iris tried to look enthusiastic as she and Claire walked to the rendezvous point for the Field Trip. She wore her twin long knives at her side, hoping she wouldn't have to use them on the excursion to the Market between the Middle Zone and Lower Region. The soft banging of the sheathed blades against her quads felt reassuring.

As usual, Claire was having a one-sided conversation about everything she had heard concerning the Market. "Max said there was a chocolate factory place near the pawn shop we're going to. I miss sweets; I still can't believe Societans dislike chocolate." She lowered her voice as they passed by a group of Instructors. "I haven't had any in years—since I moved to Upper Society. I hope we get to have some."

They turned a corner and then stepped into a supply room. Rows of weapons and clean uniforms covered the walls. Locked cabinets lined the far side of the room.

"Are you ready for the best day ever?" Eve Sanders strode in

She was followed by her cousins, Viola and Beatrice. The Cromfords seemed just as excited as their outing.

"Of course!" Claire exclaimed, letting the manic side of her personality take over. "I can't wait to see what's at the pawn shop! I've always been under the impression that Regioners were uneducated Neanderthals. But since the shop owner has gained quite a reputation for quality products, I guess not everyone is like that."

"Claire, that's unkind," Beatrice scolded. "They don't have the same advantages as we do. The Regioners deserve our pity, not our scorn."

"I doubt they want *pity*, Bea," Viola reasoned while fussing with her appearance.

"Is anyone else coming—other than us and the Vegas?" Eve asked, twirling one of her short, red curls.

"Nope, just us." Maximus walked into the room along with his brother.

"Alastair!" Eve ran forward and flung her arms around his neck. "It feels like I haven't seen you in forever!"

"It's good to see you." Al patted her gently on the back before peeling her arms off him.

Eve spoke excitedly at Alastair. "Why are we bringing weapons with us to the Market? Is it unsafe there? I've heard that Regioners can be hostile."

"Don't worry, Eve." Alastair gestured at the supply room. "The weapons are just a precaution; Max and I met up with some Gangsters the last time we were down there. So we thought we should be prepared."

The unarmed women browsed through the weapons, picking up what looked interesting, testing the weight or how well they swung.

"Alastair, the swords are all too heavy," Eve complained. "Is there anything lighter?"

"You might like knives. They're easier to swing."

"Here." Iris handed Eve a pair of blades a few inches shorter than her own.

Eve took them with a nod of gratitude and strapped on the sheath belt. "Will you show me how to use them, Al?"

Alastair shook his head. "I don't think we have enough time for a lesson. Anyways, they'll be on your hip only to prevent people from attacking you. Since you're inexperienced with them, it's more likely they will be taken and used against you--on the unlikelihood that we'll actually encounter trouble."

"I'm not *that* helpless, Alastair. I know how to use my fists. I took a month-long self-defense class before Placement Testing," Eve bragged, holding up her hands.

"And I've learned a lot of fighting basics in Agent Thomas's Sparring class.

Across the room, Claire clipped a belt full of throwing knives around her waist.

Iris checked to make sure the short blades were sharp; she didn't want her best friend trying to defend herself with blunt blades.

Max casually walked over, stepping between the women. "Pssst. Iris," he said in a low tone without looking at her. He examined a row of weapons as he whispered, "Alastair wants to speak with you privately. Claire has agreed to help separate him from *Miss Clingy* so that you two can chat. Hang behind the group on the way to the Elevators and Al will take care of the rest." In a louder voice, Max shouted over to Viola. "I think you might like these axes, darling." He removed a pair of them from the shelf and sprinted over to where Viola stood admiring a bulky mace.

"Aw, thanks, Sweetie!" Viola glanced down at his belt. "Shouldn't you bring a weapon?"

"Don't need one; these hands are lethal weapons by themselves." Max held up his arms and flexed his muscles.

Viola looked up at her giant boyfriend. In a timid voice, she said, "I'd feel a lot safer in Market if you had some steel to hack at any dangerous Regioners, Maximus." When Max gave in, she gave him an intimate kiss.

"Do you lovebirds have to do that *here*?" Beatrice grumbled, grabbing a pair of night sticks. "We're on an official mission for the Agency Board. Try to keep this professional."

"How long have Viola and Max been dating?" Claire whispered to Iris.

"Apparently they've liked each other for the past few of years. But Max finally got up the courage to ask her out last week." Iris was happy to see that the couple had decided to go public with their relationship.

Alastair raised a hand to get the attention of the group. "Now that everyone is equipped, let's head to Market."

Max led the way to the Transition Station. Viola and Beatrice walked alongside him. The ladies had a million questions about what Market was like, many of which had to do with the rumors about the purposes of the Regioner's ink Signatures.

Despite the animosity between them, Claire kept Eve company. Miss Sanders glanced eagerly at Alastair, who remained a distance from the other women. Every time the red head came up to him, he pulled out his OMNI and sent messages of "the upmost importance." Eventually, she got the hint and cheerily chatted with Miss Birch.

Iris walked by herself most of the way to Transit Station, pulling up the rear of the group like Max told her to. She wondered what Alastair wanted to talk to her about. Was he going to scold her again about beating his records? She couldn't help it if she was better than him in some respects. Having been raised by tutors in her private study, she had never been able to judge her own abilities against other people. She had no idea what kind of skills her peers possessed, so she tried her best at everything she did.

When they reached the Down Elevators, Max called all the girls—except Iris—into his Pod. The Elevators beeped, signaling the next Transition. Eve almost jumped out of the Pod at the last moment, but the doors closed on her. Iris was left taking another Pod alone with Alastair.

The Transition occurred and Alastair motioned for Iris to go inside the next Pod.

She nodded in thanks and entered the compartment. She tried to engage him in conversation to see if he was still upset with her.

"So, what was it like missing weeks of Training?"

"It was very boring and tedious," he replied. "But it couldn't be helped. I had some important plans to make for this trip. No one really understands the true significance of regaining trust from the Regioners."

Not entirely content with the response, Iris commented, "Yes. It must be extremely important since the Agency was willing to put a hold on your education."

There was an awkward silence for a couple minutes until the next stop in Transition.

As the Elevator began moving again, Alastair turned to Iris and said in a gentle-but-nervous voice, "Look, I owe you an apology. I shouldn't have been so antagonistic towards you about the whole *record thing*. You beat me and my ego was bruised. But now it's healed. I guess what I'm trying to say is that I want us to be *friends*."

Iris stared at him, trying to figure out the man's angle. Less than a month ago, he acted as though she was his greatest enemy. Today, he wanted to play nice.

She sighed, "Yes, I would like to be your friend, too."

"Great!" Alastair smiled at her for several moments. "Oh! I've been wanting to ask you: What happened at your first Sparring class? I heard something about you trying the new combat armor and defeating some Agent."

"It was sort of weird. Agent Thomas made it sound like some sort of practice thing or demonstration, but Agent Mitchell gave off the vibe that it was more than just a friendly match. He refused to tell me who it was. Well, I went into the session without any preconceptions about my opponent. But he seemed to really know what he was doing." She thought carefully before she added, "I accidentally smashed in his helmet with my fist, which ended the fight. I still don't know who my opponent was. Claire seems to think it was an advanced Dueling Dummy they were testing. But I saw blood on the shattered helmet."

"Yeah, I saw the video. You were great."

The topic of conversation began to confuse her. "Max made it sound like there was something very important we needed to discuss."

"No, I was just trying to ease into conversation with you. It was mostly the whole *friend* thing that I wanted to bring up. We haven't really been alone together; it's been hard to really get to know you."

"Friend-making isn't one of my talents," Iris admitted, shifting in her seat as she adverted her eyes.

"You and Claire seem to get along pretty well, so it *is* possible for you to make friends."

"I guess you're right," she sighed, shaking her head. Iris looked up and met Alastair's intent gaze. "I need to make more of an effort with everyone—especially Eve. She seems to despise me; I'm not sure why."

"Eve can be *difficult*," Alastair consented, shaking his head. "You should keep trying with her. She'll come around."

Iris nodded, resolving to make Miss Sanders her new friend.

"Look at us. When we met at the Agency, you looked as though I was the last person you would ever want as a Mentor. And I held a grudge against you because you bested me. Now, here we are—having a very civil conversation." Alastair paused as his face fell. "I just reminded myself of something. I never asked your pardon for what happened to you five years ago." The look in his eyes seemed genuine as he added, "I'm truly sorry that you got hurt."

"I forgive you for that, also. As long as we are apologizing, I'm sorry for my attitude towards you, too."

"Apology accepted." Al placed a comforting hand on her shoulder.

For the next half hour, Iris and Alastair exchanged information about themselves. Nothing too personal was said—just basic interests and ideologies. The more they talked, the more comfortable Iris was around him. All the unpleasantness from their previous encounters was forgotten.

When they reached the bottom of Upper Society's Sectors, they stepped out of the Elevator. The rest of the group was waiting for them.

Eve ran up to Alastair and immediately engaged him in conversation. Claire and Beatrice simultaneously rolled their eyes with a sigh. Max and Viola began descending the steps of Transit Station, motioning for everyone to follow.

Iris was surprised at how clean the Plaza looked compared to the Sectors of Middle Zone. It was by no means immaculate, but it was fairly hygienic. Cleanly dressed men and women in colorful garb burst in and out of buildings. Except for the lack of extravagance and luxury, Iris felt like she could have been an Upper Society Plaza.

As they walked, they tried to ignore the gawking expressions of the Regioners and Zonese. They put on serious faces, ignoring the urge to stare at the glowing ink on the wrists of the bystanders.

The group stopped in front of a medium-sized building. They were immediately greeted by a young man wearing a navy blue apron.

The man spoke with flourish, exaggerating words in an attempt to appear fancy. “Welcome, Societans, to our humble establishment. Will you please come inside?” He held the door open for everyone. As soon as they were all inside, he resumed his introduction. “My name is Zett. If there is anything you need, please let me know. Feel free to browse the shop while I let the Lord Rye know that you are here.” He disappeared into a room at the back. A second later, he stuck his head back out to add, “There are refreshments on the counter. Please, help yourself.” With that, he was gone again.

“What a fascinating shop!” Claire rushed forward and started picking through bins of miscellaneous electronics.

“Yeah, I thought that you in particular would like it,” Alastair chuckled.

Everyone else went to the counter to see what sort of “refreshments” had been prepared for them. The Trainees were excited to see an assortment of chocolate treats on a tray. They ignored the fruits and vegetables, munching instead on the cocoa-dipped pretzels, caramels, and nougat.

"Iris," Claire called out from across the store, seemingly forgetting her earlier craving for sweets. "You have to stop me before I buy out the entire shop. I'm holding you responsible for keeping my spending in check."

"Of course." Iris flourished her hands at Claire. "I hereby limit you to ten items."

"Thank you." Claire placed a heap of items next to the register and turned to Alastair. "When can we come back, Al?"

"I'm glad to see some enthusiasm." A man appeared from the back room, followed by Zett and another associate. "It's rare to meet another person with a passion for mechanics."

Iris found the man to be quite handsome for a Regioner. His slightly tussled black hair swept across his forehead, almost covering his brown eyes—which had a hint of green. She leaned forward to get a better view of his lean, muscular build. He wore a denim blue sweater with rolled up sleeves and a pair of grey slacks. Faint freckles dotted pale cheeks. His smile was friendly and charming; his demeanor was open and sweet. Iris blushed when she noticed his gaze resting on her. Normally, she was attracted to more than just good looks, but she couldn't help feeling drawn to this young man.

"My name is Tays Rye, and this is my shop: The Sapphire Pawn. You already met my clerk, Zett. The other man behind me is my sales associate, Roteg."

Mr. Rye led them on a tour of the shop, letting them examine the quality of his products. Everyone looked to Claire for her expertise with such things, and she expressed her satisfaction that everything was of above-average quality.

This pleased the shop owner. He then began his sales pitch. "I know all of you have heard rumors about Regioners—that we are unintelligent, apathetic, lazy, immoral beings. Those rumors are both true and incorrect. Down here, most don't have the luxuries of a decent education or a socially productive upbringing. The purpose of our meeting today is to show that there is hope of recovering the Lower Region. My Clan—the Azures—have been steadily increasing productivity. More and more shops in the Market Sectors are owned by Regioners, trying to turn their hard work into profit in order to survive the hardships of this life.

"I'm not here to convince you to give us money," the shop owner continued. "That would be counter-productive. I'm asking that the Agency take a more active role in the Region's economy. We can supply you with products of good quality for much less money than those produced in Upper Society. Help us rebuild civilization in the decaying bottom of this Megacity. Undo the mistakes of the generations before you. Work with us and we will ensure Rygom's bright future."

Iris scanned the faces of her group to see if everyone else was as inspired as she was. To her disappointment, most of the Trainees seemed to be barely listening.

Only Alastair appeared to be interested in what the shop owner had to say. "It's refreshing to see such passion in a place where so many have given up hope," Al replied at the end of Mr. Rye's speech. "We look forward to welcoming the Region back into the prosperous jurisdiction of the Agency."

Something about Alastair's response made the shop owner's face twinge, but the expression was gone almost as quickly as it appeared. He thanked Vega for the encouragement with a modest—and yet somewhat disturbed—smile.

Chapter 26

The Field Trip to Market couldn't be going any better for Eve. She had been reunited with the love of her life, Alastair Vega, and was getting to spend the whole day with him.

To top it off, her former rival started to fall for another man. Eve saw how Iris watched the cute shop owner; Miss Kayn's cheek turned pink when their eyes met and she fidgeted with her OMNI.

Eve thought it was adorable, so she decided that she would encourage the relationship—even though it was doomed to fail. Iris Kayn was a Societan. Tays Rye was a Regioner. The match would never succeed, but that wouldn't stop Eve. She would keep that woman away from her man at all costs.

After Mr. Rye's speech, there was silence as the group of Trainees processed what had been said. The only thing Eve could think about was how to bring Iris and Tays together. Although she had never been much of a match-maker, plots and schemes filled her head.

In an attempt to generate more conversation, Eve stepped forward and said to the shop owner, "You speak as though you have plans for clearing everything *nasty* from the Lower Region. What do you have planned for those sick with the Plague?"

Nothing pulled at women's heart-strings more than a man that cared for others. Well, women like Iris.

"I'm sorry to say that I have no immediate plan for helping the Plague-stricken," Tays admitted. "But isn't there is a scientist in Upper Society that is working on finding cures for all the different Plagues. Once the economy down here becomes more stable, we could set up a foundation to help fund his research."

Eve peeked at Iris from the corner of her eye to see if her plan had worked. Miss Kayn's smile grew even broader during the response—if that were even possible.

"Are there any more questions?" Tays asked. When no one else spoke up, he added, "Okay, please explore Market at your leisure. But I recommend you travel in at least pairs. And, of course, you are welcome to continue perusing my shop."

Claire instantly ran up to the shop owner, a gadget in her hand, and began asking questions. Tays motioned for his clerk to come answer her inquiries so that he could go over more business with Alastair.

Miss Birch talked animatedly at Zett, but the poor guy seemed to be rather confused by everything that came out of her mouth; he was clearly a new employee.

Max said something about wanting more of the "chocolaty goodness" and Roteg agreed to take him to a chocolaterie across the street. Viola was eager to accompany her boyfriend. She wrapped her arm around Max's waist, getting as close to him as she could as they exited the pawn shop.

In the far corner, Beatrice busied herself by reading some magazine called "The New Blue View." Eve tried to pry her cousin away from the periodical, but her efforts were unsuccessful.

Iris stood by the display window, glancing through a collection of vintage electronics. She occasionally stared in the direction of Alastair and Tays.

Eve hoped that her competitor was staring at the Regioner and not at Al. Casually, she strode towards Iris Kayn, a broad smirk on her face. "So, what do you think of the handsome shop owner?"

"He seems very passionate about what he's doing," Iris replied very professionally.

"You should go talk to him some more about his plans for cleaning up the Region. I'm going to go do some window shopping." Eve turned to Alastair and said, "Al, I'm going to go look at the boutique up the street. Would you like to come with me?"

"I'm sorry, Eve," Alastair replied, "but I have some important business to take care of—contracts and such."

"I'll go with you," Iris offered forcibly. "Claire keeps telling me I need new clothes."

"That's a *great* idea!" Alastair spoke with a degree enthusiasm that greatly bothered Eve.

"Alright," she conceded, nodding at the door. "Come on."

Eve led Iris out of the shop and the two ladies ventured to the boutique.

"I've always admired your sense of fashion," Iris admitted. "Would it be okay if I ask for your advice on clothing?"

"Sure, whatever I can do to help you improve your look. Is there any one in particular you want to look good for? Maybe a certain *shop owner*?"

"Oh, don't be ridiculous!" Iris scoffed, peering through the window of a nearby art gallery. "Besides, he'll only ever see me in my Agency uniform since we aren't allowed to wear our casual clothes on official business."

"Yes, but you could always come back here on your time off. It isn't that far—only about half an hour. He certainly can't come up to see you; his ink Signature keeps him confined to the Market levels and below." Eve moved closer and linked arms with Iris. "Have you never heard of the love trysts that happen between Societans and Regioners? They occur *all* the time. They meet, fall in love, and have secret gatherings in the secluded areas of Market."

"Okay, now you're just being silly," Iris laughed.

"No, I'm *not*."

*****

Ten-year old Evelyn Sanders ran ahead of her mother, anxious to see the beautiful items in the window ahead. It was her first time visiting the shops at Market. Some interesting characters walked about the streets, but Eve ignored them.

Claudia Sanders caught up to her. "Evie, what do you think of that purple gown on the mannequin? Do you think it's my size?"

They dashed inside and asked the clerk for the dress. Mrs. Sanders held it up to her body.

"Perfect, Mum. Papa will *die* when he sees you in it. Go try it on!"

"Okay." Claudia pointed at a shoe rack on the far wall. "See if you can find some heels to go it."

Browsing through the shelves of shoes turned out to be quite a hunt. Many looked like they would go with the dress, but they weren't the right size. When she eventually found a decent pair of grey wedges, a giggling noise caught her attention.

She followed the sound to the far end of the shop.

There was a man and a woman whispering loudly between bouts of laughter. Something about the man's voice sounded familiar. She looked to see if the store clerk was watching and then slipped into the back room.

Eve froze where she stood, dropping the shoes to the floor.

Byron Sanders sat on an over-stuffed chair with a strange woman sitting across his lap. His hands wrapped around her waist while her lips attacked his neck with kisses. Her fingers rubbed up and down his half-exposed chest.

"Papa?" Eve asked, hoping her eyes were deceiving her.

"Evie, um, this is an old friend of mine." He stood, put the woman down, and moved toward his daughter. "We were just getting…*reacquainted*." Peeking his head through the open doorway, he asked, "Is your mother here?"

Eve just nodded, tears threatening to roll down her cheeks.

"Look, Pumpkin," he sighed, "Mummy doesn't get along with my friend. I don't think she should know that I'm here with Omoni." He fished a credit-disc from his wallet. "Take this and promise me you'll go back to Mum and keep quiet. Okay?" He gave her a kiss on the forehead as he placed the disc into her hand. "I'll see you tonight, Evie."

Without another word, he gently pushed at her shoulder until she was out of the room. He slammed the door in her face.

*****

Eve shook her head to clear the awful memory from her mind. She looked up to see the front of a clothing boutique. It wasn't the same one as her memory, so she was comfortable going in. Hiding behind a large smile, she pulled a red skirt from a rack. "I think this will look cute on you." Eve put the hanger in Iris's hand.

Iris's face scrunched up as she examined the skirt. "I've never looked really good in red. I prefer cooler tones."

"Remember: you said you trusted my fashion expertise. Oh, and how about this white blouse?" Eve spent the next several minutes picking out items for Iris to try on while also shopping for herself.

By the time they went to the fitting rooms, they each had an armful of fabric between their hands. Vests of velvet, sequin belts, flared jeans, and other articles of clothing were tried on. Eve worked her powers of persuasion on Iris, convincing her to buy things she herself vowed never to own.

"Are you sure the polyester looks okay?" Iris asked as she spun in front of a mirror.

"You look *fabulous*," Eve assured her. "Wear that tank top with those leggings next time you go to The Grey Circumstance. Vintage is on its way back to the top of clothing design. Now, try on these earrings with those black leather pants and pink lace chemise."

"I *do* like leather and lace," Iris admitted as she went back into a fitting room. When she came back out, Miss Kayn said, "I'm really glad we had this opportunity to bond, Eve. I'm having a lot of fun." She flipped through half of another rack before asking, "May I ask you a question?"

"You just did. But, yes, you may ask me another."

"Very funny. Well, I was wondering, um—you like, Alastair, right?"

"*Of course* I like Alastair!" Eve admitted, throwing her hands in the air. "I thought that was obvious."

"That's why you've been snide?" Iris asked. "You thought *I* wanted him?"

"I wasn't sure if you wanted him or not. But part of me sensed he liked you."

"Let me tell you once and for all: I'm his friend and that's it. I know I'm not exactly the best person to be giving advice. However, I suggest that you turn it down a notch. Back off a little bit and maybe he'll start to miss you."

"Thanks. I'll think about it," Eve replied curtly.

"Look, I really want you and me to get along," Iris sighed, sounding even more serious than usual. "Apparently, I'm not very good at friend-making, but I'm trying. We're going to spend the next three years Training together. Odds are, we'll also have to work together once we're Agents. I just want everything to be out in the open between us."

"You're right," Eve admitted, throwing her hands up in exasperation. "I need to stop being so *needy*. From now on, I'll let him approach me if he wants to talk." She paused before adding, "As long as we are giving character instruction, can I offer something in return?"

"I welcome any counsel that helps me better understand social conventions."

"In that case, I think you should spend less time Training during free hours and more time with people. You're showing everyone up."

"You sound just like Claire," Iris groaned, putting back a see-through shrug.

"Good. Maybe now you'll listen to the advice," Eve chided. "You're already superior to everyone—except Alastair. There's nothing else you have to prove to the Agency. Go to scheduled sessions and do your homework, but do nothing *extra*. Like you said, we have three years of Training ahead. If you burn the candle at both ends, you'll exhaust yourself before graduation."

"Sorry. I didn't mean to appear superior. I grew up sort of secluded and I have been trying to prove that I belong at the Agency. I guess I could cut back on my exercise routine."

It felt odd for Eve to be talking so freely with a woman whom she had vowed to hate for eternity only that morning. But it felt nice to gain her as friend; she knew now that Iris would no longer come between her and Alastair.

Eve's OMNI beeped loudly.

She shifted her armful of clothes around so that she could reach for her device.

It was a message from her mother: *I'm going to transfer some more credits to your OMNI in case you want to buy anything on your Field Trip.*

A moment later, her father called, sounding agitated. "*Why is your mother telling me that need more money? We just sent some last week. What could you possibly have needed to buy? Did you waste all of it already?*"

"No, I still have plenty from last week," Eve replied calmly.

Claudia Sanders' voice could be heard in the background. "*Evie needs to look her best, which requires a hefty bank account! I'm sending—No! Let me go, Byron!*"

There was the sound of a struggle before Mr. Sanders sighed, "*Pumpkin, could you try* not *to bankrupt me during your Training? Both your grandfathers worked really hard to build our fortune and I'd like to enjoy it awhile longer.*"

"Stop fighting. I don't need it," Eve said before hanging up.

A moment later, there was a beep on her OMNI. She looked at the screen to see that her mother had transferred credits anyways.

The call from her parents upset her more than usual. Shopping suddenly felt strangely unfulfilling. An odd sensation took the place of her desire to browse through endless racks of clothing.

"I'll pay for your stuff," Eve said to Iris. "But then you've gotta come with me." She set their purchases on the counter, impatient to leave and address the distress that plagued her.

Chapter 27

Klev and Lom had become kidnappers. Not in the sense of being mercenary-like—even though they had done that sort of thing before—but in the way that they were helping grab a dangerous threat to the Megacity. Klev hated the term "kidnappers;" he said it sounded as though they are grabbing a child in exchange for ransom. Instead, Klev labeled himself and Lom "nabbers."

They sat atop a tall building in Market. Below, Zonese and Regioners intermingled in a bustling, moving mass between the shops.

Lom pulled out a notebook. "Should we call in our status to Master Pavoc?"

"No." Klev dug through his bulky bag of spy equipment that had been provided by their latest patrons, the Crimson Clan. He pulled out a pair of binoculars and began scanning the streets below. "Master said he didn't want to be reached unless it was an emergency. We'll create a status log. Write down what I say:

"Our mission," Klev dictated to his partner, "is to collect a young woman from the Market between Middle Zone and Lower Region. The target is suspected of being a dangerous, illegal experiment known as an Alteration.

Recently-appointed nabbers Klev and Lom were given orders by Master Pavoc of the Crimson Steels, brother-in-law and steward to most radiant Queen Romisa—"

"Is all that necessary, Klev?" Lom interrupted, looking up from his notebook. "Master Pavoc knows all this—especially who he is."

"Oh, Lom, you have much to learn about pleasing your employers. Trust me, this is *completely* necessary." Klev cleared his throat before continuing his dictation. "Nabbers Klev and Lom ran surveillance of the pawn shop, owned by the Azure Clan. The Agent youngsters in question stood inside for many minutes, discussing no doubt some very important business. A small group of them left the shop and ventured to a chocolaterie down the street." He paused a moment, looking at his colleague before adding, "Okay, you can stop writing now, Lom. Look and tell me what you see."

Lom put down his pen and notepad. He took up a pair of binoculars and peered down into the street. "Tell me again, Klev. What am I looking for?"

"Agents! How many times must I tell you, Lom? Look for people in black or grey uniforms."

After several moments of searching the streets below, Lom said, "Okay, I see three people—two are wearing grey uniforms, and the other has all blue clothing. Do ya think our target might be one of the greys?" He handed over the binoculars.

"Yes, she very well could be," Klev whispered. "Read back to me what Master Pavoc told us."

Lom flipped back through the pages of his previous entries. He scratched at his temple as he read the paper. "We're looking for a 'pretty woman in a light grey Agency uniform, approximately eighteen years old.' My notes also say that she'll be wearing a pair of long knives on her hip."

"Do we have a picture of the young woman?"

"No. I think Master Pavoc showed us a photo of the whole group of Agents that were coming down here. He pointed at the girl, but I don't remember what she looks like."

Klev zoomed in with his binoculars. He carefully examined the weapons at each person's sides. "None of these have two long knives. The man has a sword, but it's too long to be a knife. And he only has one. And he is the wrong gender."

"Partner, it's astonishing to watch your mind work!" Lom exclaimed.

"It's best if we continue our status log." Klev stepped away from the ledge. He turned his attention back to the group at the chocolaterie and watched them relocate to a café down the street. Resuming his dictation, he said, "After close inspection, we've deduced that the Agents at the café don't possess the proper weapons either. Nabbers Klev and Lom will return to scene of origin in hopes of ruling out more suspects."

They descended a rickety ladder to the Market streets and made their way up the avenue. All the while, they peaked in each store to make sure that none of the Agents slipped past them.

Eventually, they made it back to the shop and discovered that two more Agents youngsters were missing. Only three Agents remained: a man in dark grey and two women in light grey.

Klev and Lom were fairly anxious about once again dealing with the Agency. They had a long history with them in the past, but most of their years of service were nothing but wisps memory in their consciousness. Their very first encounter with the government was eerily vivid in their minds, despite the thirty years that had passed.

*****

Twenty-five-year-old Lom sat at his mirror, touching up his old man make-up; the dark lines on his face were smeared by the sweat dripping down his face. His next scene was fast-approaching. He loved acting, but he sometimes wished the stage lights weren't so darn hot. Lom was tempted to wipe his face clean and start fresh, but he didn't have the time for that.

Klev was on the stage, performing the beginning of the last act of the play *Pygmalion*. He angrily strutted up and down the stage, irritated at the disappearance Eliza Doolittle. It was Klev's favorite play to perform.

He would often drag Lom from Sector to Sector, in search of another Zonese troupe performing it. Klev would audition and automatically get the role without getting a call-back. Directors loved him, and they would give him whatever he needed—even casting Lom as Colonel Pickering in each and every theatre he went to.

Lom put the last touches on his smudged face and then quickly strode onto the stage at his cue. Having played Pickering twenty-six times, his lines were second-nature to him. He glided through the scene with Klev, hoping that the other actors could keep up with them.

At the end of the show, Lom grabbed Klev and congratulated him on yet another great performance.

"No congratulations are necessary, Lom. I don't do this for the entertainment; I do it for the pure love of the theatre." Klev waved over a group of audience members, who clutched at their programs.

Lom knew people only wanted Klev's autograph, but his friend refused to sign any scrap of paper unless Lom signed his name as well. That way, when they thought of one man from the pair, they thought of the other. Klev and Lom were quickly becoming a most famous duo in the Market Sectors.

Of course, Klev and Lom weren't their real names; they had decent Upper Society names, but they were irrelevant in the Region. It had been almost ten years since they left their stuffy, obnoxious parents that wanted them to be doctors, or lawyers, or politicians. They left home at sixteen, ran away to the freedom of Market. The boys took on Regioner names and pursued their dream of acting.

Klev and Lom sat in the theatre lobby and signed program after program for over an hour. By the time most of the crowd had disappeared, there remained a small group of men, clad all in black. The men made Lom nervous, but Klev reasoned that they were just there for the show. They had done nothing wrong and they shouldn't worry about any Agents lurking about.

When the Agents approached their autograph table, Klev put on his best smile. "What can we do for you gentlemen this lovely evening?"

A young man in his early twenties stepped forward. "Mister Klev and Mister Lom?"

"Yes," Lom replied, pointing at the sign above them that held their names in large letters. "But please drop the *Misters*."

"My name is Agent Vega." The man stepped forward and handed Klev a contact-disc. "I represent a group of researchers that are particularly interested in people with your type of *talent*. My colleagues and I were wondering if you would oblige us and come meet our benefactors. They have a business proposition for you."

Klev examined the disc warily. "What kind of *business proposition* are you talking about, Vega?"

"They'd like to offer you the role of a life-time."

*****

"Are any of them the person we are looking for?" Lom asked.

Klev had been repeating the woman's description in his head the whole way from the café. He peeked through the binoculars once again at the shop. "Nah! The women don't have the right weapons."

"Are you sure? The women appear to be the right age and they're very pretty."

"Weren't you listening? Those female Agents don't have the pair of long knives. Seriously! A man of your aptitude should have better hearing. Besides, the Agency is full of pretty young women. Now, come on."

"Hey, Klev, do you think maybe we should grab one of the Agents and make them tell us where the knife girl is?"

"No, Lom, we can't," Klev sighed, raising his binoculars once again. "The other Agents are harmless bystanders. We don't want to cause an incident. Remember what happened in Torlea? Do you want to go back to prison?"

Lom shook his head, his eyes wide with a sense of fear. "Prison doesn't appreciate our talents."

"Good, so we'll do the nabbing *my* way." Klev scanned the streets. "She shouldn't be too far; Agents like to stay close together." He stopped and thought really hard for a minute. "Hmmm. If I were a highly dangerous weapon, where would I go?"

"How 'bout clothes shopping?" Lom suggested, looking up from his notebook. "If I were an eighteen year old girl, I would go clothes shopping."

“That’s ridiculous!” Klev snatched the notebook out of Lom’s hands and stuffed it in his jacket pocket. He returned to scanning the streets. “We’re looking for a menace to civilization, not your average teenage girl.”

Lom pointed down a short alley. “But, look, Klev. I see two Agent girls coming out of the boutique over there.”

Klev handed Lom the binoculars. “What can you tell me about those girls?”

“One blonde and one red head. Both are very pretty. They have a bunch of shopping bags in their hands—Oh! Oh, Klev,” Lom groaned, lowering his vision equipment. “I think we have a problem.”

“What? What *kind* of problem?”

“They *both* have two long knives at their sides.”

“Impossible! What are the odds of that happening?” Klev grabbed the binoculars from Lom and took a look. He cursed when Lom’s observation was confirmed.

“What should we do?”

“I think the red head is prettier, so I say we take her,” Klev said with finality.

“Are you sure? The blonde is so much prettier than the other.”

“Lom, I’m never wrong. Therefore, I say we take the red.”

After a moment of thinking, Lom asked, "What if we take them both?"

Klev ignored him. As if suddenly inspired by an idea, he said, "You know, there are *two* of us and *two* of them. I bet we could take them *both*."

"Brilliant!" Lom looked into the alley and the girls were gone. "Where'd they go?"

The nabbers spent the next several minutes looking for the girls in the shops of the surrounding area. They attracted the attention of the nearby Regioners and Zonese. One clerk even kicked them out of their stores for scaring off their customers.

"If they get back to the other Agents, we'll never catch them. Lom, do you know of any other clothing stores in the area?"

Lom pointed east. "There's one a couple block back. It's owned by the Tyrian Clan."

"That's not relevant to the case. Stay focused!"

"Klev, perhaps we should go ask the people in the street which way the girls went. There are plenty of witnesses."

"Wait, maybe someone saw the direction the girls headed," Klev said. "Come on, Lom!"

They made their way to the surface street and asked around about the two Agent girls.

No one would talk to them. Regioners and many Zonese don't like getting involved in Agency business.

Klev and Lom almost gave up hope when a merchant pointed in the direction of the clothes shop Lom had mentioned earlier. The store-owner overheard them talking about "finding some decent accessories for their new wardrobe."

"Why would girls need that many clothes unless they were planning on going on the run?" Klev wondered out loud. "We must hurry and find them before they disappear forever!"

They didn't bother getting back onto the roofs; they were running out of time. Lom led the way to the shop he had mentioned. The duo stopped short, hiding in the side street as they spotted their targets.

"We'll wait for them here." Klev sat down and removed his pack. "They have to come out eventually. When they do, we'll *nab* them. Listen carefully, Lom! I'll take the red head and you take the blonde. You understand?" Klev pointed at Lom's pocket. "Pull out a notepad. I'm gonna dictate an update. Nabbers Klev and Lom tracked the elusive Agent women to a boutique. Both own twin long knives. Due to different points of view about beauty, Nabbers Klev and Lom will take *both* captive when they emerge from their hideout. If anything goes wrong, Nabbers Klev and Lom will resort to extreme and illegal methods in order to complete the job."

With that, Klev removed a gun from his pack and strapped it to his side. He tossed another one to Lom, who looked warily at the firearm.

"Are you sure these are necessary?" Lom asked, filling the gun with ammunition from his pack. "We need her *alive—not dead*. What if we accidentally shoot one of her important organs or something?"

"Have you gone mad, Lom? One of those women has *untold* power. We'll need to use *every precaution* to bring them in. But only use it if the original plan looks like it's gonna fail."

Lom pulled a burlap mask over his face. "You're in charge, Klev!"

Chapter 28

Iris was worried for her new friend. Eve had mumbled something about knowing another clothing boutique and half dragged her down a series of streets and alleys. Once they reached their destination, her fellow Trainee became agitated and unnaturally quiet.

She stepped in front of Eve. "What's going on?"

"I've been here before—about eight years ago." Looking absently at the various racks, Eve walked toward the front of the store. "My mum brought me here to shop for dresses."

"Okay, so why do you look like you had a bad experience?"

"It was stupid coming here," Eve sighed, shaking her head. "We should leave."

She began retracing her steps to the front door when the store's clerk asked, "Can I help you ladies?"

"We were just looking, thanks," Iris replied with a quick smirk.

"I know that voice." Eve turned and her face grew pale. "You worked here when—"

"You are very familiar," the clerk remarked, looking Miss Sanders up and down. "Oh, you came here with your mother and she tried on Lady Omoni's old gown. I never forget a customer."

"Yes, I met *Omoni.*" Eve took an agitated step towards the woman. "She was back there, in that room with my father—smooching and touching him." She pointed animatedly at the back room, scowling at the clerk. "So I have a few words for that seductress if you could please tell me where she is."

"I'm very sorry," the clerk said, wringing her hands together. "Lady Omoni passed away almost a year ago. If there's anything else you need, let me know." The woman disappeared into the back.

"Are you okay?" Iris placed a hand on Eve's shoulder. Although the touch was meant to be comforting, it only seemed to add to her anxiety.

"Eight years I've waited to confront the woman that stole my father's affection from my mother." Eve took a shuddering breath. "Now there's nothing I can do to fix my parents' marriage."

"It isn't yours to fix. Your parents need to solve their own problems."

"It's probably for the best, I suppose. Now that she isn't around, father can move on and love mother again."

Iris felt awkward about the whole business. She had only just gotten on a friendly basis with Miss Sanders and now she was being plunged into all her personal problems. She did her best to console Eve. "Perhaps your father loved both this woman *and* your mother. The heart can feel split and unsure when that happens."

Tears formed in Eve's eyes. "No! You're only supposed to love *one* person. That's how it works. He's married to my mother so he should only love *her*!"

"I think we should leave. This place is upsetting you."

"Wait. I need to find out who that woman was." Eve walked to the counter and said in a very loud voice, "Excuse me!"

The clerk came out slowly, a large smile plastered onto her face. "How can I help you?"

"You said this Omoni chick died. So who owns the shop now?"

"Her daughter, Lady Belana."

Eve threw up her hands with a huff. "What's up with calling everyone *Lady*?"

Iris came up to her and whispered, "I think it has something to do with the Clan Leaders. I skimmed through the next chapter of our history text and it briefly mentioned the complicated oligarchy."

"Lady Belana Lynch, like her mother before her, is the Leader of the Tyrian Clan," the clerk explained, confirming Iris' suspicion.

"Oh, great!" Eve scoffed, her hands forming tight fists. She paced the length of the boutique's front counter. "My father had an affair with Region *royalty*! Where can I find this *Lady* Belana?"

"The Tyrian Clan's HQ is on the other side of the Region, several Sectors Down. But I must warn you." The woman scanned the shop, her eyes resting on each of the other customers before lowering her voice. "Lady Belana has a very bad temper. Be careful what you say to her and how you say it. Now, I must ask you to leave."

"Thank you for your help," Iris said when Eve rudely walked away. "We should head back to the pawn shop."

"No. I want to talk to this *Belana*," Eve insisted, turning the opposite way.

She began to move towards the exit, but Iris stopped her. "Why?"

"My father is a very proud man. He wouldn't be intimate with just anyone. I have a feeling this *Omoni* grew up in Upper Society. I need to know who she was."

"Even if you're right, do you think the daughter would know about her mother's past? I mean, Societans that end up as Regioners usually have dark secrets that they are trying to hide from the world."

"I really hate your logic. Fine. Let's return to the others. Maybe I'll be able to get some answers the next time we come to Market."

They gathered their bags of purchases and headed outside.

Iris had a bad feeling as she stepped onto the street. "Wait, Eve. Something isn't right."

The crowds of people had disappeared during the few minutes they had been inside the boutique. No one was in sight except for two masked men that stood in the street. They were situated in a place that blocked off the way towards the pawn shop.

"Good afternoon," said one of the men. "Could you help me with a little problem?"

Iris set her bags down and stepped in front of Eve. "What do you want?"

"We're looking for someone," he explained, scratching at his burlap mask. "I hope you'll offer us your assistance."

The second moved forward. "We are tracking an Alteration. Have seen one?"

"I'm not sure I would know how to identify an Alteration." Iris kept her distance, backing up every time the men came closer. She gently shoved Eve back, her hands reaching for her knives. "Excuse us; we're very late for a meeting. Please let us pass."

She tried to step around the men, but they adjusted their positions to obstruct their way.

"What do you think, partner?" the first man asked. "Do you think these two match the description?"

"Oh, one of them *definitely* is," second man number two said "How do we tell which?"

"No way to tell here on the street. We need to take them *both* with us. Remember? The Master will sort it out. We need only nab them."

At that last sentence, Iris turned and ran, pulling Eve along with her. Clothes flew out of Eve's bags as she stumbled behind her. Iris nearly crashed into a barricade that jammed the street. They were forced to turn down a deserted alley. "Stay behind me!" Iris yelled at Eve, pushing her at the back wall. She pulled out her twin knives and prepared herself for the attack. "Message Alastair and tell him where we are."

She had never before used her self-defense skills in actual combat, let alone while defending someone else. The closest experience was during the final Placement Test when a squad of Dueling Dummies attacked her and Claire. Anxiety rushed through her, despite the adrenalin coursing through her system.

Behind her, Eve's OMNI beeped when the message was sent. Miss Sanders then began whispering something unintelligible. Iris tried to understand what her peer was saying, but she gave up as the men approached.

In the alley, they were cut off from the rest of the street.

The only way to safety was through the attackers. They crept in slowly, raising their own blades. Both had their own long swords ready in their hands.

"I don't want to hurt you," Iris said in a last attempt at peacemaking.

The two attackers laughed. The first man stepped forward, swinging his blade wildly at Iris's middle. She easily deflected the blow, but it distracted her enough so the other man could sneak past her.

Eve screamed.

Iris kicked her attacker in the gut and went to rescue her friend. She spun, aiming her blade right at the man's head. He deftly shuffled backward and rejoined his partner. They shared a silent look before advancing once again.

Quickly forming a plan, Iris decided to try and force the men out of the alley so that Eve could escape. She alternately sliced at her foes and they were gradually pressed back.

When they realized what she was doing, they returned with powerful blows of their own.

Soon, Iris was almost standing on top of Eve.

The larger of the men pinned Iris's blades to the side of alley while the other cleared her hands of her weapons. It all happened in a blur that she didn't know what occurred until she stood at the back of the alley, completely defenseless.

"Take these." Eve twisted awkwardly in the cramped space and slipped the extra pair of long knives into Iris's hands.

The pair of First-Year Trainees had little more moving room. Iris tried once again to push the attackers back. But they were already repeating the series of blows that had disarmed her earlier.

All of a sudden, Eve cried out, "I'm the Alteration! Take me! Leave her alone." She stepped to the side and frantically waved her arms.

When the men pressed forward again, Eve's OMNI whizzed past Iris's head on its way to smack an attacker in the face. The diversion worked; Iris was able to shove the men back to the main street.

Her next plan was a little risky. It put her in a dangerous spot. Weighing the consequences, she decided to implement it anyways. After trapping one man's blades between her own, she pushed forward. The man lost his balance and stumbled in front of the other. She flicked her wrists, causing the trapped man to drop his sword. He groaned in pain as his hand twisted backwards against her force. Iris threw an elbow at his chest and he fell to the floor.

She stepped over his unconscious body and began attacking the remaining man. He was no match for her by himself. Iris ruthlessly thrust her blades at him as he retreated towards the barricade. As he tried to climb over the barrier, she managed to disarm him.

Lowering her blades, she said, "I said that I didn't want to hurt you and I meant it. Let us go on our way." She went to go get Eve, but the sight made her freeze.

The man who was supposedly unconscious must have faked it. He hefted Eve into his thick arms. A trickle of blood ran down Miss Sanders's forehead. Iris turned to attack once again, but she couldn't go near him.

The first man held a gun in his free hand, still baring his sword. "You're good, dearie, but not good enough to dodge bullets. So, please, make our job easier and come with us quietly."

The one carrying Eve began walking away from the scene. Iris fought the urge to go after her friend, but she knew when she was beaten. She let the borrowed knives clang to the floor and placed her hands in a surrendering pose above her head. Iris positioned her face away from the man, not wanting to see the man's hilt as he knocked her out.

Wind brushed against her neck as the man swung at her, but the blow didn't land.

Iris looked to see Alastair fighting the man off. He redirected the gun and swung his own sword at the attacker. The man dodged and threw his fist in Alastair's face. Al stumbled backward, falling on top of Iris.

"I suppose we're just taking the red head after all. It's *her* we want, anyways."

Before he left, the attacker discharged his illegal weapon. It made several terrible cracking sounds as a bullet flew from the barrel.

Alastair screamed in pain. Blood gushed from the series of wounds on his left thigh.

Iris put pressure on his leg above the wound. The bleeding slowed. "Help! Someone help me. Please!"

The rest of her companions arrived at the scene. Max got out his OMNI and made a call to the nearest Agency Base. Viola and Beatrice tried to calm Alastair down while Iris continued pressing on the artery above the bullet hole. They all removed their uniform jackets and placed them on his shaking body.

Alastair kept crying out Eve's name over and over again.

The Cromfords held him down when he tried to get up. Claire unstrapped her sheath of throwing knives, removed the blades, and used the belt as a tourniquet. With the belt in place, Iris removed her bloody hands from the mangled flesh. Dozens of questions were asked by everyone at once, but her head swarmed and she couldn't give them any answers.

Minutes later, paramedics showed up and took Alastair away. Before the Forensic Agents could sweep the area, Iris controlled herself enough to quickly pocket Eve's slightly damaged OMNI from where it had landed.

Claire came up to Iris, wielding the retrieved long knives from the alley. "It wasn't your fault. I'm sure you did everything you could."

"It wasn't enough."

Chapter 29

Tobias watched as his body guards released their stress on each other in a fierce battle.

Any on-looker might think that Stella and Drew were unnecessarily cruel to each other. But their regular beatings were necessary for the two Hardings to remain "sane."

In the Sparring Ring, Stella flung her whip at her younger brother. Normally, she almost never missed, but Drew's strategy outweighed hers. The whip would crack toward him, only to miss by about an inch as he dodged.

A series of strikes failed and then Drew said, "Wait."

Stella paused with an irritated sigh, but she let the leather tail of her weapon fall limply to the ground.

Once her brother had a chance to recover, he said, "Continue," and she attacked again.

They would then resume until either one used the safe word. Drew threw a handful of knives in her direction, most of which were deflected with a snap of Stella's wrist.

"Everyone alright?" Tobias asked out of habit instead of concern.

They nodded and continued their skirmish.

"I should have the Hardings come in for a demonstration," said Agent Brant Thomas, the Sparring Instructor. The scar down his face twitch as he added, "They could teach my arrogant students a thing or two."

"Yes, they're incredible," Vega replied, typing notes in his OMNI "I just hope that someday they'll learn to control themselves in a public setting."

Stella shrieked, "Drew, that one *hurt*!"

"Good. I almost thought you had grown *immune to pain*." Drew shot another knife at his sister. "Do you remember how all your shrinks use to say that inflicting pain was your way of trying to *avoid* it? Well, I guess you haven't imposed enough hurt to the world if your soul can still *feel*."

"I'll make you *bleed*!"

When taunts grew tedious, Tobias pulled Agent Thomas away from the Ring, towards the rear office. "Can I count on your further discretion?" he asked, needing reassurance from his loyal subordinate.

"How long have you known me?"

"You've always been a valuable asset," Tobias conceded. "However, this mission is unlike all the others."

Agent Thomas was as severe as stone. He had yet to fail the Vega family. "I will personally lead the mission myself," Brant guaranteed him, scratching at his scar. "My team is ready to leave at a moment's notice. Just tell us when it needs to happen and we will fulfill our task."

Tobias looked hard at the man. Although his body showed that he was prepared for service, a subtle tremor in his eyes suggested something else. "You're not completely sure about everything, are you?"

"Of course I am, sir. It's just that—"

"You want *more* details?" Tobias interrupted. "I can't divulge anything until the job is done, just like it has always been."

"Yes, but you've never sent me to—"

Tobias's OMNI beeped. He looked at the screen to see and incoming call from Maximus. "This better be important."

"Father, Alastair's been shot! Some Trainees were attacked and he protected them."

Rage filled Tobias' body. "Is anyone else hurt?"

"The attackers took Miss Sanders, but Miss Kayn is having a hard time telling the Enforcers what happened."

"Where is your brother?"

"They took him to the Bullet Surgeon."

"I'll be right there." Tobias ended the call and turned to Agent Thomas. "Cancel the mission. I have to go take care of something." Agent Vega fumed with anger as he stormed out of the Sparring Ring and made his way to where Alastair was having surgery.

"Do you need us?" Drew asked as he followed.

"No. I have to go deal with a problem."

"You have a meeting this afternoon," Stella said, striding forward. "Do you want me to cancel it?"

"You're not my secretaries!" Tobias snapped. "Go back to Vega Manor and check the perimeter or something." He pushed past every bystander that stood between him and the path to his first born. Irritated shouting rang out past him as he shoved Agents left and right. Some moved to confront him for his rude attitude, but stopped when they saw who he was.

He made his way to the base of the nearest Transit Station, which held his personal transportation vehicle. He got in and sped away through the roads that ran below the public transports.

Few people knew about the secret tunnels below the Transit Station. Only the most important people in the city had enough prestige or money to own their own vehicle. It made getting around the city much faster than waiting for each Transition.

With great dexterity, Tobias guided his car around other vehicles in the tunnel.

The magnetic wheels hugged the metal surface of the road, preventing his car from rolling as he swerved in and out of the slower-moving cars.

In no time, he arrived at his destination.

He hit the "park" icon on the steering consul. The wheels moved from below the car to the right of the vehicle, pulling it up onto the side of the tunnel—away from the on-coming traffic. Tobias stepped out of his vehicle onto the pedestrian walkway above the road and walked to the exit.

The Hospital wasn't far from the Station. Tobias burst into the lobby and brushed past the front desk without signing in, expecting the staff to know exactly who he was. Following the directions Maximus had sent him, he made his way through the different wings.

Eventually he spotted his younger son.

"He's in there." Maximus pointed at the door.

Tobias went past without a word. Alastair was sleeping soundly. A bundle of needles were embedded in the crease of his elbow, connected to machines via a network of tubes. Screens flashed vibrant colored text that displayed his vitals.

A nurse rushed in and warned Tobias that young Vega needed his rest. Waving her off, he tapped his son on the arm to wake him.

Groggily, Alastair opened his eyes. “Father?”

“What happened?” Tobias’s voice showed concern, but it was more for the details of the event than for the wellbeing of his son.

“I need to sleep. You can ask Max.” Alastair shut his eyes and rolled over.

“Don’t shrug me off!” He stormed to the other side of the hospital bed. “What happened at Market? Start from the beginning.”

With a sigh, Alastair turned onto his back. “Everything went fine at the shop,” he explained, rubbing his face. “The Trainees went off to browse through other stores. Miss Birch, the younger Miss Cromford, and I remained behind with the pawn owner. I arranged the documents for Mr. Rye to sign—which he did. While this was happening, Miss Kayn and Miss Sanders were attacked by two Regioners. Miss Sanders was kidnapped. Max is trying to get a hold of all the Board members to issue an Enforcement Squad to look for her.”

Tobias shook his head. “Son, I’m afraid that Miss Sanders is beyond help now. She will have been given a

Signature by now, exiling her forever from Society. There is nothing that can be done."

"No!" Alastair sat up abruptly. "No, you can't give up so easily. We have to find her. I was supposed to keep everyone *safe*."

Softening his tone, Tobias said, "It's the despicable Regioners, Alastair. After the events of today, I don't think the Agency can do business with those monsters. I want you to contact Lord Rye and cancel our agreement. We will have nothing to do with kidnappers."

"Wait. You think the shop owner had something to do with this?" Alastair asked, slowly.

Tobias took a seat across from Alastair's hospital bed. "How else would Regioners know that the Agency Trainees would be in the Market today?"

"I don't think he—"

"Nevertheless," Agent Vega continued, "the Regioners need to know that we are not to be messed with. Their lack of morality just cost them their only hope of rejoining civilized Society."

Alastair sunk back into his bed with a groan. "There's something about this whole business that bothers me. Why would they want *Miss Sanders*?"

"They see our uniforms and just see talent. They probably want her for her skills. Once they have a Signature on her, she will be completely theirs. Miss Sanders will be forced to work for them."

"We could always cover her Signature so that no one knows that she has been branded a Regioner."

"If anyone ever saw her Signature, she'd just be thrown back to the Lower Region. Then the Clans would know that we tried to hide one of their residents and could sue us for theft." Tobias saw the worry on his son's face, so he added some words of comfort. "Miss Sanders knows how to take care of herself. She won't be harmed as long as she does as she is told. Now, get some rest."

With that, he left. Tobias didn't even look at Maximus as he passed. Minutes later, he was home.

"Anything to report?"

"No, sir," Drew replied, straightening up. "No one suspicious has been here."

"Notify me if that changes. Other than that, I don't want to be disturbed." Tobias entered his study and shut the door.

Stella sat lounging in his desk chair, her legs dangling over the arm of the seat. Her long black hair had been washed and straightened since her sparring match with Drew. "So, you *did* make it home for your meeting after all."

"Not today, Stel. Get out."

His fierce tone caused her to frown. After a moment of hesitation, she obeyed the command.

Tobias connected his OMNI to the wall screen and dialed a number.

The vid call was answered by a man with light hair.

"Hello, Pavoc. Can your *Mistress* take a call?"

"Agent Vega. How did everything go today?" the Crimson steward asked in a pleasant voice.

"That's something I need to discuss with Romisa. *Go get her.*"

"Touchy today, are we?" Pavoc raised an eyebrow. "Well, Her Majesty is unable to come to the phone right now. Would you like to leave a message?"

Tobias hated dealing with the smug Crimson. He would need to figure out how to get rid of the steward sometime soon. "Tell Romisa that the longer she refuses to see me, the longer she goes without seeing her *son.*"

"It's alright, Pavoc," said a woman's voice off-screen. "I'll talk with him." The Region Queen appeared in all her dark glory.

"Events in the Market didn't go as planned," Tobias said in an accusing tone.

"Really?" Romisa turned to Pavoc. "Have your men returned yet?"

"No. Not yet, Your Majesty," Pavoc answered off-screen. "But they'll come when they can. They're probably covering their tracks."

"So what's the matter, Toby?" Queen Romisa inquired, her face unusually calm.

Tobias took a deep breath. "Your men took the *wrong* woman."

"*Impossible*." The Crimson steward stepped into view of the screen. "They came highly recommended; they never fail."

Tobias shook his head in annoyance. "Why do you keep this imbecile around?"

"I find him exceedingly *reliable*," she replied with a wink.

"I find that really hard to believe. One of my sons told me they took a little red head girl. I told you that I wanted the *blonde*!"

A smile ran across the Queen's wicked lips. "*My* son?"

"It doesn't matter *which* of my sons told me! We had a deal and you didn't hold up your end of the bargain. I will not—"

Pavoc held up his hands, interrupting Tobias. "Hold on a minute. We really don't know for sure if they messed up or not. Until they have returned, we can't say for sure who they have taken."

"Are you calling my son a *liar*?" Tobias asked, finding it increasingly difficult to calm himself. "He didn't know the details of the plan so there's no reason why he would lie to me."

"Still, we can't blow up over this." Pavoc pursed his pouty lips in thought before saying,
"*If* my men took the wrong girl, it might not be entirely their fault. It probably falls with you, Mr. Vega."

"I'll pretend I didn't hear that." Tobias turned to the Queen. "Romisa, if the kidnappers screwed this up, the blame lies with you. You will never see your son—ever."

"You can't do that!" she screeched, her cheeks matching the bright red of her haloed crown. Her dark eyes filled with rage as she screeched, "You promised that I could see my *Matevak*!"

"I promised you that you could see him when Iris Kayn was safely in my custody." Tobias folded his arms to show that his decision was final.

"You're insufferable, Toby! If you think that you can keep him from me—"

"Don't worry. I'll give you another chance to be useful." With that, Tobias clicked off the call. He sat back in his chair, rubbing his temples, wondering why he had ever been involved with her.

*****

Newly promoted Captain Tobias Vega decided to treat himself to a weekend away from the compulsive needs of the Agency, his ambitious friends, and his clingy fiancé. He thought getting older would mean being able to have more freedom to have fun.

Tobias couldn't have been more wrong.

Being thirty years old wasn't as thrilling as he thought it would be; it was full of *responsibility* and *duty*. Tobias was sick of those words. He needed a few days alone where he could do as he pleased without anyone looking over his shoulder.

What better place to do that than in Market?

He made his plans and temporarily said goodbye to his life. Dressed in his common street clothes, he traveled down to the bottom of the Middle Zone to a somewhat decent hotel. Tobias checked into his suite, dumped his things on the bed, and then went looking for adventure.

Scouting several Market clubs, he decided none were worthwhile to go into. After finding one that seemed decent enough, he strode inside, had a seat at the bar, and ordered. Music blared from all over, masking most other sounds of the world. His OMNI beeped repeatedly before he finally turned it off.

"What're you drinking?"

Tobias almost spilled his tonic when the woman spoke. He turned to see who had interrupted him. Once he looked at her, he was unable to stop staring. The woman wore a tight scarlet dress that only came halfway down her thighs. A black, lacy slip showed beneath the hem. Her long, dark hair hung in ringlets over her bare shoulders. A red, two-tiered Signature wrapped around her right wrist.

When it was clear that he was unable to answer her question, she told the bartender, "I'll have what he's having." She twisted on her stool to face Tobias. "You're new here, aren't you, handsome?"

"Um, yes. I'm on vacation," he stammered, wiping his hands on his slacks. "Do you come here often?"

"It's my home away from home when I'm sick of family—which is most of the time."

"I can understand family problems," Tobias said, still recovering from the shock of meeting her.

The bar-tender placed a glass in front of the girl and poured her a shot.

"Whatever you've got going on in your fancy Societan home is nothing like what I have to deal with," she replied before downing her shot.

"How did you know I was a Societan?"

"Couple ways," she said with a wry smile. "One, you are dressed *way* too fancy. Two, you are exceptionally *cute*."

He felt he cheeks grow hot. "I didn't know that Societans were known for being cute."

"*Most* of you are." She signaled for the bar-tender to pour another drink. "So, handsome, what can I call you?"

"Toby," he responded after a pause, not sure if he wanted to reveal his identity to this pushy woman. Returning to a previous subject, Tobias asked, "So, why do you think your problems are more severe than *mine*?"

"It's complicated," the girl replied, her playful tone disappearing from her voice.

"Try me."

With a sigh, she said, "I'm Princess Romisa. My father, Matolin, is the King of the Lower Region. As his eldest child, I'm supposed to inherit his title as Monarch, as well as become the Leader of the Crimson Steel Clan."

"And you don't want to?"

A fire burned in her eyes. "Of course I do! I can't wait to be Queen!"

"So what's the problem?"

"I have no Heir," Romisa explained. "Region Law states that only someone with offspring can inherit Leadership titles. My younger sister is married and has a child—with another on the way. If I don't have a kid soon, my father will have no choice but to relinquish the throne to her."

"Sounds awful," Tobias replied, trying to be sympathetic. He attempted to hide the fact that he had no idea that there were actual Laws in the Lower Region.

"I could never raise a child," Princess Romisa continued, motioning for the bartender to pour her another shot. "But I must bear the task. I *need* to have one. Otherwise, I would be forced to start listening to my little sister."

Tobias had a thought in his head which made him smile.

This seemed to confuse Romisa. "What's so funny? Do you have a suggestion, Toby?"

"I do, but it's crazy." He finished his drink, hoping that it would soften his nerves.

"I'm all ears. Tell me your crazy idea. Maybe I was thinking the same thing." She gave him a smile that sent a shiver through his body.

"Well, you could just grab some guy off the street and—"

"Take some of his *genetic material*?"

"I guess you could word it that way," Tobias laughed.

Without warning, Romisa sprung her head at him and kissed him hard on the lips. "Would you like to donate to my cause?" She wrapped her arms around his neck.

"Oh, why not—"

*****

As fun as that weekend was with Romisa, Tobias couldn't help regretting having a child with her. The Region Queen had allowed Tobias to raise their child on the condition that she would get him as her Heir once he finished his Agency Training. Tobias had less than a year to plan his way out of their agreement.

Romisa could have told the world their little secret. But for some reason, she had kept her mouth shut for over twenty-one years. Perhaps it was because she didn't want to risk angering Tobias. This close to the end, she might do something drastic to ensure that he followed through with his part of the bargain. Tobias had to figure out a way to keep her in check, along with formulating a new plan for gaining control over Iris Kayn.

He pulled out his OMNI and selected Agent Thomas's name. "I've got a different mission for you, Brant."

"How can I be of service?"

"Meet me at your office in an hour," Tobias ordered. "We need to implement a new strategy. It's a little riskier, but it will probably have a better pay off."

There was silence on the line before Agent Thomas asked, *"If it's a better plan, why wasn't it our first option? Risk has never been a problem in the past. What is different about this next mission?"*

Tobias rummaged through his desk drawers, pulling out piles of data-discs. "It has to happen in Upper Society."

Chapter 30

Norman was in surprisingly good spirits, despite the lack of spirits inside him. Audrey had suggested having a dinner party with the Birches to help lift his mood.

He sat across from his hosts, downing a glass of scotch. The Birch children played noisily in the next room while the adults passed the time with idle chit chat. At one time, Dr. Kayn had memorized all the names of his friends' eight children, but now the information was just an echo in his head.

"Oscar and I are so pleased that Iris was able to escape those two kidnappers." Helen Birch poured him another drink. "All those years of self-defense training have paid off."

"Thank you," Norman replied, his glass held awkwardly below his chin while he was forced to respond to his host. "It's a good thing it wasn't Claire with Iris." He paused and took several sips of his scotch. "Otherwise, she might have been taken instead of Miss Sanders."

"I don't think Iris would have let that happen," Audrey Taledon said, sounding morose. "Iris would have let herself be taken instead."

Oscar Birch gave his cousin a cautionary look. "We have no idea what would have happened in that situation, Audrey. Personally, I have no desire to even think about those hypothetical situations. I'm just thankful that *both* girls are safe."

"Except for Miss Sanders!" Helen shuttered. "I can only imagine what her parents are going through."

Audrey put her wine goblet down and shook her head. "I have little pity for the Sanders. Byron is a despicable, ruthless man; Claudia is flighty and has no care for anything in the world other than her own pleasure."

"What's the matter, cousin?" Oscar asked, looking genuinely concerned for her. "You've been in such a foul mood all evening."

Audrey stood and moved to the kitchen cabinets. When she came back to the table, she placed two bottles in the middle of the group. She swatted Norman's hand away as she poured the drinks. "I almost took a job this week."

Helen poured herself some sherry as she asked, "Where was the job?"

"The day Eve Sanders was kidnapped, I was in a meeting with her father," Audrey explained. "Byron offered me a position in his OMNI manufacturing company. They're working on a new line of implants for their products. Near the end of the meeting, Claudia came flouncing in to show her all his new clothing purchases. They had a fight right there in front of me. When he shouted, she wasn't fazed, which made him shout even louder."

Oscar shrugged. "So? Couples fight. I suppose you wouldn't know being single still."

Ignoring Mr. Birch, Audrey continued, "An Agent then came in. He told the Sanders' what had happened. Claudia began to cry and her husband stopped her. Byron said that Eve was no longer their daughter; she was a Regioner now. His wife dried her eyes and left without another word. As if nothing had happened, Byron asked me if I was interested in the position."

"And you declined, right?" Helen asked, concerned as always.

Audrey nodded solemnly. "Yes, but I didn't refuse until the next day when I read Eve's obituary in the news. They didn't even *search* for her. To them, being related to a Regioner is worse to them than having a dead daughter. So they're just pretending that she died in Market. They're having a funeral for her and everything!"

Norman wondered how he would react if he had gotten the same news about Iris. Would he go and search the Megacity until he knew his daughter was safe? Would he hire mercenaries to kill the scumbags that took her future from her? He didn't want to think about what he might do. As it was, Iris was still safe and nobody knew what she was, so he had nothing to worry about.

Suddenly he had a headache. Norman drained the last bit of his drink and excused himself.

Walking down the familiar passage to the bathroom, he noticed the seven Birch children scattered in the play area. They all had dark hair—black or brown—and either brown or green eyes. One of the boys sat in an armchair, reading some sort of book. The twin girls were busy fighting over a bag of cosmetics. The little ones sat in front of the vid screen on the wall. Small toys and gadgets were clumped together in piles throughout the room.

Norman stepped into the small guest bathroom. He wet his hands and splashed water onto his face. He hadn't been told all of the details, but something about the whole kidnapping business upset him. Iris had called him the moment she arrived back at the Agency and told him quite a bit about it, but it felt as though there were things she had left out. But he couldn't pry too hard without her learning things she shouldn't know.

He returned to his friends, who had moved out of the kitchen and into a small parlor. Fresh drinks had been poured. Norman took the remaining empty seat and picked up his full glass.

"Audrey and I were just talking about the upcoming election." Helen said, putting out finger sandwiches.

"Both Vega and Cromford had originally supported the Rehabilitation Act for the Lower Region." Audrey took Norman's glass and drank it. "But after the incident with Miss Sanders, both of them have rescinded their desire to help."

"Most of the city is upset about what happened to the young woman," Helen added, mixing herself a cocktail.

Oscar nodded his head in agreement as he said, "However, many feel that the incident only warrants more support for the Act. There are rumors that there will be a third Mayoral contender in the next election. But no one knows who."

Norman accepted another glass of scotch from Helen, much to Audrey's chagrin. "It's probably one of the Agency Board Members that helped create the Renovation Act." His words began to slur together. Tired of drinking from a glass, he took possession of a bottle of wine and sipped from it.

"I think you have had enough," Audrey said as she tried to pull the wine from his grasp.

"I've barely had any," Norman retorted.

"Perhaps I should take you home."

"No, I can take care of myself; I'm a grown man."

"Norman Kayn, *give me the bottle*," Audrey ordered in a stern but gentle voice. "I'll take you home and you can have some of your *stronger* stuff before you go to bed."

This got to him. He reluctantly agreed and put the bottle on the table.

"Thank you, Oscar and Helen, for a lovely evening. We'll have to do this again sometime." Audrey carefully pulled Norman out of his seat and guided him to the Birch's front room.

They turned down a series of hallways. She seemed to lead him through the least direct path home, probably to avoid the busier sections of the Residential Area.

When they finally arrived at his apartment, Audrey sat him down on the couch in the living room and handed him half a bottle of tequila. "When you pass out, the couch will catch you. Goodnight, Norman." She patted his head and looked down at him with pity in her eyes. "I'll see you in the morning—*if* I can wake you." Audrey let herself out, locking the door behind her with her OMNI.

Norman gulped down the bottle's contents. Eventually, his mind slipped and he fell into unconsciousness.

*****

Norman fussed with his tie as he nervously eyed a waiter. The man carried a tray of some sort of bubbly beverage, presumably containing alcohol. He wouldn't have minded enduring the elitist party if his wife would just let him *drink*.

Across for him, Neil Parson prattled about something insignificant. "…and they just chatted on and on for hours, but Olivia and I just could *not* understand a word they were saying!"

Beside him, Teresa laughed loudly. She turned to Norman. "Can you believe that, Doc?"

He turned his head away from the roving waiter and gave his wife a *Sorry, I wasn't listening* look.

"I just can't believe that little Troy and Remy are already talking to each other. And they're only a year old!" Teresa slapped Norman in a playful manner. "Such delightful little babies!"

Grasping the hint, Norman added, "You should make a video and put it on-line for everyone to see." He politely excused himself and found a secluded corner.

Teresa joined him, a fake smile still plastered to her painted face. She put her arms on his shoulders in a seemingly intimate manner, but she roughly pulled him down to her level. “Come on, Doc. You have to try harder!”

“I’m doing my best, Resa. Maybe if I could have just one—”

“Do *not* finish that sentence! You promised me that you’d stay sober.” Teresa’s frown quickly disappeared as she planted a hard kiss on his lips. She pulled back and smiled at someone behind his shoulder. “I just can’t get enough of him,” she said to a pair of gawkers. Her smile remained as her attention returned to him. “We’ve worked hard to cure the Plagues. Those people out there want to be a part of it, and we’re going to *let* them in hopes that they’ll fund our research to discover the *next* one. We’re going to go out there, listen to every boring story they want to tell us and pretend like we’re enjoying this pretentious gathering. *Understand*?”

Norman gave a solemn nod, sliding his hands to her lower back. “You’re right, Resa. With your sister’s reputation under scrutiny, we can’t depend on their funding any longer.” He leaned in to kiss her, but she took a step back.

"Why would you bring that up right now?" Tears formed in her eyes. "Elizabeth and Calvin face ruin and you're being glib about it at a *party*?"

Unsure of how to respond, all Norman could say was, "No," over and over again.

"Oh, shut up!" she snapped, her face turning bright red. As a waiter passed, she quickly grabbed a glass of champagne and downed it in one breath. She chased down the next server and took another one.

Following in his wife's steps, he enjoyed a few glasses. After about five drinks each, the other party-goers caught up to them. Conversations were renewed as the Doctor and Doctor Kayn were asked questions about their research. Everyone wanted to know how their tremendous success affected their personal lives.

Having a higher tolerance to alcohol, Norman handled answering most of the questions. He briefly enjoyed the role reversal as Teresa became more inept at conversation. It soon became all too easy to charm the crowd with stories of their struggle to find the past several cures. As his wife suggested, he threw in some minor deceptions to gain their pity.

More drinks were consumed, and the events of the night grew blurry.

There was a minor incident involving Tobias Vega. The clearest image that came to mind was Resa holding onto Vega's shoulders after stumbling over her heels.

Norman's knuckles suddenly throbbed and Tobias's jaw turned deep purple.

The last few images in his mind were of Ross Harding moving in front of him and Gina crashing a glass bottle onto his head.

*****

A ringing sound awoke him. He stared at the empty bottle beside him and shook his head.

The ringing continued and he tried to stand. His legs refused to work and he crashed to the floor. His knees smashed painfully into the coffee table. Norman made his way to the front door, supporting himself by holding the furniture.

He fumbled his OMNI off his belt and somehow managed to get the sensor onto the lock. The door whooshed open to reveal a pair of men dressed in all black.

One of the men held a translucent screen that was covered in blurry letters. Looking up from the monitor, he said, "Good evening. I'm Agent Thomas; this is Agent Mitchell. Are you Mr. Norman Kayn?"

"No," Norman replied curtly. His next words slurred together. "I'm not a *mister*; I'm a *doctor*."

"Well, *Dr.* Kayn, I have a warrant for your arrest." Agent Thomas held up the screen.

He must have really been drunk to create such an illusion—one of his greatest fears coming to life.

Instead of being scared, he simply laughed and tried to close the door on the men.

The door wouldn't close. The second man had stepped through the frame and held it open. "We were hoping you would cooperate, Dr. Kayn," Agent Mitchell said, reaching for something on his belt.

Norman grinned. "May I—I know what I'm—um, you're charging me with?"

Agent Thomas replied, "You are suspected of being involved in illegal Alteration research."

Sighing, Norman held his hands out in front of him. "For your sake—saké? No, sake. Yes. I hope that for your sake you have enough proof for your, um, uh—what's the—accusations! Ha! Accusations. Yeah, cuz then I'll be back here in-da-morn'ng tah nurse my hangover."

Chapter 31

Closing her eyes, Iris held her breath as she stepped into a cloud of disinfectant. After five seconds, the mist was blown away and the glass door in front of her opened. "I seriously doubt I've picked up a germ in the last minute," she snapped at a busy-looking care-taker.

"Yeah, they're a pain," the nurse conceded, "but it's better than risking an epidemic."

Iris understood the need to have a completely sterile hospital. However, having the small gas chambers every twenty feet was overkill. It was procedures like this that caused the growth of the Plagues. The super-viruses evolved from every-day microbes and became resistant to all traditional methods of sterilization.

"What room is Alastair Vega staying in?" Iris asked, approaching the information center.

The nurse turned away from the screen she was looking at and moved to a different one. Her fingers flew over the keys. "He just finished a physical therapy session and is resting in his room. But I can't allow any visitors at this time."

"I just need a minute. He can wait *that* long before taking a nap, right?"

"Miss, we have certain procedures and—"

"He saved my life," Iris blurted out. "I need to thank him and I would rather not have to come back and be exposed to more of these disinfectant chambers."

Tapping a screen, the nurse reviewed something in Alastair's file. "That clarifies why he was shot. None of the nurses have seen a gun-shot wounds in ages. I'll let in you in if you explain what happened." The woman suggestively raised her eye brows in a manner as if to increase the shadiness of her offer. "The medical staff has a wager going about how Mr. Vega was shot. I would like to know who is right."

Iris cleared her throat, trying to figure out how to answer. "Well, that's classified. I'm unable to discuss the details—"

There was a whoosh as a chamber opened up. Alastair came hobbling out on crutches.

Stepping away from the unhelpful nurse, Iris walked towards him. "Hi. I came to see how you're doing." She rummaged through her backpack, pulled out a card-disc, and handed it to him. "The gift shop downstairs didn't have anything that said, 'Thank you for taking a bullet for me,' so I got you this instead."

Alastair put the card-disc in his OMNI and read the message. "*Get well soon.* How original!"

"I thought about getting roses or a stuffed bear, but didn't know which you'd prefer."

"That's alright. My room already looks like a jungle with all the plants and animal toys people have been bringing me. For some reason, people think those will make me get better faster." He sniffed and rubbed his nose on his shoulder. "If anything, I think all the presents are giving me allergies."

They walked for several minutes, passing through more disinfectant chambers before Iris realized they were no longer in the recovery wing of the Hospital.

"Where are we going?"

"Physical therapy makes me hungry," Alastair huffed, struggling with his crutches. "If your conscious is still guilt-ridden, you can buy me a sandwich."

"I never said I was *guilt-ridden.*" Iris frowned as she held the cafeteria door open for him.

"It's all in your eyes. Besides, why else would you be here? I mean, other than to give me a generic card-disc?"

"Okay, that's very perceptive of you. Now, select your lunch so I can pay for it." She motioned at the various shelves of foods. Alastair went to grab a tray, but Iris took it instead.

"I got it. Go find a seat and I'll meet you over there." She chose a bowl of soup for herself, headed over to the pay counter, and pulled out her OMNI.

The cashier looked her over and then stared in Alastair's direction. "How do you know Mr. Vega?"

The question threw Iris off. "He was my Mentor in the Agency Training Program."

"Oh, so this little lunch meeting isn't a *date*?"

"Um, no," she replied, slowly. Before the nosy cashier could ask anymore question, Iris quickly touched her OMNI to the cash register to sign the screen. Without another word, she made her way to where Alastair was sitting. "Everyone here seems really interested in your personal life."

"Everyone?"

"That cashier and one of the nurses." She handed him his sandwich.

Alastair sighed, "I just have that affect on people. It comes with being a Vega, I suppose. Max draws a lot of attention as well." He took a large bite of his sandwich. With a satisfied groan, he said, "I miss meat. This is the first solid thing I've eaten in a week."

This comment opened up the conversation Iris was hoping to have with Alastair, but she had no idea how to begin. She didn't want to bring up such a delicate subject, so she decided to tip-toe around it and hope he got the hint of what she was talking about. "I'm glad to see you moving around already."

"Yeah, I was lucky to get the Bullet Doctor."

Iris paused, stirring her soup absent-mindedly. But eventually, she added, "Yes, *you* were very lucky."

Alastair solemnly asked, "Did you want to talk about Eve?"

Nodding, she said, "I'm not sure how to ask this. I wanted to confirm a rumor that I heard. Is it—is it really true that no one is searching for her?"

He looked away before saying, "Yeah. She has been pronounced *dead*."

"She isn't *really* dead, right?" Frustrated, she threw her spoon onto the table and brought her hands to her forehead. "Someone should be out there looking for her. I just keep thinking: *What if it was one of us?* I would want someone to look for me." When Alastair didn't say anything, she glared at him. "If you had been taken instead, would your father and Max be looking for you? Eve and I would."

He didn't return her gaze. "It's not that simple."

"*Of course it is*!" Iris shouted, gaining the attention of the other hospital-dwellers. "Your friend gets taken and then you do everything you can to rescue them!"

Alastair closed his eyes and took a deep breath. "I've had this conversation with every Agency Board Member. Eve has been given a Signature by now. Once someone has been marked, they're unable to come further Up than Market."

"I can't believe I am hearing this." Iris stood abruptly and left in a huff.

The Sectors blurred by as she traveled home to the residential area of the Agency. Back at her Living Quarters, she slumped down onto the couch.

Some details were still hazy about that fateful afternoon, but Iris hoped that Eve's OMNI would help piece some things together. Even though it was against the law, Iris had taken the device without telling the investigating Agents. Pulling out the stolen OMNI from its hiding spot in the couch cushions, Iris began searching through the files to see if there were any clues—anything to help her fix her mistake.

Unsure of what she was hoping to find, she read the message Eve had sent to Alastair. Unfortunately, it was nothing significant.

Iris scanned through some of the other messages, eager to discover some sort of hint as to whether or not Eve really *was* an Alteration. The woman had claimed to be one, but Iris had doubts as to the truth behind the words. There was a possibility that it was just a distraction to give her a better chance to deal with the kidnappers.

Much to her disappointment, the messages held no key information. After several minutes of reading, something clicked in her brain. She recalled that Eve had an implant. Iris searched frantically through the icons, trying to find the implant file.

Finally, she found what the correct application: Voice Transcriber. Tapping the screen, Iris scanned through the thousands of files of Miss Sanders' conversations. She scanned through the vast information for several minutes before she realized that there was a search option. Iris typed in the date and approximate time of the kidnapping.

The Voice Transcriber started a new file every hour. Iris had to scroll down their conversation at the boutiques before she found what she was looking for.

Eve: *I don't know if anyone will hear this, but I want to record what's happening—just in case anything goes wrong. Iris Kayn is protecting me from two attackers. I'm absolutely useless in this situation. I've contacted Alastair Vega, but that's all I'm capable of.*

The document had a section of white space where the OMNI didn't recognizable any utterances. Iris impatiently scrolled down the screen to find the next section of dialogue.

Eve: *I'm the Alteration! Take me! Leave her alone.*

Iris skipped over the sections involving the actual kidnapping. She moved to the place where it seemed that Eve was unconscious. The two kidnappers then discussed their hostage.

Unknown Man 1: *Nice thinking, Lom. She's still alive, right?*

Unknown Man 2: *Yeah, Klev. I just hit her with my hilt to knock her out.*

The implant software was sophisticated enough to learn and recognize new voices and their names. The attackers' identities began showing up on the screen.

Klev: *Master will be pleased. However, I wish we could have nabbed the other girl, as well. Too bad that Agent showed up.*

Lom: *What's this? Hmm. She has some sort of pink plastic sticking out of her neck.*

Klev: *That looks strangely familiar. The Agent that I shot had something like that. What could it be?*

Lom: *Do you think it's some sort of spy-tracking device?*

Klev: *Perhaps. We'll have to examine it better. Put her down.*

Lom: *I think we can take it out.*

Klev: *Don't take it out! What if it activates a self-destruct?*

Lom: *Oh, oops. I pulled it out already.*

Klev: *What'd you do that for? We need to smash it now.*

The document ended. Iris looked it over multiple times, hoping to find some sort of hint about where Eve was. But the kidnappers didn't leave any clues.

Iris had thought that investigating the situation would make her feel better, but it only made everything worse. The traumatic event had brought on some unpleasant realizations. The Agency had become weary of the Lower Region and was threatening to disband the Rehabilitation Act. Without the Act, the Regioners would lose all hope of ever having a safe and happy life. Millions of lives were about to be changed as a result of her inability to operate at the point of a gun.

On top of everything, her father hadn't called her in days. It was irregular behavior for him since he usually tried to contact her every hour.

She had called Dr. Taledon, but she had no idea where he was either. Audrey had said something about her father being an adult and capable of taking care of himself. She assumed he might be in Market getting ridiculously drunk, as he often did when his mood needed "comforting."

A beeping at the other end of the room brought her out of her brooding. Reluctantly, Iris stood and trudged over to artificial intelligence's screen. She wiped at her eyes before asking, "What is it, ARHA?"

"I am sorry to bother you, Iris Kayn," the computer replied, "but I have been instructed to give you some news."

"Go ahead. It can't be any worse than the news I received earlier."

"I am unaware of what news you received earlier. However, I am almost certain that this is worse than that." The screen flashed and several files opened up. Iris moved closer to get a better look. "Yesterday morning, you father was arrested. He is currently in the Agency's custody."

She couldn't believe what she was hearing. "Wait. He was arrested *yesterday*? How come no one has told me until now?"

"The charges needed to be processed," ARHA explained. "The Agency has been building a case against him. They wanted to make sure all the channels were gone through properly before informing you."

"What are the charges?"

"That is classified. Even if I knew, I would be unable to tell you. I was simply instructed to tell you so that you knew where your father was."

"Can I at least see him?" Iris asked. "Where are they keeping him?"

"I am sorry; I cannot tell you anymore now." The files on ARHA's screen disappeared. "I will let you know when the Agent in charge is ready to pass you more information."

"Will you at least tell me who is charging him?"

Without responding, ARHA said, "Good day, Iris Kayn," and then the computer screen went black.

Iris wanted to throw her OMNI at the AI, but that wouldn't be productive. The universe had once again thrown something infuriating at her. Nothing seemed to be going the way she had imagined her life to be. Iris knew that it was unrealistic to be upset at every little hitch, but it was hard to not be despondent when very few things were going for her.

Chapter 32

A trio of Massage Agents stared as Claire stomped out of the Bodywork Lounge. She barely felt like herself; something indescribable came over her and she headed towards the one place she had sworn she would never go—the gym. Having a naturally high metabolism, she had never needed to exercise off extra calories. But this afternoon, she wanted to run the track or lift the weights—or whatever it was that Iris spent so much time doing there.

As usual, her roommate was in the far corner of the room, jogging on the treadmill. Iris didn't notice her as she approached. Claire got her attention by hitting the stop button. "I'm calling an emergency vent session." She dragged her friend towards the large, heavy bags that hung from the ceiling.

"What happened?" Iris wiped perspiration from her face with a towel.

Claire didn't saying anything at first. She let go of her friend's hand and faced a red bag. Pulling her arm back, she was about to punch when Iris caught her wrist.

"If you are going to box, you need the right equipment." Iris moved to a locker behind the rows of punching bags and came back with a duffle. "Put these on," she instructed, tossing Claire a pair of padded gloves. Iris then began strapping cushioned shoes onto Claire's feet. "Now, will you please tell me what has compelled you to take up boxing?"

"I'm not *taking it up*. I'm so angry that I feel like if I don't get it out of me, I just might explode." Claire fumbled with the glove straps, unable to figure out how they worked. "Help, please."

Iris sighed as she expertly wrapped the straps around Claire's wrists. "Okay, the first thing you have to know is—"

Claire didn't wait for her to finish. She began slamming her fists into the leather sack. The impact sent a jolt up her arm, but she continued attacking.

"Stop!" Iris shouted, putting a hand on Claire's shoulder. "You're going to hurt yourself. Straighten your wrists so they are aligned with the back of your hands." She held up her arm to demonstrate.

Adjusting her punch, she resumed striking. Throwing in an awkward kick, Claire said, "The Agency is run by a Board of idiots."

Iris held the bag in place. "Did you have another dispute with one of your Instructors?"

"No. Well, yes, but that's not the cause of my fury." Claire paused and wiped a bead of sweat from her forehead. "I've been ditching classes."

"Oh. If that's the reason you are upset, that's no excuse to be angry with the Agency." Iris strapped on her own set of boxing pads. "Attendance is *required* in order to pass the Program."

"I know all that! I just felt like it was a waste of my time to go to class. My Instructors weren't teaching me anything new." Claire threw an elbow at the punching bag. "The first week of classes, I pointed out mistakes they made, which then made me an outcast in my Program. 'Know It All' is what the other Engineering Trainees called me. So I learned to keep my mouth shut. I did my work quickly and then spent the rest of class time working on my different Projects."

Iris began attacking the neighboring punching bag. "Did your Instructors know what you were doing?"

"It didn't matter since I got top scores in *everything*." Claire let out a rather un-lady-like huff. "The professors acted as though I'm brilliant because their teaching. No one taught me how to be an engineer; I was *born this way*."

*****

One Saturday each month, Mr. and Mrs. Birch left for a date night. It was always a traumatic time for four-year-old Claire and their toddler, Sylvester.

They left their children in the care of Oscar's cousin. As much as the Birch children loved their aunt, Audrey wasn't much fun to be around. They were always plopped down in front of the video screen and forced to watch boring old-people movies for hours between dinner and bed-time.

During one weekend night, Audrey brought over several bulky sacks. Claire hoped her aunt had finally brought them some toys for her to play with. While Audrey changed Sylvester into his pajamas, Claire snuck into one of the satchels.

Something pricked her finger and she flinched. Still curious, Claire flipped the bag over and spilled the contents on the floor. Little metallic pieces covered with poky wires clattered as they landed. As she looked at the parts, something happened to her. She picked through the wires and metal coverings, connecting parts where they seemed to fit together.

Sylvester came over and asked, "Play?"

"No! They're *my* games, Syl!" Claire barked at the two year old, swatting at his hand. "Go away."

"What are you doing?" Audrey gasped.

"Playing with your puzzles," Claire casually replied without looking up.

Taking a seat next to her, Audrey examined the mechanism. "Have you ever done anything like that before?"

After thinking for a minute, Claire shook her head.

Audrey stared at her and the girl returned her gaze.

The silence was too boring for Claire, so she continued building. Grabbing different pieces, she muttered, "This goes *here* and that goes *there.*" Suddenly, she looked up, alarmed by something. "Something's missing. Where is it? Ah, there it is. Yes!"

Clearing her throat, Audrey asked, "How would you feel about coming to my lab and playing with more parts?"

"Do you have more puzzles for me to do?"

"Plenty."

*****

Twice a week for the next fourteen years, Claire had met with Audrey to build items.

But it was more than that. She learned *how* and *why* things worked, instead of only instinctually knowing how their components fit collectively to create a working apparatus.

Despite all the knowledge her aunt bestowed on her, it was still her pure-born talent that enabled her to become as skilled as she was. Claire resented anyone who tried to down-size her abilities or take credit for them.

"So what did the Board say to you?" Iris asked.

Claire took a deep breath. She didn't know if she could restate the blasphemy she had been accused of. Imagining the faces of the Agency Board Members, her padded fists made contact with the leather. "Like I said, they're a bunch of idiots." She sighed as she ripped the gloves off her hands and threw them at the punching bag. "They said I was an *Alteration*! They don't recognize that someone can be as good as me without being one of those *abominations*. Now I have to go through a series of tests and scans to ensure that I'm not a threat to Society."

The thought sent chills down her spine. She didn't like the idea that she was going to be poked and prodded like an alien.

"But you and I know that you *aren't* one," Iris urged, taking off her own gear. "You'll pass their assessments and that'll be the end of it. You'll see. This is just a minor inconvenience on your journey towards a brilliant career."

Claire finished taking off her padded shoes. Her theory about working off her anger was dead wrong. She only felt more agitated. Mixed feelings flitted about her head. She couldn't control the ideas that sprang up. As she moved to leave the gym, she found herself being tempted to share her worst fear.

Iris caught up to her and threw a comforting arm around her shoulders. "I'm here for moral support. Always. If you ever need anything—"

Losing control of her body, Claire fell to the floor, unable to hold the tears back. She almost never cried in front of people; it made her embarrassed and intensified her frustration. "Oh, Iris! What if it *is* true? What if I'm some sort of lab experiment?"

Kneeling beside her, Iris whispered, "You can't think that,"

"Why not? My dad's extended family is full of scientists. Anyone of them could have done something to me." She continued to babble on, spewing out all ridiculous possibilities that had been plaguing her until Iris slapped her across her face. "Ow! What'd you do that for?"

"You are *not* an Alteration. The whole notion is *ludicrous*."

Taking a deep breath, Claire said, "You're right. I just couldn't help remembering all the rumors that have been going around. They say that Eve was taken because she was an Alteration. But that's crazy. I mean, *Eve*! Flighty little Eve who only has one thought in her head."

Iris helped her up from the floor. "Are people really saying that?"

"Wake up and listen to the gossip, Iris!" Claire wiped at her tears, which were only replaced by ones of rage. "It's all over the Agency. It got me thinking that maybe Eve was taken by accident—that maybe the kidnappers were after *someone else*."

"Have you been reading those mystery novels again?" Iris shook her head. "It was a random kidnapping; they happen all the time in the Lower Region."

Claire felt her fears begin to melt away. She hugged Iris and strolled out of the gym.

The more she reflected on her friend's words, the more she was convinced she was absurd to think herself an Alteration. Claire strolled down the halls towards her Living Quarters, anxious for a steamy shower to wash away the grotesque layer of sweat covering her body.

Once all clean, Claire still didn't feel any better. Something must have snapped further in her brain because she found herself wanting to talk with her mom and dad. Pulling out her OMNI, she connected it to a screen in her room. She tapped a few icons to begin a vid-chat with her family.

Meredith answered the call. “It’s Claire! Hi, sissy.”

“Hey, Mere. Can I talk to mom and dad?”

“Mommy! Daddy!” Meredith screamed. “Claire wants to talk to you!”

There was a sudden burst of background noise as all the Birches began yelling excitedly. In a matter of seconds, the whole family was gathered around the computer screen—everyone asking questions at once.

“How are you?”

“What do you and Iris do for fun?”

“Did you buy us anything?”

“Have you made any new friends?”

“How are your classes?”

“Will the Agency let us come and visit you?”

“Did you go on any dates?”

Claire hit the mute button until her siblings and parents completed making all their crazy inquiries. When all the mouths stopped moving, she turned the volume back on. She chose her words carefully, still unsure of why she called them. “Um, well, it’s been a rough day and I need comforting. I've tried most of my usual cheer-up tricks—as well as a few unusual ones—but nothing's working."

"My daughter needs me?" her mother exclaimed, tears flowing down her cheeks. She heft Meredith on her hip, not caring that the toddler tugged on her hair. "Oh, Claire-Bear! How can I make you feel better?"

"Why don't you do what you usually do?" Sylvester smirked at her. "Go grab a guy and suck face until you feel better."

"Don't pester your sister about that, Syl," Helen chided her eldest son.

Oscar motioned for everyone to be silent. "Perhaps you'd be interested in joining us for dinner tonight. It might take your mind off things."

"No, thanks. I've got some things to do this evening," Claire lied. "I should get going."

She waved good-bye and ended the vid-chat.

But Sylvester's words tugged at her. Why *hadn't* she gone after the first man she saw? Determined to be promiscuous, she dressed in her fabulous blue tube-top dress and put on a hint of make-up to add a little color to her face. Once she looked desirable, she strode off to The Grey Circumstance.

Normally, few Trainees frequented the club during the week—most were busy studying or preparing for the next week's work. But there were still several viable options.

Alastair Vega sat by himself at the bar, downing a beer. Under regular circumstances, she would have ignored her former Mentor and grabbed someone else. However, it wasn't a day for regular circumstances.

"Since when do you consume alcohol?" Claire asked, taking a seat by him.

"Since I turned twenty-one last week," Alastair replied with a frown.

"Oh! Why didn't we have a party?"

"Considering that I was in the Hospital with a gun-shot wound, I didn't really feel like *celebrating*."

"Well, it looks like you're in need of cheering up, too." Claire stood and motioned for him to follow. "I know just the thing to improve our moods." She led him up to second floor. Vega Balcony was completely empty save for the lush furniture. "This is perfect."

Alastair took a seat on a couch and put his leg up on the arm of the sofa. "What did you have in mind to cheer ourselves up?" He gently massaged the side of his thigh.

Claire plopped down in front of his stretched-out body, planning her move. There was some risk involved, but she went for it. Lacing her fingers around his neck, she leaned in to kiss him.

He pushed Claire away before she made contact. "Geez, Claire! Did you run out of horny Trainees to manipulate?"

She was grateful that he hadn't called her a "slut." That insult normally followed every rejection she had received. The term usually referred to someone that exchanged sexual favors for some sort of material reasons. It didn't apply to her since she never asked for anything in return—just a good time.

"I prefer to call it 'stress relief,'" she replied, putting her hands in her lap. "There's nothing *personal* about it." She paused for a second, staring deep into his horrified eyes. "What did you do to Alastair Vega, the *ultimate lady's man*?"

Al sat up and moved as far away from her as the couch would allow. "That's a long story."

Yawning, Claire said, "I *hate* long stories." She stood, strolled over to the balcony bar, and picked the lock on the cabinet. With a click, the glass doors popped open. Holding up a small bottle, she asked, "Want one?"

"Are you trying to get me drunk, Miss Birch," Alastair chuckled.

"I think you're already half way *there*," Claire teased. She removed the cap off a wine cooler and took a swig.

"As your Mentor, I'm obligated to inform the Board of your under-aged drinking."

Losing the playfulness to her voice, she asked, "Is that why you won't kiss me? Because you're my Mentor?" Claire nervously rolled the bottle between her fingers. "I thought that role was over after the Placement Assembly."

Alastair shook his head while he pinched the bridge of his nose. "Claire, I still don't understand why you could possibly think that this is a good idea."

"What? You think I want a relationship?" She took a seat across from him in an armchair. "Al, I just want to make-out. It doesn't have to *mean* anything. Besides, I thought you liked kissing Zonese girls."

"You're *not* a Zonese."

Claire sighed, "There's no way that you're not aware of my past. I know about the stupid background checks—just like I know about your old fetish for scoping out the Middle Zone for ladies to smooch."

A look of horror spread across his face. "How do you know—"

"The young women you paid off aren't as discreet as you'd like them to be." She chugged the rest of her wine cooler before adding, "Don't worry. My lips can be sealed with a kiss."

"So this is *blackmail*? You won't tell the Societan Press about my past in exchange for letting you have your way with my body."

Walking towards him, Claire said, "No, that's not really my style. I only mentioned it in hopes that it would reignite the feelings of those memories." She sat down beside him and tossed the empty bottle away. "And, no, not your *whole* body—just your lips and hands."

Without warning, he leaned forward and kissed her hard on the mouth. Firm hands held her waist tightly, pulling her closer to him. "No one can know."

"Duh," Claire scoffed, positioning herself on top of him. "I'm the epitome of discretion."

Chapter 33

The longer Mezik lived, the more creative he had to be to find interesting ways to entertain himself.

Normally, he would waste hours listening in on people's conversations with the radio he had found in the attic. But someone must have become paranoid because all the signals were being jammed.

So he went about finding other ways to pass time. That morning Mezik had already teased the brunette triplet, Otum, for her crush on Dr. Darreth. Half an hour later, he disguised himself as a poor boy and suspiciously stalked the Jade Heir, Soha Darrow, who had been visiting Rikani on matters of business. The late morning was fairly frustrating as he and his cousin, Kumate, attempted to decipher Mutof's riddles while Uncle Dagnos and Aunt Nasiram contracted a deal with the Azure construction workers.

Now that it was the early afternoon, he was fresh out of entertainment schemes. Completely bored out of his mind, Mez decided to find the one person who never failed to be dull—his brother. He went to the garage, but Tays wasn't at his usual hang-out place.

Instead, Koen the scavenger was there by himself, unloading his latest haul of broken-down junk for Tays to fix up. "Have you seen Lord Tays, Master Mezik?"

"No. I was just about to ask you the same thing."

"I need him to sign for this shipment. He's fifteen minutes late." The scavenger held up a scanner.

"I'll sign for it." Mezik held out his wrist so that Koen could scan his Signature. "I'm assuming that everything is in order. I don't believe that Tays and Rikani have never had any problems with you."

"Sorry, no. I need someone with more *seniority*."

As he spoke, Rikani came rushing through the door. "Sorry, Koen. Tays has been M.I.A. all week." She held out her right wrist and brushed it against the scanner. Without another word, she turned around and exited the garage.

"Hey, Kani!" Mezik called, realizing his sister hadn't seen him. "Wait up."

"I'm very busy today, Mez. I don't have time for one of your scams to get out of the Azure HQ."

"No, it's not like that at all," he assured her, catching up to her brisk pace. "I was wondering why Tays is '*Missing In Action.*' What's going on?" When she didn't answer, he jolted in front of her and held his hands out.

She waved him away. "Never you mind all that. Go use your creative energy towards something useful. Or find Chera and start studying for your language exam."

"Don't change the subject. He's my brother, *too*. I wanna know what's happening."

With a sigh, she said, "I wish you'd just enjoy your childhood while you're still young. Getting involved in adult business is a sure-fire way to grow up too fast."

Mezik ignored that last comment. His mind was deep in thought. Tays had a tendency to go on long trips when he was agitated. There were a number of places he liked to go. "Maybe he went to the country side."

"No, his bike is still here. But he left a note a few days ago, hinting at his hide-hole. I can't read it, though. I hate his stupid messy hand-writing." Rikani fished out a crinkled piece of paper from her jacket and handed it to him. "We'll talk *later*. I'm late for a meeting with Zobin." She began walking away briskly, but stopped suddenly. "By the way, if you ever read Zobin's newspaper, 'New Blue View,' I *will* ground you for the rest of your life."

Mezik was tempted to ask why he was forbidden to read it, but he knew he'd end up in trouble just for asking. He already had enough upcoming schemes that he was sure to get in trouble for. Mezik decided his life would be a tiny bit better if he took a break from living in permanent penalty.

Besides, he was still being punished for one of his most dangerous schemes.

*****

For his twelfth birthday, Mezik Rye had asked for one thing: a day trip to Market.

As was expected, his brother and sister refused. They asked him again what he wanted, threatening that they'd buy him nothing for his special day if he repeated his request.

Mezik finally admitted his life-long dream of learning how to wall climb. Rikani and Tays saw nothing wrong with that gift, so they arranged for him to take lessons from one of the knowledgeable Clan members.

Mezik's coach turned out to be Sokun, a tall mass of bulky muscles. Sokun spent most of his time outside the Megacity, hunting for meat to bring back to the Clan chefs. He also had an extensive knowledge of rock climbing. Sokun took Mezik to an abandoned section of the Azure HQ that hadn't been renovated.

Three afternoons a week, the hunter showed Mezik how to create harnesses of rope to suspend him in the air if he were to lose his grip. The young Rye also learned how to fasten pulleys and hook them into the metal walls of the Megacity. Sokun showed him what were good foot and hand holds and how to tell which edges would slice his hand open without proper glove protection.

Two months passed and his teacher felt Mezik had learned about all he could. He even promised to take him outside Rygom when he turned sixteen and let him rock climb for real in the hills around the Megacity.

The next day, Mez woke early so as not to be seen by anyone. He slipped down the winding corridors until he reached his climbing practice area.

Pulling his pack from his shoulders, he began preparing for his escape. For eight weeks, he had been working on cutting through the floor. It had been such a time-consuming task because he was rarely left unsupervised. He removed a saw from his pack and made the last few hacks at the hole.

He poked his head down into the Sector below. It was still a part of the Azure HQ's property, but the construction workers had yet to renovate this area. It was the perfect place to make his escape.

After securing the riggings for his pulleys and ropes, Mezik put his pack on and tied the harness around his waist and chest.

Mezik began his descent. He picked his handholds carefully, like Sokun had taught him. It was a very long way down, but he tried not to think about that. A couple times, he slipped and fell a few feet before the ropes caught him. He regained his footing and continued on his way.

Near the bottom, Mezik got cocky, spending less time checking to find safe holds. About twenty feet from the bottom, his lack of attention caused him to put his hand on a sharp edge.

Yelping in pain, he instinctively jerked backward. He expected the harness to hold him.

It didn't.

His foot twisted in a hold, which caused him to plummet head-first to the ground. Mezik threw his hands out in front of him to protect his face. With a crunch, his body hit the floor. He tried to prop himself up onto his elbows. Pain shot up his arm. His left forearm was bent halfway between his elbow and wrist.

Cursing profusely, he rolled over as best he could with the pack on his shoulders.

A group of Azures appeared, all still in their night clothes. There was a chorus of voices above as they asked him questions and told him how concerned they felt when they heard him screaming.

A pair of Azures came running to up him a short time later. They helped the boy to his feet and escorted him to the Hospital Wing.

Dr. Darreth lay asleep on his cot.

"Darreth, wake up!" screeched one of the Trips.

"What is it, Otum?" He opened his eyes, staring at Mezik for half a second before he rose from bed. In moments, he had out his tray of shiny surgical instrument and began sterilizing a long, curved needle. "O, get him ready. Zett, go find Tays and Rikani. The rest of you need to leave."

Otum propped Mezik on a bed and shot him up with pain-killers. "Dr. Darreth will make things all better."

"You don't need to talk to me like I'm five," Mezik snapped.

"Sorry. Just lie still," the dark-haired Trip ordered. "He'll come by in a sec to set the break and sew you up. Are you thirsty?"

Mezik nodded and Otum left in search of a water pitcher.

Before she returned, Rikani and Tays came bursting through the doors.

Kani was frantic. "Mez! Are you okay? Does anything else hurt? How could you be so stupid! I'm never letting you out of my sight again!"

Tays did his best to get their sister out of Mez's face, pulling at her shoulders. But his actions were futile as Kani's adrenaline kicked in. He gave up and just stared at Mezik with a disappointed glare.

Dr. Darreth came by the bed, managing to shoo Rikani away with just the wave of his hand. He put something wooden in Mezik's mouth and placed his hands on the wound. With a quick jerk, the bone snapped into place. He patted Mezik on the shoulder reassuringly before stitching the gashed skin together.

When the doctor was done, Otum reappeared. She removed the wood from Mez's mouth and offered him cup of water.

"Maybe we should just lock him up until he's sixteen," Rikani spat, plopping onto the cot beside Mezik's. Her gaze remained on the stitched flesh on her littlest brother's arm. "We need to save him from himself."

Tays stood between Mezik and Rikani. "Kani, go home. I'll talk to him."

After shooting Tays a cautious glance, Rikani walked away with a huff.

Dr. Darreth finished sewing the last stitch. “If you had fallen differently, you might have died. Keep that in mind the next time you want to go climbing.” He gathered his things and gave them some alone time.

Tays was quiet for a few minutes before saying, “Do you know why Rikani and I hold onto you so tight?”

“You have a compulsive need to control everything?” Mezik scoffed, rolling his eyes.

“That’s only *part* of it. We’ve lost a lot. You are the last thing we truly care about. We think that by holding on tight, we’ll never lose you, *too*.”

Mezik shook his head. “I understand that you worry I’ll end up dead like half of our family. But I can’t live cooped up like a prisoner. I need some freedom, Tays! I want adventure, and I can’t get that while stuck in the Azure HQ.”

*****

Unfolding the paper, Mezik was surprised at the number of grease smears over the dark ink.

He read as he walked down the empty corridor. Only a handful of letters were legible

L□□v□□g □□□ aw□□le. Con□□c□ □nl□ □□ □□ em□□ge□□y. C□□pi□□ at t□□ Un□□□□eve□□□s.

Lov□,

Tay□

Some words were more readable than others. After looking at the note more closely, he could see some of the black lines among the grease, but the words did little to help him discover Tays's location.

Mezik was so absorbed with his project that he didn't notice that Chera had begun following him. "Whatcha doing?"

"Trying to read something."

"*Trying*? Didn't my mom teach you how to read like eight years ago?"

"Ha ha. Very funny." Mezik looked up from the note. "The paper is all smeary; I can't tell what these words are."

"Maybe I can help." Chera took the paper from his hands and looked at it silently for a minute. "Hmmm. I can't make all the letters out, but I think it says, '*Leaving for awhile. Contact only in an emergency. Camping at the—*" She paused and squinted at the last word. "I'm not entirely sure about this last part. Based on the letters I can make out, I know only one word that fits." Her pleasant smile disappeared. "*The Underdevelops*."

The way she said it sent a chill up Mezik's back, even though that word meant absolutely nothing to him. He wasn't sure if he should look scared or brave. In the end, he tried to seem indifferent. "Oh, yeah. I know all about that place," he lied. "It's not a big deal. Tays goes there all the time."

Chera gasped, her eyes widening in shock. "He does? Your brother must be some sort of daredevil or something."

"It runs in the family, I guess," Mezik replied, not sure why he felt the need to impress his classmate. "I go there to visit him sometimes. I was just about to go there anyways. So, I'll see ya tomorrow in class."

Turning to leave, he found that she began walking with him. "Do you mind if I come along?" Chera asked, hesitantly. "I've always wanted to go to the Underdevelops."

"Um, I suppose you could come along." He paused, trying to come up with a way to disguise his lie. "Would you mind if I stopped by my sister's office first? I need to get, uh, *something*."

Chera nodded, looking scared and yet thrilled.

When they reached the office, Mezik said, "Wait out here in the lobby. I just need to discuss some important, uh, business stuff with Vian. I'll be right back."

In the outer chamber of the office, Vian was busy typing at her desk. The Crimson woman barely looked up from her work as she asked, "And what can I do for you, Master Mezik?"

"I heard a startling rumor today about the Underdevelops. People seem to have the impression that they aren't safe."

"Well, what today really *is* safe?" Vian asked, rhetorically. She stopped typing and turned to face him. Her discerning eyes looked the young Rye over. "You can have accidents in the most unlikely of places."

"*Accidents*? So that's why some people are scared of them?"

"No, it's more than that. The Underdevelops are parts of the Azure HQ that haven't been renovated. It's about as dangerous as the rest of the Lower Region." After a second, Vian asked, "You're not planning an escape through the Underdevelops, are you?"

"Why does everyone think that everything I ask about is involved with a break-out?" Mezik sighed and took a seat across from her. "I think Tays has been hiding out in the Underdevelops. I'm planning an intervention—which just so happens to be supported by Rikani. For once, she's angrier at him than me."

That seemed to appease Vian. "Alright. If it will get Tays in trouble, I'll tell you what you want to know."

"How do I get there?"

Vian pulled a small brochure from a desk drawer. She flipped to a map and handed it to Mezik. "Do you know where the Trips' new green house is being built? It's right below that floor. On the main stair way, go down one more level past that. Everything beyond that is the Underdevelops."

"I owe you one, Vian." Mezik pocketed the brochure, waved good-bye, and headed back to Chera. Moving past her, he said, "Let's go."

They traveled for several minutes, chatting about the insignificant nothings of their everyday lives. Chera seemed exceedingly pleased about something, but Mezik had to try to not look bored.

"Are you worried?" he asked her.

"A little. But I have you to protect me." Chera reached down and took his hand.

Making no move to pull away, Mezik stammered, "Um, yeah. Sure, cuz I've been there before and know which dangers to watch out for."

Being so concerned about where he was headed, he didn't hear Chera's next question. They had entered the dark passages of the Underdevelops. Mezik was too busy thinking about all the scary things they might encounter to pay any attention to her. So, out of years of habit, he simply answered 'yes' to whatever she said.

"Do you really mean that?" Chera asked, moving closer to him.

"Huh?" Mezik blinked absent-mindedly at her.

"Do you really *like* me?"

"Oh, no. I don't—"

Chera stopped and pulled her hand out of his. "Then why did you *say* that you did?"

"Honestly, I wasn't listening," Mezik admitted, letting go of her hand. "Sorry."

"Sorry? You're *sorry*? Oh, that's just fine. I only opened my heart to you and you didn't even have the decency to pay attention!" She flung her fists dramatically in front of her.

Mezik stepped away. "Whoa! Calm down. It's not a big deal."

"Of course it's a *big deal*," Chera sobbed. "I told you that I liked you and you don't like me back. We still have to see each other *five days a week* for school. It's gonna be so *awkward* and weird. On top of it all, I'm in the *scariest* place I've ever been and I'm *stuck* with you! So don't tell me to *calm down*!"

She stepped toward him, causing him to retreat. He was so busy watching her hands that he forgot to watch his own feet. He tripped over a metal box and fell backwards.

Unfortunately for him, backwards was an open hole in the middle of the floor. He felt weightless for a moment as his body was in free-fall. But the sense was not long-lived. His feet were caught in something and his body swung upside-down.

"I've got you," Chera huffed as the clutched his legs. "Are you alright?"

Mezik took a quick inventory of his body. Everything felt intact. The only strange sensation he experienced was a headache from all the blood pooling into his head. "I'm fine. Are you sure you have me?"

"For the moment. But who knows how long that'll last! What should we do?"

"I was thinking about yelling as loudly as I can for my brother and hope that he hears me. What do you think?"

Chera instantly began yelling for Lord Rye.

Mezik joined her. He shouted, "Tays!" and "Help!" intermittently. No more than thirty seconds passed before a second pair of hands grasped his ankles. Before he knew it, Mezik was lying beside his brother.

"What are you—"

"Kani sent me," Mezik interrupted. "She's worried about you."

"I just wanted some alone time," Tays sighed, leaning back. "Kani shouldn't have sent you here; it's dangerous." He let Mezik go and gently touched his ankle. "Your foot is swelling. I'll need to carry you. I have to get something from my camp first. I'll be right back." He vanished into the shadows.

"We never finished our conversation," Chera whispered, kneeling beside Mezik.

"Ah, come on!" he moaned, covering his eyes with his arms so he couldn't see her hurt expression. "I don't want to get involved in all the mushy crap. We have the rest of our lives to make mistakes. Let's just be kids and have a good time. *Okay*?"

Chera nodded and hugged him. "I'll try not to think about you like that. But I can't stop caring about you, Mezik Rye."

Tays was carrying a pack when he returned. "I might as well come home for awhile. Kani might venture out here herself if I'm gone any longer." He picked up his little brother and began walking towards the safe levels of the Azure HQ.

Chera followed by closely.

Once they reached the lighted floors, Chera took off for home, promising to come by that evening to check up on him. With her gone, Mezik had the opportunity to ask Tays all the questions he had wanted to.

"Why did you leave?" Mez inquired as he was carried once again to Dr. Darreth.

"I was angry about losing a client."

"That seems like a silly thing to be upset about," Mez laughed, suddenly feeling euphoric. "There are plenty of other clients out there."

Tays shook his head. "Not like this one. This was the *ultimate* client—the answer to the Clan's financial problems. I wanted to show Kani that The Sapphire Pawn is important and that I could do something to help the Azures. But I failed. My pride was hurt, and I ran away like a child having a tantrum."

"Was it that big Agency contract that you and Kani thought I didn't know about?" Mezik asked.

"I suppose we need to learn that you pick up some of the things we talk about."

"But I don't entirely understand. It has to be more important than just money to make you leave. What else was this about?"

"So you already know that we use to be Societans," Tays whispered as they passed a group of gawking Azures. "Well, our family was in competition with another family. It was rather humiliating when father lost the company. In dealing with the Agency, I worked with this family again. Mostly it was with the sons and not so much their father. However, I got to show that I'm not the same as dad—that I can be successful even with the disadvantage of being a Regioner."

"Oddly, that makes perfect sense to me."

"Like I said, it doesn't matter anymore. They terminated the contract."

"I'm sure you'll have another shot again. Keep working hard and an opportunity will eventually open up," Mezik encouraged with a smile. "I'd like to help you the next time. I want to show that we're not a family of losers like everyone thinks we are."

Tays looked away. "I'm not so sure about *that*."

Chapter 34

Having made a promise to her new friend, Eve, Iris decided to begin wasting her precious afternoon hours by slacking off.

Under normal circumstances, she'd been in the gym, running half a dozen miles or so before dinner. Instead, she wandered aimlessly through the Plazas nearest to her Living Quarters. She had no idea what to do for the rest of the day. Maybe if she ran into someone she knew, she could hang out with them.

However, there was no one around. Very few Trainees frequented the Grey Circumstance before 7:00; on a whim, Iris decided to go anyways.

The club was practically empty. A handful of patrons were spread about the main room. She knew none of them. If Eve were there, she'd tell her to go introduce herself to the other Trainees.

But Iris needed a little confidence booster. She moved to the bar and eyed the menu. Many of the drinks were alcoholic. Since she was only eighteen—and had never been in a situation that required a fake ID—she eyed the sugary stuff. Flagging down the barista, she asked, "Can I have some of that vanilla drink, please?"

The man looked confused. "We don't usually—"

Cutting him off, she said, "I'm not in the mood to do *the usual*. Serve me up a glass." After thinking for a second, she changed her mind. "Wait. You might as well get me a whole bottle."

The baffled server handed her a fresh bottle and scanned her OMNI credit file.

Iris removed the top and took her first swig. She coughed as the sickenly sweet liquid threatened to come back up. "I think I might need some water, too." Taking another sip, she found that it went down better.

Since she only had sugary things every once in awhile, Iris wasn't use to the feeling of euphoria. Something strange came over her. Bottle in hand, she made her way over to the stage.

Several instruments stood up in their various stands, waiting to be played. Iris's extensive education didn't include music, nor any of performing arts for that matter. Setting her drink on the floor, she picked up a guitar and began plucking the strings.

The sudden noise got the attention of the other customers. They glared at the interruption. Many close to her got up and strode to the far end of the club.

Iris wasn't deterred; she kept playing, believing that she grew better with every strum.

For a few moments, she forgot all her problems. She lost herself into her impromptu performance. Closing her eyes, Iris took all her frustration out on the guitar strings. Her fingernails scrapped against the metal strings every few beats to change up the monotony of the regular strumming. When she opened her eyes, half of the scattered crowd was gone.

Growing bored of the guitar, she moved onto another instrument. The piano looked like fun; there were so many more notes to combine. She experimented for several minutes, learning what keys and pedals made which sounds.

She indulged in another gulp of her sugary vanilla beverage. With each sip, she felt a lightening of her spirit.

Iris was almost ready to go meet new people when a somewhat familiar face approached.

"Good afternoon, Miss Kayn." Agent Drew Harding sat down beside her and shut the cover over the piano keys. "How are feeling today?"

"Absolutely amazing, thank you very much!"

"Might I ask what you're doing?"

"I'm taking some good advice to heart by trying something new."

"That's wonderful, but do you have to try something new in *public*?" he asked in a low voice. "Perhaps you should go practice somewhere *private* before giving a concert. Doesn't that sound like fun?"

Iris pulled open the lid again and started composing a little song. "No, I need to show people that I *suck* at stuff. I'm not a perfect little *goody-two-shoes*."

Agent Harding raised an eyebrow. His next words were said slowly, as though he was still processing her explanation while he spoke. "So you're trying to make yourself more desirable by showing off your weaknesses?"

"Yes! It's been pointed out to me that people think I'm a robot. But I'm not!" She began to chug her bottle, but he took it from her.

He looked over the label. "You're drinking *vanilla syrup*?"

"I guess so. It's pretty good." Iris felt her lips form into a wide, involuntary smile. A few high-pitched giggles burst out of her mouth.

"Oh, I see. You're hyper," Drew groaned, easing her off the piano bench. His other hand still kept the syrup out of Iris' reach. "I was kind of hoping you were intoxicated. I know what to do with drunks—not hyper children."

"I'm not a *child*!" Iris pouted, smacking him on the shoulder.

Agent Harding went to the nearest trash chutes and dumped the bottle. "Miss Kayn, some Trainees have registered complaints against you. I need you to leave with me."

Iris pulled her knives out and swung them at him.

He easily dodged as he bore a handful of throwing knives.

"I'm not done with my song!" When Drew backed off, Iris sheathed her blades. She plopped down at a percussion set and began banging at the drums.

Drew Harding looked uncertain for a second, but he put his throwing knives back into his blazer. After typing something into his OMNI, he sighed and said, "Congratulations on successfully being beyond my control; not many can brag about besting me. Have a good night, Miss Kayn."

With him gone, Iris ordered another vanilla syrup and gulped half of it in one sitting. The barista gave her a disturbed look, but she ignored him. Recovering from the buzz-kill that Drew brought on, she began composing lyrics to go with her drumming.

Sometime later—she was unsure of how long—the Vega brothers showed up. Max looked rather amused. Alastair was expressionless.

"Hey, we've been looking for you," Max said with his usual playful grin.

Iris found the petals to the cymbals. "Now that you've found me, Maximus, what'd you want with me?"

"We thought you might want to talk to someone."

"I'm fine," she replied, continuing her rock song. "Besides, I have Claire to talk to if I need to."

"Yes," Alastair commented as he limped towards her. "But I doubt Claire really understands how you're feeling. You're probably tired of hearing, 'It's not your fault,' from everyone."

"So you're here to tell me that it *is* my fault?" Iris scrunched her face up as she tried to understand the logic in their words.

"No, not at all," Max said with a nod. "Maybe. Perhaps just a little. It's—."

Iris rocked out on the drums, hitting all the different parts to an uneven rhythm. She paused briefly to retort, "You know, I wish you Vegas would just say what you *mean*. I'm sick of all the politics of the Agency. It should be simple. Something should either be *good* or *bad* for people—no ambiguity."

"*Now* what are you talking about?" Max asked, loudly.

"Nothing," Iris shouted over the ring of the cymbal. "I just hate that the Agency is rescinding the Rehabilitation Act because of one incident!" With her hands paused over the snare, she added, "I really think we could have done some good with the Regioners."

There was something else that bothered her too, although she would never be able to tell him. One of the men that took Eve had mentioned Alterations. Whoever hired them thought that either Iris or Eve were super-humans. Iris knew it wasn't her. Miss Sanders had yelled that she was one. Perhaps it was more than a distraction. Maybe she really *was* one of those vile creations the Trainees had spread tales about.

The thought made her head hurt—either that or the ridiculous amount of sugar she had just consumed.

"Are you okay, Iris?" Alastair asked.

She hadn't realized she had shut her eyes nor that she was shaking her head. "Oh, it's nothing."

"Perhaps you should go lie down before dinner," Max suggested. "May we walk you to your Living Quarters?"

Iris nodded and dropped her drum sticks. Once home, she pressed her OMNI to the lock and the door opened. They stepped inside to find Claire Birch busy at her desk with some wire and miniature hover engines.

Claire looked up when they entered and rushed over to the Vegas. "You won't believe what I've been through today!"

"I'm going to go get some pain relievers," Iris said, heading to the stairs.

"Hurry back," Claire replied, curtly. "I want you to hear what I have to say, too."

Moments later, Iris returned to the sitting room, carrying four small pills in her palm; it was more than the recommended dose, but she didn't care. She pulled a bottle of water out of the pantry, took the pills, and drank a few sips.

Claire was already yelling at Max and Alastair. "How does it feel to have the most sinister man in Rygom as a *father*?"

Max shrugged. "We've gotten use to it."

"What did he do?" Alastair asked.

Claire fumed. Pointing a finger at the Vega brothers, she said, "I've spent the past eight hours being poked and prodded like a lab animal because Tobias Vega and the other Agency Board Members accused me of being an Alteration!" She looked so steamed that she might throw a punch at them.

"I thought you had gotten over your anger about this," Iris whispered, moving between Miss Birch and the Vegas. "We've talked it through. Yes, it sucks, but there's *no way* you could be one."

"I *was* better," Claire snapped. "I went into the examination all confident and stuff. But I'm so sore from all the pin pricks and standing still for the body scans. And *the incessant, repetitive questions!* My fury has been reawakened and it's about to get vengeance."

Max stepped forward, his hands out in front of him. "Look, Claire, you're not the first person that's been falsely accused of being an Alteration. About once or twice a year, the Board takes a handful of exceptional students and does a thorough study of their anatomy. It's mostly a precautionary procedure."

This seemed to appease Claire. She folded her hands and relaxed a bit. "I guess when you put it that way, it's not too bad. It was still really humiliating." Without another word, Claire descended the stairs.

Alastair turned to Iris. "Regarding the medical examination, the Board wants to be extra careful about Alteration rumors—especially since Eve's abduction."

In a low voice, Max said, "Al, that's probably not the best thing to say at this moment."

"No, it's okay," Iris assured them. She eased her way through the common area and carefully lowered onto a couch. "We can talk about Eve. It still feels totally surreal, but I'm learning to deal with it."

Max suddenly said, "We need something to lift our moods. I think Eve would want us all to be happy."

"What should we do? Have a party or something?"

"That sounds great, but I'm supposed to meet Viola in ten minutes. However, you and Al could plan something. See you later." Max left in a hurry.

"So, what would you like to do?" Iris asked, gesturing for Alastair to sit on the other couch. She rubbed her temples, hoping her headache would go away so she could go out with her companions. "Should we all go back to the Grey Circumstance tonight?"

"No," he said rather quickly. Alastair cleared his throat and added, "We've been to the Grey Circumstance so many times. And I was thinking of something a little more *private*. I was hoping maybe *you and I* could go get something to eat. Maybe somewhere a little fancy and fun? I know this great restaurant—"

"Alastair," Iris interrupted. "Are you asking me on a *date*?" She wasn't sure if she was hearing everything correctly; her brain was still heavily under the influence of her sugary drinks.

"Well, there isn't exactly a *name* for what I am asking. There's no word in the English language to describe two friends simply getting something to eat. You could say I'm inviting you to hang out or to have a friendly excursion with me. But, no, no—not a date."

"Okay. I guess we could do that."

"How about tomorrow night at 6:00 pm? And, if it's alright with you, I'd like to show you something afterwards." Alastair exited the Living Quarters, leaving Iris to her thoughts.

Her head swam, making her feel dizzy. Questions filled up her mind. If the outing was just going to be *friendly*, why did he seem so nervous about it? Why would he choose a fancy restaurant? And, most importantly, what did he want to show her? These things consumed her.

She didn't even realize when Claire reentered. "What's with the weird look on your face?"

Iris had no idea what her friend was talking about.

"You have this goofy smile, but your eyes seem sad or upset." Claire gave her a confused glare. "You have a secret! Tell me everything!"

Chapter 35

Pretending to take notes, Tays scribbled ideas for his shop onto his notepad. Around him, the Clan Elders prattled on about Lower Region matters. He kept an ear open to make sure that he didn't miss anything important.

"So what if the Agency is repealing the Renovation Act?" Pakoat asked, leaning back in his over-sized, emerald green chair. Even since he sold the Jade Darrow Clan to Unmare, he had enjoyed living the end of his life in bliss as an Elder. He didn't seem to care what happened to the Region. "Back when I ruled, I didn't need the democratic government coming in and fixing things. We got along just fine, thank you."

Zafrok, the oldest member of the Icterine Clan, snorted awake. "Huh? Oh, no. I don't think so. You former Leaders let things get out of control." He wiped at pastry crumbs on his nauseatingly yellow suit. "We could use a change around here."

Tays felt out of place. He was by far the youngest person in the Council. But technically he wasn't an Elder. He was only filling in for his Uncle Asdem, who refused to leave Rye Manor in the Azure Head Quarters. Someone else probably should have been appointed, but Tays and

Rikani didn't trust anyone well enough to protect their interests in Council matters.

"Well what about all the Alteration rumors?" Elder Kasta was a firm woman who didn't like dealing with nonsense. From what Tays knew about her, he figured she was once a Societan—a good friend of Lady Lurahi Bray, the Mayor's former wife. Kasta turned to Fraz, a disgusted frown on her bright pink lips. "Do you still have contacts in the Agency? Perhaps we could send one of our spies to see what the Board knows about Lizra's and Tolim's research?"

Fraz wore a freakish amount of make up on her face. She blinked her deep purple eyelids as she processed what the Magenta Elder had asked. "*Spies*? I think it's a little soon for that, isn't it?" She took a deep breath before saying, "My relations would certainly be willing to help, but that will only escalate the matter. Let's hold off a little longer."

The conversation continued around the table. As was custom, it moved to the right down the half-circle of brightly-colored chairs. Other Elders looked as though they wanted to speak, but they had to hold their tongues until control of the dialogue retuned to them.

“I don’t have anything to say,” Tesro replied to the expectant looks of the other Elders. He loosened his orange tie and set it on the table. “I pass.”

“Why do you always pass, huh?” Matolin, the former Region King, smacked the table. “Come on, Tesro! You haven’t contributed in weeks. I don’t think Lord Dagnos will be happy to hear that you aren’t fulfilling your duties.” The Crimson Elder normally spent his turns trying to motivate Tesro to contribute, which always ended in Matolin not saying anything productive either. He turned to Tays. “What about Asdem? Is he still in the loop about current events? When is he coming back to the Council?”

Tays ceased his doodling. “Oh, I’m not sure. Asdem recently started roaming the rest of the Azure Manor instead of just his room. It only took him five/six years to get to that point. So it might be another ten years before he comes back to these meetings.” He knew he shouldn’t be talking like that in front of the Elders, but he couldn’t help being cynical. “Oh, speaking of family, I have a dinner I need to get to. Can we wrap it up for the day?”

The others nodded. They all stood and left without any other discussion. Tays dashed past them, out into the streets of the Market. He made his way to the Transit

Station and took a Train three Plazas East before taking an Elevator Down six Plazas.

At the Azure HQ entrance, he entered the code and rushed by the security officers. Bilez, Hurez, and Janez saluted and returned to studying the video monitors.

Dinner had already been served by the time he arrived.

Tays patted Asdem on the shoulder, who sat picking olives out of a bowl of salad by the door.

"The Elders say hi," Tays said, taking a tomato chunk from the bowl. "They miss having you in Council sessions. Any chance you want to resume your duties, uncle?"

"I can't," Asdem replied, handing him a cucumber slice. Jomiq and the boys will be home any day from their trip. I want to be here when they do. It's been such a long time since I've seen them."

"Whatever you say." Tays smiled at him, trying to be encouraging about his uncle's tragedy-induced dementia. He then went to join the rest of his family at the table.

Rikani fawned over how smart Kumate was and Nasiram and Dagnos did their best to keep Mezik entertained with stories from the Amber Rush Clan. Tays sat at the head of the table and began filling his plate with food.

"How was the Council meeting today?" Aunt Nasiram asked, a look of sympathy on her face. "Anything interesting happen?"

"The Elders are worried about the repealed Renovation Act." Tays replied. "Kasta bickered about send spies to Upper Society. It was a nightmare." He turned to Rikani and said, "We've got to appoint a new Elder. These meetings are killing me. Who's the eldest Azure?"

Rikani turned away from Kumate. "That'd be Bast, but we'd end up with a similar issue as sending Uncle Asdem. I might make Zobin an Elder, but I'm afraid he'll publish all the Council secrets in his New Blue View magazine." She irately stabbed her lamb casserole with her fork. "I've even offered it to Tarek once, but he says he is retired and needs to relax or something."

"And I suppose you can't ask Rutab since he still has his Tyrian Signature," Mezik commented. "He'd be an interesting choice, though."

There was a lull in the conversation as everyone ate their meal. Asdem took one dish at a time to eat as he meandered around the room. The chefs, Myhus and Haben, refilled the serving plates as they emptied.

"Hey, how about Myhus?" Mezik asked. "He's pretty old, huh?"

The senior cook scooped fruit salad into a large bowl. "And what I am I old enough to do, Master Mezik?"

"You could be our new Elder! What do you think, Kani?"

"I appreciate the offer, but I'm afraid that my grandchildren need me in the kitchen." Myhus bowed and quickly left the dining room.

Roteg came in before the door swung closed. His face was sweaty and his gold blonde hair clumped to his forehead. He smoothed the long strands behind his ears. "Good evening, Ma'ams and Sirs. I, uh, need Tays for a couple minutes."

Tays piled food onto his plate and followed his employee out of Rye Manor. He gulped down his food as they walked in the direction of his garage. "Everything alright?" the Azure Lord asked as he finished his meal. He wiped his mouth of the inside of his sleeve. When the sales associate didn't answer, he began to grow concerned. "Why do you look so upset, Ro?"

"I really don't want to do this," Roteg explained in an agitated tone. He stopped outside the garage. "Please understand that I didn't have a choice."

The door opened. Exada stood over Vian, holding a gun to her older sister's head.

"Hello, handsome. Thanks for coming."

Vian let out a sob as tears ran down her face. "Ada, you don't have to do this."

"Now sis, this isn't any of your business." Exada holstered her gun and motioned for Vian to go to her fiancé. "Take your man elsewhere. I don't care what you do, so long as you don't tell anyone that I'm here."

Scrambling towards Roteg, Vian let him pull her into his arms. After giving Tays a sympathetic look, Ro carried her out of the garage.

Tays stared at his ex-girlfriend. She wore one of her usual red and black patterned leather outfit. Her platinum blonde hair was straight and sleek, tucked underneath a scarlet headband. Exada put on her innocent smile as she approached him.

"From what I've heard, you've had a rough couple of weeks." She came to within inches of his face.

He took a step back. "As much as I don't care for you sister, I don't like how you got me here." Tays tried not to notice her flowery perfume. Swallowing hard, he continued, "Now just tell me what you want."

"Always to the point, Tay-Tay. I always liked that about you." Exada moved toward him until he backed into a wall. She ran her black finger nails up and down his chest. "I've been thinking about you're little mishap with the Agency. I believe that I have a solution to your problem."

"Really? Knowing you, you're going to say go kill them all."

She chuckled loudly—a devious and yet somehow beautiful laugh. "Yeah, that sounds like me kind of thing. But, no. For my plan to work, we need to get back together."

*****

Life couldn't have been better for Lord Tays Rye. He had a wonderful sister and brother, his business was booming, and the most beautiful woman in the Megacity loved him. For the past six months, he had lived in absolute bliss as he and Exada planned the rest of their life together.

Heading home early, he stopped at the Trips' produce stand and bought a bouquet full of brightly colored flowers. On the journey home, he regularly checked his jacket pocket for the small, square box to ensure that it was still there. He rehearsed proposal lines in the Elevator as it traveled Down. In the end, he decided to just wing his speech.

Exada sat in his room, reading something on his computer. Tays crept in quietly and wrapped his arms across her chest. As he moved to kiss her neck, an elbow collided with his ribs. Stunned, he fell back and rubbed where he had been hit.

"Oh, Tay-Tay! I'm so sorry!" Exada spun in her chair, a look of shock and concern on her face.

When she got up to help him, his attention caught on the blank screen of the computer. He tore his gaze away since it made him paranoid about what she was reading when he interrupted her. Holding up the flowers, he discovered that they had been mauled by Exada's startled attack.

"Were those for me? Oh, you are the sweetest boyfriend ever!" She began picking at the unharmed buds, snapping off the crumpled stems. "I'm going to press these so that I can have them forever."

Unable to keep his mind from his computer, Tays asked, "What were you doing, Ada?"

She blinked at him. "What are you talking about?"

"I gave you your own computer. Why were you on mine?" He sat up and moved toward the screen.

"Oh, I think mine might have a virus." Exada pulled herself into his arms and kissed his cheek. She slipped her fingers through the holes between his shirt buttons and caressed his chest hair. "I was looking up ways to take care of that on *your* computer. I hope you don't mind, Tay-Tay."

He sat at his desk chair and pulled her into his lap. "You want to be careful when de-bugging a hard drive. I want to make sure that you found a credible site." Tays began going through the search history when Exada's hands took his.

"That's okay, Tays. You don't need to do that," she assured him with a smile. "I looked at multiple sources and they all said the same thing. Wanna come help me fix it?"

"In a second." He moved her hands back to his chest and resumed his search. "The history has been cleared." Tays went to the icon that showed the most recently used applications. "Exada, why were you looking in my files?"

She kissed him hard on the mouth.

"Stop!" He pushed her away. "What's going on? Please tell me the truth."

Exada stood and paced the length of the room. "Okay, I guess I can't hide the truth any longer." In an instant, the warm, loving woman he cared about disappeared. Her posture straightened and her face became fierce. "No use in pretending anymore. I'm not the helpless little girl you think I am."

Tays's mouth couldn't form words. A thousand sentences threatened to come out all at once.

"My deceased mother was Daelym Steel, Heiress of the Crimson Clan. Her sister, Queen Romisa, is my aunt. I've been sent by her and my father, Steward Pavoc, to infiltrate the Azure Rye Clan and learn its weaknesses."

"*Infiltrate*?" He rubbed his temples and let out a shuddering breath. "You've been *spying* on me for the past six months?"

"Yep!" Exada sniggered, her laugh devious and cruel. "It's probably been the best assignment I've ever had. I got to date a Clan Lord. The pampering has been quite nice. And you just made it *so easy* to manipulate you."

Tays couldn't control himself any longer. He flung himself at her, reaching for her throat.

She blocked both his hands, striking at the wrists with her fists. A kick landed in his abdomen, causing him to fly across the room in his desk chair.

Exada clicked her tongue. "That wasn't very gentlemanly, Tay-Tay. Here I am being honest and you go and attack me." She approached him, not a hint of worry in her eyes. "Now, can I finish explaining without you trying to choke me again?" When he nodded, she sat on his bed so that she was at his level. "I really tried to love you, Tays. You're just so *boring*, though. You live such a plain life for someone who has the potential to do world-changing things."

The ring box in his jacket pocket felt heavy. Tays shrugged the material off and leaned back in the chair. How could he be so wrong about someone? He was so sure that he knew Exada. He felt like a fool. Rubbing his stomach, he asked, "So none of it was real? Six months of my life were a complete waste."

"Yep—a complete waste. Well, *for you,* at least. *For me*, it's been pretty productive. I've got some good information of your Clan to give to Aunt Romisa." Exada pulled out a small aerosol can and covered her face before spraying him.

Tays barely registered what was happening before his vision went dark.

*****

"You really think I'd ever agree to date you again?" Tays scoffed, pushing past her.

Exada molded back to the soft, sweet woman he once loved. "Tay-Tay, I know you still have feelings for me somewhere. I've heard you talking with Roteg about me."

"Wait, what? You've *heard* me talking to Ro? Do you have my shop bugged?"

"Oh, silly Tays! Of course I do! I had to make sure that the LERJ Gang wasn't influencing you. Don't be mad. I did it for the Region." Exada batted her eyelashes at him. "In fact, getting back together is for the good of the Regioners as well. And I know how much you love helping people."

Tays shook his head. "I don't care what you have to say. I can't trust you, so I'll never love you again."

"Love? No, I'm not asking you to *love* me, Tays. I just want you to marry me so that we can rule the Region together." She was quiet a moment while her former lover processed her words. "Yes, that's right. I'm proposing to you now, just like you almost did a couple months ago. Together, we can de-throne my aunt and take over as Monarchs. King Tays and Queen Exada. What do you think?"

“You really don’t know me, do you?” Tays laughed incredulously. “I hate responsibility. Sure, I’d like to help people, but not while having everyone come to me with their problems.”

“Oh, Tay-Tay, I’m not suggesting we rule from the Azure Clan. I’m already in line for the throne. Technically, I have two people in front of me—my aunt’s illegitimate son and my older sister. But I’ve got a plan in place to keep Romisa’s Matevak out of the Region. And Vian has abdicated her lineage by choosing to become an Azure. Once I’m crowned, I’ll be able to approve Vian’s request to transfer Clans so that she can marry Roteg.”

Tays turned his back to her and discreetly picked a screwdriver from his work bench. After tucking it in his sleeve, he faced Exada. “I’d have to be stupid to help you achieve that kind of power. I can’t even imagine what horrors you’d unleash—no matter how many good things you promise to accomplish.”

Exada looked sincerely hurt at his comment. “*I’m not a monster*! Yes, I can be a little more abrasive and scary than most women. But that doesn’t mean that I don’t also have a sensitive side. We can do a lot of good as Monarchs.”

"It sounds like you already have a fairly solid plan. Why do you even need me?"

"I'll need an Heir. I'd prefer someone with a pedigree. Nuto would work—even though he's adopted—but he is fawning over Soha. Nasiram won't let me in the Amber HQ, so I can't get at Dagnos. Besides, he's middle-aged now. I could go for Unmare's grandson, but she keeps him locked up, ready to marry Belana on her 21st birthday. So really that only leaves you, Tay-Tay. We don't really even need to get married. All I need is to occasionally share you bed until I get pregnant. Except, I'd rather not go down the same course that my Aunt Romisa took."

Tays stared at her, rage threatening to take over his body. "You need to leave right now." When she didn't move, he shouted, "Get out!"

She didn't seem deterred. "I'll try again later. Matters in the Region are going to get out of hand soon. If only you knew what I do. Oh, well. Maybe in a few weeks you'll come begging to be with me. Only time will tell." Exada moved to the door but then paused with her hand on the controls. "I do hope little Mezik is making good use of the radio scanner I left him." Before Tays could reply, she dashed through the door and disappeared down the hallway.

Chapter 36

Feeling vain, Alastair carefully checked himself in the full-length mirror for the fifth time in ten minutes. He smoothed down his dark hair, searched for wrinkles in his white dress shirt, and adjusted his gold tie.

"Stop fussing!" Max ordered as he walked across the room. He pulled the mirror off its hook and turned it so that it faced the wall. With a huff, he plopped into his over-sized lounge chair. "Why are you so nervous? It's just a date." Max began spinning around in the chair, looking up at the ceiling as he did so.

"It's *not a date*. I'm not romantically interested in her."

"Sure, whatever you say." Max sat up quickly and blinked the dizziness out of his eyes. "But know this, Al: Viola and I were crazy about each other for years, having just 'friendly get-togethers' before I finally told her how I felt. If you really like Iris, let her know. It'll save you a lot of awkward moments—not to mention years of remaining in 'friend status' when you could be in a loving relationship."

Alastair began putting on his shoes and scoffed, "Thanks for the advice, but it isn't needed. Iris and I are just getting something to eat somewhere more private where we can, um, share our, um, feelings about, um, stuff."

"Yes, do the whole 'share your feelings' thing. Girls love it! Your tongue will be in her mouth before you leave the restaurant."

"Are you ever serious about *anything*?"

"Not if I can help it," Max chuckled, raising his eye brows at his brother. "But you keeping your feelings to yourself isn't a good thing. I mean, your last girlfriend was kidnapped and forced to be a Regioner."

"Eve wasn't my *girlfriend*," Al snapped. "And I think it's completely inappropriate to talk about her situation with such flippancy. She deserves our pity."

"She has always wanted more than just your *pity*."

"Shut it." Alastair took a swing at his brother, but his bad leg threw him off.

Max easily dodged the punch.

At that moment, their father entered the room without bothering to knock. "So, are you ready for your date with Miss Kayn?"

"Apparently it's *not* a *date*," Max said, throwing his hands in the air.

"We're going out as friends." Alastair was growing impatient with his nosy family.

"And where are you going on your little outing?" Tobias asked.

"I have a reservation at SUPERNOVA."

"Oooo! A reservation? That sounds awfully romantic!" Max teased, punching Al in his side.

Alastair resisted the urge to throw something at him.

"Is that all? Or do you have something else planned?" His father looked at him with his *I'm waiting for an answer* glare. When Alastair didn't respond, he continued, "You requested time to enter the Improvement Center for 9:00 tonight. Were you planning on taking Miss Kayn there or were you going to swing by after you dropped her off at her Living Quarters?"

"Is that a problem?"

Tobias shook his head. "No, I'm simply curious about your plans. I don't mean to pry. I hope everything works out. Have a good night, Alastair. And, Maximus, stop giving your brother so much grief."

Alastair grabbed his OMNI from his bed and left Vega Manor.

Several Sectors later, he arrived at her hall. Anxiety wafted over him. A bead a sweat trickled down his brow and he wiped it with the sleeve of his shirt. He took a few deep breaths to calm himself down.

Before he could knock on the door, it slid open.

Claire Birch stood there, smiling up at him with an amused look. "Good evening, Prince Charming. Are you here to pick up your Princess?"

There had been a surprising lack of awkwardness since his make-out session with Claire. As she left the balcony, she had muttered something along the lines of, "Now that I've reawaken your passion, will you ask Iris out?" It seemed like an odd thing for someone to say after sucking face for an hour, but that was just Miss Birch's way.

"Why does everyone think we're a couple?" Alastair sighed, coming into their Living Quarters.

"We're just having fun at your expense," she said with a wink. "I'll go tell Iris you're here." Claire disappeared down the staircase.

As Alastair stood there in the living room, his wounded thigh began to ache. He took a seat in one the chairs and massaged the area where he had been shot. The medical Agents had been able to heal the holes in only a couple weeks with the use of nanites, but it still bothered him on occasion.

"Is your leg okay?"

Iris's voice startled him. He looked up and stared. She wore a long three-quarter sleeved, forest green silk blouse trimmed with white lace. A pair of tight-fitting grey leggings stopped at her knees. Her gold hair hung over her shoulders in waves, held back by diamond-studded pins. The slightest hint of black eye liner made her blue eyes pop against her blushing face.

"Oh, yeah," Alastair mumbled, feeling embarrassed. "There was a muscle spasm, but it's better now."

"So where are you two love birds going tonight?" Claire asked, coming up from behind her friend. "Perhaps to the top of the city for a moon-lit picnic or some type of cultural extravaganza?"

"We're not *love birds*," Alastair retorted, moving to the door.

"Yes, yes. I've been getting the whole *just friends* talk from Iris. Whatever you call it, have fun."

"Sorry about Claire," Iris whispered to him as they left the Living Quarters.

"No worries. Max has been laughing at me all day. It's like two people can't go out and have fun without there being other implications."

"Exactly." Iris let out a sigh. As they strolled down the halls, she very obviously avoiding eye contact with him. "That's all we are—two *friends*. I mean, a few weeks ago we hated each other; but we got over it and we're now getting to know one another."

"Yes," Alastair agreed, "without the watchful gazes and gossiping mouths of our fellow Trainees."

They continued chatting as they walked to the restaurant, trying to define what was between them. Iris viewed it as they "were blinded by anger and jealousy but were trying to make sense of the world now that they could see properly." Unable to come up with a better description, Alastair concurred with her explanation.

When they reached their destination, he led her through large wrought iron gates filled in with glass and swirls of silver designs. The sign above the entrance read "SUPERNOVA" in large, white words over a black background. Once inside, Alastair pulled out his OMNI to show the hostess the reservation file on his screen. The middle-aged women then took them across the room to a table set for two in a secluded nook.

The walls, ceiling, and floor were painted completely black. White, glittering stars shone in patterns of the constellations throughout the room—although they technically weren't in the correct places in the sky. Above each table was painted a different colored planet with a number of moons orbiting them. The heavenly-bodies glowed brightly, illuminating the surrounding area. The metal tables and chairs were decorated into satellite-like shapes. On the floor, misty clouds of greens, purples, reds, and blues represented gas formations left over from dead stars.

Iris was also admiring the artistry when a waiter approached. They placed their orders and sat in awkward silence.

Eventually, Alastair found a subject to discuss. "So how long have you known Claire?"

"We've been friends since we were thirteen. We met after a *certain party* where I left extremely embarrassed and slightly injured." Her face melted into shock when she saw his expression. "Oh. I guess that probably isn't the best thing to bring up, either. Sorry. My hurt feelings sort of took over for a second."

"No, you're right," Alastair agreed. "We haven't completely resolved those issues."

"Do we really need to talk about what happened that night?"

Guilt rushed through his mind, causing his forehead and hands to perspire. He had acted so cruelly towards her and yet she was still willing to be his friend. Before he could answer her, he recalled how he violated her privacy almost four months ago.

*****

A week before Placement Testing, Alastair sat in Agency library, surrounded by data-discs. Max, Stella, and Drew were at different tables with their own piles of data. His unhappy volunteers inserted the discs into their OMNIs one by one and lazily glanced through the information.

"Come on! It'll take us forever if you continue at that speed. Look faster," Alastair ordered.

"We've *already* been looking *forever*!" Max complained. "Can't we take a break?"

"No, we have to keep looking; the answer is here somewhere."

"Just because I don't have to check up on my Mentees shouldn't mean that I'm required to help you study yours."

Fidgeting with a throwing knife, Drew asked, "What's wrong with *your* Mentees?"

"Everything! There's no way they have enough talent to get into the Agency, so I've been told not to bother with the background checks," Max explained.

With a groan, Stella asked, "Tell me again why we have to help you?"

"Because my father told you to," Alastair spat. "He says that the key to our future is Iris Kayn. So all of you need to be involved."

"There's nothing important in here," Drew scoffed, hurling a disc across the table. "The only thing suspicious is her mother's family's sudden disappearance after the trial. But it doesn't give us anything to go off of."

Stella knocked over a pile of data-discs, clearly frustrated with all the intellectual work of the morning. "Even if Elizabeth and Calvin made a discovery, there's little chance they had a proper lab to complete their experiment; the Lower Region isn't exactly known for its pristine working conditions."

"Still, we shouldn't give up on that lead," Alastair said, taking the disc from Drew Harding. He inserted it into his OMNI and began skimming through the file.

Their research was interrupted when Viola came strolling in. Her long red hair was tied into a pretty braid that swung across the front of her shoulder. “Any chance you guys wanna come to The Grey Circumstance?”

“Can’t. We’re busy, Vi,” Max replied with a sigh.

“I don’t accept that answer. You’re going to put those discs down and come have fun with me,” Viola ordered. “Bea’s got this dance musical performance that I’m required to go to. It looks suspicious to the public when I don’t act like a caring, supportive sister. I need someone to come with to keep me entertained.” She looked at the files they were reading. “You’re *still* researching your Mentees?”

“Yes. I have quite a family history to comb through,” Alastair said without looking up. “Not to mention thousands of files on the experiments Elizabeth and Calvin were a part of. So have fun at the concert. Say hi to Beatrice for us.”

A few minutes later, Al raised his head to see if his helpers had come up with anything else for him to glance through.

They had all disappeared.

*****

When he didn’t reply, Iris said, “Ok, so we don’t have to talk about it.”

Alastair shook his head. "No, we can talk about it—if you really want to. I mean, it was what brought upon the tension between us. Maybe we should discuss it before we move forward with our friendship. I was quite a troublesome child."

"That's a bit of an understatement; you practically scared me off!"

Iris was about to say something else before she was interrupted by the appearance of their waiter. Food was placed on the table and Alastair began cutting into his steak. Iris looked nervously at the fatty sauce bathing her chicken. After the first bite, she went at it as ravenously as Al enjoyed his meal. They ate in silence for several minutes, appeasing their appetites.

"When I got home that night, I replayed the scene over and over in my head until I had every detail memorized." Iris looked down at the chunks chicken. "I didn't entirely blame you. I knew there was something missing from my schooling, but I wasn't sure what it was. When I saw how comfortable you and Max were when speaking to other people, I realized that I didn't know how to talk to people without getting nervous. I asked my father if I could have someone to practice talking to. A few days later, I met Claire."

Alastair stared at her. That was the most she had ever said to him at one time. He knew it would be appropriate for him to share something deeply personal, too, but he was unsure of what to say.

Should he tell her what it was like for him to grow up without a mother? At least he had Max. Iris didn't have anyone to share with until she reached her teen years. What could he say to help her feel like he could empathize with her? Did she need his empathy or just sympathy? Did she want to feel that other people go through the same things she does or did she need to feel like no one else knew how she felt?

In the end, he reached over and put his hand on hers. "Thank you for sharing that with me. I think I understand you a bit better now."

Near the end of their meal, Alastair began telling her funny stories about him and Max pulling pranks on their governesses and babysitters. Alastair thought about the things they did in high school, but he kept them to himself since the stories would probably scare her away.

Iris also shared some tales about how Claire would convince her to sneak out at night when they were in high school. They would go shopping for things their parents refused to buy them. It was the most reckless thing she had done. He smiled at her definition of "getting into trouble;" he found it endearing.

Their waiter returned with a bill-disc. Alastair inserted it into his OMNI and moved the money over from his credit account. When he was finished, he left the disc on the table.

"Are you ready to go back to the Agency?"

She nodded. "Does this mean our night is over?"

"No. There's something I want to show you first." Alastair grabbed her hand and pulled her along. "Hurry! We're going to be late."

"Are we going to a movie or something? We can't talk during movies."

He let out a chuckle, amused by her naivety. "Be patient. I really think you'll like where we're going." Minutes later, he stopped. "We're here."

They stood in the large doorway with a plaque that read "Improvement Center." Alastair led Iris into the room, stopping at a small desk directly in the center. He pulled out his OMNI and showed the identification file to the man behind the desk.

The Agent clicked some keys on the computer in front of him. "Welcome, Mr. Vega and Miss Kayn. Enjoy your visit." The Agent gestured to a door behind him.

"Thank you." Alastair turned to Iris. "Shall we?"

Once inside, he expected to hear Iris gasp as she took in the setting. Instead, she just looked like she was waiting for him to take her someplace else.

"What invention are you going to show me?" Iris asked.

"You're not overwhelmed by the grandeur of the room?" Alastair gestured at the vast rows of work tables and storage shelves. "It usually takes people a couple minutes to take in the sight."

"Oh, I've been here before," Iris replied with a shrug. "Viola took a bunch of us to test something for her Guild."

The memory pricked at his mind. "Oh, yeah—the Bubble Sauna incident with Beatrice and her wrist. I forgot about that. I suppose this is a waste of time," Alastair sighed with a grimace.

"No, I'd *love* to look around," she assured him. Approaching the nearest workstation, she eyed a pair of hover boots. "Am I allowed to touch or should I just use my eyes?"

"You can pick things up," Alastair replied. "Just be careful—some of these prototypes aren't quite ready."

As they walked down the room, Iris peeked at the different work tables. Her jaw dropped deeper the further along they strolled. There were different versions of upgraded Dueling Dummies, implant studs, the latest OMNI devices, holograms, and a number of other technologies that people had once considered to be science fiction.

"Claire would love this place." Iris grinned as she inspected a counter full of the latest OMNI designs.

"I'm sure she'll end up here once her Training is complete. This is where the top minds of the Agency work. I have no doubt she will be among them in a few years." Alastair took her to the far corner of the massive room. "The Agency is working on developing new designs for melee weapons." He searched carefully through a network of storage cubes and pulled out two masses of metal.

"Knife hilts?"

"Here." Alastair put them in her hands. "Jerk your hands as though you are going to stab something with them."

Iris did what he said. As she flicked her wrists, blades sprouted from the hilts. "That's amazing." She examined the knives. "The blades are longer than the hilt. How are they stored in there?"

"I have no idea," he admitted with a shrug. "It has something to do with nanites. Most of the research done here is practical uses for that technology."

"Weaponry is considered a *practical* use?" she asked him with a frown.

"Not exactly. I believe they were developing it for something else," Alastair explained. "But they are still experimenting with the idea before sending it to the Forge. These are only prototypes. The scientists are still working out some kinks."

Iris stepped away from him and began swinging the knives experimentally through the air. "You're right. There's something not right about them." She gave the blades back to Alastair.

Al yanked them a certain way and the blades disappeared. He returned them to their bin as he said, "I thought you might want a sneak peak at what you might one day fight with."

"Thank you. This has been a pleasant evening."

"I'm glad you had fun." Alastair moved toward her.

Iris called out his name like a question.

He fixed his eyes on hers.

"Is everything okay?" she asked.

"Yeah, I'm fine," he sighed. Although he had spent hour trying to figure out the best way to verbalize what he wanted to say, he still drew a blank. Deciding to wing it, Alastair said, "Iris, this may seem hasty to you—and it probably is—but I need to tell you something."

With that, he crossed the space between them, his arms wrapping around her waist. His hands settled in the small of her back.

"What are you—"

"I care about you," Alastair blurted, his grip tightening around her. "I mean, I really like you."

There was uncertainty in her eyes. Iris was silent, only letting out a hard, ragged breath.

Taking it as a sign of encouragement, Alastair leaned forward slowly, his lips traveling to hers.

She didn't move towards him and yet she didn't pull away.

A loud noise interrupted their almost-kiss. Alastair turned his head in the direction of the sound. Footsteps echoed through the room. A dozen men and women in black Agency uniforms stormed into the room.

Chapter 37

"What's going on?" Iris asked to no person in particular. Fear consumed her—fear that the Agency knew her secret and fear that they knew she was sick. Her body shook in anticipation.

Tobias Vega strode through the Agents, followed by the Harding thugs. "Oh, dear! It seems as though we have interrupted something."

Alastair pulled Iris behind him. "How can we help you?"

"It's time for Miss Kayn to be reunited with her father." Mr. Vega turned to Stella and Drew Harding. "Escort my son home."

Iris stepped forward. "I can see him now?"

"Something's wrong," Alastair whispered to her. "Don't say anything else until I find out what's happening." To Agent Vega, he said in a pleasant voice, "I'd like to be here to comfort my friend while she her only living parent in prison."

Tobias moved toward his son, his gaze dark and firm. "Look, Alastair, you're reputation need not be sullied by what is about to happen. Miss Kayn's unfortunate connections have made her the center of some vicious gossip. By being close friends with her, you're likely to join her in ridicule."

"Wait." Alastair held his hands out in front of him as though he was trying to push his father away. "First you wanted me to befriend her. And now that we're finally getting close, you're forbidding me from seeing her? I don't understand what you want from me!"

Iris couldn't believe what she was hearing. "You were being nice to me because you're dad *told* you to?"

He spun to face her, shocked confusion in his eyes. "Let me explain."

"Stay away from me!" she spat, backing away from him.

The surrounding Agents pulled out their weapons and shifted their formations as she moved. A wall stopped her from going any further.

"Agent Vega, why have you brought so many Enforcers with you?" Iris asked as she eyed the group of black-clad men and women. "If you were just taking me to my father, you wouldn't need this many people."

"Very perceptive, Miss Kayn," Tobias replied with a smile. "It seems that I can't hide anything from you. I have reason to believe that you, your father, and Dr. Taledon have partaken in illegal Alteration research. These fine Agents are just my way of ensuring that you come peacefully."

"*Alteration research*?"

It was absurd. Her father studied the pathology of the Plagues. He didn't alter human beings. It just wasn't possible.

For a moment, Iris played with the idea that this was just a precautionary measure—like Max had mentioned the day before. But that thought quickly fizzed out. This was too elaborate a scheme to be a safeguard. And yet, the two Regioner kidnappers had thought that she was an Alteration.

The seriousness of her situation finally kicked in. She needed to discredit any foundation of the absurd claim. "I have absolutely no idea what you're talking about. Alterations are myths. They *can't* be made."

There was a glint in Tobias's eyes as he asked, "How well do you really know your father, Miss Kayn?"

She glared at Agent Vega, her eyes burning with fury. "My father is a *good* man. Dr. Norman Kayn would never risk harming anyone for some foolhardy scheme to make super humans."

"I have a theory." Tobias strode a little closer and folded his hands behind his back. "Try and stay with me as

I paint a picture for you. An intelligent young man meets an equally stunning and bright woman and falls in love. Courtship ensues and they marry. Powered by the same vision, they work hard to make the world a better place."

Iris didn't like where he was headed. She wanted to bury her ears beneath her hands, but her curiosity was piqued. She couldn't help but listen to every word that spilled out of the man's mouth.

"For years, they study and research together to cure the Plagues that curse the Lower Region," Tobias continued. "But this isn't enough for them; they are *tired* of doing things through traditional means. One day, the wife has a breakthrough. She tells her husband she wants to change the makeup of human beings so they cannot be harmed by things such as diseases and ailments. Spurred on by this idea, they begin their experiments. However, tragedy strikes."

How could Tobias know anything about her parents? They weren't friends. Could any of it be true? Was it lies mixed with the truth? What could she believe? She was on the verge of tears—all the emotions coursing through her mind threatened to burst out.

"Stop!" Iris cried out in an attempt to release some of the pressure building inside her. "Please, stop."

Tobias halted for a brief second, but resumed his narrative. "The wife becomes ill with the same disease she had spent most of her life trying to fight. She dies while giving birth to a beautiful little girl. Consumed by sadness, the husband directs every fiber of his being towards bringing his wife's vision to reality, without any worry about consequences. His sorrow compels him to use his own daughter as a subject for his project." He paused before asking, "Does any of this sound *familiar*?"

"It sounds like *lies*," Iris said in a low voice. "I am *not* an Alteration. I'm as *normal* as you and your sons." It wasn't the absolute truth, but she couldn't tell him that she had contracted a Plague through her mother. He hadn't mentioned anything about it. And, as far as she knew, her medication was hidden safely within her Living Quarters. "What proof do you have that any of it is true?"

"I have hundreds of files," Tobias explained, holding up a pack of discs. "But I don't have enough evidence to verify my theories. I was hoping you would be more cooperative than your father. Are you sure you don't want to help me find the answer?"

"Where is he? Tell me where my father is!" Iris reached behind her and pulled out the experimental knives from their bin. With a flick of her wrists, the blades shot out of the handles. She flung herself at the nearest Agent and swung the prototype knives. Catching their spear between the blades, she pulled back and ripped the weapon from the owner's grasp. Iris used the Agent's weapon against him, smacking the man in the head with the spear.

The next Enforcer in her way was a woman wielding a battle axe. She proved to be more of a challenge, dexterously jumping away from the strikes. But Iris quickly disarmed her and sent her flying into a nearby shield.

Iris continued fighting off the Enforcers one at a time. Occasionally, two or three tried to approach her at once, but she would slip behind a work bench. One Agent attempted to climb over the barrier. Iris sent an elbow at his face. It scared the others into removing that as an option.

The most difficult opponent was Drew Harding. He blocked her swings with ease and was unfazed by the force of her blows. The more she attacked, the more violent he became. In the end, she subdued him by stabbing the knives into his arm sleeves, pinning him to a table.

While the Enforcers recovered from the shock of their wounds, Iris strode weaponless towards the Vegas and Stella. She had an overwhelming urge to rip the flesh from Agent Vega's bones. Before she could do perform any of the gruesome acts pictured in her head, she found herself on the ground. Something hard and leathery tied her hands together.

Miss Harding stood over her, whip in hand and amused smile on her lips. “Good luck trying to get out of that, dearie.”

Alastair gently helped her sit up.

As soon as she was right-side up, Iris shrugged away from him.

Agent Vega sighed as he freed Mr. Harding from the prototype knives. “I think you need to have a little chat with your father. How do you feel about a Simulation reunion?” He tapped his OMNI the screen up to her face.

The Improvement Center vanished, replaced by a dark, empty room. Iris stepped forward, looking for something other than the grey nothingness that surrounded her.

There was a flash of light and her father appeared, slumped on the floor.

“Dad? Are you okay?” Iris scanned his image for signs of injury. “Did they hurt you?”

“Iris? Is that you?” Dr. Kayn righted himself and stood. “Yeah, I’m fine.” He blinked and looked around. “What is this place? I was in a jail cell.”

“We’re in a Simulation.” Reaching out, Iris touched the virtual version of her father. The scruff of his beard felt so real, as did is soft hand when he stroked her cheek. “Dad? Something happened. I don’t understand.”

Norman whispered, “Audrey was right.”

“Mr. Vega says I’m an Alteration.” Iris stifled a sob. “It’s not true.”

He stayed silent and averted his gaze.

“What’s going on? Talk to me!” She grabbed at him. It wasn’t really his body she was touching, but he would *feel* the sensation of her shaking him. “What did you do to me?” The void consumed her. Iris groaned as her mind left the Sim. “Dad!”

“Now are you ready to talk?” Agent Vega asked.

Iris closed her mouth and tucked her lips under her teeth. She coldly stared at the man who was ruining her life.

Tobias sent the all the Agents away except for the Harding siblings and Alastair. “I really hate being the *bad guy*, Miss Kayn. All I want to do is help you. But I need you to cooperate first.”

“How can you possibly *help* me?” she inquired with a hint of mockery and disbelief. “If I *am* an Alteration, are you going to put me in some sort of recovery center? Is there an Alteration Anonymous support group that I can attend? Or will you just do away with me like a failed *experiment*?"

Drew chuckled lightly as he freed himself. "*Alteration Anonymous*? Very amusing title. That's not quite what we call it."

Iris faltered, trying to process what Agent Harding said. She struggled against the pressure of the whip that remained wrapped around her wrists. "What do you mean? There really *are* Alterations that have survived?" she asked, unsure if her ears were functioning properly.

"The world fears them," Tobias replied, calmly. "And yet, they're what we need to save everything. You can help, Miss Kayn. Show Rygom and the other Megacities the potential for humanity. We could do so much! But we need your father's data to make it possible. Agree to help us and we'll take care of you."

"I—I'm not sure," Iris sputtered, taking in ragged, uncontrolled breaths as she began to lose her temper. "I'm still not convinced that I'm an Alteration. Where's the proof? The fact that I beat your son on a stupid Placement Test? That I took out an entire Squad of Enforcers?"

Tobias took a step closer to her. "I think you've overlooked something. I haven't *accused* you of being one.

I simply *implied* that you've been used as a subject for your father's Alteration research. Your abilities don't seem to have manifested yet. I have reason to believe that something is hindering them."

Growing more confused as the conversation progressed, Iris asked, "So I'm an Alteration and yet I'm also not an Alteration?"

"You have the potential to become one, but you need have to be removed from whatever is blocking your abilities. I think you need a peaceful night in a holding cell—away from whatever it is that's keeping you from your destiny." He turned to Miss Harding and nodded.

"Come on, little dearie." Stella pulled on her whip, forcing Iris onto her stomach. "You've got a reservation in a lovely jail cell."

Terror struck her. The thought of missing an injection made Iris nauseous. "Hold on! I'll tell you something you don't know, but I need something first. I need something from my Living Quarters."

"I'm afraid that I can't let you return to your room." Tobias stared down at her, a mixture of delight and disappointment in his eyes.

"Please! I really need—" The thought of missing a dosage filled her with so much panic that she couldn't get any more words out. The terror suddenly turned to rage and she formed a quick plan. She rolled onto her back, wound a leg around Agent Harding's whip, and pulled. The tension on her wrists ceased.

Taking Alastair by surprise, she sent her fist straight into his nose. Resisting the urge to tear him apart with her bare hands, Iris ran. Dodging Enforcers was hardly new to her; she had spent countless hours doing it in the Simulators. Fortunately for her, Agent Vega had sent away most of his squad. Iris headed towards one of the Testing Rooms, but something large and metallic blocked her escape route.

A trio of the newest prototype of Dummies surrounded her and raised their weapons. Instead of the fleshy outsides, these robots were coated in a sleek, dark substance that looked identical to the material of the combat suits. Even if she could get her hands on a weapon, it'd be useless against the nanite armor.

Iris grabbed the discarded spear of a defeated Enforcer. She quickly blocked the blows of two of the Dummies and lunged out of the way of the third. Stella's whip flew towards her and wrapped around the spear. Miss Harding tugged and it was yanked from Iris's grip.

As the robots reoriented themselves, she ducked into Testing Room #2 and looked for a decent hiding place. The Bubble Sauna sat in the middle of the room—its top lowered down to cover the tub. Iris shot forward and slid inside just as the Dummies came clonking in with their heavy footsteps.

With no weapons, she almost made up her mind to surrender. However, she remembered the features of the Bubble Sauna. Moving towards the controls, Iris selected the "steam" icon and adjusted the setting to "high." Puffs of hot, cloudy air rose from the bottom of the Sauna.

"Come on out, Miss Kayn," Tobias said from outside the chamber. "You're only making things more difficult for yourself."

She opened the hatch, letting the steam pour out into the Testing Room. It hung low to the floor like fog. With that as cover, she aimed the bubble hoses out of the chamber. A series of clangs echoed into the room and the floor shook.

From the Sauna entrance, Iris could see the Dummies slipping on the bubbles. As the robots fell, there was a sound like shattering glass as the robots smashed into each other. Iris wished she could thank Beatrice for the inspiration of the tactic, but she'd probably never see the youngest Miss Cromford again.

With the Dueling Dummies destroyed, Iris figured she had the tactical advantage to escape her four remaining pursuers. She hit the button that controlled the Sauna ceiling and quietly slipped out the back way.

As she moved around the side of the room, something smacked into her abdomen. Iris fell to the floor with a grunt. A set of knuckles landed on the side of her face.

Dazed, she looked up to see Alastair frowning over her.

"I'm really sorry for this," he said, quietly. "If there's any truth in what my father says, I need to know."

Iris tried to sweep his legs with her foot, but he was too quick for her. He counter-grabbed her ankle and pulled her around so that she was on her stomach. Before she could turn onto her back, Alastair jumped on Iris and held her tight while Mr. Harding cuffed her.

"Why did that have to be so hard?" Tobias grabbed her jaw, pinching until Iris met his gaze. "Don't you see that I'm trying to help you?"

His words made no sense to her. How was locking her up going to help?

Agent Vega let go. “Goodnight, Miss Kayn. I shall see you in the morning.”

The Harding siblings forced Iris to her feet and escorted her out of the Improvement Center.

The thought of missing her injections raced back to her mind. A fresh wave of fear consumed her and brought her to tears, but they were all for naught. All she could do was shout, “Please!” over and over again as she was dragged through the Agency.

This concludes "Iris: Book One of The Rygom Narratives."

Thank you for reading. If you'd like to learn about Amy Engle and her other works, visit **AMYENGLE.COM/CONTACT** and subscribe to her Newsletter.

"Alteration: Book Two of the Rygom Narratives" will be released early 2019.

Other forthcoming books from Amy Engle in 2018:

- "Reps and Royals"
- "Mended by Ashes"
- "The People's Order"
- "Not So Anonymous"

CPSIA information can be obtained
at www.ICGtesting.com
Printed in the USA
FSOW01n0544070218
44115FS

9 780996 723022